"This place is . . . Shedai."

Frowning, Jetanien shook his head. "I'm afraid I do not understand, Your Excellency. This place is taboo? Quarantined? Forbidden?"

"From long ago," Sesrene said, *"our people avoided this place. It is said the unspeakable occurred here. Of all places, this is where we are not to be."*

Lugok released a hearty laugh, one Jetanien recognized as derisive. "Folk tales," he said. "Stories to frighten the meek and mewling. These Tholians truly are cowards."

Jetanien, however, found himself listening with intent to Sesrene's words. Could this supposed fable have a foundation in ancient fact? Might the ambassador's seemingly ingrained fear of the Taurus Reach possess roots to a danger so dreadful and frightening as to leave an impression lasting millennia?

What if they fear whatever it is we're looking for? What if the very builders of the artifacts—the originators of the meta-genome—have struck millennia of terror in the Tholian people? All of this is connected. It simply has to be.

It has to be.

STAR TREK®
VANGUARD

SUMMON THE THUNDER
DAYTON WARD & KEVIN DILMORE

Based upon STAR TREK
created by Gene Roddenberry

POCKET BOOKS

New York   London   Toronto   Sydney   Erilon

An *Original* Publication of POCKET BOOKS

POCKET BOOKS, a division of Simon & Schuster Inc.
1230 Avenue of the Americas, New York, NY 10020

This book is a work of fiction. Names, characters, places and incidents are products of the authors' imaginations or are used fictitiously. Any resemblance to actual events or locales or persons, living or dead, is entirely coincidental.

This book is published by Pocket Books, a division of Simon & Schuster, Inc., under exclusive license from Paramount Pictures.

ISBN-13: 978-1-4165-2400-7
ISBN-10:   1-4165-2400-2

This Pocket Books paperback edition July 2006

10 9 8 7 6 5 4 3 2 1

POCKET and colophon are registered trademarks of Simon & Schuster, Inc.

Cover art by Doug Drexler; station design by Masao Okazaki; background image courtesy of NASA and the Hubble Heritage Team (STSci/AURA)

Manufactured in the United States of America

For information regarding special discounts for bulk purchases, please contact Simon & Schuster Special Sales at 1-800-456-6798 or business@simonandschuster.com.

*For Michi and Michelle—this is what
we were doing all that time.
Really.*

Watch ye therefore, for ye know not when
the master of the house cometh.

—*The Gospel According to Mark,* 13:35

THE TAURUS REACH
2265

1

Commander Hirskene found that, try as he might, he could not stop pacing.

Lost in thought, he was oblivious of the ever-present sounds enveloping the command deck of the Tholian battle cruiser *Aen'q Tholis,* and all but ignored the activities of the subordinates working around him. The only thing he heard was the staccato echo of his six feet against the metal deck plating. He had been at this long enough that he now allowed the sounds to guide him back and forth across the command deck, counting off the steps before he reached either the forward or the rear bulkhead and was required to reverse his direction.

His unease refused to release him from its unyielding grasp, and he felt as though it might fracture him at any moment. The sensation had plagued him for the past several cycles, starting when he received his first orders from the Ruling Conclave on Tholia and intensifying as his ship made its way toward the destination specified by those orders.

The Shedai Sector, or as the Federation had taken to calling it, the Taurus Reach.

We have crossed the territorial boundary, Commander. The report, offered by his second, Yeskene, pushed across the SubLink and broke into Hirskene's troubled reverie. Accelerating his movements across the deck plating, the younger officer almost was scampering in order to stay in step with his superior, while the sapphire hues that had warmed the local thoughtspace deepened as the subordinate made his report. *I never would have believed that I might visit this place.*

Indeed, Hirskene replied. Like his second and the rest of the ship's complement, he too was traveling into the Shedai Sector for the first time. For as long as he could remember, this area of space was a place to be avoided. The reasons had been lost to the ages, of course, having fallen into a vast chasm of mystery that lay somewhere between truth and legend. All that remained were the stories, and Hirskene had lost count of how many times he had heard them throughout his life.

He did not doubt them now.

This anxiety he nursed was not his alone, of course. Hirskene could sense it in every member of the ship's complement, even without having to commune through the Lattice. Still, were he to make use of the vast telepathic network which linked all his people, he surely would perceive the same trepidation being mirrored by every Tholian in the Ruling Conclave.

"Status report," Hirskene said aloud, amber hues coursing through the SubLink as he moved toward the center of the command deck. "Are there any indications of other vessel activity?"

There was a momentary pause before the subordinate manning the sensor display console replied. "Negative, Commander. We are alone here."

To its credit, Hirskene's crew appeared to be allowing neither their own feelings nor the actions of their superior to distract them from their duties. All around the command deck, members of the lower echelons—menials who served as conscripted crew aboard Tholian military vessels—kept their attention on their consoles and monitored the current status of every shipboard system as well as the area of space through which the *Aen'q Tholis* currently traveled. While his position as commander and a member of the Leadership Conclave saw to it that he never would carry out such proletarian and yet necessary work, Hirskene was in fact envious of the subordinates in his charge.

At least they have something with which to occupy their time, and their thoughts.

He had known for many cycles that this day would come. Once the Ruling Conclave had begun reporting incursions into the Shedai Sector by forces of the Klingon Empire and the Federation, Hirskene had realized it would be only a matter of time before Tholian vessels were diverted from their regular missions to deal with this rapidly unfolding situation. What he had found disconcerting was that it had taken so long for the supreme leaders of the Political Castemoot to act.

The Federation's foray into the region had happened seemingly without warning, followed by notifications of more recent, pronounced incursions into the area by more of its ilk. Of course, it was the latter occasions that had brought the most concern. As part of this series of overt actions, the humans and their allies had established a permanent presence in the sector. A mammoth space station, its size surpassing even the largest deep-space outposts of the Tholian military, now stood watch over Federation activities in the region.

And what was the nature of those activities?

Even before the advent of the space station, Federation vessels had been dispatched throughout the sector. Long-range sensor telemetry as well as reports from civilian merchant ships traveling within the region offered accounts of colonies and smaller settlements taking root on a host of worlds. If the information Hirskene had reviewed about the Federation's supposed primary interests were true, then their motivation to extend the boundaries of their territory rivaled even that of the Assembly.

Though a young organization, the Federation was composed of species from numerous planets, most notably the Vulcans, who had been journeying across space for uncounted generations. Still, one of their prominent member worlds, the inhabitants of which called themselves "humans," had in addition to their proclivity for expansion displayed an unnatural desire for making peaceful contact with anyone they might encounter during their travels. Since leaving the confines of their home planet, the humans had introduced themselves to a number of other spacefaring races, some of whom had proven to be enthusiastic about the overture.

The Assembly, of course, was not so welcoming.

While stories of Tholian exploration of the galaxy dated back to the earliest recorded history, Hirskene, like most of his brethren, always had harbored an intrinsic distrust of the aliens with whom he had been forced to interact. For the most part, the Assembly's territorial annexing of neighboring star systems was a one-way proposition. The system being annexed usually became a servile province. Bipedal species in particular—races physiologically similar to humans, Vulcans, and other Federation members—had proven quite useful in the lesser echelons, though naturally they remained subservient to even the lowest-ranking members of Tholian society.

That did not mean Hirskene had to be content with their presence.

And so it was with the humans and their compatriots. Encounters with them had been infrequent since that initial contact, but each instance had been only a stark reminder of why they were to be avoided. Their aggressive movements into space—areas farther away from their homeworld and ever closer to territory claimed by the Assembly—had caused no small amount of unease. So far as the Ruling Conclave was concerned, the Federation was not to be trusted, particularly now. Something had attracted the humans and their allies to this part of space, something that necessitated abandoning their customary methods of expansion in favor of a more aggressive strategy. What had brought them here with such speed and fervor?

Hirskene suspected it had something to do with the mysterious phenomenon that had afflicted him—and every known Tholian—several cycles ago. Everyone had been gripped by an almost identical fear: a primordial sensation that coursed through the Lattice and forced its way into their minds, to the very core of their beings. This thought-pulse, while defying identification or explanation, led all who had experienced it to the same conclusions. The pulse originated somewhere in the Shedai Sector, and it must be destroyed.

How the Federation factored into that, Hirskene did not know. Perhaps their very incursion into this remote, mysterious region had prompted this violation of the Lattice? That might explain the sense of anger experienced by Hirskene and other Tholians linked within the Lattice at that dreadful moment, one that lingered long after the thought-pulse itself had faded. If that was the case, then the Federation's continued presence in the sector—to say nothing of their ongoing efforts to push farther into the area—surely would continue to provoke whatever it was that had been . . .

. . . *awakened*.

Until this very moment, Hirskene had never considered the incident in just that way—but the notion now made perfect sense to him. The presence that had forced itself upon the Lattice and encroached upon his people's most sacrosanct form of harmonious unity now felt to him as though it were a slumbering giant, one roused insolently from its sleep by the thoughtless, arrogant actions of those who knew not what they violated. And now, the giant sought restitution for this trespass, a demand it would not allow to be denied.

A reckoning, Hirskene feared, was at hand.

Even if the Federation is the cause, Yeskene reminded him, *they are but one problem.* His second-in-command and most trusted friend of course referred to the other party that had expressed an unabashed interest in the Shedai Sector: the Klingons.

Having decided that the Federation's interest in the region must have something to do with acquiring an advantage in the ongoing political and military stalemate that currently existed between the two powers, the Klingon Empire had wasted no time dispatching ships of its own. From what Hirskene knew of Klingon practices when it came to usurping other planets, their tenacity rivaled even that of the Assembly. Those caught up in such action would find life to be unpleasant at best.

There already had been a few minor skirmishes with the Klingons as Tholian forces were dispatched into the region in a bid to counter the empire's stratagem. Were the Ruling Conclave to decide that more overt action was necessary to stave off the aggressions of both the Federation and the Klingons—or even to undertake a bold, concerted effort to drive both parties out of the Shedai Sector—the only outcome Hirskene could foresee involved war with both powers.

If such challenges do await us, he wondered, *can we truly be victorious?*

"Commander," Hirskene heard, the interrogative wrapped in stark scarlet as Yeskene allowed his concern to be discerned. Only then did Hirskene realize that he had been so lost in thought that he had failed to comprehend that it was the third such time his second had called to him.

Feeling Yeskene's concern spreading among those subordinates who had turned from their stations to look upon him, Hirskene turned his full attention to his second. "What is it?"

"The sensors, Commander," Yeskene replied, the bright red colors currently permeating the SubLink deepening in hue as his rearmost right leg tapped absently on the deck plating while he spoke. "They are detecting an unidentified energy surge." The tapping was an unconscious habit of his, one that Yeskene displayed during times of uncertainty but that disappeared whenever a situation worsened. Hirskene had learned to accept the nervous tic as a barometer of whatever circumstances he and his crew might find themselves facing. Hearing it was usually a sign that something unexplained might be happening, but nothing inherently dangerous.

"What is the source?" Hirskene demanded as he turned back to the subordinate operating the sensor console.

"Unknown," the menial replied, maintaining his watch over the computer-generated graphic displays floating in the air before him. "All I am able to determine is that it is not coming from inside the ship. It is an external phenomenon."

"Are you able to localize it?" Yeskene asked, his six legs skittering across the deck to bring him alongside Hirskene.

The subordinate nodded. "I am attempting to do so now." The two, long fingers of his uppermost left extremity played across his console's smooth, translucent interface panel, each tap of a control slightly altering the array of sensor displays hovering over his head. "At first, I considered the possibility that the system might be experiencing a malfunction," the menial said, "but such is not the case. All internal and external sensors are operating within nominal parameters."

Hirskene nodded, pleased with the subordinate's initiative. It was yet another example of Yeskene's exceptional training and disciplinary regimen. He did not need to offer the menial any further instructions on how to proceed; the worker already was carrying out the proper protocols with exemplary proficiency.

"I believe I have pinpointed the source of the anomaly, Commander," he said. "It is almost directly aft, maintaining a steady distance."

Alarm flashed through Hirskene's mind even as his training and years of experience automatically suggested the next steps. *Defensive status,* he ordered through the SubLink. *Arm weapons and raise shields. Pilot, bring us about.* There was a chorus of acknowledgments as his subordinates moved to carry out the orders, and Hirskene could sense the heightening tension as their anxiety permeated the Lattice and applied a deep crimson tinge to the thoughtspace he immediately occupied.

Ignoring the sensations, he turned to the menial at the sensor console. *Let us see it,* he projected, and then looked at the command deck's largest display monitor, situated on the room's forward wall. *Transfer sensor data to central observation.*

The first thing he saw once the image shifted from that of a static starfield was . . . another static starfield. For all intents and purposes, the picture had changed not at all.

Where is it? he asked, feeling only the first hints of his impatience coursing through the Lattice and beginning to assert themselves as he turned from the monitor. *I do not see anything.*

According to the sensors, the subordinate replied, *it should be centered on the screen.*

There, Yeskene said suddenly, pointing to the display. *Do you see it?*

Looking back to the monitor, Hirskene at first saw that nothing appeared different, but then his eyes caught sight of . . . something.

A shape was coalescing, its form gaining substance with each passing moment. A vessel, though it was like nothing Hirskene had ever seen. Flat and compact, the craft appeared to be of simple construction. Its main hull appeared to be composed of gray metal, with no identifiable markings. What could only be engine

nacelles angled away from the hull, giving the entire vessel an up-
swept appearance as it moved through space.

Even as he felt harsh red waves ripple through the SubLink and
the alert tone echo across the command deck, Hirskene realized
that the ship which had materialized from nothingness was heading directly for the *Aen'q Tholis*.

2

"Cloaking device disengaged, Commander," the voice of the weapons officer echoed across the *Bloodied Talon*'s cramped bridge. "Weapons armed and ready to fire."

Commander Sarith did not need to hear the report, knowing that the subtle increase in the intensity of the bridge's violet-hued lighting signaled the deactivation of the cloaking system and the halting of its formidable demands on the ship's main power systems. Likewise, the telltale computer tone beeping at Centurion N'tovek's weapons station told her that the vessel's armaments were prepared for her next command.

In truth, given how sophisticated the automated defensive systems were aboard this vessel—one of the newest in the Romulan military arsenal—she truly had no need for the centurion at all.

Well, he does have one particular useful talent, she reminded herself as she glanced to where N'tovek stood at his post, garbed in the crisp gray tunic and trousers of a Romulan centurion, his head all but obscured by his polished gold helmet. Occupying one of the four stations that formed the central control hub at the center of the *Talon*'s cramped bridge, for once he actually appeared to be concentrating on the matter at hand.

If he ever learns to approach his duties with the same enthusiasm he demonstrates in other areas, he may one day become an acceptable, if not noteworthy, officer.

Forcing the errant thought away, Sarith took a final look at the lone Tholian battle cruiser on the screen. With its communications already jammed thanks to interference generated by the *Talon*'s tactical countermeasures, there was no way the vessel's commander would be able to summon help. Sensor data had revealed that even at its maximum speed, the Tholian ship could not escape. Their only choice was to make a defensive stand, which sensors led Sarith to conclude would be laughable, at least against the state-of-the-art weapons currently under her command.

Perhaps they'll make a fight of it, anyway, she hoped. *If nothing else, it will alleviate my boredom for a time.*

"The Tholian vessel has raised its defensive screens and is arming weapons," N'tovek reported, his attention still focused on his tactical displays. "Shall I commence firing, Commander?"

Rational thought won out over her misplaced pride and potential overconfidence. While sensors suggested the Tholian vessel itself was no match for the *Bloodied Talon,* they could not rule out the ingenuity and simple guile of its commander. Better to dispense with this matter now and leave nothing to chance, Sarith decided.

"Fire."

N'tovek wasted no time, his fingers moving over the weapons station's firing controls before the echo of her command faded from the bridge. Moving to the station immediately to the centurion's left, she peered into the viewfinder in time to see the twin bursts of crackling yellow disruptor energy lance across the void at the same instant the overhead lighting flickered in response to the weapons' power draw.

The bolts closed the distance to the Tholian battle cruiser in an instant, impacting on its shields, causing them to flare in violent response to the attack. N'tovek fired again without waiting for the order, and this time the assault pierced the cruiser's defensive screens. In the viewfinder, Sarith watched as plumes of freezing gases escaped from holes punched through the ship's hull. The vessel banked to its right, attempting to evade further salvos, but N'tovek already was plotting new firing coordinates.

"Their main engines are offline," reported Darjil, the centurion to N'tovek's right, whose own face was bathed in gentle blue light from his station's viewfinder. "Sensor readings also show a loss of primary life support."

Never even a chance to fight back, she mused. *A pity.*

"Finish it," Sarith said, her voice offering no trace of emotion as she gave the order. The sooner this business was concluded, the better.

With equal detachment, she watched as the *Talon*'s targeting scanners locked on to the Tholian vessel before the ship's weapons unleashed another burst of disrupting fury, which enveloped the retreating battle cruiser in a halo of undulating golden energy. Even at this distance, she could discern easily the separation of hull plates as the Tholian ship came apart. Explosions and fires from within the vessel snuffed out the instant their own raging chaos came into contact with the airless void surrounding the ship. Those parts of the cruiser that were not disintegrated quickly collapsed into a cloud of debris that began to expand in all directions—paltry evidence that a ship had ever existed there.

"Powering down weapons," N'tovek reported.

"Lay in a course away from here," Sarith ordered as she began to pace the perimeter of the utilitarian bridge. "They may have managed to dispatch a call for assistance."

Looking up from his station, Darjil said, "Commander, our countermeasures to scramble their transmissions were active throughout the encounter. I detected an attempt to dispatch a subspace message, but it was dispersed. There was nothing for anyone to receive."

"It seems that someone hasn't read the intelligence briefings on the Tholians," a voice said from behind Sarith, and she turned to see her second-in-command, Subcommander Ineti, entering the bridge from the service corridor. A small smile tugged at the corners of his mouth, warming his cragged, angular features. "Or the very least, the material appended to those briefings by the senate's liaison from the Medical Division has been overlooked, specifically the information pertaining to the Tholians' formidable telepathic abilities."

Despite a paternal, almost mentoring tone that was a perfect accompaniment to his aged countenance, there still was no mistaking the rebuke in Ineti's voice.

"I apologize for my oversight, Subcommander," Darjil reported as he snapped to attention. "There was much information to review, and I felt it prudent to concentrate on the military aspects of the vessels we were likely to encounter during this mission."

Sarith suppressed a smile as the centurion delivered his weak attempt at an explanation. Despite this being his second long-term assignment aboard the *Bloodied Talon*, Darjil still had not yet learned that the best response to Ineti's frequent observations on how the crew might go about improving themselves was simply to acknowledge the proffered recommendations and commence acting on them as soon as possible.

"Considering the tasks the Praetor has given to us," Ineti replied, crossing his arms as he commenced a leisurely circuit of the bridge, "I commend you on your sense of priorities. However, if I may be so bold, Centurion, perhaps upon the conclusion of your current duty shift, rather than spending your time and your funds engaged in games of chance with the misguided hopes of increasing your meager wealth, you might instead attempt to extend your knowledge of the Tholians into areas that do not directly pertain to their military capabilities. After all, an enemy can pose a threat in many ways that do not relate to their ability to brandish a weapon. Would you not agree?"

It was the executive officer's habit never to raise his voice or vary his inflections even to the smallest degree when addressing perceived deficiencies in his subordinates. Not that it mattered, because only a fool would mistake the subcommander's suggestions as anything less than an ironclad directive that he expected to be followed without hesitation or stipulation.

"Absolutely, Subcommander," Darjil replied, an unmistakable tremor now evident in the junior officer's voice as he stood ramrod straight and stared straight ahead—even when Ineti came to a stop and leaned forward until his face was less than a finger's length from Darjil's right ear.

"Learn everything that you can about your enemy, Centurion, and not just those aspects which dovetail with your chosen area of expertise. Only then can you hope to truly be victorious. Now, return to your station."

Not even bothering to wait for an acknowledgment of his order before turning away from the control hub, Ineti stepped closer to Sarith, waiting until he was out of the line of sight of any of the centurions manning the bridge's stations before allowing a wolfish smile to grace his wizened features.

"Youthful exuberance," he said in a low voice. "So much energy, so little focus. Was I ever like that, I wonder?"

"I don't believe our historical records chronicle events that far in the past," Sarith retorted as she turned from the bridge's main deck and moved toward the small alcove that served as both her station in the ship's command center and her office. Its dominant feature was a simple desk, fashioned from the same metal as the deck plating and jutting out from the bulkhead. Atop it sat a computer terminal and a control pad, which allowed her access to the ship's communications system. A pair of functional chairs, bolted to the deck and the only two to be found in the already cramped control room, completed her station's furnishings. While it was not nearly as lavish as the private chambers allotted to the commanders of larger vessels, the alcove adequately served Sarith's purposes.

Taking the chair positioned on the outer edge of the alcove, Ineti offered a knowing grin as he settled himself. "So, another glorious victory for the Praetor, yes?"

Sarith looked about the bridge, wondering whether any of the bridge crew had overheard him. Thankfully, the omnipresent thrum of the *Talon*'s engines had muffled his voice, preventing it from carrying across the cramped chamber. "I wish you would learn to be more . . . guarded with some of your observations, Ineti," she said. "It would better serve you in your quest to end your career on a positive note."

"I'm afraid it's more than a bit late for me to make such a fundamental alteration in my admittedly flawed approach to life, Commander," Ineti replied. "Besides, it's not as though I'll ever be considered for a ship of my own. Such opportunities have long since traveled beyond my reach, I'm afraid." Shrugging, he added, "As it happens, I'm content to ply my skills as a teacher, and to keep *you* out of trouble."

Smiling in spite of herself, Sarith shook her head. In truth, she knew that Ineti was all but untouchable in the eyes of the

Senate, Fleet Command, or even the empire's intelligence
bureau. His career, already long and distinguished even before
she was born, had all but assured him a place of prominence
not only in the halls of Romulan power but also in the annals of
their history. A decorated veteran of numerous conflicts—
including campaigns waged alongside her father during the
war against the forces of Earth and its allies more than a century ago—Ineti could well have ascended to the Senate itself
had he ever sought such prominence.

However, his propensity for speaking his mind—regardless of
the subject or whoever might overhear—had soured him in the
eyes of those who oversaw the advancement of officers into the
higher echelons of military command and political office. While
popular opinion prevented them from taking direct action against
him, those individuals nevertheless found more surreptitious
methods for making their displeasure known to him.

At least, Sarith thought with no small amount of amusement,
that's what Ineti chooses to let them believe. So far as she was concerned, the shortsightedness of certain narrow-minded cowards at
Fleet Command was to her advantage, as it allowed her to continue benefiting from the aged warrior's learned counsel.

"Keep me out of trouble?" she repeated after a moment. "If
that were true, then where were you when the Tholian vessel detected us?"

"In the engine compartment, trying to learn how it was
possible in the first place," Ineti replied. "Apparently, the
cloaking device's energy dissipation rate is such that it can register on another vessel's short-range sensors within a certain
distance."

Sarith nodded, considering her mentor's report. "So, we approached too close to our enemy."

"I believe that is what I said," Ineti replied, mild amusement
playing across his otherwise stoic expression. His features hardened, however, as he leaned across the narrow desk. "We were
fortunate on this occasion that it was a single vessel that we
easily outmatched. Such providence may not visit us next time,
particularly if the Tholians were able to dispatch a distress call.

We need to exercise more caution if we are to continue our mission undetected."

"I would have preferred to avoid contact altogether," Sarith said, leaning back in her chair and allowing her head to rest against the bulkhead behind her. Her standing orders to avoid detection at all costs made no other decision possible. "Unfortunately, the cloak's power requirements tend to degrade the performance of other onboard systems." In addition to its impact on the ship's weapons and defensive systems, the cloaking device also compromised the sensors such that the only way to obtain decent telemetry was to approach objects of interest much more closely than normally would be required.

"Even with its effects on our sensors, the Tholians should not have been able to detect us," Ineti said. "Drawing power directly from the warp engines is the most likely cause, and perhaps is a design flaw. We should alert Fleet Command of the unexpected discrepancy as soon as possible." With another knowing smile, he added, "Whenever that might be."

Allowing the cool, slightly vibrating surface of the bulkhead to act as therapy against the headache she could feel descending upon her, Sarith finally opened her eyes and glanced at the chronometer displayed on her desktop computer terminal. She quickly calculated the interval of time remaining until her next planned subspace communication back to the empire and noted that several hours remained—more than enough time for her to compose a thorough account of their current situation and status.

Finally, something new to report.

The journey to this region of space, far beyond Romulan boundaries, had taken months, thanks in no small part to the circuitous route that had been required in order to skirt Federation and Klingon territory, not to mention their paying particular attention to avoid the network of observation outposts the Federation had deployed along their border with Romulan space. To the best of Sarith's knowledge, it was the first time any military vessel had left the confines of the Romulan Star Empire since shortly after the war against Earth.

All so that we might spy on our former enemies.

"I know that expression," Ineti said after a moment. "Once again, you wonder if this assignment is worthy of an officer of your stature."

Sarith smiled. As always, she failed utterly at concealing her thoughts and feelings from her oldest friend. "I do not question the Praetor's orders, or the directives of Fleet Command," she said, the words sounding rehearsed even as she said them. "I would simply have appreciated more information. It is preferable to know for what exactly we are undertaking such risk, would you not agree?"

"Of course," Ineti replied, "just as I've agreed with you on each of the seventeen occasions since our departure when you have raised this same question."

Sighing, Sarith shook her head. The old man certainly could be exasperating at times. "I have to wonder what interest the Praetor might have in happenings taking place so far from home," she said. Her vessel had traveled almost the length and breadth of explored space, and for what reason? To gather information on the recent upswing of Federation, Klingon, and even Tholian activity in this heretofore isolated region of space, to relay that information back to her superiors, and to do so without alerting anyone to her ship's presence. It was of paramount importance to the Praetor that no one know of the Romulans' first slow steps toward emerging from an isolation that had lasted more than a century, and that their interests were piqued by whatever might be unfolding here.

"Just because we do not see the threat," Ineti said after a moment, "does not mean it does not exist. Such prudence has guided us for countless generations, my friend. Do not forget that."

"Some would call that philosophy nothing more than simple paranoia," Sarith countered. In fact, judging from the scant intelligence data received from undercover operatives positioned within the ranks of the Federation Starfleet, the Earth-centric political body seemed almost obsessed with expanding their influence into this region of space, which apparently had provoked the Klingon Empire into dispatching their own vessels. The activities of both entities appeared to have angered the Tholians, and by all accounts, war in this region seemed inevitable.

Among the many things missing from the intelligence reports was what had set these events in motion.

What had brought the Federation here, possessing it to venture into territory flanked by two rival powers who both considered the humans and their allies to be a threat? Had the Klingons learned of some potential military advantage the area offered, and were they now determined to seize it before the Federation staked their claim? How did the Tholians factor into the equation, apart from simple xenophobia and a desire to be left well enough alone?

Sarith's mission was simple: Find answers to those questions.

3

"Go away."

The words were spikes piercing Cervantes Quinn's head even as he said them, aided as they were by the fact that he was speaking while pressing his right cheek into the cool surface of the bar in Tom Walker's place. The wood—or whatever material simulating wood that had been used to construct the bar—vibrated beneath his face, sending renewed waves of pain into his skull and giving him cause once again to utter his oft-used yet never-honored entreaty to any benevolent deity who might be listening.

Please, just let me die in peace.

"Quinn," Tim Pennington said, repeating the summons for the third time while simultaneously placing a hand on Quinn's left shoulder and shaking it. "Come on, we're going to be late. We're due to ship out in less than an hour."

"Huh?" Quinn said, the word coming out as much a gargle as it was anything remotely intelligible. Pulling his head up, during which he discovered that some of his long gray hair had become stuck to the bar by way of a congealed green substance equally likely to be Aldebaran whiskey or engine coolant, he turned and regarded Pennington—all six of him—dancing in his unfocused vision. "What are you talking about?"

Pennington rolled his eyes. "The shipment, Quinn, don't you remember? The replacement parts for the load lifters that farmer on Boam II ordered? You contracted with the station to deliver them in a week. We have to leave this morning if we're going to keep that schedule."

Watching as the six dancing Penningtons continued their fluctuations before his eyes in a frenzied attempt to meld into a single irksome speaker, Quinn came to the conclusion that the journalist's slight Scottish brogue was even more irritating to hear first thing in the morning, particularly when Quinn was nursing a hangover that harbored enough force to initiate a warp-core overload.

"Right," he said finally, nodding in acknowledgment to Pennington and immediately regretting the movement. He reached up to cradle his forehead in his hands. It was going to be a long day, but ultimately one he had no choice but to survive, at least if he wanted to get paid.

Vanguard's quartermaster division had already taken pity upon him by offering him a contract to transport supplies and other requested items from the station to the various colonies that were springing up throughout the Taurus Reach. So far the work had been marginally profitable, if not exciting, at least enough to keep him fed and his ship, the *Rocinante,* in working order. It also provided him with at least some funds that he could put toward his outstanding debts, the number and amount of which escaped him at the moment.

I wonder if I've got enough to buy a new skull, he thought as another stab of pain wormed its way behind his eyeballs.

Regarding him skeptically, Pennington shook his head. "Did you spend the night here?"

"Possibly," Quinn replied. "I think so." He pondered the question for an additional moment. "Yeah." Like many of the other establishments located within Stars Landing, Starbase 47's commercial and entertainment district as well as home to the majority of the station's civilian population, Tom Walker's was open around the clock so as to better serve personnel assigned to each of the station's three standard duty shifts. The bar was also one of the few places aboard the mammoth station where Quinn normally could find solace at this ungodly hour of the day, as evidenced by the fact that the bar was empty of other patrons.

Almost empty, anyway.

"Well, you look like hell," Pennington replied, making no effort to hide his disdain. "Are you going to be able to pilot that flying death trap of yours, or not?"

"I've flown when I felt a lot worse than this," Quinn said as he rubbed sleep from his eyes. "Feel free to stay behind, if you're worried."

Shaking his head, Pennington replied, "Ordinarily I might take you up on that, but I've got my own reasons for tagging along."

"Oh, yeah," Quinn said, recalling that the onetime reporter for the Federation News Service had lined up a series of interviews with several members of the colony on Boam II, one of the first such settlements to be established at the start of Federation expansion into the Taurus Reach. Pennington planned to write a story about how the colony had thrived in the sixteen months since its founding, in the hopes of showcasing some of the positive progress being made in this region.

"It's not going to win me any prizes," Pennington conceded, "but hopefully it'll let me pay a few bills, assuming I get to write it."

Nobody's gonna buy it, he mused, *but why rain on his parade?* Under most other circumstances, Quinn probably would not have cared less that the journalist's life lay all but in ruins—that he'd been fired from his job and dumped by his wife.

Of course, given that Quinn himself had played a hand, albeit unknowingly, in demolishing Pennington's career, things were different. Acting on direction of the station's intelligence officer, Lieutenant Commander T'Prynn, Quinn had planted information that she had given him and that she had designed as bait to trick Pennington into writing a damning article for the FNS about the destruction of the *U.S.S. Bombay* at the hands of Tholian vessels last month. The information was fake, its sources either liars or phantoms created by the Vulcan for the sole purpose of luring the journalist to craft a story which could then—along with Pennington himself—be discredited. Her tactics had proven successful, with the FNS wasting no time firing Pennington and Starfleet using that opportunity to cloak in shadow whatever had really happened to the *Bombay* somewhere deep in the Taurus Reach.

Whereas Quinn could accept that his chosen line of work might entail visiting hardship or even harm on others, he had his limits. He did not believe in killing except in self-defense, and he studiously avoided cheating or otherwise harming innocent people. Pennington's only apparent crime had been one of unchecked enthusiasm as he wrote and published his story with the information he had obtained. Because of that, he was now a laughingstock in the professional journalism community and an outcast even here, aboard this station in the hind end of space. It was because of the guilt Quinn felt over his role in Pennington's professional demise that he had befriended the disgraced reporter, without cluing him in to the true reasons behind his decision, of course.

I'm not a complete idiot.

"So, are we going or not?" Pennington said, his voice seeming to acquire an even thicker accent as his annoyance level rose, and each syllable tapping a new nail into Quinn's alcohol-ravaged brain.

Holding up a hand to silence his friend, Quinn said, "Yeah, yeah, we're going. Just hang on a minute." His brow furrowed as he recalled the previous evening's activities. "The cargo's already in the hold, and I took care of preflight last night." Seeing the look of concern on Pennington's face, he added, *"Before* I started drinking, all right?"

Pennington appeared to relax. "Fine. Let's go then."

"Get your stuff and meet me at the docking port," Quinn said as he began searching through the numerous pockets lining his shirt, trousers, and jacket. "I need to settle up with Tom."

An expression of surprise appeared on Pennington's face. "You're settling your tab? Is this some sort of special occasion?" He frowned. "You're not dying, are you?"

"I'm not that lucky," Quinn retorted before waving Pennington toward the door. "Go. I'll meet you there in five minutes. We'll be out of here on schedule."

Pennington pointed a cautioning finger at him, his frown turning skeptical. "Don't be late," he said as he turned and headed for the door. "I need this job, and so do you."

"Don't worry, dear. We'll be fine," Quinn said to the reporter's retreating back before his gaze returned to the bar.

Once Pennington was gone, he shook his head. "Two weeks with that," he said to no one, imagining the round-trip voyage to Boam II and back. "Mommy, make it stop."

And with that, he laid his head back down on the bar. Within seconds, the few innocuous sounds drifting through the tavern faded away as Quinn once more allowed sleep to reach out for him.

He had no idea how much time had passed before he felt another poke in his left shoulder.

"Dammit, Tim," he said, jerking his head up and squinting in pain at the sudden movement. "You're worse than my second wife." He whirled around on his barstool, seriously considering punching Pennington for the second time since meeting the aggravating journalist.

Instead of Pennington, Quinn found himself staring into the face of Zett Nilric. Impeccably dressed, as always, in a tailored slate-gray suit with polished black shoes, the trim Nalori regarded him with an expression cold enough to freeze warp plasma. The tavern's low overhead lighting reflected off his oily black skin and shaved head, making his expression appear all the more sinister.

"Mr. Quinn," Zett said without preamble, his tone reserved and almost lyrical as he spoke, "Mr. Ganz wants to see you."

Quinn sighed. That the Orion would send his right-hand man and most trusted enforcer to personally escort him to see their mutual employer could not bode well. "What did I do now?"

Zett, of course, did not smile. "Why, nothing. At least, not yet."

4

Occupying his customary table at the rear of Starbase 47's officers' mess and without moving his eyes from the data slate lying atop the table near his left elbow, Commodore Diego Reyes reached with the fork in his right hand to stab at his eggs.

The fork scraped against the plate, alerting him that he had already consumed his breakfast. Looking over at the empty plate with an aftertaste of the meal still in his mouth, he realized that he had been so engrossed in his morning reading that he had failed to recognize how utterly horrible the eggs had tasted.

"What the hell did I just eat?" Reyes asked, frowning, as he reached for his glass of orange juice in the hope of washing away the aftertaste of . . . whatever.

Across from him, Dr. Ezekiel Fisher's brown face warmed as he offered a wistful smile from over the rim of his coffee cup. "Ktarian eggs. I made a change in your diet profile for the galley after your last physical. Those are lower in cholesterol, and they've got all sorts of vitamins and minerals a growing boy like you needs."

Reyes frowned at his longtime friend. "You know I hate Ktarian eggs," he said. "Always have. I'd rather chew on my boot."

"Your boot would offer more nutrition than what you usually eat. Besides, they taste better when you mix in green peppers," Fisher countered, indicating Reyes's plate with a nod of his head. "You didn't seem to mind them this time."

His scowl melting somewhat, Reyes said, "Is it part of a chief medical officer's job description to harass and harangue those in his care in as many ways as possible?"

"Absolutely," Fisher replied, nodding with conviction as he took another sip of his coffee. "It's the second verse of the Hippocratic Oath, the one you never hear because most doctors are going on about doing no harm and whatnot. Me? I skipped right to the good part."

"I thought all that stuff about doing no harm wasn't even in the Hippocratic Oath," Reyes said.

Fisher smiled. "You have to look for it. Which is all the more reason to get to the harassment and haranguing, such as telling starbase commanders that their eating habits are atrocious, and that if they don't start taking better care of themselves, more of their favorite dishes will be deleted from their diet profiles."

Deciding that he probably would survive this particular breakfast—while at the same time making a mental note to get with the quartermaster about clandestinely shipping in some care packages from Earth as soon as possible—Reyes pushed the plate away and reached for his data slate. It contained various morning reports submitted by the station's department heads as well as a distillation of message traffic and other updates received from Starfleet Command in the past twenty-four hours.

"Do you remember Terrance Sadler?" he asked as he held up the tablet for Fisher to see.

The doctor nodded. "Sure. Left Starfleet about six years ago to settle down on some colony planet."

"Right," Reyes said. "Hell of a security chief. Probably the best I ever had." As he spoke the words, he looked about the mess hall to ensure that his current security officer, Lieutenant Haniff Jackson, was not in earshot. It was not that he doubted Jackson's abilities or potential, of course, but Sadler had served under Reyes for three years aboard the *U.S.S. Dauntless*. Nearly every member of their ship's crew for one reason or another owed his or her life to Terrance Sadler, who had proven to have a knack not only for anticipating trouble but for handling it, as well.

A real bad karma magnet, Terry was.

"What about him? Did he send you a note, bragging about how exhilarating life is on the frontier?" Fisher asked, reaching for a carafe at the center of the table to refill his coffee cup. "Unlike here, where nothing ever happens."

Ignoring his friend's sarcasm, Reyes replied, "The last I heard, he settled on Ingraham B." He held up the data slate for emphasis. "According to Starfleet Command, all contact with the colony there has been lost." He frowned as he glanced over the report for the fourth time. "That planet's nowhere near Klingon space, or any other known threat."

Was something new making its presence known in that still isolated area of Federation territory? Ingraham B, while not a military target by any means, was still home to a thriving agricultural and scientific colony. Terrance Sadler had elected to resign his commission and accompany his wife, herself an accomplished xenobiologist, to the planet in the hope of settling down, starting a family, and leaving behind the stresses of life aboard a starship.

Yeah, but if trouble comes knocking, you can bet Terry will be the one answering the door.

"You know, it could be something as simple as a power failure," Fisher offered, "or whatever else that might knock out their communications gear. It doesn't always have to be something malicious causing problems."

Shaking his head, Reyes pointed to the data slate again. "It's been three days since contact was lost. They're sending a ship to investigate, but it'll take weeks just to get there."

"Space is big, Diego," Fisher said, in that paternal manner of his which allowed him to state even the incredibly obvious without coming off as patronizing or insulting. "For all we know, they'll have comm up before that ship can get halfway there."

While he wanted to think that something innocuous could be responsible for the apparent communications blackout, Reyes's gut told him that simply was not the case. His feelings of apprehension only deepened when coupled with the pain he still carried over the loss of the *U.S.S. Bombay.* The captain of the ship, Hallie Gannon, had been his first officer on the *Dauntless.* She and Sadler had also been friends, and their notorious late-night poker games had seen more than a few credits whisked from Reyes's own pocket.

I hope everything's all right out your way, Terry.

The report regarding Ingraham B was one of more than twenty received from Starfleet Command since yesterday morning, and those were but a percentage of the briefings and updates transmitted to Starbase 47 during a given week. The reports were a lifeline of sorts for the station, connecting it with the rest of the Federation and reminding all aboard that they were but one act of an immense, multifaceted play that was being written anew with each passing day. While much of what Reyes reviewed was positive—details from dozens of newly explored worlds, a few first contact situations, and so on—there also were several reports that caused him concern. Heightened activity from within Klingon and Tholian borders was at the top of that list, of course, particularly as they related to his current assignment.

What the daily briefings never failed to do, regardless of whether they contained encouraging or disquieting news, was remind him that this was a time of unprecedented potential—for Starfleet and the Federation as a whole. Never before had so many opportunities to make so much progress in so many different areas of knowledge—science, technology, relations with new civilizations—been within such seemingly easy reach.

Of course, much of that excitement was unfolding very far from where Diego Reyes currently sat.

That's okay, he mused, though with more than a small amount of melancholy. *We have our own unique brand of excitement here, don't we?*

The initial discovery of virtually identical samples of incredibly complex genomes—collected by the *U.S.S. Constellation* two years ago from five different star systems and all separated by several light-years—had ignited a firestorm of policymaking and strategizing at the highest echelons of Starfleet Command. Theories raged over the origin of the "meta-genome," as it had come to be known. Was this a clue to some future step in natural evolution, one that humans and humanoid species throughout the galaxy might eventually take? There were those in the Federation science community who believed the intricate DNA might be artificial in nature. If that was the case, who was responsible for it? Was it someone with whom the Federation might ally itself, or was it a possible—and potentially staggering—new enemy?

Vanguard's primary mission, so far as the public was concerned, was to provide logistical support for the extensive exploration and colonization effort already well under way in the Taurus Reach, as well as to be a nucleus for Starfleet operations in the area. In reality, that duty provided cover for the station's true purpose—directing the efforts of Starfleet specialists to learn as much about the meta-genome and its origins as was possible. It was a tall order, especially considering that, with precious few exceptions, Starbase 47's entire complement was unaware of the meta-genome's existence in the first place.

The strain of commanding this effort, so far from home, had already taken a personal toll on Reyes, its harshest blow coming with the news of his mother's death. That loss had weighed heavily on him, along with his inability to even be present at the end, bound as he was by his duty to Starfleet, this station, and the growing number of secrets it harbored.

Suppressing the truth behind the loss of the *Bombay,* not to mention the steps that had been taken to prevent the ship's destruction from igniting all-out war with the Tholians, had been distasteful enough. Compounding that dilemma was the willful scuttling of the professional career of journalist Tim Pennington, who had reported the incident via the Federation News Service. The reporter had been used—duped into writing a story using information both fabricated and manipulated so that Starfleet might discredit him in the eyes of the public. Their sacrifice of Pennington cast off suspicions that the *Bombay* tragedy had resulted from anything more than an unfortunate accident.

Reyes could only hope that whatever secrets the Taurus Reach held, they would prove to be worth the costs already incurred in discovering them. Such feelings of guilt and uncertainty had visited upon him no small number of sleepless nights, a situation made worse by the fact that there was no one on the station with whom he felt he could discuss his troubles.

Including my two closest friends, Reyes reminded himself as he looked across the table at Fisher, who sat back in his own chair, sipping his coffee and watching the random procession of Starfleet personnel moving about the officers' mess.

"You're awfully quiet this morning," the doctor said after a moment, returning his attention to Reyes. "Even for you." It was as much an observation as it was a joke, Reyes realized. The two old friends long ago had left behind the necessity to fill dead air with inane conversations, and the irregular breakfasts they shared were often as not eaten in almost total silence, with Fisher enjoying his customary fruit plate and coffee, while Reyes ate whatever the food slot produced as he pored over the contents of the data slate his yeoman delivered without fail each morning.

Reyes shook his head. "Sorry. Lost in thought." Shrugging, he added, "Just trying to get geared up for another exciting day of reading supply requisitions, status reports, and whatever complaints have been levied against me by some irritated colony administrator."

"You're irritating colony administrators again?" Fisher asked. "What'd you do this time?" No sooner had he spoken the words than he raised a hand as if to wave them away, adopting a knowing smile as he did so. "No, wait. Scratch that. What did Rana *say* you did this time?"

Reyes replied, "Nothing yet, but the day's just getting started." He and Captain Rana Desai, the station's representative from Starfleet's Judge Advocate General Corps, already had faced off several times on matters involving several of the newly established Federation colonies in the Taurus Reach. Most of those cases had involved Starfleet's attempts to secure needed resources from planets upon which colonies had been founded. To him, what appeared to be a straightforward situation—Starbase 47's need to remain self-sufficient by acquiring raw materials from worlds in neighboring star systems—often was made more complicated by a variety of legal and public-relations issues he was both unqualified and unmotivated to understand.

For that, he relied upon Captain Desai, and his attitude often resulted in conversations with her on these and related topics that could be, for lack of a better word, animated.

"We've been butting heads a lot lately," Reyes said after a moment. "A lot of it's just the usual—not seeing eye-to-eye on this or that." He shrugged. "She's got a tough job to do, enforcing or even making law this far out in the middle of nowhere, but sometimes I think she forgets that she's not the only one carrying a heavy pack." Indeed, Starbase 47's assignment to oversee the legitimate and burgeoning Federation presence in the Taurus Reach was becoming more demanding with each passing day, bringing with it an increasing number of situations and issues between Starfleet and civilian entities that required not only his own attention but also that of Captain Desai. That the pair sometimes exuded diametrically opposing viewpoints in some cases was—in Reyes's opinion, at least—a galactic understatement.

Leaning back in his chair as he stroked his beard, Fisher offered one of his trademark knowing smiles. "I imagine the ethical and philosophical debates alone make for pretty stimulating dinner conversation."

Despite himself, Reyes winced in reaction to his friend's comment, quickly looking about the mess hall to see if anyone else might be overhearing their conversation. While he and Desai both took steps to keep their personal relationship as low-key as possible, the commodore was nagged by the constant feeling that everyone on the station—along with anyone sitting aboard one of the dozen or so ships currently making use of Vanguard's docking facilities—knew exactly what was going on.

Reaching for his orange juice, he sipped from the glass before answering. "They don't really aid in my digestion, though."

"I have no doubt," the doctor said, the words almost consumed by the chuckle that came with them.

Of course, Reyes was hampered in his dealings with Desai by the fact that he was required to keep from her the host of secrets regarding the station's true mission, a situation made all the more complicated by the fact that the two of them were sleeping together.

One of these days I've got to quit half-stepping, he reminded himself, *and just find some way to be* completely *miserable.*

Fueling that misery for sure was his need to monitor the aggressive movements of both the Klingons and the Tholians into the region. So far, their incursions had brought about several very tense encounters, including the destruction of the *Bombay* and the Starfleet outpost on Ravanar IV.

The incidents had ratcheted up the already strained relations between the Federation and the notoriously xenophobic Tholians, coming much closer to igniting a war between the two governments than was generally known. It had taken a supreme effort on the part of Ambassador Jetanien, the Federation's diplomatic envoy currently assigned to Vanguard, to head off that conflict by conducting a series of heated negotiations with his Tholian counterparts. In the end, hostilities had been avoided, but how long would the fragile peace last?

One way or another, Reyes mused, *we're going to be ringside when that question gets answered.*

Draining the last of his coffee, Fisher placed the cup back on the table before retrieving the cloth napkin from his lap and wiping his mouth. "Time to go to work," he said as he rose to his feet, taking a moment to wipe a stray crumb from his blue uniform tunic. Reaching up, he ran a finger inside the shirt's black collar. "Whoever designed this new uniform must have been an executioner in a previous life. At least the old collars didn't feel like I was sticking my head through a hangman's noose."

Reyes smiled at the comment. In actuality, he found that he preferred the recently introduced uniform redesigns. The only thing he had found out of sorts was the proliferation of red tunics, worn by personnel who at one time might have sported gold. The new color scheme was taking a bit of getting used to.

"Maybe it's just too small for you," he offered as he gathered the data slate and stood up from his own chair. "Might want to check your own diet card, Doctor."

Fisher chuckled. "Comments like that won't get you invited to my retirement party, Commodore."

"At this rate, I'll retire before you do," Reyes said as they crossed the officers' mess toward the door. "How long are you going to milk that, anyway?"

Shrugging and with perfect deadpan delivery, Fisher replied, "As long as it irritates you, why rush it?"

The station's CMO had been contemplating retirement for a while now, Reyes knew. After more than five decades, Fisher had seen his share of what life in Starfleet had to offer. To say that he had grown tired of that life would be an egregious understatement, and Reyes had to wonder why he had accepted assignment to Vanguard in the first place.

Whatever the reason, I'm sure as hell glad he's here.

The door leading from the mess hall opened several paces before Reyes and Fisher should have been in range of its proximity sensors, and through it stepped Captain Rana Desai. As usual, she presented an immaculate appearance in her Starfleet uniform, tailored with utmost precision to her athletic yet still quite feminine physique. Her black hair was cut in a short style that kept it free of her face, and once again Reyes found himself drawn to her high, smooth cheekbones, delicate nose, and narrow chin, made all the more attractive by her choosing not to apply cosmetics.

She looked great even when she was angry, Reyes decided, which was a good thing considering Desai's dark, stern expression as she stepped into the room.

"Commodore," she said by way of greeting, "we need to talk."

"This can't be good," Fisher said, smiling to Desai.

Resisting the urge to elbow the doctor in the ribs, Reyes offered his own weak attempt at pleasantries as he regarded the JAG officer. "Looks like we're getting started early today." Desai's only response was to stand silent and allow her scowl to deepen.

It's going to be one of those days.

"I'll be in sickbay when you need me," Fisher said, nodding to Desai as he stepped past her on his way through the door. "Good morning, Captain," he offered before exiting the room.

"What can I do for you, Captain?" Reyes asked as the doors closed behind Fisher, knowing even as he gave voice to the question that he was not going to like her answer.

Holding up the data slate in her left hand for emphasis, Desai said, "Explain to me why it seems you cannot grasp even the basic concepts of civil liberties."

Reyes shrugged. "That could take a while. How's your schedule this morning?"

Yes, he decided, watching Desai's eyes smolder as if in preparation of unleashing phaser beams through his heart, *she looks fantastic when she's mad.*

5

As she stepped from the turbolift, Commander Atish Khatami paused a moment to sip at the cup she cradled in her hands, letting the tea it carried warm her mouth. She had tucked her data slate under one arm so she could hold her hand over the top of the grayish standard-issue beverage cup, being mindful not to let her drink slosh over the cup's side while on her way from the *Starship Endeavour*'s recreation room. At this point, she thought as she sipped again, she surely did not want to bobble it now.

Making her way down the corridor, Khatami sorted through a mental list of her morning routine. As the *Endeavour* had returned to Erilon while she slept, she had awakened early enough to gather and review reports from the gamma-shift crew as they ended their duties, knowing as she did so that she probably had made a bit of a pest of herself. Khatami secretly enjoyed that she was a "morning person," a quality that seemed to rattle her colleagues more often than not. She had even managed to sneak a bite of breakfast, and now everything seemed to be in order for her next item of business.

Rounding a bend in the corridor, she spied the ship's chief medical officer, Anthony Leone, his left hand holding a drink of his own as he stood propped against the bulkhead outside the door to the *Endeavour*'s main briefing room. The wiry, sandy-haired man saw her and nodded silently, folding what looked like a pained grimace into a smile of greeting.

"Tony," she acknowledged him in return, noticing Leone's attention focused not on his mug but rather on a small device he held in his other hand. "Captain inside?"

"Nope," Leone said, his eyes not wavering from what Khatami now recognized was a palm-sized chronometer.

"Good," she said, comfortable that she was keeping to schedule. Khatami had learned quickly that while Captain Zhao liked his meetings frequent, he also liked them brief and to the point. Above all, he expected everyone called to a meeting to arrive before he did—and be ready to go. "Shouldn't be long then."

"I'd give him about . . . six seconds," the physician said, "if I make my mark."

It was then that Khatami heard the distinctive clatter of rapid footfalls against the deck plates. Turning to look past Leone toward the sound, she caught a glimpse of a bare-chested man in Starfleet-issue athletic shorts rushing their way.

"One minute, forty-two seconds, Captain," Leone called out to the approaching runner. "Step it up, sir!"

"One more lap," Captain Zhao Sheng huffed in a metered breath as he ran past. "Good morning, Commander." His words echoed against the bulkheads as he disappeared around the bend of the corridor.

"Morning, sir," Khatami called out to the now empty passageway. She had caught a slight scent of perspiration mingling with an almost spicy fragrance that lingered in the air of Zhao's wake, and she smiled to herself in a subtle admission that she found it rather appealing. She chalked it up as another way that the captain reminded her of her husband, Kenji, whom she hadn't seen since her last visit to their home on Deneva, more than four months before. Calculating the time between stops home was only going to become more involved the longer the *Endeavour* was assigned to Starbase 47 and its subsequent duties in the Taurus Reach.

This place is a far sight from home for everyone here, not just me, she thought, *but we all knew that going in.*

"I dunno," Leone said after a moment to break the silence. "Running around, dripping with sweat. What kind of captain parades around his ship like that, with no shirt on and all?"

Khatami chuckled, something she typically found easy to do in Leone's company. "I think he's setting a great role model for the crew by staying on top of his physical training," she said, and smiled as she stepped toward him. "As ship's physician, you certainly can appreciate that."

Leone shrugged. "You just remember that the next time you see Mog running half-naked down the corridor," he said, referring to the *Endeavour*'s burly chief engineer, shaking his head and turning away from the chronometer in his hand long enough to sip from his drink. He swirled the cup and Khatami could see the thick, tan broth within.

"How do you drink that stuff?" Khatami had a high tolerance for the Federation's wide assortment of food and drink, but Leone's palate for his preferred morning beverage escaped her.

"Blame Mog, I guess," he replied. "He got me started on it. Everyone on Tellar drinks it. Tastes sort of like . . . caffeinated mushroom soup or something."

"What's it called again?"

"Like I can pronounce it?" Leone sneered a bit as he brought the cup to his lips, barely getting a sip before they both heard the sound of Zhao's approaching footfalls. The doctor's attention returned to his chronometer as the captain slowed and came to a stop before them. Touching a key on the device, Leone nodded in approval. "Shaved five seconds, sir," he said. "Not bad."

Zhao was expressionless and drew in a deep breath as Leone passed him the chronometer. As usual, Khatami was impressed with the captain's disposition even after the brisk run. His hairless chest gleamed with a thin sheen of perspiration, but that was the only evidence of the exertion he had just completed; his face was not flushed with color and he showed no sign of being winded. He was in peak physical condition, something Khatami could not as easily say for some of her fellow starship captains with whom she was personally acquainted, particularly the ones who had been on the job as long as Zhao.

Maybe I can expect this from Kenji when he's the captain's age?

The captain glanced at the chronometer before looking to Khatami. "I appreciate your indulging my run, Commander," he said. "With my schedule today, this was the best time to fit it in."

"Of course, sir," she said. "Actually, we're starting right on time."

"Excellent," Zhao said as he led the way into the briefing room and proceeded to the far end of the conference table. He grabbed a towel slung over the back of his chair and began wiping the perspiration from his chest and arms. Khatami was not at all surprised by the towel being at the ready, nor by the sight of a crisply folded standard gray Starfleet physical training shirt and a tall tumbler of water resting at the head of the table. Captain Zhao was nothing if not suitably prepared for any situation. "I hope you'll forgive the lapse in attire, everyone," he said as he scooped up the shirt and put it on. "I promise not to make it a habit." To Leone, he said, "Doctor, please consider scheduling my next physical-fitness test so that it doesn't clash so squarely with my duty schedule."

"And deprive the crew of your sterling example to health and fitness?" the physician asked, his tone one of pure mockery as he held up his cup in mock salute. "What a waste of a morale booster that would be."

Smiling at the good-natured jab, Zhao waved the matter away as he reached for his water. "So, shall we start and let Lieutenant Xiong catch up on his own, or am I being too presumptive in thinking he'll be here at all?"

Knowing full well that Xiong's cavalier attitude toward Zhao's penchant for regular staff meetings put the two at constant odds, Khatami held her tongue as she took a seat at the briefing room table. She trusted that the room would not remain silent long, however, as the concept of knowing when a question could go unanswered typically eluded Dr. Leone.

His predictability fell into form this morning.

"I'm sure I just passed him on deck eight coming with a tray of sweet rolls for everybody." As soon as Zhao shot a narrow-eyed look at him, Leone quickly added, "Um, sir," and slid into his chair.

"Dr. Leone," Zhao said, pausing to take a long swig of water, "maybe you could start with your report on the status of the Erilon encampment's staff and their acclimation to conditions?"

"Yes, sir," the physician said in a voice Khatami found suddenly officious. "The Corps of Engineers and survey-team members have adapted to the arctic climate on the planet as well as we can expect. Dr. Catera's incident log for the last few weeks looks pretty routine. A few cases of frostbite in the extremities, fatigue, bumps and bruises. It's what you'd expect at any installation trying to get up and running in Class-P conditions."

"Any illnesses or reported reactions to anything indigenous?" Zhao asked.

"Besides the sniffles?" Leone frowned. "No, nothing out of the ordinary, illness-wise. As for reactions or interactions or any other kind of actions, nothing. There've been no reported encounters with indigenous life beyond any bacteria or mold thawed out and stirred up by our activities. There's been no higher-order life detected down there, Captain. The place is an ice cube."

Listening to Leone's report, Khatami knew that, like her, the captain was waiting for information that to the doctor might on its own seem new or unusual but which might have additional meaning when coupled with other facts to which she and Zhao were privy. Researchers at the Erilon encampment were among the first Federation personnel with long-term exposure to bacteria and other life imbued with the Taurus meta-genome, and no one had any idea of the potential implications of such prolonged contact.

As the doctor completed his report, Zhao quietly took another long draw from his tumbler before looking to Khatami. Their eyes locked only briefly, but in that instant she saw that his thoughts mirrored her own: *Nothing new.*

"So much for Erilon," Zhao said with a small smile. "Ship's status, Commander?"

"As far as the *Endeavour* goes, all main systems are working normally," she said before consulting the data slate she had brought to the meeting. "Chief Nelson resolved that pattern-buffer problem in the transporter room. Commander Mog replaced a faulty backflow to eliminate an intercooler issue he reported yesterday. Oh, and Doctor, I received a memo thanking me for correcting the food-slot situation."

"Situation?" Zhao knit his brow. "I wasn't informed of any situation."

"Oh, it was nothing, sir," Khatami said, wincing a bit as she heard the words escape her lips unchecked. The captain never liked hearing an incident aboard ship or a status report on an *Endeavour* system reduced to "nothing."

"If it was nothing . . ." Zhao let his voice trail off, offering a knowing smile because Khatami and everyone else on the senior staff could finish the sentence for him.

. . . then why bring it up in a meeting?

Mentally resetting herself as Leone sighed audibly, she said, "I meant that more for Dr. Leone, sir. Ensigns th' . . . th'Shendileth and sh'Dastisar—"

"Say *those* three times fast," Leone said, which made Khatami laugh in spite of herself.

Zhao seemed to almost crack a smile himself, though it was quickly suppressed as he glanced over at Khatami. "Continue, Commander."

"Well, sir, the ensigns in question had complained that the food slots had not been programmed for Andorian cuisine," she said. "I told them that the problem lies in their meal cards, so I consulted Dr. Leone and he issued me amended cards to pass to them."

"And another shipboard dietary crisis is averted," Leone said dryly. "Good work, Commander."

"So," Zhao said, "let's move on." He made a show of looking about the conference room. "We seem to be missing some representatives from the planetary survey team."

Khatami fidgeted a bit in her seat, uncomfortable at her being the bearer of frustrating news. "Well, sir, Lieutenant Xiong informed me that he would forward his report to me in time for the meeting. Then when you asked for his attendance at our meeting, I presented that request to him as well."

"And his response?" Zhao's voice was flat and his eyes just slightly narrowed.

"He indicated that he would come to the meeting . . . if he had time," Khatami said, eliciting a single cough of a laugh from

Leone. "Those were his words, sir, and I made it very clear that you wanted your report in per . . ."

Khatami abruptly closed her mouth as Zhao rose from the table and sharply tugged down the front of his shirt, the same automatic gesture he would have made had he been wearing his standard Starfleet duty uniform. The glint in his eyes was not one of anger or irritation, but of ice.

"Considering the lieutenant's busy schedule, perhaps I'll just take my report from him in his lab."

"Captain!" Khatami exclaimed, surprised at the sharpness of her own voice as it echoed around the briefing room. Rising to her feet, she continued in a more reserved tone. "That is, sir, allow me to retrieve Lieutenant Xiong and escort him back here. There's no reason for you to go to the surface yourself."

"On the contrary," Zhao said, his voice remaining neutral as he strode to the door. "I think there's every reason. Our Mr. Xiong is a busy young man. I'd hate to inconvenience him any more than is absolutely necessary."

Khatami hustled to keep pace with Zhao as Leone fell in behind her. "But sir, please at least wait long enough for me to assign a security detail to accompany you." By way of reply, Zhao offered an odd, almost amused expression, and she expected him to deliver a sharp denial of her suggestion, but none came. "Starfleet regulations, sir," she said, hoping to lighten the tone. "I'm offering only a reminder."

After a moment, the captain nodded. "Very well. Have Lieutenant Nauls muster two of his team and meet me in the transporter room in one hour." As Zhao walked toward the turbolift, his words echoed back to her. "We'll give that pattern buffer its first run."

As Zhao left the room and the doors closed behind him, Leone sidled over to stand next to Khatami.

"I've never seen him that mad, have you?" Leone asked in a wide-eyed whisper with as much seriousness as Khatami had ever heard from the doctor. "Good idea about the security, Atish. I think the captain's gonna *kill* Xiong."

6

As he always did when summoned to the inner sanctum aboard the *Omari-Ekon*, Quinn stood between the pair of ominous black obelisks while facing the raised dais upon which Ganz reclined in unrepentant splendor. He tried not to fidget as the muscled Orion crime lord looked down upon him, his emerald green skin glistening from a recent application of body oil no doubt provided by one or more of the concubines with whom he surrounded himself. For several moments Ganz said nothing, and Quinn had to restrain himself from speaking first for fear that he might start blabbering incoherently.

He also feared he might simply throw up all over the room.

Rising up from the pile of multicolored cushions and pillows covering the dais, Ganz maneuvered himself into a sitting position, resting his bare green feet on the polished deck plate less than two meters from Quinn's own dingy boots.

"You don't look well, Quinn," the Orion said, his voice low and ominous. "You need to start taking better care of yourself. All that drinking is going to kill you one day."

Quinn, of course, held no misconceptions that Ganz was at all interested in his health. "I plan to cut down later today," he replied. "I figure that's when I'll run out of money." Looking around the lavishly appointed chamber, he added, "What can I do for you, Ganz? I don't mean to sound like I'm rushing, but I've got a charter this morning. I'm leaving in less than an hour. I'll be gone for two weeks."

"I know all about your itinerary," Ganz said, his thick brow furrowing. "I've got a change in your schedule."

Quinn knew better than to protest, but he still could not help

the resigned sigh that escaped his lips. He braced for whatever retribution his minor loss of bearing might bring, but Ganz merely
shook his head.

"Don't worry," the Orion said, "I've already made arrange-
ments to ensure your shipment gets where it needs to go. Zett will
give you all the details when we're finished here, but suffice it to
say that your so-called employment with Starfleet provides a nice
cover should I need you, so it's in my best interest to ensure you
don't do anything which might make them decide to termi-
nate your services." Shrugging, he added, "Of course, this extra
effort on my part comes with a price. I figure sixty percent of your
fee from the station quartermaster should be sufficient to cover
my end."

Naturally, Quinn thought, this time taking pains to suppress
any reaction to Ganz's words. *Why can't I just die from alcohol
poisoning like other drunks?*

As if on cue, a bell rang from somewhere down on the gambling deck, announcing another lucky winner at one of the table
games. At least somebody was having some good fortune this
morning.

"What do you want me to do?" he asked.

Ganz nodded, obviously pleased with the way the conversation was going. "I need you to leave on schedule. After you rendezvous with one of my ships to transfer your cargo for that
Federation colony, you'll head to the Yerad system and retrieve an
employee of mine."

A few salient factoids about that system managed to work
their way up from the depths of Quinn's liquor-deadened and
sleep-deprived memory. "Aren't they under Klingon control?"
With the Federation and Klingon Empire each taking pronounced interest in the Taurus Reach in recent weeks, the
region had seen a sharp upswing in ship traffic, particularly
from the Klingons. Based on what he had gleaned from gossip
overheard in various places around the station, the Klingons
were sending numerous ships into the area, hopping from system to system and planting the flag of the empire on a number
of worlds. While most of those planets were reportedly unin-

habited, a few were known to contain sentient populations, which the Klingons had "conquered."

Ganz nodded. "More or less. The Klingons staked a claim, but they're interested in the dilithium mines on one of the outer planets. They're leaving Yerad III alone, at least for now."

"For now?" Quinn repeated. "Ganz, you're a smart man. Surely you're following the . . . how should I put it? The chaotic political climate in that region?"

Fixing him with a stern glare, the Orion paused for several seconds before one thick yet impeccably groomed eyebrow arched upward. "Do I present the appearance of someone who follows politics, Mr. Quinn?"

Good point, Quinn conceded, as a faint yet noxious odor—one he recognized as a more exotic blend of Rigelian tobacco no doubt being enjoyed by someone on the gambling deck—drifted past his nostrils. A brief wave of nausea washed over him, and he wondered once again if he might escape the *Omari-Ekon* with the contents of his stomach.

Reaching to a small table set to the right of the dais, Ganz retrieved a sizable mug with a flared base that seemed small and fragile in his massive hand. After taking a large gulp of the mug's contents, he said, "What I do know is that there's no way to be sure when the Klingons might adjust their priorities, so I need to take a few steps to protect my business interests. You understand. Right, Quinn?"

Yerad III was not unknown to the privateer. The planet was located within a system outside the actual boundaries of the Taurus Reach, but close enough that the Klingons had deemed it a good strategic point for ship servicing operations as well as the dilithium mining Ganz had mentioned. Essentially a third-rate imitator of Risa or Wrigley's Pleasure Planet with its numerous self-styled resorts, spas and other destinations of questionable morality, the remote world also was home to a loose collection of assorted nefarious characters who preferred to blend in with the comings and goings of the planet's uncounted visitors. Away from the prying eyes of Federation or other law-enforcement entities, the planet's teeming underworld took advantage of the isolated location to carry out all manner of questionable activities.

"So," Quinn said, hating where this conversation was going. "You want me to go to Yerad III and get your . . . ?"

"One of my accountants," Ganz finished for him. "He safeguards a substantial portion of my . . . financial records and other information related to several of my various business activities. Bring him to me along with all of his data files. He knows someone's coming to get him, so he should be ready when you get there." He leaned forward, his expression growing even more menacing. "No matter what happens, those files have to make it here. You understand what I'm saying, Mr. Quinn?"

Doing his best to maintain an even keel as he listened to the details of his coming assignment, Quinn affected what he hoped appeared to be a genuine smile. "Perfectly. Does this bookkeeper have a name?"

"I'm sure he does," Ganz replied without hesitation. Turning to Zett, he asked, "What's the bookkeeper's name?"

"Sakud Armnoj," the Nalori replied. "He's a Zakdorn."

A Zakdorn? Quinn only barely prevented himself from visibly flinching at the thought. His few encounters with members of that perpetually fussy, pretentious species had almost always ended with him wishing for a blunt object of some kind and five minutes without any witnesses. Performing the mental calculations for the voyage to and from Yerad III did little to raise his already plummeting morale. *Almost a week with a Zakdorn. If I'm lucky, we'll get blown to hell by a passing Klingon ship, or maybe I can just fly into a star.*

"Any other questions?" Ganz asked.

Figuring he had nothing to lose, Quinn replied, "I don't suppose this little errand—assuming that I get this bookkeeper of yours back here safe and sound—makes us even, does it?"

"No," Ganz replied. "Not even close."

Of course.

After a failed assignment last month to Ravanar IV, during which he had lost a very valuable piece of technology that Ganz had sent him to retrieve, the Orion had seen fit to place Quinn into perpetual servitude as payment for the blunder. Further, the item turned out to be a component for a Starfleet sensor screen in use on the planet, and Ganz's displeasure at Quinn's inability to obtain it was but one consequence of that botched task.

Your actions led to the loss of a starship and the deaths of hundreds of Starfleet personnel, Mr. Quinn.

The accusation, levied by Lieutenant Commander T'Prynn during his first clandestine meeting with her, deep in the bowels of the station, still rang in his ears. In a manner of speaking, she was correct. The *U.S.S. Bombay* had been dispatched to Ravanar IV with a replacement component for the sensor screen he had incapacitated, and shortly thereafter had fallen victim to ambush by Tholian vessels. T'Prynn had used that information to press him into service for her own purposes, none of which she felt inclined to share with Quinn, leaving him with the burden of attempting to serve two masters who appeared to have more in common than either would ever readily admit.

If there is a Great Bird of the Galaxy out there, then the only reason it's interested in me is so that it can swoop in low and fast and take a big . . .

"Anything else?" Ganz said, interrupting his momentary reverie.

Quinn shrugged. "Why me?"

"To be honest, I need somebody I can count on not to screw this up," the Orion said before drawing another long pull from his mug. "Don't look so surprised, Quinn. I'm a businessman, and I'm smart enough to know when I've got a useful employee working for me." He leaned forward, his thick brow furrowing. "So . . . don't screw this up. Understood?"

Unsure of what to make of Ganz's abrupt, unexpected show at what for him passed as civility, Quinn nodded. "You got it."

His departure from the *Omari-Ekon* was much like his arrival. As Zett walked behind him and just to his right, no doubt ready to kill him if he so much as breathed in a suspicious rhythm, Quinn looked longingly at the festive atmosphere surrounding him as he passed through the gaming deck. Throughout the room, all manner of humans and aliens—none of them

Starfleet—were engaging in the sort of whimsical ribald behavior that had made Ganz's vessel a premier destination for those seeking solace from the more conservative, restrained venues available aboard Vanguard. High-stakes gambling, high-priced liquor, and equally expensive "companionship"—male, female, and a few Quinn honestly could not categorize—all were on stark, uninhibited display here in the ship's festive sanctuary.

They're happy now, he reminded himself. *But just wait until they see the bill.*

Zett, naturally, opted out of any casual conversation as they reached the airlock, offering only a perfunctory nod of farewell to Quinn. Now alone with his muddled and unorganized thoughts as he continued on down the gangplank and toward the docking corridor, the privateer wondered about his chances of surviving a mission into Klingon-occupied territory only to travel to a world teeming with all manner of despicable cretins and abscond with a whiny, nasally Zakdorn whose name his employer had not even bothered to learn.

The outlook was not encouraging, he decided as he rode a turbolift up to the station's small-craft bays, wondering at the same time whether his day would get any worse before he even had a chance to get the *Rocinante* under way.

Rounding a bend in the corridor, Quinn was almost to the docking bay where his ship was berthed when he stopped short, coming face-to-face with Lieutenant Commander T'Prynn. The Vulcan intelligence officer stood ramrod straight in her crisp red Starfleet uniform, hands clasped behind her back and looking as though she might have been waiting there for a hundred years.

"Good morning, Mr. Quinn," she said.

Dammit, the privateer thought as a fresh wave of hangover pain chose that moment to course through his alcohol-saturated brain. Reaching up to rub his forehead with the heel of his right hand, Quinn wondered if there was any chance of a hull breach occurring right where he stood.

7

Sweat dripping from her black hair to sting her eyes, Rana Desai lunged forward, her arm and racquet extended to meet the ball as it bounced off the court's well-marred forward wall and came out short and shallow. Her opponent had placed a wicked spin on the ball with the perfection of a seasoned pro, draining its inertia and forcing Desai to scramble in a desperate attempt to reach it before its second bounce.

She was too slow, groaning in defeat as the ball dribbled past her and rolled toward the rear corner of the racquetball court.

"Nice play," she said, mopping perspiration from her brow with the sweatband on her right wrist. "If I'd known you could kick my ass all over this court, I might not have recruited you for my office in the first place."

"Thanks, Captain," replied Lieutenant Holly Moyer, offering an apologetic smile as she pushed a lock of her long auburn hair out of her face, tucking it underneath the black band she wore around her head. "You almost had that one, though. I may have to get more creative." Walking toward the small door at the rear of the court, she said, "That's two games. Want to go best out of five?"

"Don't push your luck, Lieutenant," Desai said, maintaining her poker face though her words carried a jovial tone. Though she was Moyer's superior officer in Starbase 47's office of the Starfleet Judge Advocate General, she had established a policy among her staff that rank did not extend to off-duty activities. Given that she and her subordinates spent upward of ten to twelve hours each day within the confines of the station's JAG office, which itself was ensconced within the larger container that was Vanguard itself, the ability to leave behind work and all of its trappings was of paramount importance to her. In addition, Desai also made it a point to schedule one-on-one meetings—preferably in an informal atmosphere—a tactic she had learned often helped her junior lawyers to gain new perspective on a difficult case or some other troubling aspect of their day-to-day duties.

Desai followed Moyer off the court to a low-rise bench atop which sat their respective racquets. "What's happening with McIlvain's Planet?" she asked, reaching into her bag for a bottle of water, randomly selecting one of several cases she knew currently sat in Moyer's open file and which had been causing the lieutenant no end of grief.

Moyer drank from her own bottle before shrugging. "Tellar and Rigel are bringing their cases for arbitration," she said. "Meetings are scheduled for early next month." Shaking her head as she took another swallow of water, she added, "The place isn't big enough for both of them, I guess, even though their respective colonies aren't even on the same landmass."

"One big, happy Federation, aren't we?" Desai grabbed a towel from her bag and wiped her face as she took a seat on the bench. "It sounds like something for the C.A.'s office," she said, referring to Aole Miller, Vanguard's colonial administration liaison.

"Will do," Moyer replied. Adopting a wistful smile, she added, "You know, if the planet really *is* McIlvain's, then why doesn't he just come take it back from these guys?"

Desai offered a mock wince. "Okay, you're not allowed to make jokes again." Leaning against the wall, she considered the next item on her mental checklist. "What about that follow-up statement from Lieutenant Ridley? We need to make a ruling on that bar fight."

Moyer shook her head. "Not yet, but I expect it by the end of the day. As it stands now, I'm leaning toward simple assault rather than domestic battery."

"They weren't married?" Desai asked.

"One guy is the second husband of the other guy's third wife, or something. I can never keep that stuff straight," Moyer replied, examining the strings of her racquet. "I'll call a Denobulan JAG I know on New Bangkok and get her opinion."

"Fair enough," Desai said, rising from the bench and moving back toward the court. Feeling energized after the brief respite, she nodded to Moyer. "Let's go. Three out of five."

"It's your funeral, Captain," Moyer said, the words punctuated by a mischievous smile as she followed Desai onto the court, closing the access door behind her.

Stretching her arms over her head, the captain asked, "What's up with that cargo-theft case?" While crime, particularly theft, had so far been rare on the station, there had been a handful of notable exceptions, one of the most recent of which involved the attempted pilfering of medical supplies and equipment from a docked cargo hauler. The perpetrators were a band of privateers, and initial interviews with the group suggested they were a loose-knit lot who with magnificent clumsiness had bungled the execution of an equally insipid scheme seemingly plotted over more than a few bottles of Aldebaran whiskey.

Despite a curiously ample collection of evidence and confessions, Desai's instincts told her there was more to this case than what was visible on the surface.

"Well," Moyer said, "if they hadn't botched the job, they would have turned a tidy profit selling that stuff on the black market." Shrugging, she said, "Somebody's paying their bills. I'm following the money and seeing where it leads." She shook her head. "Otherwise, it's a pretty weak case, Captain. Security's screwup hurt us."

Desai could sympathize with her plight. The case currently hinged upon sloppy paperwork submitted by one Ensign Donovan Collig, a member of Vanguard's security team. "I ripped Lieutenant Jackson a new . . . well, let's just say he didn't sit comfortably the rest of that day."

She had wasted no time addressing the matter with the station's chief of security in no uncertain terms, particularly given the fact that it was not the first time she had heard members of her staff complain of poorly assembled incident reports submitted by the security section. Thanks to Collig's failure to retain key foren-sic samples from the crime scene, Moyer's evidentiary chain was broken, severely fracturing any chance the JAG office had of con-necting the attempted burglary to where Desai believed it origi-nated: the Orion trader Ganz.

It was not the first time such a setback had occurred during one of her staff's investigations where the goal had been to link something tangible to the merchant prince who for reasons defying logic and common sense was allowed to maintain a vessel docked with the station. Were such failures truly acci-dental? Was it possible that Ganz had friends embedded within the station's security force?

"Hey!"

A voice from above and behind them echoed off the walls. Startled by the outburst, Desai and Moyer looked up to the spectator stands situated one level above the court to see Ezekiel Fisher regarding them from where he sat reclined in one of the seats. Leaning forward until his arms rested atop the safety railing, he offered one of his paternal smiles. "Are you going to play or not? And quit talking shop. It throws off your game."

Desai laughed, running her free hand through her sweat-dampened hair. "It's already off," she replied. "And who invited you, anyway?"

"I'm never one to await an invitation to witness a demonstra-tion of athletic prowess," Fisher said, rising from his seat. "You've looked better, though."

"I can only hope," Desai replied, watching as the doctor de-scended the narrow, spiral staircase leading from the observation deck. Turning to Moyer, she said, "I guess I'll quit while I'm be-hind. Your game, Lieutenant."

"I'll take it any way I can get it," Moyer said, breaking into a wide grin. She nodded to Fisher as he moved toward them. "Good to see you, Doctor," she said before looking to Desai. "See you at the office, Captain."

Fisher's gaze followed the lieutenant's willowy form as she disappeared through the door at the back of the court. He waited until Moyer was out of earshot before glancing at Desai. "Always liked redheads."

Offering a mock scowl, Desai punched him playfully on the arm. "What are you doing down here?"

Fisher gestured to the door and they started toward it. "You know me. If somebody's playing a sport anywhere on this station, I'll find it. I'm a serial spectator."

"Ever think you'd have more fun if you played instead of just watching all the time?" Desai asked as she once again sat down on the bench.

Waving away the suggestion, Fisher said, "There's no senior circuit on the station." He smiled at his own joke as he sat down next to her. "Okay, you got me. Haven't seen much of you lately, and figured I'd see how you're doing, and all that."

"Making a house call, Fish?" Desai regarded him with a lop-sided grin.

"Not if you keep calling me that," Fisher replied, grimacing at the nickname she knew he hated. "You've been working hard these past few weeks, hiding in that office of yours. Do you ever get out of there?"

Desai nodded as she rummaged in her bag for her bottle of water. "Sure. I get to eat every so often, and I've read about this phenomenon that's supposed to relieve fatigue and stress. Sleep is what I think they're calling it." In truth, the workload had been enormous during the past month. The inquiry into the loss of the *Bombay* had resulted in many other cases and issues being repri-oritized, and she and her staff had been playing catch-up since then.

"So you're saying that your social life has been drawing the short straw," Fisher said, leaning back against the wall and reaching up to stroke his beard.

Is he kidding? Desai looked askance at the doctor as she sipped her water. Fisher was the only person on the station—so far as she knew, anyway—who possessed knowledge of her relationship with Commodore Reyes. As he also had been a friend of Reyes for decades, she was certain he knew that same relationship had been strained during recent weeks. Despite that, in all the time she had known Fisher, the man had made it clear that getting involved in the personal affairs of others, even his close friends, was an activity he preferred to avoid if at all possible.

If he's here, then he's worried about Diego, she surmised. *And maybe even worried about me.*

"Fish," she said after a moment. "How's he doing?"

Eyeing her from beneath a furrowed brow, Fisher asked, "Like he'd tell me?"

"He'd tell you before he told me."

"Well, that's because I've courted him longer," the doctor countered, his deadpan delivery making her laugh. "He's carrying a lot of weight around. His mother's on his mind. Hallie Gannon and everyone else on the *Bombay* are on his mind." Sighing, he glanced about the corridor before saying, "He loves being here, Rana. Challenges, mystery, lots to learn. It's just the place for him at this point in his life. But, he hates to lose people. Always has."

Desai nodded. "I know." She had seen as much during the inquiry into the destruction of the *Bombay,* during which she had been duty-bound to sit and listen as the prosecutor she'd appointed grilled Reyes for hours on his actions—or lack thereof—which may or may not have contributed to the tragedy. He had been forced to relive the incident through grueling testimony, every moment of which Desai was sure had rubbed at the wound inflicted by the loss of the starship and its crew, the captain of which had also been a close friend.

"What's odd," Fisher said, "is that he's endured thirty years of losing people. You'd think he'd have found a way to cope with it by now."

The blunt comment stung Desai. "That seems a little harsh. You know that inside he's not what we all see in the uniform." While he presented a gruff, commanding exterior in public, she had seen firsthand the vulnerability Reyes contained with exceptional skill. That he managed it so well was a testament to his force of will, and was one of the many qualities she admired—no, loved—about him.

"Oh, I know," Fisher replied, "and that's my point. He closes off. Keeps people out, and keeps the hurt all caged up in him. That's not any way to heal, Rana."

Desai nodded. "Well, you're the healer. What do you suggest?"

"I have no idea," Fisher said.

"And once again, your sage counsel proves invaluable," Desai replied, releasing a humorless chuckle as she busied herself tucking her racquet into her bag. For all the problems she had faced dealing with Reyes on a personal level, confronting him in a professional setting had proven almost as daunting. Much of that was her fault, she knew.

"We've disagreed on any number of issues, Fish, and some of those disagreements have been volatile." She chalked that up to her passion for upholding and defending Federation law, even when it became inconvenient to Starfleet missions and interests. "I know he understands on an intellectual level that I'm just doing my job, but sometimes I wonder if our professional . . . spats . . . are having an effect. You know, gradual but detrimental effects."

Frowning, Fisher shook his head. "Give the boy some credit, Rana. He'd know if you were shirking your responsibilities in order to ease tension, either what's between you two or whatever he's carrying around on his own. He'd never forgive you for that."

"Now you're talking like a doctor," Desai said, rising from the bench. "I should make appointments to see you more often."

"Come by anytime," Fisher replied, smiling. "Don't even need to call ahead first." Standing up, he regarded her in that mentoring manner she had come to appreciate. "Don't worry, Rana. In addition to all the responsibility he has on his shoulders right now, it's been a long time since Diego's been able to care about anyone that didn't just take orders from him. He'll find his way, and so will you." Reaching out to pat her on the arm, he indicated the racquetball court with a nod. "In the meantime, don't let it throw you off your game."

After leaning in to give her a peck on the cheek, the doctor turned and walked out of the room, leaving Desai to finish gathering her belongings as well as her thoughts. In his customary fashion, she realized, Fisher had managed to offer comfort, confidence, and support, all without really conveying anything in the way of helpful advice.

How does he do that?

Meanwhile, Desai knew she was faced with a choice. She could strive ever more diligently to ensure that her relationship with Reyes did not suffer because of their sometimes conflicting responsibilities, or she could surrender to what many might consider to be inevitable. It would, after all, be easy to concentrate solely on her work, committing herself to the career she had chosen and allowing the professional gap to widen between them, taking with it any chance for personal harmony and happiness.

Most troubling to her, Desai realized, was that the question seemed to possess no easy answer.

8

Sitting cross-legged on the floor of her quarters, her back straight and her hands clasped gently in her lap, T'Prynn closed her eyes. Feeble illumination offered by the lone candle resting atop the squat table before her was the only source of light in the room, its flickering luminescence still visible through her eyelids. The rest of the room was consumed by darkness, offering no distractions and allowing her to concentrate on clearing her thoughts and opening her mind as—for the second time—she began to meditate.

And the second time, she failed. As with the first attempt, the serenity she sought within her own mind was interrupted by a single, pervasive demand.

Submit.

The voice of Sten, her long-dead fiancé, called to her as it had almost constantly since that day fifty-three years earlier when, while enveloped in the violent yet passionate embrace of *Plak tow,* T'Prynn had killed him, snapping his neck during ritual combat. The act had been in accordance with Vulcan traditions and had come while in the throes of ceremonial *kal-if-fee,* where she had fought Sten to the death for the right to be freed from their betrothal. Even in death, he had forsaken everything that Vulcans held dear, forcing his *katra* into her mind as her hands broke his neck.

Submit.

Since that moment, fueled as it had been by long-suppressed emotions run amok—anger, betrayal, unrequited lust—Sten's living spirit had dwelled alongside T'Prynn's own consciousness, carrying on the sacramental duel and challenging her for supremacy of her own mind.

Submit.

While there scarcely was a moment during which T'Prynn was not aware of its presence, Sten's *katra* seemed to be intruding upon her thoughts of late with increasing frequency, to say nothing of amplified force. She suspected it was due to a lowering of her mental defenses in the face of working long hours and not allowing herself sufficient time for sleep and meditation. There was also the distinct possibility that her infrequent yet fervent trysts with Anna Sandesjo, the inexplicably alluring woman who—among other things—served currently as attaché to Ambassador Jetanien, might also be a contributing factor.

An intriguing notion, that, she mused.

Still, the occurrences were not unknown, and in the past T'Prynn had been able to cope with the incursions using one of several techniques imparted to her by the Adepts. Indeed, she owed her sanity and even her life to the centuries-old order of masters who safeguarded not only the ancient teachings of Surak but also the writings and rituals surrounding *Kolinahr* and other mental and physical disciplines designed to reinforce the Vulcan people's edict of wisdom through logic and the careful, deliberate mastery of passion.

Submit!

Despite their best efforts, however, the Adepts had been unable to rid her of Sten's constant, hammering attacks against the fortification she had erected around her consciousness. All such attempts had failed, with the high masters informing T'Prynn on each occasion that the *katra* of her dead fiancé would remain with her unless it left of its own volition, or upon her death. Until either of those events occurred, she would forever be locked in mortal combat within the depths of her own mind.

I will not submit to you! Her mind all but screamed the rebuke. *I will never surrender.*

Deciding with no small amount of irritation that further attempts to meditate would meet with the same result, T'Prynn made one more concerted push against Sten's *katra,* succeeding once again—if only temporarily—in forcing her late fiancé's ubiquitous presence into a deep, dark corner of her mind. That accomplished, she leaned forward and blew out the candle before rising to her feet.

"Computer, lights."

In immediate response to her commands, a quartet of recessed red lights, one set at eye level into each of the room's four walls, glowed to life and cast their harsh crimson glare toward the ceiling. As she crossed her quarters to the small, austere desk that occupied the corner nearest her bed, she opened the closure of her meditation robe, removing the garment and folding it carefully before laying it on the edge of her bed. "Computer, display docking-bay departure schedule," she said, pausing long enough to retrieve her uniform before continuing on to her desk.

Atop the workstation sat a standard-issue bulky gray computer terminal. A collection of data cards, each labeled and ordered with meticulous care, rested within the storage niche molded into the terminal's base, but aside from that the polished surface of the wood desktop was bare. In accordance with T'Prynn's request, the computer screen flared to life and coalesced into a text display featuring several columns of precisely arrayed data. Pulling on her uniform and smoothing it into place, she leaned forward to review the report on the monitor. It took her only a moment to note that Cervantes Quinn's small vessel was still scheduled to depart the station on time.

Her plan to conscript the freighter pilot carried no guarantees of success, of course. She was confident that the Klingon sensor drone, one of however many such devices dispatched into the Taurus Reach by battle cruisers of the empire, would be at the coordinates she had calculated based on information gleaned from a furtive review of intercepted Klingon subspace communiqués. While she initially had doubted Quinn's ability to find the device and obtain the data it would contain, she reminded herself that the man made a living scrounging and scurrying about space, somehow obtaining that which should by all rights lie beyond his limited grasp. For all the faults the trader possessed, prudence demanded he not be underestimated, regardless of whether he was acting upon her instructions.

However, T'Prynn was surprised and somewhat concerned that Quinn had defied her instructions to avoid contact with Tim Pennington, particularly after the role the trader unwittingly had played in her harsh yet necessary ruination of the man's credibility as a journalist. Quinn, for reasons as yet unknown, had befriended the disgraced reporter, with the pair spending a great deal of time in pursuit of their mutual interests. So far as T'Prynn could discern, those hobbies involved little more than their repeated attempts to deplete the inventories of Stars Landing's various tavern owners in methodical fashion.

Whereas she originally was confident that Quinn never would reveal his own complicity in Pennington's professional downfall, now she found herself doubting that certainty. Quinn would be required to manufacture some sort of falsehood in order to explain the necessity of retrieving the sensor drone. Failing that, and assuming their friendship had strengthened as much as T'Prynn believed it had, the higher the possibility that Quinn might actually find the moral fortitude within himself to confess his sins. If that were to occur, T'Prynn would find herself faced with carrying out another unpleasant yet quite necessary act in the name of preserving the secrecy surrounding Vanguard's presence in the Taurus Reach.

Until then, Quinn is useful, she reminded herself, *and the journalist may yet prove to be, as well.*

Assuming the unlikely duo managed to accomplish the comparatively simple feat of capturing the sensor drone, T'Prynn had estimated the odds to be severely against the mismatched duo escaping detection and successfully retrieving the information she sought before the drone could transmit it to a waiting vessel.

As for that sensor data, what would it contain? Of that, T'Prynn had no idea. Indeed, nothing at all was known about the area of space the drone was scheduled to scan in six days' time. Named by the Starfleet stellar cartographers tasked with cataloguing the plethora of stars and planets revealed by the Federation's own array of unmanned long-range sensor probes deployed into the Taurus Reach nearly two years earlier, Jinoteur had at first appeared to contain nothing of even passing interest. With all that Vanguard was currently tasked to oversee in respect to the legitimate colonies, remote Starfleet outposts, and trading vessels scattered throughout the region, the apparently nondescript system might well have gone unexplored for the foreseeable future.

That notion was revised even before Starbase 47 itself had become fully operational, when it was discovered that a series of rampant, unexplained malfunctions aboard the station were not due to onboard systems errors as might be expected aboard a starship or starbase that had been rushed through construction and into active service. Instead, the anomalies had been caused by interference from what specialists from Starfleet's Corps of Engineers had described as a "carrier wave" emanating from somewhere within the Jinoteur system, all but imperceptible except by sensors specially modified to detect it.

Computer analysis eventually had determined that the wave was in effect a previously unknown variety of communications signal. Further, translation software also had offered the theory that the signal might in fact be transmitting a warning. Station and corps engineers had devised a means of answering the signal, after which the carrier wave abruptly had ceased its transmissions. Yet, even after several months of continued analysis, the reason for the strange signal—as well as the identity of those responsible for sending it or any intended recipients—remained a mystery.

Was there a connection to a larger riddle, the one that Vanguard and its crew had been assembled to solve? Might the originators of the carrier wave somehow be connected to the same ancient beings who appeared to have created the equally intriguing meta-genome that Starfleet researchers were seeking even now?

There was only one way to find out—though doing so carried with it a need for care and stealth so as to prevent attracting the unwanted attention of either the Klingon Empire or the Tholian Assembly. Both powers were making their own forays into the Taurus Reach in response to Federation expansion into the region, though by all accounts the Klingons appeared to have been taken in by the extensive disinformation campaign currently in play. Dozens of colonies and remote outposts, all of them genuine efforts on the part of Federation citizens, were springing up throughout this area of space. Only a handful of people knew that some of those colonies were in fact providing cover for research operations tasked with studying artifacts of ancient alien technology and construction, chiefly to determine whether there was any connection to those responsible for the meta-genome.

It had taken significant effort on her part to infiltrate Klingon communications networks in order to determine the routes and timetables related to the array of unmanned sensor drones the empire was dispatching into the Taurus Reach. Determining the schedule and travel path of the probe assigned to the Jinoteur system had been difficult, but it was a simple matter when compared with the larger challenge of actually devising a means of intercepting it in a manner that allowed Starfleet to collect the drone's information while at the same time denying it to the Klingons. Only fortunate happenstance had allowed her to commandeer Cervantes Quinn's furtive journey to Yerad III in order to meet her needs, saving her from having to employ someone from her expansive network of operatives and informants.

Submit.

The voice sliced through her thoughts with the force of a keenly sharpened blade, ringing in her ears and her mind.

Without her conscious control, T'Prynn's right hand formed a fist and slammed down onto the surface of her desk. The sound of wood cracking echoed across the confines of her quarters, and she looked down to see that she had punched a hole through the desktop and fractured the surrounding wood. Momentary physical pain registered as she noted the sting of several splinters piercing her flesh, and she welcomed the fleeting respite from the mental anguish currently plaguing her. For a moment, her attention was riveted by the six green splotches of blood welling up from where the splinters had penetrated her skin.

You are weak. The words goaded her, though this time she could not be sure if the voice was Sten's or her own. *Eventually, you will have to surrender to me. It is inevitable.*

Ignoring the patent threat, T'Prynn slowly and methodically removed each of the splinters from her hand before moving to the small bureau set against the wall near her quarters' compact, utilitarian lavatory. From the top drawer, she retrieved a small hand towel and a protoplaser. She wiped her hand clean before waving the small medical device over it. The tiny wounds—as well as any bruising they might later generate—were healed in seconds.

If only I could erase you as easily, she thought as she returned the protoplaser to her bureau. She thrust the taunt into the deepest recesses of her mind, where she knew the enduring consciousness of her onetime betrothed still lurked, waiting for the moment when she was at her most vulnerable so it could seize control and finally achieve what it had demanded for so long.

Submit, the voice said again.

"Never," she said aloud, tossing the bloodied hand towel into the matter-reclamation slot near her lavatory door, before turning on her heel and marching out of her quarters.

9

Squinting into a desk-mounted viewer, Lieutenant Ming Xiong ignored the gritty sting of his tired eyes as they played across yet another chromatographic analysis of samples taken from around the Erilon encampment site where he had lived and studied these past weeks. His mind fogged a moment as he scanned over the colored bands of data. Were these soil samples? Rock samples? Ice samples? Yes, ice samples, he remembered, ones from cores drilled a few meters from the base of the massive black structure—the *artifact,* as the survey team now called it—that rose from the surface of the cold, hardened soil almost half a kilometer from the encampment.

The artifact that had consumed his every thought since its discovery.

Xiong had spent weeks sorting through dozens of new affinity readings relating to proteins collected from various depths of the planet's glaciated ice pack, hoping to unlock even the slightest clue to the meta-genome. While Starfleet researchers of the highest caliber had been subjecting samples of the complex genetic structure to battery upon battery of tests, Xiong still spent what time he could doing his own intensive study. It was either that or sleep, as he did not have much inclination to mingle with the several dozen of his colleagues "doing time on this ball of ice," as he heard a few put their situation.

What he possessed that those Starfleet researchers did not were samples of the artifact itself. However, particles of the construct raised more questions than they answered. The material alone was a conundrum, not completely glass and not completely stone. There were no detectable seams in the artifact's assembly, leading to speculation as to whether it was cast whole or perhaps even grown organically. The material's age was indeterminate, at least so far as the latest scans could detect. In Xiong's mind, it only reflected in substance all of the mystery embodied in the artifact as a whole.

As he looked through the new samples and compared them to the artifact's base material, Xiong let his enthusiasm fan the spark of his unspoken hunch that, somehow, the meta-genome and the artifact were connected. More time and study, he was convinced, would reveal how a key woven deeply within the meta-genome's bases and sequences would unlock just the information necessary to reveal the artifact's unknown nature—and its true purpose.

So, I just keep looking, Xiong thought.

"Lieutenant?" The voice's ring through the darkened and otherwise quiet room startled him, prompting a sharp intake of breath that in turn offered a vivid reminder of the coppery tang of the stale air within the encampment's enclosed spaces. "I need to interrupt you, sir."

"No, you don't, Ensign," Xiong said, recognizing the voice as that of Colleen Cook, one of the junior archaeologists assigned to the site. He turned his head from the viewer just enough to let its bluish light spill forth onto his chin and cheek before speaking again. "I'm sure someone else can assist you because right now, I'm busy."

"But no one else can assist *me,* Mr. Xiong."

The crispness of the words was like a blast of cold air rushing down his spine. He jolted upright and spun around to find himself staring into the implacable expression of Zhao Sheng.

"Captain!" Xiong said too loudly as he noted the other man's narrowed eyes. "This . . . is a surprise, sir. What brings you down here?"

Zhao nodded a dismissal to Cook, who appeared more than happy to duck back outside the research room. "You missed our meeting this morning," he said. "I decided to collect your report in person."

Xiong felt a pang of sheepishness and found it hard to hold the captain's gaze. "I . . . don't have a report for you, sir," he said. "Speaking freely, sir, I don't report to you in this matter."

"*Permission* to speak freely granted, by the way," Zhao replied, his eyes narrowing as he crossed the small room until he was less than a meter from Xiong. The young researcher squared himself against the uneasy encroachment on his personal space.

"I am well aware, Lieutenant, of the command structure and that your detached duties place you under the direct authority of Commodore Reyes on Starbase 47," Zhao said evenly. "Your report on your activities here is expected as a courtesy to me, particularly when it's my ship and crew who are acting as chaperones for this little field trip of yours."

Xiong swallowed, realizing that Zhao would interpret that as a sign of weakness of will. *So be it,* he thought. The lieutenant knew all along that such a dressing-down would be coming, but his intentions had been honest, even though Zhao was the last person who would hear his excuse at this moment. He simply had not found the time to prepare for the captain a complete report that would truly be useful. Xiong could have submitted the finished "alternative" version of his research that Starfleet Command had ordered he draft for personnel with lesser clearance—one written with the intent to obfuscate the true nature of his findings—but that would have brought him more problems with Zhao than he had even now.

Besides, the very idea of that alternative report gnawed at Xiong's conscience. Given the choice, he would proudly share with Zhao—or anyone else, for that matter—everything he knew to date about the meta-genome and the artifact.

But I have my orders.

With that in mind, he simply nodded. "Yes, sir," he said, continuing to meet the captain's stern glare.

"And this is your last reminder that your presence at my staff meetings is expected," Zhao continued. "I might phrase it as a request for you to be there, but you will regard it as an order."

"Understood, sir."

Zhao held his stance for a moment before stepping back. He

drew a breath and released it through his nose as he took a look around the room, and Xiong noticed the captain's eyes had settled on a makeshift cot with rumpled bedding shoved against one wall. Zhao rubbed his chin before continuing in a somewhat warmer tone, "You look worn, Lieutenant," he said. "Can I assume that your studies have kept your attention more tightly than they should?"

Xiong released a small laugh as he allowed himself to relax. "I'd like to say that we're finding more to examine each day, but in truth it seems that we're finding more to examine about every ten minutes."

"And what *have* you found?" Zhao asked with a glimmer of interest in his dark eyes.

"I could tell you, sir," Xiong said with sincerity, "but we're just not sure what it all means yet."

Zhao nodded, seemingly willing to accept that for an answer, at least for now. As the captain turned away and quietly paced a few steps, Xiong felt compelled to offer at least a few morsels of undiluted factual information. Besides, engaging someone in actual conversation was something that had eluded him since his arrival on Erilon. "I can tell you that the artifact, what you see on the surface . . ."

"Yes?"

Xiong smiled. "It's nothing compared to what we've seen underneath it. We didn't expect there to be any kind of structure supporting the thing at all. I was sure it was grounded in bedrock. But there's an entire system of subterranean chambers and passages, all artificial in origin. We've found interface consoles and storage and who knows what else is actually there. For security reasons, investigations have been restricted to sensors-only except for a couple of key areas."

"Key areas," Zhao repeated. "Such as?"

"Well, the most interesting one is what we think is a control room," Xiong replied. "The problem is, we're not sure just what it controls or what anything else actually does."

"So," the captain said, "there's equipment connected with the artifact at a central point?" When Xiong nodded, he added, "And it's completely powerless?"

"No, sir. Not completely," Xiong said. "We've tried interfacing a generator to what we think is a power-distribution coupling, but nothing's worked. Candidly, sir, we're not even sure it's a power hub that we've hooked into."

A table-mounted intercom panel next to his viewer beeped twice, and he reached across to activate it. "Research Room. Lieutenant Xiong."

"Ming, it's Spence," said a voice in tinny but audibly excited tones. *"We're picking up a new power reading down here. It just popped on. You might want to see this for yourself."*

Xiong felt a surge of excitement charge his tired frame. "On my way!" His mind whirling with what such a reading could mean, he crossed to an equipment locker, threw open its door, and started rummaging through his belongings—all before remembering that he was not alone in the room.

"Uh, Captain," Xiong said as he tugged a parka from the locker, "Ensign Spencer is working in the artifact control room and I need to join him there."

Zhao's face sobered a bit, his own eagerness to learn more about the unknown visibly dashed. Then he stood a bit straighter, almost as if accepting the unpalatable situation that he simply would be nonessential personnel in the control room. "Understood, Lieutenant," Zhao said. "I won't keep you from your duties."

Xiong slid into the parka and headed past Zhao, but then he stopped. He could not push himself through the doorway, not if doing so meant leaving another explorer behind. He paused, recognizing in that moment that he and Zhao were very similar in certain respects. They likely had joined Starfleet with the very same hopes and dreams of seeing just what awaited them in the farthest reaches of uncharted space.

Despite a nagging, cautioning voice in the back of his mind, Xiong turned back into the room.

"You're welcome to join me, Captain," he said, and offered a small smile, "but only if you brought your winter coat."

Zhao's expression brightened in amusement, displaying more emotion than Xiong could recall seeing before now. "I'm always prepared, Lieutenant," he said, "but I'll have to bring a few friends along as well. Regulations, you know."

Xiong shrugged. *I'll guess I'll just have to swear them all to secrecy when we get there.*

10

"A little groggy there, son? You look all slumped over!"

Ensign Stephen Klisiewicz raised his head from his console at the sciences station and looked across the *Endeavour*'s bridge to the source of the voice. Pointing to where his attention had been focused, he said, "This device is a viewer, sir. It requires the user to hunch down and look into it. I understand how that might be a new concept to an engineer such as yourself, Commander. You're more used to *crawling* into things rather than just looking into them."

Bersh glov Mog released a laugh that sounded more like a belch—one that rose over the rest of the bridge's ambient noise—and that was enough to set Klisiewicz to laughing a bit on his own.

"Well, we all learn by doing," Mog replied, offering the Tellarite equivalent of a smile, which to Klisiewicsz still looked like the fierce rictus of a rabid dog.

The engineer's sentiment underscored the sense that, in its own slow way, the *Endeavour* was becoming something of a teaching vessel. Mog seemed to run engineering more as a training lab, mixing up duty rosters and making sure his staff became highly proficient at all aspects of operations rather than focusing on a single area of specialization. Khatami seemed to follow his lead by rotating untried personnel into roles of greater responsibility when opportunities arose. Even Captain Zhao seemed to make himself available to officers fresh out of the Academy, such as Klisiewicz, to discuss matters of life and duty aboard a starship.

Okay, so maybe not so much in sickbay, he thought, *but every place else is pretty open to a new guy like me.*

Two hours into his duty shift, and the chief engineer had

started tossing wisecracks across the bridge at his expense. Had the remark come from someone other than Mog, he surely would have held his tongue in reply. While Klisiewicz was becoming fast friends with the Tellarite chief engineer, he noticed in his first scan around the bridge that other than Mog's, there were few familiar faces.

He knew Commander Khatami, of course, who in Captain Zhao's absence now occupied the *Endeavour*'s center seat, but his conversations with her typically did not stray from whatever task was at hand. Specifically, she was the one to pass to him any information he might need in the course of his duties regarding his continual search for class-V forms of life, otherwise known as anything containing the Taurus meta-genome. Those conversations rarely were chatty; it seemed to be a sobering subject for her, he sensed.

The communications officer looked familiar, but his name escaped Klisiewicz at the moment, and the navigator, Lieutenant McCormack, well, he did recognize her, as she was one of his favorite objects of secret unrequited affection on the entire ship.

Turning back to the science console, the ensign noted the white blinking indicator and toggled the controls to transfer the sensor data to an eye-level display. Looking over the readings, he knit his brow before turning to Khatami, who already was regarding him expectantly.

"Commander," he said, "we're registering a new power reading from the surface."

"Location?" Khatami asked, spinning her chair to face him.

Klisiewicz keyed in a few commands, allowing the computer to correlate the sensor data. "It's about five kilometers northwest of the encampment and . . . about two kilometers beneath the planet's surface."

"Anything else?" Khatami asked.

"The energy signature is weak, but pretty distinctive, Commander," Klisiewicz replied as he entered new commands to the console, self-conscious of getting her more information as quickly as he was able. "It's definitely a geothermal source, and it's slowly building in temperature."

"Keep an eye on it, Ensign," Khatami said, her eyes turning to the main viewer, "Provide regular updates as appropriate, and relay those sensor readings to the survey teams on the surface."

"Aye, Commander," Klisiewicz said as he keyed the required commands to route the data. The swiftness of a starship's response to human command was something for which he was sure he would never lose a sense of marvel.

Then another alert indicator flashed on his console.

"Commander!" he called out to Khatami even as he bent over the hooded viewer once more. Reviewing the new stream of sensor telemetry being fed to his station, he said, "We're picking up a second power reading now."

"And?" Khatami asked.

"It's confirmed, sir. Same energy signature as before," he said, checking his calculations. "Bearing due south of the encampment this time, less than five kilometers out."

"Any ideas, Mr. Mog?" the first officer asked after a moment. "Could they be activating the artifact?"

"Well, we could ask," the engineer replied before turning back to his station.

"Mr. Estrada, hail Lieutenant Xiong at the encampment," Khatami said, "and let's see what's going on down there."

Activate the artifact? Can they do *that?*

Klisiewicz involuntarily rubbed his arm as he felt goose bumps rise beneath his sleeves. His thoughts turned to Ravanar IV and the destruction dealt to the research facility there by the Tholians, who apparently had taken issue with a Federation presence on that world. According to what he had learned from rumors and other scuttlebutt around the ship, Lieutenant Xiong, who had been there along with a landing party from the *U.S.S. Enterprise* investigating the aftermath of an earlier Tholian attack, had barely escaped with his life.

And Ravanar didn't even have an intact structure, he thought, *but the Tholians still wanted us to leave it the hell alone. Could the same thing happen here—or something worse?* As he turned his attention back to the incoming stream of data from the planet's two newly energized power sources, Klisiewicz could not help thinking that someone, somewhere, would learn what was happening on Erilon—and not like it one bit.

Xiong jumped from the driver's seat of the encampment's all-terrain vehicle, his face chilled by icy wind as he made his way quickly to a black, manually operated hatch—the only distinct feature on the snow-encrusted front of a temporary structure at the base of the artifact. He turned and squinted through the bright white of swirling snow to see his five passengers step out of the side hatch of the vehicle, which had been adapted for use on Erilon with rear treads and an assembly of shock-absorbing skis mounted in place of its front axle.

He waved them forward, unable to hear any crunching of their boots on the snowpack from the howling of the arctic wind. Xiong had not been on the planet long enough to get a feel for impending white-out conditions, but as he placed his gloved hands on the hatch's center wheel and strained to turn it, he had to wonder whether this was the start of some weather he did not want to witness firsthand. A form stepped alongside him to grip the wheel as well, and they both attempted to turn it again.

"The automatic locks keep freezing shut!" Xiong yelled over the wind to his helper, whom he now recognized as Captain Zhao. The two tugged to break the wheel loose of the outdoors' frozen grip, and after spinning it freely, Xiong pushed his weight against the door and opened it enough to admit them into the airlock.

Stepping back so the others could pass, Xiong clanged the hatch shut behind the last of them and started to twist the interior mate to the locking mechanism to seal it. Once the wind's whine was shut out, the room filled with the clatter of feet stamping against floor plates and hands slapping against parkas to loosen the ice crystals that had accumulated on their protective clothing just in the short amount of time they had stood outside. Xiong pushed back the fur-lined hood of his parka and moved to the opposite door.

"This one's a bit easier," he said, slipping his hand from a glove and keying a security code into a panel next to the door. As it slid open, a rush of warmer air greeted the new arrivals. They made their way briskly into a darkened, ebony-surfaced corridor, one with a graded slope that led under the planet's surface, with Xiong leading them toward a dim source of light and sound several hundred meters into the structure. Their footsteps rang crisply against the smooth floors and walls of the low-ceilinged corridor, and no one spoke as Zhao stepped up into the point position of the group a few strides before they entered the control room, a move that Xiong dismissed as being more out of habit than arrogance.

"Report," the captain snapped in a voice loud enough to capture the immediate attention of the three researchers in the room. Xiong saw Lieutenant Spencer, the young, blond-haired officer with whom he had worked most closely since his arrival, draw himself up from a crouch next to a power generator and approach the group.

"Uh . . . yes, sir," Spencer said hesitantly to Zhao before looking at Xiong. "Isn't this information . . . ?"

Nodding as he slipped out of his parka, Xiong said, "Captain Zhao's presence is authorized, Spence. Just tell us what's going on."

Spencer spoke as he turned and walked deeper into the room, prompting Xiong and Zhao to keep up. "When I called you, we'd just picked up a power source activating below the surface a few kilometers from the artifact. We thought that was interesting enough to notify you. But now we have three of them."

Xiong felt his jaw go slack, and it required physical effort to keep his mouth from dropping open in surprise. "*Three?* Where?"

Spencer turned and pointed to the screen of a portable computer viewer propped up on a pitch-black console top in front of them. "One northwest of us and two others south. They're building in output, and we're detecting some deep melt—there!" Spencer poked at the screen where a blinking amber dot indicated a fourth budding power level, this one situated northeast of the artifact and apparently equidistant from the others. "They just keep activating, no rhyme or reason."

"Lieutenant Spencer," Zhao spoke, "how long have you been attempting to transfer power from that generator into the artifact's control center?"

"Not long, sir," the younger officer replied. Looking past the captain's shoulder, he called out, "Hey, Bohanon, how long has our generator been up and running?"

A large-built Denobulan in a blue jumpsuit stepped to the pulsing generator and stooped over it. "Two-point-three-seven hours, Spence."

Looking to Zhao, Xiong asked, "You think we may be activating those power sources, Captain?"

"Or," Zhao countered, "are they activating as a *response* to your activities here?" Any further discussion was interrupted by the sound of the captain's communicator beeping. Unzipping his parka, Zhao retrieved the device and flipped it open in a practiced motion. "Zhao here."

"*Khatami here, Captain,*" said the voice of the *Endeavour*'s first officer, filtered through the communicator's small speaker. "*We're not getting a strong signal. . . .*"

"I can hear you," he spoke back. "What's your status?"

"*We're fine, sir,*" Khatami continued, "*but we're monitoring multiple power spikes from the planet in the vicinity of the artifact.*"

"We're on top of the situation, Commander," Zhao said in a voice that exuded more confidence than Xiong himself was feeling at the moment. "I'll presume you are transmitting your readings to the research base?"

"*You know me too well, sir,*" Khatami said, her voice easing a bit. "*We'll keep you apprised.* Endeavour *out.*"

As Zhao closed his communicator, Xiong said, "If this is a response, I don't see why it's . . ."

The ground trembled beneath his feet and he reached out toward the nearby wall to steady himself as a heavy metal clanking suddenly rang once, then again from within the structure. Everything in the chamber seemed to register the vibration, which also rattled equipment and made Xiong look to the ceiling for any sign that they might be facing a cave-in. He fell silent along with the rest of the men in the control room and, just like each of the others, found himself instinctively looking to Zhao.

Evenly, almost quietly, the captain said, "We're leaving. Collect any data you can carry and get moving, now." Pointing to Bohanon, he added, "Disconnect that power coupling."

"Wait!" Xiong said in a loud whisper, drawing Zhao's narrowed gaze. "That'll kill the computers. I need time to transmit our data to the *Endeavour*. We can't afford to lose it." When Zhao did not answer after a moment, the lieutenant took a step forward, his expression anxious. "Captain, please!"

"Do it quickly," Zhao ordered before turning his attention to the others. "The rest of you, continue the evacuation."

Xiong dashed to the portable console and his fingers sped across the buttons and switches, dumping all of their accumulated raw data into a central file and pushing it upstream into a communications feed. Once he had begun the data transmission to the *Endeavour*'s main computer, he snatched his parka from a chair back and was just beginning to shrug into it when another resounding crash echoed through the room. Instead of the low rumble that just moments earlier had washed over everything and everyone in the chamber, this clamor was localized, sounding as though it had come from the control room.

Frowning in confusion, Xiong looked toward the adjoining room in time to see a pair of *Endeavour* security guards scrambling back through the entrance, their phasers drawn and aimed toward the way they had come.

"Everybody out!" one of the men shouted. "Now!" Even as he shouted the order he punctuated the words by firing his phaser into the control room.

"What's going on?" Zhao shouted over the weapons fire, and Xiong saw the captain reaching into his parka to extract his own phaser an instant before the entire room was plunged into darkness. The sound of the generator faded, as did the gentle hum of the portable computer and communications equipment.

"Report!" Xiong heard Captain Zhao shout as other members of the team cried out in alarm.

Fumbling into one of his parka's larger pockets, Xiong drew out a flashlight and activated it, its narrow beam playing across the darkened interior of the ancient control room. He quickly found the group of *Endeavour* security guards and other members of his own team gathered near the airlock.

"There's something in here!" another voice shouted, and Xiong recognized it as the *Endeavour* security guard who had fired his phaser. "It came through the damned wall!"

Xiong felt his heart beginning to race as he sprinted across the room to join the group. A loud crash echoed in the chamber somewhere behind him. Spinning around, he aimed his flashlight beam toward the source of the noise in time to see a blur of movement in the control room. A cry of pain echoed through the room, followed by a flurry of phaser fire as beams of blue energy sliced through the darkness.

Something was attacking? What was it? How could it have forced its way through solid rock? Was it native to this world?

Later! his mind screamed at him. *You need to move, now!*

"The door won't open!" said another voice from somewhere to his left, sounding like Bohanon's.

"Force it!" shouted Zhao.

Nervous bile stung Xiong's throat as the screeching howl of metal against metal pierced the air and echoed against the hard, flat surfaces of the corridor. A second, longer grinding moaned from the yielding door as several men grunted from their effort, which sent a blast of chilled air from the airlock to surround them and immediately permeate Xiong's uniform.

As he felt the huddle of men start to push beyond the doorway into more darkness, a frantic scream stabbed his ears. He looked toward it only to have his eyes burned by the flash of phaser fire. The brightness of the beam held for a couple of seconds, plenty of time for a vivid image to sear into the young researcher's mind: one security officer's grimacing face glowing sapphire in the flare of a thin, lancing beam, and that beam finding its mark against . . . something else—a shapeless, black form that seemed to envelop another guard and squeeze him at the torso, compressing his body to inhuman thinness.

Blind panic reached out to snare Xiong in its grip, his eyes wide as he looked all around for potential threats. Memories of Ravanar IV exploded in his mind—scrambling from danger, the near-blinding pain of his shattered knee, the shock waves of the energy blasts unleashed by Tholian demolitions as they obliterated all evidence of the similar artifact on that world.

"Where the hell's the door?" he heard a voice shout, before another flashlight beam flared into existence and he saw Spencer, Bohanon, and one of the *Endeavour* security men moving toward the airlock's inner door.

"Xiong!" Captain Zhao called out, and the lieutenant saw him standing near the door, waving the others into the airlock. "Move it!"

He pushed his way into the airlock, followed by Zhao, who pulled the inner door closed behind him and engaged the manual lock. While Bohanon and Spencer fought with the outer hatch's wheel, the captain reached into his parka and drew his phaser before turning his attention to Lieutenants Nauls and La Sala. Both security officers had drawn their own weapons, with Nauls standing near the outer hatch while La Sala had taken up a defensive stance, her back to the wall of the cramped vestibule.

"Once the door's open," Zhao said in a quiet voice that managed still to convey the tension of the situation, "sweep the area outside and make sure our way to the transport is clear."

After some tussling and slight groaning of metal on metal, Xiong heard the hatch wheel give way and spin with the slapping of bare hands over hands to punctuate its process. Without warning, a thick slice of whiteness cut the room in half, the abrupt change in illumination momentarily blinding him as crisp, cold wind flooded the airlock.

One by one, the group began to duck quickly through the hatch and onto the cold, snow-covered ground outside the artifact just as a loud surge against the inner bulkhead rocked the temporary airlock and spilled Xiong and the others off of their feet. As he tried to regain his footing, another blow hit and a visible dent appeared in the airlock's inner door.

La Sala suddenly stuck her head back into the airlock, her dark hair already smattered with snowflakes. "All clear! Let's go!"

Xiong was almost through the outer door when another thunderous hammer blow rocked the airlock, and he turned to see that the inner door now was partly caved in.

A dark, amorphous blur sprang from the forced gap of the doorway, striking Spencer and yanking him by the arm against the door and wall. Xiong froze in shock, unable to look away as the researcher howled and kicked his feet, lashing out to free his limb from the gap. A hand slapped Xiong on the shoulder and spun him around, and he found himself looking at Zhao.

"*Go!*" the captain yelled as he all but tossed Xiong out of the airlock. Behind him, Spencer's shouting turned more guttural for a moment before stopping altogether.

Shoving Xiong toward the all-terrain vehicle and nearly knocking him to the snow-covered ground in the process, Zhao shouted, "Get that thing moving!"

As he rushed for the vehicle's driver compartment, Xiong looked over his shoulder to see the captain and La Sala frantically climbing aboard through the passenger door. Throwing himself into the driver's seat, Xiong stabbed at the control to start the vehicle, relieved when the engine powered up and the array of gauges and display readouts flared to life.

"Move!" Zhao shouted just as Xiong fed power to the transport's drive, remembering at the last moment that a fast acceleration would cause more problems than it solved while trying to navigate the snow-laden path. As the vehicle came up to speed, he heard Zhao flip open a communicator. "Erilon base! This is Captain Zhao of the *Endeavour*. We are under atta—"

Bohanon's shout cut off Zhao's words. "Whatever it is, it just destroyed the airlock! It's coming right at us!"

Trying to keep his attention on the snow-covered trail in front of him, Xiong still managed to look at one rearview monitor set into the panel above the windshield. He saw fragments of the airlock strewn across the frozen ground, though this was quickly obscured by a dual wake of snow and ice flying several meters high, stemming from a dark, undulating blur in the center of the path left by the vehicle's passage through the snow.

And it was getting closer.

"Everybody hang on!" Zhao called out, and Xiong felt himself tensing up even as he tried to coax more speed from the lumbering vehicle.

Then the blur struck.

Like a jellyfish, Xiong pitched backward and hard against the back of his seat; then his world upended with the sounds of yelling and groaning metal as he felt the entire vehicle rise off its back wheels and tumble onto its side. Everything spun to the right as he was thrown against the driver compartment's door, pain stabbing his shoulder. Then his head struck the doorframe and Erilon's bleak white landscape was swallowed by unyielding darkness.

11

Waves of pure, focused thought-power rippled through the Lattice, disrupting the unity and tranquillity of Tholia's Great Castemoot Assembly and all but crushing it in the suffocating sensations of oppression and raw, stark terror.

Harsh crimson tinged the boundaries of the immense telepathic network as Eskrene [The Ruby] maintained her tenuous union with the Ruling Conclave, defying every instinct that told her to flee the SubLink and seek out a safe haven.

Such pain! It suffocates me! The crimson now washed over the SubLink as her mind shouted to be heard over the cacophony enveloping them. All around her, Eskrene felt the other members of the council struggling under the onslaught, each of them torn between the almost irrepressible need to escape whatever it was that violated the thoughtspace and the imperative to maintain control over the supreme nerve center of the Great Castemoot Assembly to which they had been entrusted.

This was far worse, much more intense than the thought-pulse that had gripped them all several cycles ago. The brutal, hostile surge of psionic energy, emanating from that area of space long ago forsaken and shunned by the Assembly, had disrupted the Lattice for many cycles after its immediate effects and distressed the totality of the Tholian race.

Clamoring sirens of havoc and dread all but drowned out Falstrene [The Gray]. *Anger! Vengeance!*

Eskrene resisted the urge to sever her connection, fighting instead to maintain her telepathic balance and restore focal harmony with the Castemoot. *It harbors a greater purpose.*

Indeed, she realized even as she fought through the pain, this latest violation of Tholian serenity scorned description and resisted comparison, shrouding itself in veils of opaque black even as it mercilessly trampled through their collective essence.

Reaching out with her mind, Eskrene sensed the disorder stressing much of the SubLink, though already she could feel the minds of Tholians across the Lattice toiling to reassert its harmony and balance as the force of the thought-pulse began to dissipate, taking with it the rage and turmoil it had wrought. She also perceived that despite their combined efforts, the peace of the expansive Castemoot was severely fractured.

The conclave and—Eskrene also realized with growing dread—all of the Assembly now cowered in fear.

It will return. We must stop it.

12

On the bridge of the *Endeavour*, Khatami watched as Klisiewicz worked feverishly at the science station, all the while fighting the urge to push the ensign aside and take over manning the console herself. Annoyed even for considering that course of action, the first officer issued a silent order to herself to remain seated in the captain's chair and to carry out her own duties, part of which entailed trusting the people around her to see to their own assigned tasks.

"Ensign," she called out, "what's happening?"

Pulling away from the hooded viewer dominating his station and turning to face her, Klisiewicz replied, "Holding at seven active power sources, Commander. Each seems to have a central power core, with temperatures ranging between eleven hundred and fourteen hundred degrees Kelvin and rising."

"Are we continuing to update Erilon Base?" she asked, but waved the question away before Klisiewicz could answer. "Of course you are. I'm sorry, Ensign. Keep monitoring those power readings and update me as needed."

Stop acting like a mother hen, and let your people do their jobs.

"Commander," Lieutenant Estrada called from the communications station. "We're receiving an emergency call from the camp. They say they're under attack!"

Khatami's mind quickly flooded with questions, but she pushed them aside, following her thoughts to lead by the book. Slapping the control panel on the arm of the command chair with her open palm, she activated the shipboard communications circuit. "Bridge to transporter room two. Commence emergency beam-out procedures!"

"Commander!" Klisiewicz shouted over her order. "Power readings just spiked off the scale! We . . ."

The ensign's next words were lost as a hammer blow rocked the *Endeavour*. Khatami felt the deck disappear beneath her feet as the bridge pitched almost on its port side, tossing her out of her chair and sending her slamming face-first against the bridge railing surrounding the command well. Stars danced in her vision and she felt a distinctive pop as her jaw struck the rail. A bitter metallic taste flooded her mouth and she reached to feel where she was certain teeth were either loose or missing. She winced as her fingers made contact with her jaw, and when she pulled them away their tips were tinged dark red.

Lighting flickered and red-alert klaxons wailed across the bridge as Khatami forced herself to her feet, shaking her head in an attempt to regain her senses and keeping her jaw clenched tightly shut against the dull pain enveloping the lower half of her face. The smell and taste of acrid electrical smoke gagged Khatami as she staggered to her feet. Over the din of sirens and unfettered chatter exploding from the communications station, she heard one voice shouting to he heard.

"Damage report!" Mog called out, pulling himself up from where he had fallen near the turbolift at the rear of the bridge. With speed that belied his bulk, the Tellarite engineer moved across the upper deck to where Khatami now saw Estrada's unmoving form at the floor of the communications station, a pool of red widening from his head. "Klisiewicz!" he bellowed as he knelt before the fallen lieutenant. "Get a medic up here, and get me that damage report!"

Grabbing a Feinberger receiver from his own console, Klisiewicz retuned it to accept information from Estrada's station before jamming the cylindrical silver device into his right ear. Khatami saw him wince, as if overwhelmed by the initial onslaught of status reports and requests for assistance that had to be sweeping across the ship's internal communications network. Squinting his eyes as if trying to ward off the wave of information he was receiving, the ensign reached to adjust a volume control.

"Casualties all over, sir," he said a moment later. "Hull

breaches on decks seven, eight, and nine. Damage-control parties are responding. Artificial gravity is out in the primary hull below deck five. Weapons control reports that phasers are offline. Transporters are also offline."

"Shields?" Khatami asked as she fumbled toward the command chair. *What just happened to us?*

Klisiewicz nodded. "They activated automatically the moment the sensors detected . . . whatever it was that hit us. They're holding at sixty-seven percent, but shield generators are online and recharging."

Cradling her jaw in the palm of her right hand, Khatami all but fell into the center seat as she noted a shadow fall across her. She looked up to see Mog standing next to her chair, his expression one of concern.

"You all right, Commander?"

Khatami nodded silently, every attempt to talk bringing with it a stabbing pain along her jawline and inside her mouth. Gripping the sides of her face with both hands, she took a deep breath before jerking to her right, realigning her jaw with an audible pop and an agonizing jolt of fire that would have dropped her to her knees if she had not already been sitting. As it was, she felt herself begin to pitch forward only to be stopped by Mog's meaty hand.

"By Kera and Phinda, woman," the Tellarite said. "What can I do?"

"Tell . . . them," she said in a strained whisper through gritted teeth, each of which felt like spikes driving into her gums. "Give . . . the orders."

"I have to coordinate damage control," Mog replied. Looking up, he pointed to Klisiewicz. "Ensign, you are the commander's mouth. Relay her orders wherever they need to go. Understand?"

Her vision blurred owing to the tears welling up in her eyes as she fought back pain, Khatami saw Klisiewicz offer an uncertain nod as he stepped down into the command well, moving close enough that she could keep her voice low.

"Hail the captain," she whispered, every word a knife plunging through her tortured jaw, "the camp, anyone. And I want . . . transporters up . . . *now!*"

Klisiewicz looked around until he spotted Ensign Halse at the environmental-control station. "Halse, take over the comm station. Hail the captain." As the nervous young man rose from his chair to cross the bridge, the ensign added, "And get engineering on those transporters!"

"My people are on it, Commander," Mog said from where he sat at the engineering station. Completing his preliminary survey of the ship's onboard systems, he turned to lean over the bridge railing so that only Klisiewicz and Khatami could hear him. "And there's no need to get carried away, Ensign." He delivered the words with a grunt and a weak smile as he clapped Klisiewicz on the shoulder before returning to his station.

If not for the pain in her jaw, Khatami might have smiled. She let herself ease back in her seat, comforted somewhat by the knowledge that if she was going to face this situation—whatever it turned out to be—without Captain Zhao, she had Mog at her right hand.

I'd even tell him that, if it didn't hurt so damned much.

The sharp stings of agony in her jaw had started to subside into a dull, constant throb, and Khatami sensed a wave of nausea coming over her. Allowing herself to settle back into the command chair, she reached out to touch Klisiewicz's arm. "What happened?"

"A massive energy pulse," the ensign replied. "It started as individual bursts, originating from the location of the seven power sources we've detected. They coalesced into a single beam before striking us." Shaking his head, he added, "I've never seen anything like it."

She found it doubtful that he would have, given his lack of experience, but Khatami had never heard of a weapon with such capabilities before, either.

The doors to the turbolift hissed open and she turned to see Nurse Sikal step from the turbolift. The prim young Vulcan took only a moment to survey the scene on the bridge before turning and moving to where Lieutenant Estrada still lay unmoving on the deck.

At Khatami's prompting, Klisiewicz asked, "Nurse, the commander is asking about casualty figures."

Without looking away from the medical tricorder in her left hand as she waved a scanner over Estrada's head, Sikal replied, "Dr. Leone is assessing the situation as we speak, Ensign. He will have a full report in short order."

Satisfied with the report, such as it was, Khatami returned her attention to the rest of the bridge. Directly in front of her, her helmsman and her navigator, Lieutenants Neelakanta and McCormack, were already back at their stations. At the front of the bridge, the same steady—and deceptively calming—view of Erilon continued to fill the main viewscreen. That serenity was an illusion, she now knew. If whatever had attacked them could do so once, what was to stop it from doing so again?

Over her right shoulder, she heard Halse say, "No response from the captain or any of the landing party, Commander. Erilon Base isn't answering us, either."

"Tell him to keep trying," Khatami said, drawing a breath that whistled through her teeth. As Klisiewicz relayed the order, she asked, "What about those power readings?"

Klisiewicz stepped back to his station, bending over his viewer as he adjusted several controls on his console. After a moment, he reported, "They're still active, and their temperatures are increasing again."

"It has to be some kind of planetary defense system," Mog called out from the engineering station. "They're probably recharging for another shot. Stephen, calculate how long it'll take for them to get to pre-firing temperatures. Quickly!"

"Helm," Khatami called out, straining to talk in a voice loud enough to be heard by the two officers less than a meter in front of her. "Break orbit. Move us out to maximum communications range with the surface." Even as she gave the order, she heard the question in her mind, wondering if that was enough distance between the *Endeavour* and whatever was targeting it from the planet's surface.

"What's the status on transporters?" she asked.

From behind her, Mog replied, "A few minutes, Commander. They're having to reroute power from undamaged systems."

At the science station, Klisiewicz looked up from his viewer. "If my calculations are correct, those power sources will reach target temperature in forty-five seconds . . . mark."

"That doesn't seem very efficient for a defense system," Mog said. "Too long between volleys, especially if you're fending off multiple ships."

Maybe the idea is that one shot should be enough, Khatami thought. She knew from Lieutenant Xiong's reports that the planet had been uninhabited for millennia, and that the structures he was investigating were even older. Perhaps age had compromised the ancient technology to the point that it had lost much of its power, or at least enough to have spared the *Endeavour* from being destroyed after just a single attack.

"Halse," she said, agony enveloping every word, "keep trying to contact the captain. Mog, get those transporters up, now. Helm, stand by for evasive maneuvers."

With orders issued and everyone on the bridge turning to their tasks, Khatami found that—once again—she could only sit, let her people do their jobs, and wait.

If Captain Zhao can wait, then so can I.

"Xiong! *Xiong!*"

A stinging slap to his face snapped Xiong's eyes open suddenly. He rubbed his hand against wetness on his brow, and pulled it back to see his blood smeared across his fingers.

"Get up," called the form in front of him, whom he now recognized as La Sala, the surviving *Endeavour* security guard. "We've got to get out of this thing."

Xiong stood on wobbly legs, his feet perched on the beveled side panel of the upset all-terrain vehicle, and squinted straight up through its open side hatch into the bright white of the Erilon sky. He then looked around the cabin of the vehicle and saw that he was the only one left to climb out—of those who could climb out, apparently. He saw one of the Erilon researchers slumped between the side and roof of the vehicle, his neck bent at an unnatural angle, and behind him was another jumpsuited researcher, also unmoving. He felt a moment of guilt for never even knowing their names.

La Sala reached up to grab the lip of the hatch before pulling herself through the opening. Lying down atop the vehicle's exterior, she reached down to give Xiong a hand, and working with her the lieutenant was able to climb out of the transport. Almost immediately he felt the harsh, biting air on his exposed skin. He and La Sala dropped to the ground, hunkering down behind the wrecked vehicle in an effort to hide from the brunt of the wind that now was kicking up.

Next to them, Bohanon, who had been dressed only in his jumpsuit while working inside the structure, was shrugging into a parka that was too small for his portly physique. Xiong saw that blood ran down the right side of the Denobulan's face, trickling from a cut in his head that looked even worse than his own. Behind him, Zhao and Nauls were checking the power settings on their phasers, the captain returning his to a pocket of his parka. Picking up another weapon from the ground at his feet, Zhao offered it along with a communicator to Xiong.

"Take these," the captain said. "The *Endeavour*'s suffered an attack, as well. Transporters are out, but they should be back up in a few minutes. We'll have to stick it out as best we can until then."

Under attack? The question screamed in Xiong's mind, and his thoughts flashed to the ill-fated *Bombay*. "Who's attacking them?" he asked.

Zhao shook his head. "Unknown. Weapons placements on the surface appear to be targeting the ship." Looking to Xiong, he asked, "Something related to your mysterious archaeological expedition, I wonder?"

"Wh-What about the thing that attacked us?" Bohanon chattered in the frigid air. "Where did it go?"

"I hope back where it came from, once we left," Xiong said. "Or else—"

"Captain!" Nauls said, pointing toward the ridgeline where, through the snow billowing around them, Xiong now saw a column of thick black smoke rising from the distant structures at the end of the road.

Oh, no.

Zhao's sigh made a visible cloud of vapor that quickly dissipated. "We have to assume it struck the camp and that it's coming back," he said. "We need to be ready." Waving across the roadway, he pointed to La Sala. "Take Xiong and Bohanon and go for cover behind those rocks. I'll stay with Lieutenant Nauls." Zhao paused a moment to look La Sala in the eyes. "You know what to do, right?"

"Yes, sir," La Sala replied, offering a confident nod. Rising to her feet, she looked to Xiong and Bohanon. "Let's go."

As they jogged across the snow-packed trail toward the small outcropping of rocks that he was sure would offer nothing resembling adequate protection, Xiong had to ask. "So, what is it you're supposed to do?"

"Keep you quiet," she said, "while they attract that thing's attention."

"Commander, transporters are back up," Mog said, his voice a mixture of fatigue and pride.

"Allah be praised," Khatami said, sighing audibly through her still throbbing jaw. The past moments had passed with agonizing slowness, with little word from the planet's surface as to the current situation. Communications with the base camp had terminated at the same time the *Endeavour* was attacked, and all attempts to reach any member of the Corps of Engineers team assigned to the temporary research facility had failed. Captain Zhao's report of the mysterious entity that had attacked him and his landing party only deepened her anxiety, which Khatami knew would not ease until everyone on the surface was safely aboard ship and they were well away from this planet.

With transporters still under repair, Khatami had been forced to order the *Endeavour* out of orbit as the planetary weapons unleashed a fresh barrage at the starship. The cycle had been repeated once more, with the vessel dodging the worst of the attacks and avoiding further damage to already stressed systems. Only now, with transporters once again operational, could an attempt be made to retrieve the landing party and anyone else who might still be alive on the planet's surface.

She looked at Klisiewicz, who remained steadfast by her side. "Ensign," she whispered through pain-numbed teeth, "get us back into transporter range, and hail the captain again. Tell Neelakanta I want to try and draw fire from the surface using evasive maneuvers, and then move back into transporter position while it recharges."

As the ensign stepped forward to relay her orders to the *Endeavour*'s Arcturian helm officer, Khatami turned to the communications station where Halse still manned the console. "Ensign," she said, immediately reaching up to massage her still aching jaw, "anything from the encampment?"

His expression forlorn, the young officer turned from the console and shook his head. "Nothing yet, Commander. I'm still trying to hail them on all frequencies."

Having issued her last set of instructions, Klisiewicz returned to stand beside the command chair, and Khatami looked up to see the tension in the ensign's blanched features. He was gripping the railing to his left and staring straight ahead, doing his best to maintain his composure. She placed her hand on his arm again and forced a smile in an effort to calm him. "Resume your post. I'll take it from here." Klisiewicz paused until she nodded her affirmation, and then stepped out of the command well.

Turning her attention to the main viewscreen, Khatami flinched from the pain in her jaw as she asked, "Time to the next attack?"

Now back at the science station, Klisiewicz replied, "About twenty-five seconds, Commander."

"Go to red alert," she said evenly. "Helm, initiate evasive maneuvers. This is going to be close."

"Aye, Commander," Neelakanta replied as his long, thin fingers played over the helm console's rows of multicolored controls, and Khatami felt the starship heave to starboard. Then they tipped downward, faster than the inertial dampeners could compensate, in a maneuver that seemed to bring them close enough to touch the stark white features of the frozen planet centered on the viewer.

To her right and just on the edges of her peripheral vision, she saw Klisiewicz turn from the science station. "Incoming! All hands, brace for impact!"

The volley blow seemed to slam into the ship from astern, nearly throwing Khatami from her chair a second time. She clutched at her armrests and dug in her heels as she felt the entire bridge vault upward. The force drove her back into her seat, the spastic motions only serving to batter her already aching body. In front of her, Neelakanta held on to the helm console, but McCormack was thrown from her navigator's chair, falling flat on her back at the bottom of the command well. Red-alert klaxons bellowed across the bridge once more as the ship's systems attempted to recover from the new attack.

"Shields are down," Mog shouted above the alarms. "We can't withstand another attack!"

"Transporters, now!" Khatami ordered as loudly as she could muster.

"Commander!" Klisiewicz shouted, panic clear in his voice. "Sensors only detected weapons signatures from three locations. Four are still reading preattack temperatures. They're primed and ready!"

"It's *coming*!" Bohanon said, wide-eyed.

Crouched next to the frightened Denobulan, Xiong heard it, too. The soft whirring, all around him as if something were moving—no, cutting—through the snow and ice. He looked up from his place of concealment behind the rocks, squinting into the whiteness in search of the threat. Panic swelled within him as he beheld the same twisting wake of flying snow surging across the frozen, desolate plain leading to the encampment, fanning out behind a blurred, dark, vaguely humanoid form.

Then he heard both his and La Sala's communicators emit an identical pair of soft beeping tones. Fumbling into his parka pocket, he retrieved the device and flipped open its antenna grid. "Xiong here."

"This is Transporter Chief Schuster," a deep baritone voice echoed from the communicator's speaker grille. *"Stand by for beam-out. We'll be in position in forty-five seconds."*

Any reply Xiong might have offered was lost as the very air around him seemed to hum and vibrate. He felt an almost electrical sensation playing across his exposed skin at the same instant snow and small bits of ice were stirred up around him. The ground was shaking now, with thunderclaps charging the air as the pale white sky melted into a bright, harsh orange maelstrom.

What the hell . . . ?

Then the ominous, approaching figure was upon them, veering across the frozen plain and descending upon the wrecked all-terrain vehicle—just as Zhao had anticipated.

The whine of phaser fire reached his ears, and Xiong saw a bright ray of energy erupt from Nauls's concealed position near the vehicle. The beam bored into the onrushing figure, which seemed to simply absorb the energy from the phaser volley even as it continued to move with unreal speed across the snow-packed ground. Nauls fired again and achieved the same effect, with the creature maintaining its course before slamming headlong into the ruined transport.

A sharp metallic crack filled the air, and Xiong saw metal cave inward as the vehicle lurched out of the small depression its crash had created, spinning away from where Nauls crouched and skidding across the snow to settle into a ditch on the other side of the narrow path. Nauls, his position now exposed, scrambled away from the creature, moving backward uphill and fighting to keep his balance as he tried to keep his phaser trained on the assailant.

"What the hell is that thing?" La Sala whispered. Though her own weapon was aimed at the creature, she did not fire, apparently continuing to follow Zhao's last instructions.

Xiong felt his pulse racing in his ears and his heart beating as though it might push through his chest as he got his first good look at the . . . whatever it was. It appeared to be humanoid in only the most rudimentary sense; dark, towering more than two meters in height, glistening and steaming next to the vehicle in stark contrast to the snowpack surrounding it. Its physique was devoid of clothing or in fact any discernible qualities. He saw no indications of hair or skin tone or even facial features. No muscle tone was apparent in any of its extremities; the arms instead appeared to be faceted like glass or polished steel and honed to razor-sharp points that gleamed in what feeble sunlight managed to penetrate the dense cloud cover.

He, La Sala, and Bohanon watched as the thing stalked Nauls, covering ground in massive strides and closing the gap between itself and the security officer in seconds. Nauls fired again at near point-blank range, the cobalt blue beam simply disappearing into the creature's torso as it continued forward. Then the thing swung a massive, shimmering arm that caught Nauls at the midsection, slicing him in half and sending his body falling in two different directions. Blood stained and melted the surrounding snow, rapidly expanding away from the luckless man's tortured corpse as it ran in rivers down the embankment.

Xiong heard Bohanon scream in abject terror at the same moment the air was filled with the whine of another phaser.

Captain Zhao's.

This time the report sounded louder and more powerful while the energy beam that struck the creature looked brighter, its drone more intense. Xiong guessed that the captain had increased the setting on his phaser in a renewed attempt to stop the horrific monster in its tracks.

As before, the weapon seemed to have no effect. The creature appeared almost oblivious of any attack on itself as it turned and lunged toward the source of the weapons fire. Zhao, unfazed by the imminent danger he faced, held his ground and fired again even as he reached into his parka with his free hand to extract his communicator.

"Xiong!" La Sala said as she thumbed the power setting on her phaser all the way forward. "Set to maximum and fire! Now!"

Fumbling with his own weapon, Xiong raised it and aimed at the thing advancing on Zhao. The whine of tightly focused energy rang in his ears as his phaser's piercing blue beam

joined La Sala's in a frantic attempt to force it into breaking off
its attack.

Ahead of the creature, Zhao finally moved as it lashed out at
him, dodging to his left and scrambling toward the transport vehicle. Xiong gasped in horror as the captain slipped and fell
face-first to the snow-packed earth, jarring his phaser and communicator from his grip. The devices skittered across the ice-
slickened ground, only to stop well beyond his reach.

"No!" La Sala screamed, rising up from behind the rock outcropping and firing at the creature once again. The thing turned,
its featureless face seemingly looking right at them, and Xiong
felt the icy fingers of terror close around his heart at the same instant he felt Bohanon jerk on his arm.

"Shoot it!" the Denobulan screamed.

The thing was moving again, this time directly toward them.
Snow, ice, and dirt whipped into a frenzy around him as Xiong
held his free hand up to protect his exposed face. At the same time,
he brought his phaser up to strike in one last stand against the
rushing creature. Once again, the weapon tingled in his hand as it
discharged its powerful beam of energy, which again proved useless as the menacing black form loomed closer, blocking the very
sun from his view.

The tingle in his hand then seemed to cascade over his entire
body. Only after he saw the first hints of gold sparkles start to coalesce around him did he realize he had been caught by a transporter beam. Everything faded into blinding white light . . .

. . . only to be replaced by the stark interior of a transporter
room and the terrified face of a crewman standing behind the
chamber's bright red console. On the pad ahead of him and to his
left, Lieutenant La Sala found herself aiming her phaser at the
crewman and hurriedly lowered the weapon.

"Sorry, Chief," she said as she stepped down from the pad.
Turning, she looked to Xiong. "Lieutenant . . ." she began, but the
rest of her words died in her throat. Her eyes grew wide with new
fear and her mouth dropped open in unbridled shock as she stared
at something to his right.

Xiong turned to see Bohanon standing next to him, his features frozen in terror and surprise. His arms were held up in front of him as if trying to fend off an invisible enemy. Between his collar and his abdomen was a nearly perfect circle of nothingness, penetrating his torso from front to back.

The lifeless Denobulan collapsed to the transporter pad just as Xiong felt his own legs go out from under him. Color washed from his vision before everything was consumed by black.

"Incoming!"

Yet again, Khatami employed a death grip on the arms of the command chair as the *Endeavour* did its best to buck her out of her seat, pummeled once more from the planet's surface. This time the blow hit her from the side, driving her rib cage against the sharp contours of the command chair's armrest. Smoke and sparks issued from the bridge's now unmanned environmental-control station.

"Transporter room, report!" she shouted into her chair's intercom, continuing to endure her jaw's relentless ache.

"We have three . . ."

"The captain?"

The pause from the other end fed her fears. *"No, Commander."* Khatami pressed her fingers into her brow in frustration. "Keep trying!"

"I'm working on it," the transporter chief said, *"but there's nothing else to lock on to down there."*

Thoughts of Zhao and the encampment, along with all sorts of wildly imagined terrors, flashed in her mind, though the anguish and torture was short as Halse called for her attention.

"Damage reports coming in, Commander," he said. "Secondary hull compromised. Critical breach of the hangar deck. Life support is down to forty-four percent."

At his own station, Mog turned in his seat. "They're having to seal off engineering to contain a coolant leak." Looking to Khatami, he said, "I should probably get down there."

"I need you here," she snapped, the words startling her even as they sprang from her lips. The Tellarite regarded her with torment in his eyes, the need to see to his people and his allegiance waging war with each other. She held his gaze and in a near-whisper added, "Please. . . ."

Mog nodded once. "They've got it contained, and I can direct damage control from up here." The delivery of his report was such that Khatami wondered if it was more to assure himself than anyone else. Returning to his console, he rechecked the row of display monitors before straightening in his seat. "But we've got another problem, Commander. The hit to the secondary hull has cracked the base of the port nacelle strut. It needs emergency repair and we can't do it here." Indicating the planet on the viewscreen with a nod of his massive head, he added, "Without shields, if we take another hit, the support will shear off and we're done. Simple as that."

We can't leave yet, she thought. *I can't.*

"Power is cycling up again on the planet," Klisiewicz said. "We've got about forty seconds, Commander."

Khatami jammed the intercom button. "Transporter room! Who's down there?"

"This is Chief Schuster, sir. I've got Lieutenant La Sala and two members of the research team here. Lieutenant Xiong and . . . I'm not sure what the other person's name was. Xiong's pretty shaken up, but he's okay."

"What about the captain?" Khatami shouted into the intercom as if it would help her be heard better. "Xiong, wasn't he with you?"

A new, weak voice replied, *"He wasn't . . . beamed up . . . I . . . I don't know . . ."*

From the science station, Klisiewicz turned to look at her. "I'm not picking up any life signs, Commander."

Khatami felt her mind slowing as if bogged down by a tremendous weight. Her mouth was dry, her tongue thick even as her jaw continued to throb in pain.

I can't . . . I can't . . .

"Intensify your scans," she heard Mog say even as he hauled himself out of his chair and toward the command well, "and send anything you find to the transporter room. Hurry, boy!"

"*I can't find anything to lock on to,*" Schuster's voice echoed from the bridge speakers. "*Commander, I'm sorry.*"

No . . . no . . .

"Power readings are spiking!" Klisiewicz shouted. "Ten seconds!"

"Atish?" It was Mog, speaking softly at her side. He placed a meaty hand on her forearm. "We have to go. Now."

NO!

The word screamed at her, but Khatami knew there was but one course of action.

"Get us out of here," she said flatly, hoping against hope that her demeanor masked even a portion of the rage and anguish and guilt that started to crush her insides. She barely registered anything as Neelakanta input the necessary maneuvers to pull the *Endeavour* away from the planet and out of harm's way. She could hardly listen as Mog advised the helmsman of the ship's maximum safe speed even as the viewer displayed the pale, unforgiving ball of ice that was the planet Erilon receding from view.

She said nothing as the rest of the bridge crew regarded her, silently splitting their attention between halfhearted attempts to carry out their duties and looking into the face of the person who seemingly had left their captain behind to die on that frozen world.

Beaten and exhausted, Khatami could do nothing save remain at her post, her body struggling to occupy a chair that now seemed far too big to accommodate her, one that felt all the more uncomfortable in the absence of its rightful owner.

Sheng. Please forgive me.

13

Again, I am being . . . again, it is pain.

The Shedai Wanderer surveyed the scene of her final stand to reclaim this world for her heritage and her people. She had left the sanctity of rest, roused to action not as herald of the great vision but as its defender—and against what? The fragile, the limited, the selfish, the pitiful. Encroachers, plunderers, opportunists, what the Shedai had once labeled *Telinaruul*: those dismissed as criminals and subject to swift, merciless punishment.

Surrounding her was a frozen wasteland littered with broken husks; their essence voided, their purpose dashed. Looking upon them only honed her clarity of resolve, yet it also intensified her desire to escape being and return to the peace of the void. In this state, she resembled them.

She did not relish that.

Agony surrounds me . . . being brings suffering . . . but it is necessary in the now.

The knowledge she gained through being racked her, for as it was before, so it was now in this place.

How long had she slept? Ages? Mere moments? When the song of the Conduit first beckoned, the Wanderer awakened to witness the savaging of what could have been. Sandswept ruins of her people's former triumph mocked her. Burning heat gnawed at her being.

Then again came the song.

By heeding its call here and now, she was greeted by a world ravaged not by fire but by ice. Biting needles pierced her being, a sensation different but nonetheless torturous. Sorrow, rage, vengeance, roiled within her. Once more, the world she joined was lifeless, unfit, defiled by forces that dared to compromise the great vision.

But here, the Conduit remains. Hope is preserved.

The Wanderer moved across the desecrated land to the place of the known—within the Conduit—taking some comfort in the embrace of the stoneglass, a tangible legacy of her people's achievements in millennia past. Simply looking at the meager attempts by the *Telinaruul* to defile the legacy, to seize control of its capability, seemed a grievous insult against the heritage of the Shedai. Such tampering, which had brought forth the song, enraged her.

Clarity revealed to the Wanderer three actions she deemed sufficient to rectify the arrogant encroachment of this apparent new breed of *Telinaruul.*

First: Become being and eradicate the individual threats. She had accomplished that goal for the now, but it seemed likely that others would soon come.

Second: Summon the dormant energies of the world itself and channel them against the collective threat. However, she had underestimated her quarry's ability to elude destruction, which now forced her to plot new strategies if she was to achieve success in defending this world.

Third: Prevent future violations of this Conduit—if necessary—by destroying it.

Only this action gave the Wanderer pause. While this world no longer was viable, the small flicker of life placed upon it long since extinguished, she recognized the critical role this Conduit played for realizing the great vision.

No, it is not yet time. Through me, this Conduit can yet serve.

The Wanderer approached the Place of Joining, embraced an even deeper pain of being than she had yet endured, and began calling forth the power she needed for what was to come.

14

"Rocinante, *this is Vanguard Control*," said a female voice that was all business but still sounded more than a bit alluring to Tim Pennington. "*You are cleared for departure from bay fifteen.*"

Sitting in the cramped cockpit of Quinn's dilapidated Mancharan starhopper, Pennington remained silent and watched as the privateer's fingers moved as of their own volition, entering commands to the well-worn helm console. Pennington felt the increase of the subtle yet still noticeable vibrations running through the bulkheads that were too close and the armrests of the seat that was too rigid and uncomfortable for him as Quinn increased the power of the *Rocinante*'s fusion drive. Feeling the body of the ship shudder around him, the journalist briefly wondered if the freighter would self-destruct before even clearing the station's landing bay.

"Thanks, Control," Quinn said. He moved his hand to the joystick that offered him control of the ship's maneuvering thrusters, while using the other hand to pinch the bridge of his nose before rubbing his temple. To Pennington, the other man looked like he might throw up, pass out, or simply keel over and die at any moment.

"You okay, mate?" Pennington asked, finally unable to keep from saying something.

Tapping a series of keys on the helm console, Quinn replied without looking up. "I'll live."

"Long enough to keep from flying us into the wall?"

The bedraggled pilot ignored the question as he engaged the *Rocinante*'s maneuvering thrusters, guiding the freighter past the doors of docking bay fifteen and into open space. Pennington, keeping his hands in his lap and away from any of the cockpit controls—lest he accidentally engage some form of autodestruct sequence—watched as the walls of thick duranium composing Vanguard's inner and outer hulls slid past.

He always had enjoyed space travel, particularly when he could do it aboard a small craft such as Quinn's. With only the cockpit's transparent canopy separating him from the airless void beyond, the unfettered view of distant stars was one Pennington relished. When starlight was unfiltered through a planet's atmosphere or free from the obscuring light of a nearby sun—and certainly not as rendered via a ship's viewscreen—his enjoyment of this aspect of space travel never had diminished. For him, it seemed as fresh as the first time he had taken in such a view. He had been eight years old and in the company of his father, then an attaché for the Federation Diplomatic Corps, to Vulcan on a goodwill trip. As he had learned then, and reaffirmed once again here and now, the vastness and beauty of space could only truly be appreciated when viewed in this manner.

The pleasure of the moment faded, however, as he reminded himself of the reason he was aboard the ship in the first place, and of his concerns that Quinn might just be getting ready to screw up his carefully laid plans.

"Rocinante," said the woman currently acting as the voice for Vanguard Control, "*you are clear to navigate. Safe travels. Vanguard out.*"

Waiting as Quinn engaged the ship's impulse engine and began his computations for taking the ship to warp speed, Pennington turned in his seat to ask the questions that had been gnawing at him since before the privateer boarded the vessel.

"All right, Quinn, you planning to tell me what's going on? What kind of trouble are you getting me into?"

Looking up from the helm console, Quinn regarded him with a skeptical expression. "What are you talking about?"

Pennington rolled his eyes. "Bloody hell. I saw you talking to T'Prynn in the corridor before we left. Why's she pulling your leash this time?"

His eyes narrowing in suspicion and irritation, Quinn's voice dropped in volume as he replied, "Now hang on, I don't know what you might have heard, but . . ."

Holding up a hand to forestall any more of what he was sure would be Quinn's attempt at skirting the truth, Pennington said, "Look, I know all about you and T'Prynn. She's got something on you, just like she seems to have her bloody claws into a lot of other things on that station. She wants you to do something while we're out here, doesn't she?"

He knew it was a risky move, revealing his knowledge of Quinn's clandestine relationship with the Vulcan. For that reason alone, he elected to keep private the fact that he had observed the freighter pilot's first meeting with T'Prynn, deep in the bowels of the station's massive storage facility and supposedly away from prying eyes and ears. Her plan for the covert rendezvous had been sound, save for the random combination of chance, bitter fate, and guilt that had conspired to have Pennington down there at the same time.

I'm trying to dispose of one secret, and I find myself dealing with someone else's.

After the loss of the *U.S.S. Bombay* and her crew, including Lieutenant Oriana D'Amato, the ship's helm officer and the woman with whom he had been sharing a short but fiercely passionate love affair, Pennington had gathered everything he could find that might link the two of them. Personal belongings, gifts they had exchanged, anything that might inadvertently be discovered and delivered to her widowed husband, Pennington had collected it all while still in the throes of his own grief. While seeking a garbage-disposal chute to dispose of the illicit evidence, he had chanced across Quinn and his would-be handler.

Of course, T'Prynn's agenda soon would expand beyond inflicting misery upon the life of a tramp freighter captain, as Pennington was to learn firsthand.

Looking back on it now, I might have been better off if I'd put myself down one of those chutes.

Not that he would ever seriously consider such a course of action, and not that it mattered right now, anyway. What was important was that he was certain T'Prynn had coerced Quinn into doing something questionable, perhaps even dangerous, during this flight to Boam II, and he needed to know how it affected him.

To his credit, Quinn appeared to consider the question before nodding—more to himself than Pennington—as if reaching a decision.

"Okay," the pilot said, "but you have to swear you'll keep your mouth shut about this. None of that damn reporter 'on-and-off-the-record' crap of yours, you understand?"

Pennington held up his hands in mock surrender. "Fair enough."

Pausing to draw what might have been a calming breath before releasing a heavy sigh, Quinn said, "Here's the deal. We have to go and pick somebody up."

"Dammit, Quinn," Pennington shouted, cutting off the pilot's next sentence. He rose from his seat, fully prepared to launch into a tirade that would question Quinn's integrity, intelligence, manhood, and genealogy—but the rant never made it past his lips as his head struck a control panel that formed part of the cockpit's sloping overhead. Stars danced in his vision as he reached for his head, dropping back into his chair and wincing as a warning alarm wailed through the confined space.

Grunting in his own form of pain and irritation, Quinn fumbled for a bank of instruments near his left hand. A few frantic presses of controls later and the siren ceased its ear-piercing screech. "You mind watching what the hell you're doing? You almost purged the life-support system."

Still grasping the top of his head, Pennington glanced up at the control panel, which featured far more pieces of adhesive tape and what looked to be grease stains than he considered sanitary. "Sorry," he said. After another moment spent probing his scalp in a search for blood that, thankfully, produced no results, he looked to Quinn once more. "I said I heard you talking to T'Prynn. I didn't catch it all, but I heard her say she wants you to pick up some kind of sensor drone."

Quinn sighed again. "Okay, okay." Reaching into the pocket of his dilapidated jacket, he produced what Pennington recognized to be a trio of standard Federation data cards. He fanned the multicolored squares in his hand as though playing poker. "She wants me to track down a sensor drone, download the data it contains, and replace it with whatever's on these."

"What's on them?" Pennington asked.

Shrugging, the pilot replied, "Damn if I know. I figure she's up to something with Starfleet Intelligence, trying to mislead the Klingons or something."

Given the pain he still was feeling, it took an extra moment for that last part to register with Pennington.

"Wait," he finally said, sitting up in his chair. "Klingons? You mean she asked you to intercept a Klingon sensor drone?"

"You got it," Quinn said as he returned the data cards to his pocket. "Figure the drone's data is important to her, and whatever's on these is fake. Maybe she's trying to monitor ship movements or something."

"And you don't think this might get us killed?" Pennington asked, making no effort to rein in his rapidly escalating anxiety.

"Oh, I'm absolutely sure it could get us killed. If we get caught, that is." Turning back to the helm console, Quinn looked up once more and smiled. "So, we should probably avoid that."

"Fine idea, mate." Shaking his head, the pain he still felt making him regret the action, Pennington tried to get comfortable in his seat. "Okay," he said finally. "So, we go to Boam II, then catch this thing on the way back?"

Quinn shook his head. "Not exactly. T'Prynn gave me a set of coordinates and told me that I have to intercept it at a certain location at a certain time, otherwise I don't get what she's after. She says these things don't have a lot of power, or computer memory, or whatever. They do whatever scanning they're supposed to do, transmit their data to a predetermined point of receipt, and then wipe their data cores to make room for whatever they're tasked to scan next."

"So if we get to the probe after it transmits whatever data T'Prynn wants," Pennington said, "then we're out of luck."

"You got it."

Nodding, the journalist leaned forward in his seat until he could get a better look at the computer display on Quinn's console. He recognized a series of Federation star charts, though he could not read the entire screen thanks to a smudge or smear of something on the panel. Reaching out, he rubbed away the offending obstruction with the sleeve of his shirt. "So, what systems are near the rendezvous point?"

"That's what I'm checking." Quinn pointed to the monitor. "According to the charts, we'll be near the Jinoteur system." Shaking his head, he added, "Never heard of it."

"Neither have I," Pennington said, though he knew that his and Quinn's knowledge of the Taurus Reach meant little to nothing in this situation. With so much of the area still unexplored, even by unmanned sensor probes, there simply was no telling what mysteries lay within this unknown region of space.

Or, why T'Prynn might be interested in one of them.

As Quinn resumed his warp calculations, Pennington considered the privateer's original theory about the Vulcan's reasons for the assignment she had given him. "Why would she need data from a Klingon sensor drone to learn about Klingon ship activity? Starfleet's already got listening outposts and sensor arrays strung out all over the Taurus Reach." Indeed, he knew that a line of monitoring and relay stations had been brought to bear in this part of space and dedicated to Vanguard's oversight of the region. Making use of state-of-the-art technology, such fully automated outposts also were currently being deployed along the Federation-Klingon border. Reportedly, they soon would replace the asteroid-based outposts and their crews who stood vigil along the Neutral Zone separating the Federation from territory claimed by the Romulan Empire.

What could a lone sensor drone of admittedly inferior capabilities offer that Starfleet's own sensor arrays could not?

Curiouser and curiouser.

There was also the point to consider that the *Rocinante,* being a civilian merchant vessel, would conceivably be able to move through the Taurus Reach without attracting too much in the way of official attention—particularly if Quinn held to whatever course and timetable T'Prynn had given him. On the other hand, if the Klingons discovered what was going on, at worst Quinn and anyone unfortunate or stupid enough to be with him at the time would likely be captured or killed, leaving T'Prynn and Starfleet untainted by any accusations of illegal or antagonistic actions against the empire.

With Quinn involved in preparing the *Rocinante* for warp speed, Pennington mulled over this new information, taking pieces of it and putting it together with what else he knew of T'Prynn's activities aboard Vanguard. Was the unusual assignment she had given Quinn—and by extension, himself—somehow connected to some of the other things for which he knew she was responsible? Did it somehow dovetail with the questions that troubled Pennington himself, the answers to which he had pledged to answer by any means available to him?

While the story he had fed to Quinn about interviewing colonists and how they were faring in the Taurus Reach was not technically a lie, it was only part of the reason he had asked to accompany the privateer on his journey to Boam II. After several weeks of careful contemplation, the journalist had decided that in the wake of the personal and professional setbacks he had suffered, the only way he would ever regain his status—and his sense of self-worth—was by aggressively striving to solve the mystery that had taunted him for weeks.

What really happened to the *U.S.S. Bombay,* and who was responsible? Further, why did Starfleet already possess these answers while taking extraordinary steps to keep that truth from the public?

Pennington had found himself caught in the middle of that conundrum a month earlier when a tip, received from an anonymous source, had led him to information about the starship's tragic loss at the hands of Tholian vessels while in orbit of Ravanar IV. More evidence—in the form of log entries, requisition and status reports, and transcripts of subspace communiqués—indicted Starfleet, specifically Commodore Reyes and members of his senior staff, as participants in a secret intelligence-gathering operation on the planet, which also had been destroyed by the Tholians. The evidence, which Pennington painstakingly had corroborated by interviewing people named in many of the reports and logs, should have formed the foundation for the story of his career while simultaneously bringing justice for the crew of the *Bombay*.

For Oriana, he thought, reminded once again of the captivating woman with whom he had shared a bed. That loss and the pain he still felt were made worse by the fact that he had been unable even to say goodbye to Oriana D'Amato before she had left on what turned out to be the *Bombay*'s final mission. The unexpected arrival of the *U.S.S. Enterprise* at Vanguard, aboard which her husband served as a geologist, prevented him from seeing her in the days leading up to her ship's departure.

While her death gnawed at him, Pennington's grief and ire also were driven by the fact that Starfleet seemed hell-bent to keep the truth about the *Bombay*'s fate a secret. That alone was deplorable, but the measures that had been taken to accomplish the cover-up were beyond the pale. Evidence, sources, and testimony Pennington had acquired all had been manufactured in a deliberate scheme to draw the reporter into a web of lies, which he then had written and submitted to the Federation News Service. No sooner had the tremendous news story been published than it was immediately discredited, with Starfleet able to demonstrate that the information Pennington had used for his report contained incorrectly time-stamped log entries and notations by people either already deceased or not known to exist at all. And almost as immediately, he was fired from the FNS.

He had been set up. Deliberately. Everything was a fraud.

Not everything, he reminded himself. *It can't be.*

Pennington was certain that the data itself—the sensor logs, communications transcripts—was simply too detailed and voluminous to all be a sham. Somewhere, beneath the surface of the lie which had been perpetrated, the truth lay concealed. He was certain of it—just as he knew that T'Prynn had been behind the entire affair. The intelligence officer had denied the accusation of course, but despite her best efforts he had seen the truth peeking out from beneath her rigid Vulcan façade.

Part of him understood the reasons for the cover-up. Any open acknowledgment of the Tholians' role in the destruction of the

Bombay would damage the diplomatic relations the two powers currently enjoyed, which doubtless were already strained by the simple fact that Starfleet knew the Tholians were guilty and had called them on it. Pushing the issue would almost certainly lead to war.

Still, it made no sense to Pennington that the Federation should back away from the issue now. A strong, vibrant façade during its movements into the Taurus Reach seemed critical, not only with the Tholians watching their every move but also the Klingon Empire and any other power throughout the Alpha and Beta quadrants. To him, this action only seemed to further drive home the notion that this mysterious region of space contained something that the Federation—or more specifically, Starfleet—wanted to possess. Their apparent need was sufficient grounds in official eyes to downplay the loss of a starship and its crew.

Well, that's just not bloody good enough, Pennington decided. *Not for Oriana.*

He was pulled from his thoughts by the unmistakable shift in the *Rocinante*'s engines as the freighter's warp drive engaged. Beyond the cockpit's canopy, he watched the stars stretch and distort into multicolored streaks as the ship entered subspace. Such would be the view, he knew, for however long it took to get to wherever Quinn's formidable Vulcan master was sending them.

Turning in his seat, Pennington regarded the interior of the dilapidated cockpit before looking down the short corridor leading to the ship's equally cramped and decidedly untidy passenger compartment.

"Three days to get there," he said. "Maybe you could spend some of that time straightening up around here, mate."

Quinn leaned back in his seat, releasing another sigh as he reached up to rub his bloodshot eyes with the heels of his hands. "I had to fire the maid. Feel free to strap on an apron if you're bored. I'm getting me some shut-eye." As he closed his eyes, he added, "And it's twelve days, round trip."

"Twelve days?" Pennington repeated, aghast. "Where the hell are we going?"

Several moments passed before Quinn opened his eyes once

more. "Oh yeah, I forgot. What I said before, about picking up somebody? That wasn't a lie. We're going to Yerad III first, to pick up a guy and bring him to Ganz."

"You're kidding." In the month that had passed since first meeting Quinn, Pennington had taken the time to learn as much as he could find about the Orion merchant prince whose ship currently was docked at Vanguard. From what he had learned, the journalist had decided that Ganz was a most unsavory individual, someone to be avoided if indeed one possessed an ounce of common sense or self-preservation instinct.

When Quinn spoke this time his voice had already taken on the groggy drawl of someone fighting to stay awake. "It'll be fine. Trust me." There was something else, but by that point the man's voice had deteriorated to little more than an incoherent mumble, though Pennington thought he picked up something about T'Prynn and what sounded like an observation of how her legs looked in the newest version of Starfleet uniform for female officers.

This wanker is going to get me killed.

15

Looking across sickbay in the dimmed light, Anthony Leone could only shake his head.

I like to stay busy, sure, but . . . come on.

He took little comfort in the lame attempt at sardonic observation, and in fact he felt a bit guilty that he might even think such a thing given the current circumstances. Forcing away the errant thought, Leone walked to the nearest diagnostic bed, one of four in the *Endeavour*'s intensive-care unit of sickbay—each of which was occupied—to better study the readings on the patient status panel overlooking Ensign Karen LaMartina. The young woman had suffered upper-body burns and a concussion when a circuit panel blew out in the second round of strikes against the starship.

When she arrived in sickbay across the shoulder of a burly engineer, Leone noticed that her rescuer had taken a bit of a beating himself from the same explosion. Rather than hang around to have his own wounds examined, the engineer instead remained only long enough to offer a hasty report of what happened before dashing off, full of adrenaline and the desire to resume his duties so long as he was able. Leone had yet to see him return, which made the physician wonder whether the man truly was more able to perform than he appeared or had instead collapsed somewhere in the bowels of the ship.

And that's just one of five thousand things going on aboard this ship right now, none of which I have a damned clue about. The thought only fueled his already mounting frustration as he gritted his teeth and forced himself to focus on the one thing of which he was most aware at the moment: the number of casualties crowding his sickbay.

Before him, LaMartina wrestled in obvious discomfort from her injuries. Stepping closer, he placed a hand on her arm. "Pain?" he asked, and the young ensign nodded. Leone reached for a hypospray that had already been positioned nearby by Dr. Bruce Griffin, his ever-prepared assistant CMO. Adjusting the dosage on the hypospray, Leone pressed the device to LaMartina's neck and injected the analgesic, the medication entering her bloodstream on the heels of the hypospray's compressed hiss. He saw the sedative's effects begin to take hold immediately, with his patient's eyes fluttering and her facial features beginning to relax.

Weakly, she reached out to touch his arm. "I've been . . . sleepy. . . ."

"It's the medication, Ensign," Leone said, his short-sleeved tunic allowing him to feel the clammy touch of her fingers on his bare skin. "You'll be fine."

"Wait," LaMartina said, tightening her grip around his slender forearm. "I thought I heard . . . did you say . . . the captain was killed?"

Leone's own throat tightened a bit as it did every time he bore bad news to a member of the crew, patient or not. "I'm sorry, Karen," he spoke softly. "Yes, Captain Zhao is dead."

He watched as the woman pressed her eyes closed and sighed deeply. Leone never was one to couch his words in circumstances such as these; he knew it really did not soften the news of someone's death by coming up with some euphemism. Captain Zhao had not passed away. He had not merely left behind this mortal plane in order to enter another realm of existence. He had died. Attempting to dull or deflect such a grievous tragedy in large, flowing vocabulary, Leone had learned, never succeeded in making death any less painful or worrisome to those still living.

"But, we're going to be okay," he said after a moment, reminding himself with a small amount of irritation that his priorities now remained not with the dead but with the living. "*You're* going to be okay." He patted her hand before placing it at her side. "Rest now, and I'll be back in a bit."

Looking up, he saw Dr. Griffin regarding him from the foot of

LaMartina's bed, the younger man's expression one of concern. Sensing this was not a conversation he wanted held in front of his patients, Leone directed his assistant to his office. He fell more than sat down in the seat behind his cluttered, disorganized desk, waiting for the door to hiss shut before looking to his colleague and friend.

"Something wrong, Doctor?"

"Well, I was just wondering," Griffin said as he ran his hand through his sandy brown hair, "if you've heard anything about what happened back at Erilon."

Leone released an exhausted sigh. "Maybe you were on break or something, but I've had my hands full the last couple of hours. Wanna enlighten me?"

Obviously put off by Leone's remark, Griffin clasped his hands before him. "I'm only bringing it up because, to hear some people tell it, the captain might not be dead."

Frowning, Leone allowed a scowl to darken his features. "Really? And what makes them say that?"

"The word is that Commander Khatami just left him behind when she pulled up and ran," Griffin said, his eyes growing wider as he offered the unpleasant notion. "He could still be fighting it out against . . . well, whatever happened down there."

Leone knit his brow and made a fist with his right hand while cupping it in his left. He admitted to himself that he would have given a limb right then and there for a full report of just what actually occurred back at the encampment, but he could trust only what little information he did have, along with his gut instinct when it came to Khatami as he had known her for these past couple of years. "And you . . . buy into that account of events, Doctor?"

"Dr. Leone, I'm only saying . . ."

"And I'm only saying that you have an opportunity to put a lid on whatever rumor mill you seem to be tapped into," Leone said, leaning forward in his chair and adding an edge to his voice that made Griffin straighten his posture. "From what I've been told by people who were actually down on the planet, whatever it was that tore through the base and our landing party did so quickly and aggressively. There's no reason to believe that anyone survived." At least, that was according to what little information Lieutenant Xiong was able to articulate before Leone escorted the Starfleet archaeologist to his temporary quarters and sedated him.

Well, that, he thought, *and the gaping hole where that Denobulan's chest, lungs, and spine used to be.*

"If you and your party of conspiracy theorists need proof of what they were up against," Leone said, actual anger now beginning to lace his words, "I can arrange a tour of the stasis chamber. We can get all of this sorted out right now."

To his credit, Griffin meekly shook his head. "That won't be necessary, Doctor. I didn't . . . I didn't have that other information at my disposal."

"Ah," Leone said. "So, tell me, just how did *you* do on your battery of command examinations at Starfleet Academy? You know, that *Kobayashi*-whatever-the-hell-it-is test?"

"I never took those courses or that test," Griffin said, embarrassment and his own ire beginning to color his features. "You know I only undertook Starfleet medical training."

Leone placed his hands flat atop his desk and pushed himself to his feet. "Well, then," he said, glaring at the other doctor, "until you do, maybe you and your fellow gossipers can keep your damn second-guessing of command decisions to yourself. Got that?"

"Very clearly, sir," Griffin said crisply and nodding his head vigorously.

Holding his stare for an additional moment, Leone finally relaxed and allowed himself to return to his seat. "There's a lot more to healing a ship, Doctor, than just patching up its crew. Attend to that, and we'll all be better off," he said, reaching for the data slate lying atop the chaos that was his desk. "Now, unless there's anything else, I have a report to finish."

Griffin turned and left without another word, and Leone watched the young physician wander back into sickbay, then turn and look back over his shoulder for a moment before returning his attention to his patients. The chief medical officer narrowed his eyes as he watched Griffin work before shaking his head and turning to regard the data slate in his hand.

Didn't take long for the natives to get restless, Leone thought as he reviewed his final list of crew casualties. *Damn, this is gonna be a long trip home for all of us.*

Poking at reconstituted corned-beef hash, Stephen Klisiewicz decided, did nothing to imbue it with additional flavor.

And it was not merely the food before him that seemed drained of its essence, he thought. Looking around the *Endeavour*'s mess hall, every aspect of the environment seemed lifeless and dry to him. Crew members moved slowly, as though walking with leaden weights draped invisibly around their necks. Aside from the omnipresent hum of the ship's engines, chairs scraping against deck plates and the occasional grinding of cutlery against dishes offered the only audible backdrop. What few conversations actually did take place at surrounding tables seemed muted in tone and abbreviated in conduct, as if people were exchanging only the barest information necessary to keep working.

Much more than just Captain Zhao died this morning, Klisiewicz decided, *and it shows.*

He had come straight to the mess hall more as a mechanical response than anything else. After the *Endeavour*'s departure from Erilon—and after Commander Khatami left the bridge—Klisiewicz had spent the remainder of his shift at the science station, halfheartedly running diagnostic checks of the starship's computer core and data systems and quietly absorbing the pall that had settled on the bridge crew. Although Neelakanta had moved from his seat at the helm into the command chair, Klisiewicz felt that it was Mog who had lent more of a commanding air to the situation, calling across the bridge for updated condition reports and coordinating repair efforts from his engineering console. The burly Tellarite also found time to move from station to station and engage members of the bridge crew in personal conversation, a move Klisiewicz felt had done some good in restoring a measure of his own morale—maybe everyone's—as *Endeavour* made its fastest possible speed back to Starbase 47.

When an officer he did not recognize relieved him from his post, Klisiewicz simply left, his parting glance at Mog unreturned as the engineer focused on a computer readout. Halfway to his quarters, a growling in the pit of his stomach diverted him to the mess hall. Still, even though he had skipped breakfast, that hunger seemed to have been a miscue, as he found himself toying with his hash while the events of the past few hours unreeled in a continual loop in his mind.

Was I the right one for the job today? Did I really do enough? Could I at least have been fast—

"Ensign Klisiewicz?"

A flash of yellow in front of him snapped Klisiewicz from his reverie, and he looked up to see Lieutenant McCormack standing across the table from him and holding a meal tray. The navigator's face was framed in strawberry-blond hair and her smile was tentative, one he had never glimpsed during their time together on the bridge. At that moment, however, even a hint of something friendly was a welcome bit of comfort.

"Lieutenant!" he said, perhaps a bit too eagerly.

"Please," she replied in a quiet voice seemingly pitched lower than her petite frame might have suggested. "I'm Marielise. I figure at this point, we're past just ranks."

Happy to take her up on the offer, Klisiewicz rose from his seat. "I'm Stephen, then," he said as he pulled a chair out for her. "Please, sit down."

McCormack set the tray on the table and lowered herself into the proffered chair, casting a wary eye toward his tray while plucking a napkin from atop her own to reveal her selection: a cold salad of chicken, apples, and nuts on a bed of greens. He found himself a little embarrassed, somehow wanting to offer a defense for his meager meal, and a little anxious about her motives for seeking out his company in the mess. She offered no immediate answers, choosing instead to eat in the same silence as the diners around them.

"How do you find an appetite?" Klisiewicz asked, embarrassed at the question even as the words left his mouth. Frowning, he added, "I mean, you know, after everything that's happened."

Shrugging, McCormack moved greens and small bits of chicken around on her plate. "To be honest, I'm not really that hungry. I found myself here after my shift ended, without even realizing it." She offered a small smile. "Habit, I guess. Besides, I figure I'm not exactly helping anyone if I don't eat. The last thing you want is Dr. Leone chasing after you because you're not taking care of yourself."

Though he nodded in understanding, Klisiewicz felt less than inspired by the lieutenant's observations. Instead, he opted to poke some more at his hash.

"So," McCormack said after a few moments and after she had consumed half her salad, "was that really your first time in combat?"

Guess she cuts right to the heart of things, he thought as he felt his shoulders slump. "Was it that obvious?" he asked.

"Not at all," the lieutenant replied. "I only ask because I thought I heard someone mention it. I was surprised, actually."

He felt buoyed. "You were?"

McCormack nodded as she took another bite of her salad. Klisiewicz hung on her affirmation, and kept hanging as she chewed bite after bite, seemingly disinterested in pursuing the conversation. Still, for some reason, Klisiewicz did not find the silence awkward. Aside from the obvious fact that McCormack was very attractive, he found her presence a calming one. Oddly enough, he even felt some of his own appetite returning, and finally took the first bite of his own meal.

They carried on wordlessly for the rest of their meal until McCormack dropped her fork onto her now empty plate and wiped her mouth with her napkin. Rising from her seat, she looked at him and offered another smile, though this one was broader and more lively than when she had first arrived. "It was nice getting to know you, Stephen," she said.

Getting to know *me?* Klisiewicz almost choked on his hash. "Likewise," he said around a tentative mouthful of food. "Maybe I'll see you next time?"

McCormack nodded once in agreement as she picked up her tray, pausing long enough to hold his gaze. "For what it's worth," she said, "you're a good guy to have on the bridge during a fight."

And with that, Lieutenant Marielise McCormack spun on her heel and was gone, leaving a baffled Klisiewicz to watch her as she disappeared through the door leading to the corridor. It was not until several moments had passed, with him trying to assess his enigmatic dining partner, that he realized he had finished his meal and that he felt better than he had in several hours.

Wow.

Space had never felt colder for Atish Khatami than it did at this moment.

In the stillness of her quarters, she sat upright in a tall-backed seat behind her desk. The desk was unadorned except for a standard tabletop viewer, which bathed her face in a soft glow of light as she stared unwaveringly toward its screen and into the faces depicted upon it, those of Commodore Diego Reyes and Lieutenant Commander T'Prynn.

Khatami figured that if she looked straight into their faces, then maybe she could keep on blinking back any stray tears that she still could not manage to suppress. So far, through her whole report on the incident at Erilon, she had managed to do so. She believed she had held herself together on an even par with Reyes himself, which given her experience with the base commander's reserved demeanor was saying something.

Khatami knew better than to hold her disposition up for comparison against T'Prynn's.

"Have you interviewed Mr. Xiong?" the Vulcan intelligence officer asked flatly from the other side of the screen.

"Not beyond the basics of what I just told you," Khatami said, ignoring the dull ache in her bruised jaw. "Dr. Leone ordered that he be allowed to rest before he is debriefed."

"There's no need for you to speak to him, Commander," Reyes said, almost too quickly. *"We'll just do it again here, anyway. Let him rest and maybe work up his written report."*

"Yes, Commodore," Khatami replied, nodding in understanding.

"*Now, as for the* Endeavour," Reyes said, "*your chief engineer has already transmitted a complete list of the outstanding repairs and needed replacement components. We'll be ready for you as soon as you get home.*" Leaning forward, the commodore knitted his fingers together and tapped his thumbs, looking down at his hands a moment before releasing a sigh. "*Commander, I'm going to need your people prepared to ship out as soon as we can get you ready, and you know my people work fast. I'm going to need the* Endeavour *back at Erilon as soon as possible, to investigate . . . what happened there.*"

I know what happened there, and I didn't want to leave in the first place.

Khatami nodded again. "Understood," she said, refusing to give in to the burning in her eyes. If she had learned anything during her brief tenure assigned to Starbase 47, it was that the station's mission paused for little, even tragedy.

As if satisfied with the report, at least for the moment, Reyes nodded. "*Commander, Captain Zhao was an exemplary leader, and I have no doubt the others who gave their lives today were equally capable,*" he said, the tone of his voice softening. "*You have my deepest sympathies for your losses. Reyes out.*"

"Thank you, sir," Khatami whispered to the now darkened screen as she finally allowed the fresh tears to come forth.

I left them behind.

The words had been whips, mentally flogging herself during these past hours. They showed no signs of letting up, and Khatami did not want them to stop.

I left them. But he would have left them, too, even me. Or would he . . . ?

Her tortured silence was jarred by the sound of her quarters door chime. Quickly blotting the tears from her eyes, she drew what she hoped was a calming breath. "Come in."

The door slid aside to reveal a somewhat hesitant-looking Dr. Leone, holding a data slate in one hand and a medical pouch in the other. He shuffled a bit as he grimaced from one side of his mouth. "Commander," he said after an awkward pause.

"Tony," she said, allowing a bit of relief to seep into her

voice. Leone, at least, was unlikely to require too much of her in a decision-making capacity, a role she admitted she was most uncomfortable assuming at this moment. "What can I do for you?"

"Well," the doctor said, "you haven't checked in to sickbay yet, and I'm told you need to." He stepped into her quarter, allowing the door to close behind him. "So, how are you?"

Khatami rubbed two fingers along the line of her jaw. "Better," she said, not altogether lying. "At least, I don't think it's broken."

Leone nodded, reaching into his medical kit and producing a scanner. He cradled the device in his fingers as she leaned closer, and Khatami imagined a prickly sensation beneath her skin as she watched the scanner hover a hairsbreadth over her cheek and jawline while Leone moved it slowly up and back. After a few moments, he consulted its readings.

"Wow," Leone said. "That's gonna hurt awhile."

Khatami leaned back, not feeling very relieved by the assessment. "Is that your informed medical opinion, Doctor?"

"Absolutely," he said in all seriousness as he traded the scanner for a hypospray. "But it's not fractured. This'll help."

No sooner did Leone inject the contents of the hypospray into her shoulder than Khatami felt its analgesic effects begin to soothe the throbbing ache she had endured these past hours. Closing her eyes for a moment, she allowed herself to enjoy the welcome relief.

"That ought to do the trick," he said after a moment, returning the scanner to his medical kit before extracting a green computer data cartridge. He moved across the room to Khatami's personal food slot. "A colleague once told me something about doing my job when it comes to the senior staff," he said as he inserted the data card and pressed a pair of control buttons set into the bulkhead above the slot. "Something about knowing when to be a physician and when to be a bartender."

He turned to face her, now carrying a small tray that bore two iced drinks in short, square glasses. Crossing the room to her desk, he set the tray down, and a wafting scent of alcohol teased

Khatami's nostrils. Despite herself, she could not help but smile for the first time in what felt like forever.

"You know I don't drink, Tony."

Leone shrugged. "Exactly my point," he said, snatching one of the glasses and downing its contents in a single slug. "The guy didn't have a clue what he was talking about. Some people just shouldn't be on starships, you know?"

She laughed as she watched him exchange glasses, almost forgetting the pain in her jaw as he sipped from the second drink. "I'm beginning to think so, yes."

Leone nodded, then froze as if only then realizing his words carried the great likelihood of landing completely albeit unintentionally wrong. He squeezed his eyes shut and sighed. "You gotta throw me a bit of a lifeline here, Atish," he said, still looking pained. "This isn't my thing, you know?" Shaking his head, he took another, larger sip from his drink. "Dammit, we need some sort of psychiatrist out here full time or something." He froze again but this time recovered more quickly. "Not that you need a psychiatrist," he clarified before looking away and swearing one of his preferred, earthier oaths.

Khatami reached across her desk and put her hand on his arm. "Your effort is not going unappreciated, Doctor."

"Yeah, sure," Leone said, his head bobbing quickly in a birdlike nod. "I mean, uh, thanks, Commander." He quaffed at his glass again, draining his contents. "Now, I suggest you try to get some rest," Leone instructed as he packed away his medical pouch. Looking to her, he added, "If you'd like to talk, you know, later . . ." he added, still fidgeting a bit.

"I know where to find you," Khatami replied, putting sincerity in her voice more for his benefit than for hers. Still, as she spoke the words, the idea of talking to Leone didn't seem all that unpalatable.

He nodded, offering what on him appeared to be a pained grin before crossing her quarters toward the door, which slid open at his approach. "For what it's worth, Atish," he said and paused to secure her attention, "your place is right here on *Endeavour*."

"Thanks, Tony," Khatami said, feeling a little warmth return to her spirit. Leone held her gaze for a moment more before stepping out of her quarters, leaving her to stare blankly at the door as it slid closed.

Sitting alone, she let the brief reprieve from her anguish comfort her, hoping that it would keep the cold loneliness of space from returning to her, at least for a time.

16

Anna Sandesjo entered her private workspace, aware that she at best had five minutes before Ambassador Jetanien returned to the offices of Starbase 47's Federation Embassy but knowing also that she could not afford to waste this opportunity.

A pity I cannot enjoy the peace and quiet even for a moment.

While it was true that she often found it nearly impossible to tolerate the effusive diplomat's lecturing, ostentatious personality, the fact of the matter was that the Chelon ambassador's political prowess was formidable. That much had become evident in the short time since his assignment to Vanguard and the legion of diplomatic obstacles he had been entrusted to navigate as a consequence of the Federation's recent and pronounced movements into the Taurus Reach. Despite the uncertain and currently tumultuous nature of the political relations that seemed to characterize this region of space, Jetanien had risen to the challenge with tenacity, quickly forging ties with the diplomatic envoys from both the Klingon Empire and the Tholian Assembly, both of whom had been provided embassy space aboard the station.

Of course, having such a gifted ambassador on hand also made Sandesjo's job that much easier.

Closing the door behind her, she engaged the lock before moving behind the small, functional desk that faced the front of the room and was the office's dominating piece of furniture. She ignored the clutter of papers, data slates, and other administrative detritus which characterized her very legitimate responsibilities as Jetanien's senior attaché. Indeed, it was all of little importance, save for its single redeeming quality in that it supported the role she played here. Her position within the Chelon ambassador's organization naturally provided her with access to a wealth of information which might have been all but impossible to access via other avenues.

Like now.

Reaching beneath her desk, Sandesjo retrieved the thin, unassuming metal briefcase she kept there and laid it atop her desk. She entered a combination—one of two the case's lock would accept but the only one known solely to her—and opened the unit, releasing the false panel set inside and revealing the miniaturized subspace transceiver hidden within. It took a moment for the device to activate before she could key in the string of coded commands that would send an encrypted hail to her contact, Turag. After a moment, the transceiver's compact display screen coalesced into an image of the Klingon, staring out at her with his usual expression of annoyed boredom.

Once the protocol for establishing identities and the security of their covert transmission was complete, Turag offered a brusque nod. *"You were not expected to submit a report at this time."*

He was right, of course. Like other long-term intelligence operatives scattered throughout the Federation and Starfleet, her primary consideration when undertaking any action was maintaining her cover. Stealth and virtual invisibility were her watchwords and her lifeline while spying on this most formidable enemy of the empire. Getting to this point had been a trying and time-consuming process, requiring her to remain dormant as she carried on in her assumed role as a member of the Federation Diplomatic Corps. That task had proven to be even more trying than enduring the demeaning process of having her Klingon countenance surgically altered to appear human, which she had done more than ten Earth-standard years earlier. Only after that much time had passed had the opportunity to serve on Jetanien's staff presented itself, allowing her to be activated as a fully operational intelligence agent.

Part of the ongoing and even greater need to maintain her secrecy also meant adhering to the strict protocol regarding communications with her contacts. Turag, acting as her handler in addition to his own covert role as a member of Vanguard's Klingon delegation, had enacted a schedule for her to submit reports on an irregular basis so as to assume the minimum amount of risk against detection. Naturally, there were measures in place for emergencies, which Sandesjo felt justified in employing now.

Nodding in response to Turag's blunt introductory statement, she said, "I know, but I've just received new information that needs to be delivered to our superiors. A Tholian vessel has been destroyed, and the Tholians believe a Klingon ship may be responsible."

His brow furrowed in suspicion. *"We have not heard of any such action. How do you know this is true?"*

"Jetanien," Sandesjo replied. "He had an unscheduled, private meeting with the Tholian ambassador early this morning. While I've not been briefed as to the full details of the entire conversation, he did inform me about this incident. A ship on patrol near the outer boundary of the Taurus Reach bordering Tholian territory was attacked by a vessel of unknown origin, and destroyed before its commander could make a thorough report. No description of the ship was offered, only that it registered no familiar weapons or propulsion signatures, and appeared capable of evading sensors."

Assuming the action was not one sanctioned by the Klingon High Council, it was possible if not probable that Klingon intelligence operatives might soon learn of the incident. However, that Jetanien had learned of it only thanks to a private conversation held with the Tholian ambassador suggested to her that the Tholians were—for the moment, at least—keeping such knowledge classified. With this in mind, Sandesjo had decided the value of the information gleaned from Jetanien was more than worth the risk of offering an impromptu report to Turag.

Leaning forward in her chair, she added, "I was unaware that the empire possessed any ships with such abilities."

"That is of no concern to you, Lurqal," Turag replied, addressing her by her Klingon name. *"Do you believe the Tholians may be planning a reprisal?"*

Sandesjo shook her head. "I don't know, and neither does Jetanien. Of course, if they were planning such action, they would not inform a Federation ambassador of their intentions."

"Is it possible the Federation is responsible?" Turag asked.

If not for the Klingon's serious expression, Sandesjo might have laughed at the notion he offered. "You are as much aware of Federation policies on aggressive action as I am. They do not attack without provocation, nor are they in the habit of concealing their actions when they are forced to defend themselves. Besides, the Tholian commander said that the vessel presented no indications that it was from any familiar power."

"The Federation is notoriously reluctant to construct weapons for purely offensive military purposes," Turag said, *"despite the conflicts in which they've found themselves over the years. Perhaps someone in their Starfleet—someone with* naghs—*has finally learned the lessons imparted by their history and chosen to shoulder that burden."*

Pausing to consider that theory, Sandesjo decided it an unlikely scenario. Still, to appease her handler and keep this conversation moving, she nodded in agreement. "Even if that's the case, it's unlikely anyone assigned to this station would be aware of such a vessel's existence, with the potential exception of Commodore Reyes."

"A logical conclusion," Turag replied, making no effort to suppress the sneer that curled the corners of his mouth. *"Perhaps all the time spent with that Vulcan has influenced you in more ways than one."*

Despite her formidable self-control, Sandesjo still felt her blood warm in response to the other Klingon's unvoiced yet undisguised accusation. "Explain yourself," she demanded.

Shrugging, Turag offered a lascivious smile as he replied, *"Rumors, naturally. According to 'unnamed sources,' you and the Vulcan have been observed in situations that—shall we say—appear to be something other than purely professional."*

Sandesjo schooled her features and her voice to remain impassive as she regarded Turag over the comm link, at the same time relishing the image of the handler's severed head impaled upon the point of her *mek'leth* as she sang a song of triumph and enjoyed a hearty mug of deliciously aged bloodwine. What did this filthy *petaQ'pu* know? Had he somehow become privy to the more intimate moments she shared with T'Prynn?

No, she decided. While Sandesjo expected that Turag would have her under constant surveillance, T'Prynn, being a seasoned intelligence operative in her own right, would almost certainly have taken steps to ensure she was protected from covert scrutiny.

Maintaining her neutral tone and demeanor, Sandesjo asked, "Do you wish to hear the rest of my report, Turag, or continue this clumsy attempt to fuel your fantasies? I don't believe I have sufficient time to assist you in rousing that pathetic excuse for a *loD-mach* you claim to wield."

His jaw clenching in response to her rebuke, Turag's head bobbed in a curt nod. "*Continue.*"

Satisfied for the moment, Sandesjo said, "According to a subspace communication I was able to intercept and decrypt, the *U.S.S. Endeavour* was attacked near Erilon and sustained several casualties, including its captain. The ship is making its return to the station now."

"*Who is responsible?*" Turag asked. While his own inflection was measured, Sandesjo could see that he still was stinging from her admonishment.

Sandesjo shook her head. "Unknown. From what I have been able to learn, the ship was attacked by a planet-based weapon of considerable power, enough to drive them from orbit. It's not Tholian, and based on the *Endeavour*'s report as well as information gathered since the station became operational, there may be other repositories of such technologies scattered throughout the Taurus Reach."

Shrugging, Turag said, "*Planetary defense systems are nothing new, Lurqal.*"

Sandesjo braced against the sudden rise in anger at hearing her given name again. "I've told you not to call me that." She had no desire to be reminded that her Klingon heritage had been buried beneath a façade. "The technology itself is not the issue. Personnel on the planet's surface were also attacked, by an unknown alien life-form. Details on that are sketchy, no doubt due to security protocols, but I was able to gather that this development is of paramount concern to Commodore Reyes."

"*How so?*" Turag asked.

Shaking her head, Sandesjo replied, "There's no way to know, based on the limited amount of information that was shared over the communications channel. I'll pass on more information as soon as possible." Of course, she had no idea at this point how she might accomplish that, given the apparent secrecy that seemed to enshroud much of the activity taking place among the station's most senior officers and civilian advisors.

On her transceiver's display screen, Turag nodded. "*See that you do. Qapla'.*"

The communication was severed without even offering Sandesjo a chance to return the traditional farewell. Absentmindedly, she reached out and pressed the control that deactivated the unit and returned it to its hiding place inside her briefcase's concealed compartment. Once more, her cover was back in place.

Reviewing the information she had gathered and reported, Sandesjo found herself with as many new questions as Turag had posed. Who had destroyed the Tholian vessel? The Klingons? If so, why?

She realized that the commander of a Klingon battle cruiser in the middle of barely charted space did not need any compelling reason to unleash his weapons—on anything or anyone. Still, most officers in such positions of responsibility still tended to exercise a modicum of restraint, even in this age when personal honor and discipline seemed to be out of favor with many Klingon warriors. After all, Sandesjo knew of no officers so bold that they would risk the wrath of the chancellor of the High Council, who had expressly forbidden any vessel operating in the Taurus Reach from taking aggressive action against Federation or Tholian interests in the region unless acting in self-defense. It was an uncharacteristic position for the chancellor to take, suggesting to her that there indeed was more occurring in this area of space than met the eye.

What that might be, of course, was the question which now taunted Sandesjo.

17

Once again, the call rang out through the Conduit. Once more, the Shedai Wanderer answered.

Doing so was difficult. Many of the channels, which long ago had allowed for limitless movement of information as well as the ability to oversee everything and everyone the Shedai once had ruled, now possessed only a fraction of their former capabilities. Navigation was problematic, with only a few scattered interface points available for reference. While transiting the Conduits had at one time been as effortless as drawing breath into one's own body, their current lack of power and cohesion now presented a hazard to anyone who might now choose to navigate them. It was a distinct possibility that one of the few remaining thought-strands might fail.

Traveling to this world also had involved an additional risk, given that the Wanderer had left behind the shell she had worn on the frozen world. She had no way of knowing what awaited her at her destination, and should the channel falter while she was in transit before she could acquire a new host, there would be nothing to prevent her being extinguished from existence.

Regardless of the risk, the song cannot be ignored.

As before on the cold, barren world she had left behind, the Wanderer found that the call had been uttered as a consequence of the clumsy actions of *Telinaruul* attempting to understand that which was far beyond their comprehension. She recalled that this planet—which possessed vast potential perfectly suited to the needs of the Shedai in their quest to regain what once had been theirs—also was home to what once had been a primitive and inferior species that nevertheless held great promise. From what the

Wanderer could remember from the time before the long darkness had laid claim to her, these life-forms had only just begun to display the most basic levels of sentience.

There had been fierce debates about how best to proceed with these beings, but ultimately they were left to develop at their own pace and without external interference. In doing so, it was believed, these life-forms might eventually be of some use when the time finally came for the Shedai to ascend once more to their rightful place as rulers of their vast empire.

Arriving on this world in response to the song resonating through the Conduit, the Wanderer was surprised to discover that a different species of sentient life—more advanced though still hopelessly primeval when compared with the Shedai—now was present on this planet. These new life-forms—nothing more than the lowest form of *Telinaruul* ever to plague the rule of the Shedai—apparently had come and asserted their will over the native inhabitants. They had found the temple as well as the support structures that housed and protected the anchor point for the Conduit on this world.

Their vessel, now hanging in orbit, was a conventional if archaic mode of transportation, at least according to the Wanderer's scans. Like the conveyance she had engaged above the frozen world, it appeared to rely upon a crude method of controlled matter-antimatter annihilation in order to achieve a form of hyperspatial warping, which allowed it to reach the velocities necessary for interstellar travel. The ship's capabilities were interesting, but she suspected it too would be no match against the weaponry she might bring to bear against it. Such was the primitive nature of the craft—to say nothing of the *Telinaruul* who crewed it—that the Wanderer was curious as to how such unevolved beings could even have survived the harsh, unforgiving environs of space.

Still, despite their obvious limitations, the newcomers had learned enough about the ancient Shedai technology to activate a portion of the structure's intricate network of control mechanisms, a chance accomplishment which had signaled the Wanderer to this latest incursion and allowed her to travel to the violated site.

Perhaps they possess abilities I have overlooked or under-estimated.

That concern had weighed upon the Wanderer even as she willed the activation of other power sources and control systems, breathing new life into that which had lain dormant for uncounted generations. She at first was apprehensive that the long-neglected temple and its complex arrangement of command and oversight systems would not be up to the tasks she had set for it, to say nothing of the rest of the control network spread out across the planet. That anxiety had been short-lived, however, when she determined that the ancient structures and the technology they housed had been remarkably well preserved, a much different state of affairs when compared to the frozen, lifeless world from which the Wanderer had transited. Even in their aged and compromised state, the assets at her command were more than enough for her immediate needs.

Feeling her way along the Conduit's thought channels, she discerned that the fractional progress made by the primitives had in fact been in the restoration of power to a key control facility inside one of the temple's ancillary structures. Judging from their actions, the usurpers did not seem to grasp the purpose of the technology they had plundered; that they had chanced into a monitoring station for part of the planetary defense network still escaped their knowledge. Still, the Wanderer realized it was possible that—if left unchecked—they might discern the technology's purpose and perhaps even seize it for their own use.

That cannot be allowed.

18

"Let me see if I've got this straight," Reyes said as he sat behind his desk, rubbing his temples in a vain attempt to stave off the headache he already felt bearing down on him. "We've gone from the Tholians and the Klingons being upset with us, to having the Tholians and Klingons angry with each other, and Starfleet Command is now angry with us. Have I missed anything?"

From where he stood behind the pair of chairs situated before the commodore's desk, neither of which was capable of supporting his oversized and stiff-backed figure, Ambassador Jetanien rolled his shoulders in an elliptical manner that Reyes had learned was the Chelon equivalent of a shrug. "No. I believe that to be a succinct and accurate appraisal of the situation." As if punctuating his observation, the ambassador emitted a series of intermittent clicks from his blunt beaklike mouth.

"Thanks for the clarification," Reyes deadpanned, shooting the ambassador a tired scowl. Rising from his chair, he made his way around his desk and moved to where T'Prynn stood before the viewscreen set into the wall on the left side of his office. She turned at his approach, stepping aside to give Reyes an unobstructed view of the screen and the information displayed upon it.

"While we know there has been a pronounced increase in both Tholian and Klingon ship activity during the past month," T'Prynn said, "the past three days have brought the most alarming developments. According to data received by our network of long-range sensor arrays, there have been at least four skirmishes between Tholian and Klingon vessels. Each incident was an isolated, one-on-one encounter. To the best of our knowledge, no ships have been lost as all of the engagements were ended when the Tholian ships retreated."

Four incidents in three days. Reyes repeated the statistic over and over in his mind as he studied the star chart showing a cross section of the Taurus Reach, upon which T'Prynn had highlighted four locations where the clashes had taken place.

As for the rest of the chart, the commodore was struck once again by just how much of it remained without detail. Despite numerous mapping missions conducted by automated sensor probes as well as the charting conducted by the crews of the *Endeavour,* the *Sagittarius,* and even the *Bombay* before its tragic loss, much of the Taurus Reach was still unknown.

In more ways than one, Reyes reminded himself.

"Is there anything to suggest that either the Tholians or the Klingons know why we're here?" he asked, not turning from the viewscreen. "Are they simply maneuvering in response to our expansion into the region, or are they carrying out their own exploration and survey missions?"

"The Klingons are conducting planetary surveys," T'Prynn replied, "but it appears to be consistent with normal expeditions to locate resources, such as dilithium deposits, for example. There are no indications they suspect our true motives."

Reyes nodded. He knew at least two different star systems in the region had been claimed by the empire due to the presence of vast quantities of dilithium. The Klingons had wasted no time planting their flag, though thankfully those worlds had turned out to be uninhabited. Such was not the case with other systems in that sector, though Reyes knew there was nothing to be done about that at the present time.

Hopefully, we can correct that injustice one day soon, before it's too late.

"What about the Tholians?" he asked. "Are they offering up any weak explanations for their actions like they did with the *Bombay?*"

"With regards to your first question," Jetanien replied, "only the Tholians know what they believe about our presence here. As for their actions against the Klingons, this is different than the earlier tussles we've heard about." He turned away from the Starfleet officers so that he might pace the width of the office. Waving his right hand in the air before him, he added, "The Tholians admit to launching offensive action against those Klingon vessels. While we know full well they're not afraid to instigate hostilities, they are usually more methodical in their actions than what we're seeing in these cases."

"It's retaliation," Reyes replied. "They blame the Klingons for the destruction of their ship earlier in the week. Given how fast and aggressively the Klingons are moving into the region, it's easy to see how the Tholians might draw such a conclusion."

Turning from the viewscreen, T'Prynn clasped her hands behind her back. "There is no evidence to suggest Klingon complicity in that action. Further, based on what information the Tholians have elected to share with us, the way in which their vessel was destroyed is decidedly out of character for the Klingons."

"While it is true that residual energy readings taken at the scene indicate the presence of weapons of unfamiliar design," Jetanien said as he halted his pacing, "that itself does not rule out Klingon involvement." Looking to Reyes, he added, "However, I must agree with the commander that the reports of the incident are not consistent with Klingon behavior."

Feeling the dull ache behind his eyes beginning to assert itself with authority, Reyes frowned as he held up a hand. "I know what you're going to say. Klingons aren't subtle in their battle tactics. They don't sneak around, they don't cower in the shadows, and they're never afraid to take credit for a victory. In case you've forgotten, I've had some experience with them."

"I did not mean to imply otherwise, Commodore," T'Prynn replied, her manner and expression unchanged. "However, given your own knowledge of how Klingons typically conduct themselves, surely you would agree that for them to be responsible for that action in a manner consistent with the Tholians' accusations seems unlikely?"

Reyes waved away the suggestion. "What seems unlikely is me taking anything a Klingon does or doesn't do at face value."

He indicated the star chart with a nod. "Besides, if not them, who *did* destroy that ship?" Looking to Jetanien, he asked, "They don't think we—?"

"There were initial rumblings to that effect, of course," the ambassador said, interrupting Reyes's question. "However, their own long-range sensor data confirms that no Federation vessels were detected anywhere near that location before or after the incident occurred." Shaking his head, the Chelon added, "Naturally, that did not halt the initial barrage of invective, but cooler heads did indeed prevail."

"Small wonder," Reyes replied, feeling both fatigue and relief wrapping around the words as they left his mouth. Barely a month had passed since the *Bombay* incident, which still lingered like an open wound in the political relations between the Tholians and the Federation, refusing to heal no matter how much care and attention it was given. The Tholians had been expecting some form of reprisal despite promises from Jetanien and other Federation diplomats that no such action would be forthcoming. Even with those assurances, Reyes knew that everyone was watching and waiting for the precarious truce to disintegrate into full-blown hostilities.

That can't happen, regardless of the cost.

"So," he said after a moment, "if it wasn't the Klingons and it wasn't us, who the hell was it?"

T'Prynn shook her head. "We do not yet know, sir. As has already been indicated, the weapons employed were of a type unknown either to the Tholians or to us. I have run an extensive search of Starfleet's weapons identification banks and found nothing resembling the energy traces detected by the Tholian sensors."

Turning his attention once more to the viewscreen, Reyes folded his arms across his chest and said nothing as he rubbed his chin with his right hand. He was surprised to note the presence of beard stubble along his neck and jaw line. What the hell time was it, anyway? How long had he been on duty today?

Maybe that's why you're so damned tired.

Ignoring the question, he instead concentrated on the chart. A two-dimensional representation of this area of the Alpha Quadrant, the display outlined the gap of space sandwiched between Tholian and Klingon territory. The Federation border was to his left, while nothing on the right rimward side of the image was labeled, signifying the area as unexplored.

Had someone from that section of uncharted space come calling for their own purposes? Perhaps the explanation was even simpler, with a species indigenous to the Taurus Reach acting out against what they perceived as aggressive action. If that were the case, would such people make distinctions between Klingon, Tholian, or Starfleet ships? Were Federation colonists in danger from a known enemy, or instead a foe that had yet to make itself known?

Considering what had happened to Captain Zhao and the others on Erilon, Reyes knew these were not unreasonable questions. Every piece of new information regarding the Taurus Reach begged another question: If a new player is moving into the neighborhood, is it in any way connected with the meta-genome? If so, how might that affect the tenuous political situation already permeating the region?

We'll be in the front row of the biggest conflict we've seen in more than a century.

"What are the Tholians planning?" Reyes asked, his attention remaining focused on the viewscreen. "So far, the attacks—if that's what you want to call them—that have been carried out on Klingon ships don't seem to amount to a whole hell of a lot. Why aren't they attacking in force? They didn't seem to have a problem going after the *Bombay,* so what's stopping them now?"

"Lack of resources, I suspect," Jetanien replied, moving across the office to stand next to Reyes. "So far, Tholian attacks on Klingon vessels have been scattered, and they've been forced to employ fewer vessels than they're accustomed to using. As a result, their tactics have been largely ineffective and they've been forced to retreat. Likewise, the Klingons lack the ships, personnel, and matériel to truly escalate matters on their own, though I suspect that is a temporary handicap that both sides will remedy in short order, provided the situation is allowed to continue along its present path."

Cocking his head in the Chelon's direction, Reyes eyed his friend warily. "Do they teach you to talk like that in ambassador school?"

"Absolutely," Jetanien answered without hesitation. "It's a required course of study, you know."

Reyes shrugged as he turned to move back behind his desk. "I can see how it comes in handy when you're negotiating," he said as he lowered himself into his seat. "You just bore everyone to the point they'll do anything just to make you shut up."

Bowing formally, the ambassador held his rather large right manus to his chest. "Yet another veil pulled back from the shroud that protects the grand secrets of diplomacy."

"Gentlemen," T'Prynn said tersely, as Reyes noted that despite her typical measure of self-control the intelligence officer was becoming perturbed at the casual banter. "If I may point out, Ambassador Jetanien made a valid observation regarding the likely heightening of tensions between the Tholians and Klingons. At least, it was valid at the time he first offered it. Since then, it is possible that circumstances may already have worsened past the point of no return."

Despite himself, and the personal and professional stresses he had shouldered during the past month, Reyes chuckled at the Vulcan's perfectly delivered, straight-faced observation.

Remind me never to play poker with her.

"Don't tell me," he said as he regarded the commander, "you've got a plan to make this all go away." In the short time since she had been serving aboard Vanguard, T'Prynn had demonstrated an uncanny knack for resolving or disarming volatile issues with the easy, calm assuredness of a seasoned professional.

Her right eyebrow rising in a distinct arch, T'Prynn's posture seemed to adopt an even more pronounced stiffness than she already had been demonstrating. "While I appreciate your confidence in my abilities, Commodore, I feel that the ambassador is perhaps better qualified to address this situation."

"Humility? That's a first for me," Reyes said. He could not readily recall T'Prynn, or any Vulcan for that matter, ever admitting that they were incapable of carrying out a task, whatever it might be.

It was especially true in T'Prynn's case. Following the *Bombay*'s destruction, it had been her actions which had helped prevent word of that unspeakable tragedy at Tholian hands from snowballing into a full-blown interstellar incident. Though her methods had proven to be unorthodox, unethical, and even illegal, they had fostered the results Reyes needed at the time and thereby alleviated—for a while, at least—the danger of pitting the Federation into a war with the Tholians. While he could not argue with the outcome of T'Prynn's various schemes—the complete details of which she had yet to divulge—Reyes had lain awake on many nights afterward contemplating the morality of activities he had sanctioned, if only by virtue of his acceptance after the fact of what they had accomplished.

Had the ends justified the means?

Pushing away the thoughts while knowing they would revisit him in due time, Reyes turned to Jetanien. "Okay, what've you got up *your* sleeve?"

"It seems the most prudent course of action would be to bring our resident Klingon and Tholian delegations together for a summit of sorts," the ambassador replied. "Perhaps by working together here, we can hammer out some form of accord that's agreeable to all parties."

The very notion of the Klingons, Tholians, and Jetanien all corralled into the same room for any length of time sent a fresh stab of pain to Reyes's temples. "Why don't I save us some time," he said, "and just activate the station's self-destruct protocols?"

Though Vanguard currently played host to diplomatic envoys from the Federation as well as the Klingon Empire and the Tholian Assembly—a measure seen as a judicious forethought at the time of its institution—Reyes himself had questioned the prudence of the idea. Tholians of any professional stripe could be counted upon to be reserved and paranoid in all their dealings with those not of their own race, and in that regard could be somewhat predictable. Klingon politicians, on the other hand, could be annoyingly fastidious in how they chose to comport themselves,

switching indiscriminately between slavish devotion to their warrior caste's honor code and the more nuanced, duplicitous nature
that seemed to characterize their own diplomatic corps.

Or any politician, for that matter.

Despite his misgivings, Reyes was forced to admit that having
representatives from the other governments had to be of some
benefit with regard to the current situation. What he wondered
though was whether Jetanien, even with his impressive record of
diplomatic achievements, was up to confronting the formidable
task of bringing the Tholians and Klingons to the same negotiating table.

As if reading his thoughts, the Chelon leaned toward Reyes. "I
have no doubts that what I propose will be difficult, Commodore,"
he said. "However, I see no alternative if we are to pursue a peaceful resolution to what is quickly becoming a volatile state of affairs. Rest assured that I will employ all methods at my disposal
toward meeting that goal."

"I don't doubt that you will, Ambassador," Reyes replied, and
he meant it. He only wished he could view his own role in what
might lie ahead with equal confidence.

While he was content to keep his concerns to himself, it was
T'Prynn who gave them voice as she turned to regard Reyes.

"With no disrespect intended toward the ambassador, sir," she
said, "if a diplomatic solution cannot be reached, we may have to
be ready with a more direct course of action in order to protect our
interests in the region."

Though couched in words that were not immediately provocative, there was no mistaking the meaning behind T'Prynn's statement.

If there's going to be a fight, we have to be ready to get bloody.

19

With the bedcovers carelessly tossed to the floor of her quarters, Sarith lay atop her bed in soft repose, allowing the sweat of their lovemaking to cool her body as she watched N'tovek rise and begin to gather the components of his uniform. Her right hand absently stroked the sheets beside her, still warm to the touch from the heat of his body.

"Are you in that much of a hurry to make your escape?" she asked as she watched her lover fumble for his clothes, her tone teasing. "Is that fear I see in your eyes, Centurion?" Her eyes traced the lines of his unclothed body, noting the fresh scratches across his back and the tinge of green blood highlighting them. It seemed her enthusiasm had gotten the best of her, again.

Retrieving one boot from where it had fallen next to the small wardrobe positioned against the bulkhead opposite the bed, N'tovek looked to her and returned the smile. "I don't think there is a safe answer to that question, Commander," he offered with mock formality as he began dressing. "Not that it matters. I must report for duty."

Lying naked in her bed, her body still aglow in the aftermath of the brief but passionate interlude they had shared, Sarith for a moment was tempted to exercise command prerogative and simply call for a replacement to be assigned to N'tovek's station. She just as quickly dismissed the notion, however. While Sarith knew it was unwise to fraternize with members of her crew, it would be far more damaging if word spread across the ship that she was allowing anyone to shirk his responsibilities in favor of being her consort.

In truth, she had considered simply halting any further clandestine rendezvous, but had decided against it. At first, she had argued with herself that this lone indulgence was understandable, given the long-term nature of their assignment and the very real possibility that the *Talon* might not return home. Finally, however, she had offered a solitary confession to the reflection in her lavatory mirror that her reasons for keeping N'tovek's company were simple: She enjoyed it, and him.

Further, she could trust the centurion to maintain discretion with regards to their surreptitious relationship, and the advantages to be gained by keeping his silence on the matter. Both of them understood also that if she suspected that was no longer the case, Sarith would simply dispose of him out the nearest airlock.

I've already made one mistake, she reminded herself ruefully. *There is nothing to be gained by compounding it.*

Dressed once again in his uniform, N'tovek smoothed his tussled black hair down atop his head before reaching for the gold helmet that would complete his ensemble. Donning the helmet, he melodramatically came to a position of attention and offered the traditional military salute. "Request permission to take my leave of the commander."

A small laugh escaped Sarith's lips even as she made a mental note to have N'tovek wear nothing but the helmet the next time he came to her. "Permission granted, Centurion," she replied, clasping her clenched fist to her bare chest before returning the salute. "Glory to the empire; crush the Praetor's enemies."

That bit of mockery completed, N'tovek relaxed his stance and smiled, stepping closer until he could lean forward and kiss Sarith's forehead. "I enjoyed this morning."

"As did I," Sarith responded with genuine contentment, though she caught the barest hint of worry clouding that sensation. Despite the risks that came with involving one's self with a subordinate, the brief intervals of reprieve that N'tovek offered when they were together were a welcome distraction from the demands of her command.

Still, as N'tovek turned and departed, leaving her alone in the solace of her quarters, she continued to hear his last words. The look she had seen in his eyes danced in her memory. Was the centurion perhaps considering their trysts to be the start of something more meaningful—or dare he think it permanent? For both their sakes, Sarith hoped that was not the case, for such was a complication she most certainly did not need at this point in time.

Perhaps that airlock isn't such a bad idea after all.

Gathering the sheets around her, Sarith reveled in the comfort and warmth of her bed. She glanced at the chronometer on the far wall and decided she could afford herself an additional hour before returning to the bridge. A brief nap followed by a refreshing bath, and she would be ready to face the remainder of the day.

Sleep was just beginning to tease the edges of her consciousness when the all-too-familiar tone of the intraship communications system echoed across her quarters from the computer terminal perched atop her desk.

"Commander Sarith, your presence is requested on the bridge."

Duty calls, she admitted with amused resignation, tossing the bedclothes aside as she began the hunt for her own uniform.

"Report."

Everyone on the *Bloodied Talon*'s bridge stiffened to attention as Sarith made her entrance, all save Ineti, of course. Like the mentoring taskmaster he was, her trusted second-in-command was pacing the perimeter of the small room, keeping a careful eye on the activities of the centurions on duty. He nodded in respectful greeting to Sarith.

"Our long-range sensors have detected three vessels," Ineti said, "two Tholian and one Klingon, exchanging weapons fire." Looking to her, he added, "The cloak is cluttering our sensor returns, however, and I was about to order a course correction to bring us closer."

Listening to the irregular chorus of status indicators and humming machinery packed into and behind the bulkheads forming the ship's control center, Sarith nodded at Ineti's report. "Can we do so without risking detection?"

Ineti nodded. "Yes, Commander, if we reduce our power output as we draw closer, we should be able to remain concealed."

"Make the course change," Sarith ordered as she crossed the deck to a computer terminal. Like the other workstations on the bridge, the monitor and interface were built directly into a console molded into the angled bulkhead. As she activated the display, she called over her shoulder, "Do we know where either side's ships came from?"

Still pacing around the central hub of control stations, stopping only to correct the settings on one centurion's console, Ineti replied, "It appears the Tholians ambushed the Klingon ship, which we initially detected traveling from the direction of a nearby system. According to the star charts our agents were able to intercept from Klingon data transmissions, their military refers to it as the Palgrenax system. Four planets, only one inhabited by a preindustrial culture. From the subspace communications we've already decoded, the Klingons have laid claim to the system."

"No doubt it offers something of value to them," Sarith said as she called up to the computer display one of the pilfered Federation star charts. Stellar cartographers had already translated the Klingon chart's various notations into native *Rihannsu* text, and she was pleased to note that someone had also taken the initiative to remove much of the vibrant—and distracting—color schemes that seemed to saturate the original versions.

According to the chart, the Palgrenax system was well away from the travel and patrol routes that had already been established by Starfleet vessels traversing the Taurus Reach, at least if Sarith was to believe the intelligence reports provided to her prior to the *Talon*'s departure from Romulan space. It was, however, clearly within the area that seemed to have been dominated by Klingon ships since their incursion into the region some weeks ago. It was possible that—in addition to whatever natural assets it might offer to the resource-deprived Klingon Empire—the system's lone inhabited planet might also be providing a base of operations for Klingon vessels working in this sector.

Worth investigating, Sarith decided.

"Commander," said N'tovek from where he stood before his station at the central hub, "we approach the enemy vessels."

Turning from the computer terminal, Sarith moved across the

bridge until she could see into the viewfinder at the centurion's station. As she leaned closer to better see the sensor displays, she made a conscious effort not to look at N'tovek. To his credit, he stepped aside to allow his commander unfettered access to the station, as always conducting himself like the acceptable, if not outstanding, officer he was and offering no clue to anyone who might be watching that he was anything more than a subordinate sworn to live and die by her command.

Why, then, do I get the feeling that neither he nor I are fooling anyone with this pretense?

Forcing away the errant thought, Sarith focused her attention on the viewfinder. Inside the miniaturized display, which provided N'tovek with images translated from the abundance of information being received by the suite of sensor arrays positioned all around the exterior of the *Talon*'s hull, she could see the sensors' depiction of the skirmish taking place far ahead of them. Reduced to cold, lifeless bits of computer-generated icons and commentary text, it was easy to forget that the digital caricatures represented lives thrown into the chaos; violence surely gripped the participants of the conflict she observed.

Or, in the case of the Klingons, the exhilaration of heading once more into battle.

One line of sensor data caught her eye, and she noted the distance separating the *Talon* from the pitched battle. "Maintain this position," she ordered as she stepped away from the viewfinder. "Transfer the sensor feed to the main display."

She felt the change in pitch as the *Talon*'s engines cycled down, sensed the slight pull as the inertial dampening systems lagged ever-so-slightly behind the ship's abrupt deceleration. For a moment she wondered if their arrival and the sudden bleeding off of power, despite the still active cloaking device, might attract the attention of the Tholians or the Klingons. The earlier close call with the lone Tholian vessel was still fresh in her memory, and she was not yet ready to dismiss that occurrence as a stroke of random good fortune on the part of the Tholians' sensors.

Moving to stand before the large display screen built into the bridge's forward-facing bulkhead, Sarith folded her arms across her chest as the image on the monitor coalesced into a view of black, barren space. Otherwise serene darkness was peppered by the dim illumination of distant stars as well as the frenetic movements of two Tholian ships darting above, below, and around a single Klingon battle cruiser.

Though the small, arrowhead-shaped Tholian ships were of a design Sarith had never seen firsthand, the Klingon warship was of the same basic configuration as had been employed by the empire for more than a century, its distinctive orblike primary hull at the forefront of a long, narrow boom extending from the vessel's angular main drive section. Warp nacelles mounted to the underside of the hull gave the cruiser an illusion of menace, power, and speed even now as it struggled against a more maneuverable and decidedly tenacious enemy.

While other militaries—including her own—often attempted to create something new and improved in the hopes of enhancing the abilities and efficiency of their ships and technology, Sarith knew from experience that the Klingons approached such matters from a much different mind-set. Though upgraded and enhanced over time, the well-worn design had in its basic form served the empire with distinction for longer than she had been alive. She suspected it would continue on in some fashion well after she had left this plane of existence.

On the viewscreen, arcs of energy flared into existence as particle-beam weapons impacted on the Klingon ship's deflector shields, its movements to evade and engage its harassing enemy seeming sluggish and ineffective against the pair of smaller and faster vessels.

"The Klingon cruiser's shields are almost depleted, Commander," reported Centurion Darjil, standing just to Sarith's left and not looking up from his own control console. "One Tholian ship has lost all shields and has sustained damage to its main engines."

Other than the centurion's report and the usual telltale harmony of background noises that filtered through the room, the bridge was silent as the battle unfolded before her. Studying the battling vessels with a practiced eye, Sarith could tell from its somewhat slower and less graceful maneuvers which of the Tholian vessels was the more vulnerable. The commander of the battle cruiser must also have made that assessment, either via his own expertise or thanks to his ship's sensors, as the larger ship rotated on its axis as if to bring its weapons to bear on the compromised enemy attacker. As its primary hull moved into view, Sarith noted the blackened and pitted sections of hull plating where damage had been inflicted near the ship's forward torpedo launcher.

"It's unusual for a Klingon ship to be caught in such a compromising position," Ineti said as he moved to stand next to Sarith. "Were I that ship's commander, I might consider ritual suicide were I to fall victim to such a pedestrian blunder."

Sarith frowned at her friend's observation. "It's not like you to underestimate an adversary, Ineti," she said. "We know the Tholians can be formidable opponents. I'm not about to let our earlier encounter set the tone for how I approach this particular enemy. That victory was little more than fortunate happenstance."

On the screen, the Klingon cruiser unleashed a barrage of weapons fire as it completed its turn, catching the wounded and now noticeably slower-moving Tholian vessel in a vicious onslaught. Even without the assistance of magnification to enhance the viewer's image, she could see explosions wrenching apart hull plates as the smaller vessel twisted and spun to retreat from the barrage. Brief plumes of fire and rapidly escaping atmosphere—the noxious combination of superheated gases that contributed to a livable environment for Tholians—appeared from the new gashes in the ship's hull. Fragments of hull and whatever might have been blown into space from inside the wounded ship sailed out, leaving behind a rapidly expanding cloud of debris.

"The Tholian vessel has lost all main power," Darjil reported, "including life support. Its companion remains undamaged."

"What about the Klingon ship?" Sarith asked.

Still at his own station, N'tovek replied, "They have sustained major damage to their primary propulsion system, aft shield generators, and forward disruptor banks."

"That should still be more than a match for the Tholians," Ineti offered. "The Klingon commander should strike now, while the other ship exposes itself to attack as it attempts to render aid."

While she and Ineti watched, the undamaged Tholian ship swept toward the Klingon cruiser. It released a fresh volley of weapons fire as it described an intricate series of rolling, twisting evasive maneuvers that succeeded in avoiding most of the return fire the warship could muster, compromised as it was due to the loss of its forward weapons emplacements. New wounds were gouged into the ship's hull as the Tholian weapons found their mark, punching through the thick armored plating like a wild animal sinking its teeth into the soft flesh of newly captured prey.

The tactic seemed to work, as the cruiser abruptly rotated once more on its axis in what to Sarith appeared a desperate attempt to protect severely damaged sections of its exposed hull. Taking advantage of the momentary respite as the Klingon ship ceased its attempts to return fire, the Tholian vessel darted away from the point of attack, coming alongside its wounded companion. It produced a bright orange beam of energy that lanced out to envelop the damaged ship before accelerating again, this time away from the scene of battle.

"Retreat?" Sarith said, reacting with genuine surprise to what she was seeing on the screen. "No stomach for conflict when the tide turns against them?"

Still standing next to her, Ineti frowned. "Most unexpected. It appeared they had the tactical advantage."

"Is the Klingon vessel giving chase?" Sarith asked.

There was a distinct pause, but before she could turn to rebuke her subordinates for the delay in answering her question, N'tovek suddenly looked up from his station. "Commander, they're altering their course and heading in this direction."

What?

"Disengage all power systems except for the cloak and passive sensors," Sarith ordered without another moment's hesitation. "Now!"

They had been detected. It was the only logical explanation, she decided, but how?

All around her, consoles went dark as power generated by the

Talon's engines was severed. The bridge was plunged into darkness as life-support and illumination disengaged, and Sarith felt a momentary twinge in her stomach when the artificial gravity was first lost then restored, low-power battery backup systems automatically engaging to compensate for the loss of primary power. Dim red lighting flickered on, distorting the shadows and the expressions on the faces of the crew around her.

"Report," she said, involuntarily adopting a hushed whisper as she issued the order. Logic told her the measure was ridiculous, as sounds could not travel through the vacuum of space, but nevertheless she felt somewhat eased by not disrupting the shroud of quiet that had fallen over the bridge.

Apparently, she was not alone. "All primary systems are offline, Commander," N'tovek replied, his own voice low and subdued yet clearly audible now that the control room's characteristic background noises had faded. "The Klingon vessel is moving in this direction on half-impulse. Its sensors are active at full power."

So, they had somehow been detected. Sarith looked to Ineti and saw even through the shadows masking her old friend's face that the subcommander shared her deduction.

"How?" she asked him, neither of them requiring her to elaborate.

"I suspect the Tholians," Ineti replied, also employing a reserved tone. "Perhaps the vessel we encountered was able to transmit information on what their sensors recorded before we destroyed it."

That made sense, Sarith decided. If indeed the Tholians had relayed information on whatever sensor readings they had registered prior to their destruction, it was possible that data had been disseminated to other vessels traveling the Taurus Reach. For all she knew, her vessel might already be a quarry hunted by the forces of the Tholian Assembly.

Her jaw clenching as she regarded that alarming theory, Sarith turned to where N'tovek manned the bridge's only operational workstation. Almost all of the controls and gauges before him were darkened in response to operating on battery backup systems. Only the soft blue glow of the sensor viewfinder into which he peered offered any sign of activity across the otherwise lifeless control room. "Where are they?" she asked.

"Four hundred *mat'drih* to port and closing," N'tovek replied. "They are executing a series of irregular steering maneuvers, Commander." Looking up from the viewfinder, he fixed Sarith with a knowing gaze. "It appears to be a search pattern."

The Klingon vessel already was closer than the first Tholian vessel had been when its sensors apparently had detected the cloaked *Talon*. Were sensors aboard the battle cruiser at least as proficient as their Tholian counterparts?

The angled bulkheads of the bridge seemed to press in around them as Sarith counted off the intervals until—based on her calculations—the Klingon warship would either pass by or perhaps even run headlong into her ship. Without power for the viewscreens or even the ship's more active sensors, there was no way to watch the enemy vessel's approach or to see just how much danger she and her crew currently faced. N'tovek was her only source of information, and she could see even in the control room's reduced lighting that the strain was beginning to show on his normally passive features.

"We are drifting," the centurion called out softly, and Sarith's heart beat harder against the walls of her chest. Given the Klingon cruiser's movements as it searched for whatever had spooked its commander and the Tholians, there was no way for her to predict whether her vessel's path would cross that of the warship. Should she order restoration of thruster power to make a course correction? Would that action reveal their presence? She knew she had only moments to make a decision that regardless of the option she chose almost certainly would result in disaster for her ship and its crew.

"Maintain present status," Sarith ordered, instinct telling her to stay the course. The odds of them drifting into the path of the Klingon ship had to be lower than her vessel being detected due to rash action on her part. She issued the directive with a confidence she only partially felt herself, hoping her reservations had not been understood by anyone else on the bridge. Glancing to Ineti, she was reassured by her mentor's gentle nod of approval.

Moments that seemed to stretch into infinity passed in silence. Despite the notable drop in temperature as the bridge cooled thanks to the thinner hull plating separating the bridge from the harsh void of space, Sarith felt perspiration moisten her arms and her back. How much longer? Would there be any warning if the Klingon ship detected them, or would her last sight be of her vessel imploding around her as it fell prey to the power of the larger vessel's weapons?

"They have moved past us," N'tovek said after Sarith felt she had aged an eternity. Looking to her once more, he seemed almost too afraid to offer the report for fear that it would trigger some act of fateful retribution. "They are continuing their search pattern, but do not appear to have detected us."

A collective sigh of relief crossed the bridge at the realization that fate apparently had chosen to smile yet again upon the *Bloodied Talon*. Still, everyone maintained their silence, each of them looking to Sarith for guidance.

"Are we in any danger if we don't correct our course?" she asked N'tovek.

The centurion shook his head. "Only if the Klingon vessel backtracks along its search pattern, Commander." Glancing into the viewfinder again, he added, "They are continuing to move away, along what appears to be their original course before the attack. I suspect they may abandon the search in short order."

"Sound reasoning," Ineti replied, offering a paternal pat on the younger man's shoulder. "Klingon commanders are notoriously ill-tempered and impatient. They want an enemy to reveal itself and announce its desire to do battle. They're not in the habit of sitting idle and waiting for a ghost to appear."

"Still, we wait," Sarith said, now talking in a normal tone of voice that echoed across the otherwise silent bridge. "Once they go to warp, we'll restore main systems." She was satisfied that the frantic tactic of disabling primary main power might well have been the one thing which had saved the *Talon* from detection. An appropriate notation would have to be included in her next report back to Romulus. The Science Ministry, which had developed the prototypical cloaking technology more than a century earlier and had spent the interim constantly introducing modifications and improvements, certainly would want to know about the results of the very radical field tests to which the latest model of their creation had just been subjected.

In the meantime, Sarith and the *Bloodied Talon* had but one objective: Continue their mission.

"Prepare a course for the Palgrenax system," she told Ineti. "We need to see what the Klingons find so interesting there."

20

The balcony outside Governor Morqla's office exploded.

Leaping from the chair situated near the open door, the Klingon felt heat wash across his face as the wooden deck burst into flames, ignited by the crudely improvised fuel bomb hurled from someone on the ground outside the building. No doubt whoever had thrown the primitive explosive had been hoping for it to land inside the room, but their aim obviously was lacking.

Drawing his disruptor pistol from the holster strapped along his right hip, Morqla stepped closer to the doorway, ignoring the flames licking those sections of the burning balcony nearest him. Peering down from his perch on the second floor of the stone building, he saw three native Palgrenai scampering across the open courtyard of the small town square. Their drab woven clothing blended with the bland façades of nearby structures, and the claws on their bare feet churned up the dry soil as they ran toward a smaller building. The villagers moved with surprising speed despite their bulk, though even from this distance it was easy for Morqla to tell that the oldest of the trio could still be only an adolescent.

He saw harsh crimson disruptor bolts follow after the Palgrenai, evidence that at least one of his subordinates still retained a functioning brain within his thick skull as they responded—albeit belatedly—to the pitiful attack. The energy blasts tore into the ground behind the three upstarts, then into the stone wall of the squalid structure as the villagers disappeared behind it, no doubt heading for the perceived security of the dense forest surrounding the settlement.

Yet Morqla found himself smiling. Despite the laughable

tactics and net result, the youths' audacity still was quite refreshing.

Even the whelps are joining the fight now. Perhaps these jegh-pu'wI' *have some redeeming qualities after all.*

The door to his office opened, and two subordinates rushed in, disruptors drawn and searching for threats. Seeing the flames working to consume the balcony, the senior *bekk* looked to Morqla. "Governor? Are you injured?"

Waving the question away as he returned his weapon to its holster, Morqla replied, "Of course not." He turned and headed for the door leading out of his office. "Extinguish that fire."

Morqla hurried down the wide, low-ceilinged hallway and bounded down the stairs to ground level, remembering only at the last moment to duck his head and to be mindful of the shorter steps constructed for Palgrenai physiology. An open door led to the courtyard, beyond which stood a quartet of troops from his garrison. They had taken up defensive positions behind the waist-high stone wall separating the courtyard from the grounds immediately surrounding the building that Morqla had chosen to be his headquarters.

Like the two soldiers up in his office and most decidedly unlike himself, these subordinates were *QuchHa'*, Klingons descended from an offshoot of his native race but whose forebears had fallen victim to the strange genetic mutation that affected many of his people nearly a generation ago. *QuchHa'* were small and weaker and did not possess the prominent bone structure dominating the cranium.

So far as Morqla was concerned, many of these lesser Klingons also were weaker in a number of other ways, particularly in their sense of honor and the ways of the warrior. He had no idea whether this was but one of the multiple reasons why so many *QuchHa'* had been cast out from most sects of Klingon society, or whether in fact it was a consequence of that banishment. He did not care, either. Those who served under his command had proven themselves to be at least competent soldiers, ideally suited for the most unglamorous duty to which they had been assigned on this all-but-forgotten dust ball of a planet. Their lack of honor—real or perceived—might prove their undoing, but they had sworn to serve the empire, and that was all he required of them.

Morqla exited the building, noting as he did so that the late-afternoon humidity seemed even more oppressive than normal. Waves of heat rose from the rooftops of the nearby buildings, and dust kicked up by the comings and goings of people across the dry dirt of the courtyard lingered in the air. Taking stock of the situation, he was pleased to see that there appeared to be no other evidence of attacks on any of the other structures—particularly those housing members of his garrison.

Still, in accordance with regulations, soldiers around the town square were in the process of rounding up those Palgrenai villagers outside at the time of the attack. Occupation orders stated in terms devoid of ambiguity—orders conveyed to the Palgrenai in their own languages once translators had devised a means of communicating with the primitive people—those taken into custody would be questioned, possibly tortured, and summarily executed . . . if not already dead.

Some of the villagers resisted attempts to arrest them, but their squat, ungainly bodies were no match for the large, muscular physiques of his own troops. To Morqla, the Palgrenai, with their dark, oily hides, their short extremities, and the large, angular ears that drooped from the sides of their narrow, hairless heads, appeared almost reptilian, perhaps resembling what might result were a targ and a Denebian slime devil able to mate and produce offspring.

Such comparisons were not at all easy to dismiss, particularly in light of the Palgrenai propensity to slobber over anything and anyone within their reach. It was not uncommon to see villagers with dried and fresh drool coating the edges of their mouths and even their clothing. While he had not yet had the misfortune to witness a Palgrenai in the act of consuming a meal, Morqla reckoned it could not be that far removed from watching a herd of *bolmaq* at a feeding trough.

The less time spent envisioning that, he decided, *the better.* How such a species had managed to rise even to the level of civilization the Palgrenai currently enjoyed was a mystery that likely would baffle Morqla for the remainder of his days. With luck, he one day would die in glorious battle and be spared the need to ponder such inane questions.

"Report!" he shouted as he stepped further into the small yard in front of his headquarters building.

One of the soldiers—Morqla could not remember his name but saw from the rank insignia on his uniform that this *QuchHa'* was the highest-ranking *bekk* among the quartet—snapped to attention as he replied, "A covert attack by insurgents, Your Excellency." Pointing up toward the still smoldering balcony outside Morqla's office, the subordinate added, "They used crude explosives, but only managed the one attack before they were driven off."

Morqla made no effort to stifle the bellow of laughter that exploded from his gut. Seeing the expression on the soldier's face as the subordinate attempted to maintain his bearing only made the governor cackle that much harder.

"Insurgents? Covert attack?" he asked as his laughter subsided. Stepping forward, Morqla clapped the soldier on the shoulder. "Did you not see the face of your enemy, *Bekk*? Three children, no doubt carrying a bottle of their father's favorite spirits, and yet they were able to attack and escape almost undetected by the finest troops under my command." His smile abruptly vanished. "Perhaps I should enlist them as sentries. They would almost certainly be an improvement over the current arrangement."

To his credit, the soldier said nothing in response to the obvious threat. His only reply was to draw himself up even straighter and taller. Morqla glared at him for an additional moment, counting off the seconds until the subordinate's limited ability to withstand such prolonged scrutiny finally failed him.

"What are your orders, Excellency?"

Stepping away from the soldier, Morqla turned his attention back to the town square, where other members of his garrison had completed gathering what he counted to be nearly three dozen Palgrenai villagers. They were in the process of shepherding them toward the building that had been designated as the unit's detention facility.

Indicating the bedraggled cluster with a dismissive wave, he said, "Tell them to release the *jeghpu'wI'*. Interrogating them will be a waste of time. It was a child's prank."

"Excellency," the soldier said, "with all due respect, this is not the first such insurgency we have faced since our arrival."

Morqla turned to face the soldier, bristling at his blunt comments. "Do you consider me ignorant of this occupation's current status, *Bekk?*"

Once more the subordinate straightened his posture, so much so that the governor wondered if he might snap his own spine. "Certainly not, sir."

The troop had a point, Morqla admitted to himself. Though the Palgrenai were a primitive people, a preindustrial society closely resembling that of Qo'noS perhaps eight or nine centuries ago, since the garrison's arrival they had engaged in an irregular yet frequent series of haphazard attacks on Klingon forces and equipment across the planet. All such acts had been carried out even while the natives conducted themselves as a passive people who had accepted their status as subjects of the empire. Most of the assaults had been only slightly more sophisticated than what Morqla had just experienced, with the Palgrenai using whatever primitive means were at their disposal to disrupt what the governor initially had expected to be a routine occupation of this world, referred to by its native inhabitants as Palgrenax.

It was not an unexpected outgrowth of being conquered, Morqla knew. There were more than a few instances of attempts by *jeghpu'wI'* to overthrow their conquerors on worlds throughout the empire. Some of those attempts even had been successful—for which songs had been sung as Klingon warriors celebrated the tenacity and courage of their enemies in battle—though Morqla held no suspicions that such would be the case here. The Palgrenai, though obstinate, had no hope of standing against his garrison.

Though it is entertaining to watch them try, Morqla mused, suppressing the urge to grin at the amusing thought.

"Sir," the soldier said after a moment, "they targeted your office specifically. We must capture the *petaQ* that are responsible and punish them publicly, to show the *jeghpu'wI'* that such actions cannot be tolerated."

Glaring at the subordinate once more, Morqla was sorely tempted to kill him where he stood. "Is there any other information you think I've forgotten, *Bekk*? Perhaps you have guidance to offer regarding my hygiene or eating habits?"

In truth, his options in light of this most recent event were clear-cut: Acts of insurrection, no matter their size or scope, could not be tolerated. Strict discipline had to be enforced to minimize the risk and crush the desire and ability of a subjugated planet's indigenous population—which typically outnumbered the occupying force by orders of magnitude—to attempt overthrowing their conquerors. It was a simple and often brutal strategy, one Morqla understood and for the most part always had endorsed, at least in his younger days as a lower-ranking soldier participating in several such occupations.

Now, on his first assignment as planetary governor overseeing *jeghpu'wI'*, things were different.

Though he had enforced imperial directives—more or less—Morqla actually had welcomed the Palgrenai's laughable attempts to break up what had already become a dull, monotonous state of affairs. In truth, none of the attacks had proven to be anything more than annoyances. While the natives might be brave to even consider standing up to a superior force, their choice of tactics left much to be desired. Morqla guessed that might have much to do with their largely pacifistic nature. The Palgrenai were simply ill equipped to ever present anything resembling even a marginal threat.

And yet, they continue to try. There's something to be admired about that.

"The security of the empire will not be compromised if we show a measure of leniency," he said after a moment. "Gather the village population in the square at sunset, and we will remind them of the occupation orders. I will decide then whether to select members of the crowd for summary execution." He had no intention of doing any such thing, of course, but it was enough to satisfy the *bekk* for the time being.

"As you command, Excellency," the soldier said. He saluted, turned on his heel to instruct his companions to return to their normal duty posts, then left to carry out Morqla's instructions.

The governor watched him go, his eyes drawn toward the southwest where he saw a line of storm clouds gathering over the distant trees. It was the first time since his arrival on this planet that he had seen any sign of precipitation. Given what he had been told by more than one of the villagers about the dry seasons—including the current one—that could grip this hemisphere, any rainfall would be welcomed. Rain would quell the dust that seemed to permeate the air, his clothes, his skin—everything.

What a worthless pile of dirt this planet is.

So far as Morqla knew, Palgrenax offered nothing of military or political value. Mineral ores lacing its bedrock were of only marginal use for refining or energy generation, particularly of the type needed to power the empire's fleet of warships. The planet itself was too far away from those areas of the Gonmog Sector where Federation colonies and patrol routes had been established, therefore making it impractical as a base from which to coordinate any sort of effective combat operations against Starfleet vessels.

The only thing of interest this world offered, from what he could tell, seemed to be its collection of ancient, crumbling ruins scattered across this continent. For some reason, Chancellor Sturka and the Klingon High Council were most interested in the primeval structures, though of course they had not deemed it necessary to inform a lowly planetary governor what that reason might be.

It is of no consequence, he reminded himself. *I serve the empire, wherever they might send me, and for whatever reason.*

Feeling the stifling heat beginning to work its way underneath his uniform in earnest, Morqla turned and headed back inside his headquarters building, but he stopped short at the sight of his aide, K'voq, waiting for him. Small by Klingon standards, the younger officer further maligned the warrior stereotype with his unnaturally lightened hair, which he wore tied at the base of his neck rather than allowing it to flow freely about his shoulders like most soldiers. Despite his appearance, Morqla knew from experience that K'voq was a fierce and loyal warrior, which included a proficiency with the *bat'leth* that rivaled some Dahar masters the governor had known.

"Excellency," K'voq said as he held out a communicator, "Captain Kutal wishes to speak with you."

Morqla released an audible sigh, which to his own ears sounded like air escaping from a compromised hull seal. While he was a creature of duty, he had no trouble admitting that there were some aspects of his current assignment for which he had little patience. Having to speak to Captain Kutal ranked at the top of that list. Responsible for the science contingent which had been transported from Qo'noS, Kutal had chosen to remain aboard his vessel, the *I.K.S. Zin'za,* currently in orbit over Palgrenax. Though his authority did not extend to the planet's occupational garrison, the captain nevertheless chose to regard his dealings with Morqla as though he were addressing a subordinate or perhaps even one of the *jeghpu'wI'* he oversaw.

For his sake, he should hope he remains out of my d'k tahg*'s reach.*

Sighing in resignation, Morqla took the communicator from K'voq, clearing his throat before speaking into the unit's pickup grid. "This is Governor Morqla. What do you want, Captain?"

"*I await the latest status report from the survey team,*" Kutal replied without preamble. "*They are late, as they are every day.*"

"They are scientists," Morqla said. So far as he was concerned, that was more than enough information to explain the matter. "I've never bothered to learn how they view time management, or even if they care about it at all."

Kutal's coarse laughter echoed from the communicator. "*At least we agree on that much. However, I'm required to submit my own update to the High Council, and I cannot do so until I hear from those insolent bookworms.*"

"What do you want of me?" Morqla asked. "I have no authority over their activities, nor any knowledge of why they're here in the first place."

"*They billet in the village you use as your headquarters, do they not?*" the captain barked. "*I was hoping you might exercise some hands-on means of motivating them to tear themselves away from those piles of rocks and carry out their other duties. The chancellor is most interested in their latest findings.*"

Given the disdain with which the chancellor normally viewed scientists and others who did not directly support the empire's military agenda, the governor suspected that the decision to devote time and resources to an archaeological expedition, like many of the council's recent choices, was made due to the empire's desire to match or counter the Federation's expansion into this region of space.

Perhaps one of those undercover operatives the chancellor has sprinkled throughout the Federation has finally offered something of value.

Despite his low and unglamorous role within the empire, Morqla was not ignorant of the covert program that Sturka had initiated. Thanks to the trust of friends situated within the more prominent echelons, he knew that Sturka had begun placing covert agents at all levels of the enemy's political and military ranks. From high-ranking officials to lowly enlisted Starfleet personnel, Klingons surgically altered to appear as human or members of other species now permeated the Federation, collecting information in the hope that it might allow the planning and execution of an overwhelming offensive designed to assert Klingon dominance throughout this quadrant of the galaxy once and for all. Morqla had no idea if such a massive campaign was anywhere near becoming a reality, but he suspected the chancellor's scheme must be paying some dividends for him to continue supporting it even after all these years.

Even so, had one of those agents unearthed some morsel of information regarding the Gonmog Sector?

From what Morqla had read of the reports already presented by the scientists dispatched to Palgrenax, it was estimated that the ruins, which exhibited architecture not at all consistent with anything the planet's current population might have developed, were supremely ancient. Further, it appeared that many of the materials used to build the structures were not native to this planet. According to other reports submitted more recently by the leader of the science cadre, Dr. Terath, a vast storehouse had been established to amass artifacts and examples of ancient technology found cached at numerous underground locations scattered across the planet. Based on the scientist's preliminary indications, the millennia-old technology—and its builders, whoever they might have been—were possessors of tremendous power.

One such repository was located deep beneath the village where Morqla had chosen to headquarter his garrison, though the governor himself had not taken the time to explore the ancient structure for himself. Such things had never held much interest for him, though Terath's latest reports had given him cause to reconsider that position. Given how uneventful his duties had been of late, he figured such exploration might prove to be an entertaining diversion, if nothing else.

Did Sturka believe these millennia-old ruins to be the key to some kind of mysterious, ultimate weapon which might be brought to bear against the enemies of the empire? It sounded like something Morqla might read in the pages of poorly written fiction, barely serviceable as a children's story; most definitely not something to which Chancellor Sturka would pay any mind, let alone commit time and resources.

Still, if there are alien artifacts bearing some strange, powerful quality, then I would appear to be in a good position to benefit from such a discovery.

"I know there has been some minor success understanding the ancient technology found here," Morqla said. "They've managed to channel power to some manner of control console, but they don't know what it does or how it acts in concert with other mechanisms they've found." He shrugged, though only K'voq, standing silently nearby, could see the gesture. "Even I have to admit to a degree of fascination."

"*That is your weakness,*" Kutal replied, "*not mine. The chancellor requires updates and progress. Either you can instill that motivation to those petulant glob flies, or I will.*"

"I will see to it, Captain." With that, Morqla severed the connection before tossing the communicator to K'voq. "That *petaQ* would not make a boil on a flatulent targ's rump." As he turned to head back into his office, he cast one final observation to his aide. "Find Dr. Terath and bring her to me. It seems more and more people are becoming interested in our little out-of-the-way planet."

21

Quinn was snoring. Again.

Pennington glared sideways at the disheveled privateer who sat slumped in his pilot's chair, dozing and oblivious of the stink of stale sweat and distilled, recycled air permeating the *Rocinante*'s cockpit as he slept off his latest drunk. Of course, Pennington realized, it could be argued that this was in fact an extension of the same continuous state of intoxication the hapless rogue had seemingly fostered throughout the last several decades of his life.

After three days aboard Quinn's cramped and none-too-pleasant refuse scow of a ship while en route to Yerad III, Pennington's exasperation with the vessel's messy interior had all but reached its limit. Though he had made an attempt to tidy up, as a way of passing the time as much as anything, he soon had surrendered to the unalterable, unkempt reality that was the *Rocinante*.

The small galley at the rear of the passenger compartment boasted stains and particles from sources that might have once been intended for human consumption. Nothing short of sand-blasting—or perhaps a photon torpedo—would likely prove effective at cleaning the place now. The "sleeping quarters" consisted of a pair of hammocks, one for himself and one for Quinn, fashioned from sections of woven cargo netting. While the lavatory had given him cause for concern, the shower area was reasonably sanitary, though Pennington figured that owed to Quinn's evident disinterest in using it.

Charming, Pennington had thought upon getting his first look at the accommodations.

If there was any consolation to be had during this journey, the journalist decided that it came from its lack of interruption by representatives of the Klingon Empire or the Tholian Assembly—or the Federation, for that matter. Despite several long-range sensor contacts detecting ships from all three parties, the *Rocinante* had managed so far to avoid attracting unwanted attention. How that even was possible was a mystery to Pennington, particularly considering the ability of the starhopper's pilot, or apparent lack of same.

As though offering a blatant show of reinforcement to his assessment, Quinn remained as he had been during the bulk of the past three days: sleeping. His jaw slack as his stubbled chin rested against his chest, a line of drool ran from the corner of his mouth, extending to the edge of his collar and quivering like a violin string every time Quinn drew a tortured, snore-racked breath.

Grimy bastard.

Any remaining nerves Pennington might still possess after seventy-two hours spent with the near comatose trader fled as an indicator tone echoed through the cramped cockpit. Startled by the abrupt alarm, he leaned forward in his chair to examine the rows of dials, gauges, and digital readouts cluttering the helm console.

"Finally!" he said, breathing a sigh of relief. At long last, they were about to set down somewhere, anywhere. Fresh air, chilled spirits, and perhaps something to eat that did not come from a ration pack awaited. Turning to the slumbering Quinn, Pennington kicked the pilot's seat. "Get up, dammit."

Quinn roused with a startled snort, coughing and hacking as he wiped spittle from his mouth. Looking about the cockpit with eyes still dulled from sleep, he turned to Pennington.

"What the hell was *that* for?"

"We're about to drop out of warp," Pennington said, shaking his head. "While I have serious doubt as to your ability to set us down in one piece, I trust you marginally more than I do this bucket's automatic pilot."

"Huh," Quinn said as he straightened in his seat, wiping sleep from his eyes. "I've got an autopilot?" Pennington sneered as the privateer offered a sloppy smirk.

Guess that's his idea of a joke.

His attention focused on the console before him, Quinn said, "This'll be no big deal, you know. We'll be in and out. The guy knows we're coming to get him."

The words offered no assurance to Pennington whatsoever. "Does he know we're coming *today*?"

Looking up in response to the question, Quinn cocked his head as if lost in thought. "Huh," he said. "Damn if I know."

"Oh, that's just bleeding *fantastic*," Pennington said. "Is that supposed to be funny?"

Quinn shrugged. "With me, it's hard to tell." An indicator light flashed on the helm console and he pointed to it. "Here we go. Dropping to impulse."

His fingers moved over several of the smudged controls and Pennington felt a shudder run through the *Rocinante*'s hull. Beyond the cockpit's transparent canopy, blue-red streaks shrank to distant points of light as the ship emerged from subspace.

Dropping into or out of warp so close to a planet was supposed to be dangerous, according to what little Pennington had read or heard on the subject, though Quinn certainly seemed comfortable with the notion. No doubt he had experienced many occasions where such a maneuver was necessary. Pennington had no time to ask, as the first thing he saw was the green-brown sphere of Yerad III looming ahead of them. Then a shadow fell across the cockpit and Pennington lurched back in his seat as he found himself staring at the underside of a Rigelian merchant freighter.

"Holy hell!" he shouted, his fingers digging into his chair's armrests.

"Relax," Quinn snapped, his hands dancing across his console, and Pennington sensed inertial dampeners kicking in as the *Rocinante* angled down and away from the other ship, aiming for the atmosphere of Yerad III. "I've got everything under control."

Pennington's entire body still shook along with the ship as he glared at the scruffy pilot. "Sometimes, I really hate you."

"Yeah?" Quinn asked as the trembling finally began to subside. "Feel free to catch a ride home with the next guy."

Grunting in irritation, Pennington said nothing more as the

Rocinante sliced through the skies of Yerad III. A check of the ship's rudimentary scanners told him that the area of the planet over which they were flying was devoid of any cities, settlements, or other indications of civilization. He knew nothing about the planet—or the Yerad system at all, in fact—an admission that put him ill at ease. As a reporter, he prided himself on being well informed when going anywhere or meeting anyone, but he was ignorant of just about anything pertaining to this remote rock at the hind end of space. For the sake of his slowly returning professional pride, Pennington rationalized his situation as understandable, given the lack of notice he had about their destination combined with the *Rocinante*'s all-but-useless library computer.

Figures I have to be stuck aboard the one ship in the Taurus Reach that's even dumber than its pilot.

"Just leave the talking to me, okay?"

Pennington shrugged in response to Quinn's request as the pair made their way up a stone walkway leading from the busy market street toward an area of calm and serenity. An immaculately groomed lawn, replete with trees, shrubbery, and several small gardens teeming with exotic plants and flowers, surrounded what the journalist saw as an unassuming home. The quaint, one-level, unpainted prefab structure reminded Pennington of the houses built by the dozens on flourishing colony worlds throughout the Federation. Rustic, peaceful, and isolated, the place struck him as downright pleasant to behold.

Stepping onto the house's porch and approaching the heavy wooden door that was adorned only with a large brass knocker and a small circle which Pennington recognized as a peephole, Quinn wasted no time shattering the courtyard's tranquillity. "Hey!" he yelled as he pounded on the door with his fist. "Sakud Armnoj? You home? *Hellooooo?*"

"No need to shout, you know," Pennington said, his hands in his pockets as he moved to stand beside the pilot.

From behind the door, a nasally, whiny voice called out, "You don't have to shout. And thanks for using the knocker. Moron."

Pennington noted a flash of light through the peephole, realizing that they were being watched by whoever was inside the house. "Oh, pardon me. *Morons*," the voice amended.

"Just open up," Quinn said, putting his hands on his hips. "My name's Quinn. Ganz sent me to get you and take you to him."

"How do I know you're not lying?" the voice asked. "You could be trying to kill me for all I know."

"Assassins don't announce themselves by banging on your door, you wanker," Pennington snapped, earning him an appreciative glance from Quinn. "Now open the bloody door."

There was a pause before Pennington heard the occupant disengage a series of bolts and locks—enough to sound as though a prison cell were being opened—before the door swung aside to reveal a Zakdorn dressed in what appeared to be a geisha's robe and thong sandals. His pasty complexion was broken only by the series of ridges jutting from his cheeks. What little hair he possessed on the sides of his head was brown and cut close to his scalp. He regarded Quinn and Pennington with black eyes.

"No need to be testy about it," he said. "One has to be careful around here, after all. You can't go opening your doors for strangers."

"Your door's open now," Quinn said, his expression deadpan. "We might still be here to kill you."

The Zakdorn—Armnoj, presumably—waved away the suggestion. "I've known you were coming for three days. Ganz's people contacted me and sent me a complete file on you." His eyes narrowing as he regarded Pennington, the wormy little humanoid added, "They didn't send anything about you, though."

"I'm his caddy," the journalist replied, making no effort to hide his mounting annoyance. To Quinn, he asked, "Can we get on with this?"

The pilot nodded. "Absolutely." Turning his attention back to the Zakdorn, he said, "Mr. Armnoj—if that's who you are—we need to be going. Ganz wants you and your accounting records in front of him before the end of the week." He shrugged. "Of course, you could always just transmit the files to him over subspace. You know, save us all a lot of heartache."

Armnoj released a boorish grunt. "That would hardly be helpful. All of my files are encoded with a multi-quad encryption algorithm capable of thwarting any attempts at unauthorized access. I designed the software myself, including a self-regenerating cipher that allows for unparalleled data security."

"Wonderful," Quinn said, rolling his eyes. "Well, you and your encoded multi-quad whatever-the-hell-you-call-them need to get packed. We're a bit pressed for time, here."

Shaking his head, the Zakdorn affected an expression of disapproval. "You'll have to come back later. I'm on my way to the sauna."

Pennington noted that Quinn was making a valiant effort to maintain his composed demeanor. Drawing a deep breath, the privateer clasped his hands behind his back and attempted to smile. "No time for that, sir. Ganz said he wanted you back as soon as possible. It's a long trip, and the sooner we get started, the happier everybody will be."

Armnoj sniffed the air with evident disdain. "Very well, but you'll just have to wait while I change into traveling attire and pack a few things." Eyeing them both, he added, "You may come in, but kindly refrain from sitting on my furniture." He turned and walked back into the house, muttering something Pennington could not hear before saying, "You can be sure Mr. Ganz will hear about your lack of courtesy. I'm not in the habit of being treated this way."

Alone on the porch, Quinn and Pennington exchanged stares and shrugs.

"Nice guy," Quinn growled. "Reminds me of my first wife."

"She was that ugly?" Pennington asked.

"That, and talking to her for two minutes was usually enough to make me want to launch her out a photon torpedo tube."

Stepping through the door after Quinn, Pennington noted that the inside of the accountant's home was as well appointed as its exterior. His boots sank into plush woven carpeting, and he looked longingly at the trio of overstuffed chairs positioned around the sitting room. The rest of the chamber's furniture was equally opulent, and a collection of expensive-looking curios populated shelves and hutches. He recognized the spiced aroma of a notably expensive Zakdorn incense scenting the air.

Being a crime lord's bookkeeper definitely has its advantages.

"You live here alone?" Pennington called out toward the room into which he had seen Armnoj disappear.

"Of course," the Zakdorn replied from what Pennington presumed was the accountant's bedchambers. "I like it that way."

"Yeah," Quinn said, low enough so that only Pennington could hear, "because the ladies are kicking and scratching to get in here." In a louder voice, he asked, "Aren't you afraid someone might come by to cause trouble?"

"Never happened before," Armnoj replied. "Besides, I have Sniffy."

Exchanging looks with Quinn, Pennington frowned. "Sniffy?"

"Guy doesn't get out much, does he?" Quinn remarked. "File me under 'shocked,' why don't you?"

As if in response to the conversation, Pennington's attention was attracted to the sounds of movement across the carpeted floor and he turned to see . . . something . . . waddling into the room. Seemingly a cross between a dog and a walrus, the animal appeared to be encased in blubber draped in smooth, brown hair. It whipped its spindly front legs while dragging its hindquarters more or less uselessly. With wide nostrils and puffy cheeks, the creature managed to make its way close to the duo before settling in and squinting at them with beady, black eyes.

"Sniffy, I presume," Quinn said.

Frowning as he regarded the animal, which appeared harmless, Pennington asked, "What the hell is that?"

Armnoj emerged from his bedroom, dressed in a colorful silken shirt and matching trousers. "Why, he's a *slijm*," the Zakdorn said, "and a fine one, too. Pedigreed."

Uh-oh, Pennington thought.

As if reading his mind, Quinn held up a hand in warning. "It can't go with us."

"Out of the question," Armnoj declared. "He's hardly been out of my care his entire life. He means everything to me. I can't leave him."

Rolling his eyes, Pennington said, "Surely you have contingencies when you travel on business." *I can't believe I'm even having this conversation.*

Armnoj crossed his arms, saying nothing.

"I don't have any room on my ship, anyway," Quinn said. Casting a doubtful look toward the animal, he added, "Besides, it doesn't look like it'd even make it to the spaceport."

"Spaceport?" the Zakdorn repeated, his eyes wide with anxiety as he shook his head rapidly. "That simply won't do. I don't fly suborbital. You'll have to fetch yourself a suitable ship and come back."

" 'Fraid that's not going to happen, either," Quinn said, his patience obviously nearing its end. Stepping forward, he reached to take Armnoj by the arm. "We're wasting time. Let's go."

"I can't fly, I tell you. I *can't!*" The accountant attempted to wrest himself from Quinn's grasp just as Sniffy reacted to the commotion.

"Calm down, will you?" Quinn asked as he tightened his grip. "We've got a schedule to keep."

"Stop it, Quinn," Pennington said, forcing a calm voice and trying to restore some measure of peace as he stepped closer. "Mr. Armnoj, please . . ."

Armnoj cried out in what seemed like dire pain, the tone and pitch of his voice so loud and piercing that Pennington feared for the nearby glassware. At the same time, Sniffy moved with more animation than the journalist ever would have expected, rearing up a bit on its flabby, wedge-shaped body and loosing from its snout a booming sneeze.

Throwing his arm up as a cloud of yellow-green mucus flew from the animal's nose, Pennington ducked as the viscous outburst saturated his arm and hand. Then his eyes widened in fear as he realized that his bare hand, sprayed with the tacky fluid, seemed to burn and tingle as if he had reached out toward an open flame.

"Bloody hell!" he cried as he wiped his hand on his shirt, an action that only seemed to heighten the sensation. "Oww!"

"That's a boy, Sniffy," Armnoj said, leering in Pennington's direction as he kneeled down to pet the spent beast. "That's a *good* boy."

"Good boy, my ass," Quinn said, reaching into his jacket to retrieve a stun pistol, essentially the civilian equivalent of a phaser. He aimed the weapon at Armnoj. "Now, get the hell up!" Looking over his shoulder to Pennington, he called out, "Are you all right?"

"I'm fine," the journalist replied, his eyes widening upon seeing the weapon in Quinn's hand. "Put that thing away!" With relief, he noted that the burning on his skin was subsiding, and he detected no other injury to his hand. "I'm okay. It fades after a minute." He noticed that the pilot somehow had managed to avoid the mucous shower save for some spotting on his soiled jacket.

Figures.

"Yeah? Well, so does this," Quinn said as he fired his stun pistol. The whine of energy filled the room and an ice-blue beam lanced from the weapon, washing over Armnoj and the *slijm*. The two slumped to the carpet.

Pennington stood frozen in place, keeping his still tingling hand wedged under his opposite armpit. Staring at Quinn, he noted the odd expression that crossed the pilot's features.

"Damn," Quinn said, suddenly appearing as forlorn as he might be upon learning that the alcohol content of every intoxicant in the quadrant had been neutralized. "Ah, shit."

"What?" Pennington asked, dreading the answer.

"I'm supposed to bring Ganz this guy's accounting records," Quinn replied, "and I don't know where they are."

Nodding in resignation, Pennington said, "Probably should have gotten that information before you shot him."

"Thanks for the tip," Quinn replied as he returned the stun pistol to the inside pocket of his jacket. Looking around the room, he shook his head. "We'll never find them in this place."

"You *think*?" Pennington exclaimed, starting to pace around the perimeter of the room. "What in hell do we do now?"

"Wait for him to wake up," Quinn said. Nodding in the direction of the door, he added, "If you're bored, you could try to rustle up a Sniffy-sitter."

Releasing an exasperated sigh, Pennington shook his head as

he considered their current situation, which was becoming more ridiculous with each passing minute. Even if and when they finally managed to get off this godforsaken planet, they still had to travel to the Jinoteur system in order to complete the mysterious assignment Quinn had been given by T'Prynn.

Bollocks.

"We're never getting to Boam II, are we?" he asked.

Quinn shrugged. "Don't see why not. To be honest, we're ahead of schedule."

"Right." Pennington replied as he reached for the unconscious Zakdorn's arm and pulled him to his feet. Dragging Armnoj across the room, he allowed the sleeping accountant to fall without ceremony onto a nearby couch. That done, he indicated the stunned Sniffy with a nod. "You get that one."

He was sure he saw Quinn's hand flinch toward his stun pistol.

22

His satchel slung over one shoulder and leaving behind the growing crowd of station personnel who had come to welcome home crew members departing the *Endeavour,* Xiong made his way with all due haste from the gangway and away from the spacedock's main terminal. No one awaited his arrival, and he certainly had no desire to engage in any of the emotionally mixed greetings currently being bestowed upon his shipmates.

They're not your *shipmates,* he reminded himself as he stepped along with three other passengers into a waiting turbolift.

Even as the thought surfaced, Xiong pushed it away. While he might not be a permanent member of the *Endeavour*'s crew, he had stood beside them during crisis and tragedy. Their captain had died saving his life, sacrificing himself with bravery and resolve as he likely would have for any of the men and women under his command. In all the ways that truly mattered, those people were his brothers and sisters, and the grief they endured over their loss was his to bear, as well.

Forcing away the unpleasant line of thought, Xiong instead tried to focus on his surroundings as the turbolift descended into the depths of the station. He waited patiently as the lift slowed to a stop at different levels, allowing the other patients to disembark. Thankfully, no one else arrived to take their place, and he was able to complete the rest of his own journey in solitude.

The lift brought him to a stop on one of the station's cargo decks, and Xiong adopted a casual stride as he made his way down the corridor, doing his best to affect the illusion of just another member of the crew going about his duties. He maintained the charade until he arrived at his destination, an office marked like those around it with a simple location designator label: CA/194-6.

Entering the room, which was furnished with standard-issue Starfleet office furniture—a desk and two chairs—and featured no extraneous decorations of any kind, Xiong ensured the door was locked before stepping around the large gray desk and without preamble placing his right hand flat against the room's rear wall. A soft, ruby glow emanated from the wall panel underneath his hand, after which a section of the bulkhead slid aside without so much as a whisper of sound to reveal a pair of red doors. They slid apart, revealing a corridor illuminated in stark, bright white.

Home at last.

His eyes squinting as they adjusted to the sudden shift in light intensity, Xiong stepped through the doorway and into the quite familiar passageway, which extended fifteen meters to another set of doors. These were transparent, offering the lieutenant a view of the hive of activity carrying on behind them. Only when the doors slid aside at his approach was he bathed in the ambient sounds and atmosphere of this, the surreptitious heart of the Vanguard station.

To those who even knew of its existence, it was referred to simply as the Vault.

Xiong entered the expansive laboratory area, not for the first time thinking that if the hallway was a river of white then this place was the milky sea into which it emptied. Floors, tabletops, furniture, and equipment, nearly all of it appearing pristine and colorless. The main floor was partitioned into groupings of smaller rooms, some outfitted with tables and chairs for conferencing while others housed scientific equipment designed for specific and sensitive studies. Nearly all of the sectioned-off areas featured at least two walls composed of transparent aluminum, adding to the lab's sense of enormity.

More than a dozen scientists and researchers were in view as Xiong moved through the lab, manning assorted workstations and equipment. A quartet of workers sat huddled in one of the conference niches, their attention so focused that they did not notice the lieutenant as he walked past on his way to his private lab and office.

While they and the rest of the twenty-two people working in this facility all were listed among Vanguard's crew as serving a variety of assignments ranging from stellar cartography to waste reclamation—duties for which they actually were qualified, as a matter of fact—those designations were almost exclusively a cover for their real activities supporting Lieutenant Xiong. Despite their myriad functions, they as well as all of the assets in this part of the station—which included its own self-contained dormitory and dining areas—were gathered here for a single goal: solving the mystery of the Taurus Reach.

Unlike the main lab's meeting areas, personal workspaces offered more in the way of privacy. Tapping a code on the keypad next to his door granted him access to his office. Ignoring the stacks of reports, data slates, books, computer cartridges, and other detritus cluttering the room, Xiong was barely able to toss his satchel onto the cot occupying space along his workspace's far wall when he heard a voice from behind him.

"Lieutenant!" came the loud, boisterous call, and Xiong turned to see a short, portly Tellarite lumbering across the lab toward him, dressed in a white lab coat that hung well below his knees. "You're back!" With large tufts of gray hair sticking out from the sides of his wide, wrinkled face, and moving with a speed that belied his age, Dr. Varech jav Gek offered a wide smile filled with jagged, irregular teeth as he approached with spread arms.

Smiling, Xiong nodded in greeting. "Hello, Dr. Gek," Xiong said, stepping around his desk as his colleague walked into the office.

"It is good to see you," Gek said as he dropped without invitation into the only chair besides Xiong's which was empty of assorted flotsam. "We've been hearing many different stories, you know."

Frowning, Xiong sat down in his own chair. "Stories? From whom?"

Gek waved as if to clear away the lieutenant's skepticism. "Oh, you know how we all tend to talk down here." He offered a small, nervous laugh. "After our data feed from Erilon was cut off, well, you know how rumors can start. Then, Commodore Reyes told us about the attack on the *Endeavour* and the research team, and then, well, I mean . . . the idea of a life-form being found among the ruins? Well, that's just . . ."

Certain he was unhappy with the notion of the *Endeavour*'s last mission and the tragic circumstances surrounding it becoming gossip fodder, Xiong tapped his finger atop his desk. "Don't believe everything you might have heard and misunderstood, Doctor. As yet, we have no explanations for what happened at the site."

Gek chuckled, a gesture Xiong found as obvious as it was clumsy. "Oh, I know, I know! But, you have to admit it's fascinating to think about. After all, the Erilon artifacts are a million years . . ."

"We don't know that," Xiong interrupted.

"Um, hundreds of *thousands* of years old," the Tellarite amended. "Regardless, the idea of finding a life-form inside is astounding!" He paused as if awaiting affirmation. When Xiong remained silent, Gek cleared his throat and sat a bit straighter in his seat. "What did it look like? The life-form, I mean."

"It looked pretty damn *deadly* is what it looked like," Xiong snapped, doing nothing to curb the irritation brewing in response to Gek's callous badgering. As the Tellarite regarded him in wide-eyed silence, Xiong recognized that part of his colleague's insensitivity stemmed from his cultural upbringing. As a race, Tellarites typically exhibited the same temperament and level of interpersonal tact as . . .

As you.

"Well, that is . . . I was merely curious, Lieutenant," Gek said, breaking the suddenly awkward silence.

Sighing as he sank back into his chair, Xiong shook his head. "I know, Gek. I'm just . . . tired, that's all." While he was not at all interested in recounting what had occurred on Erilon, he recognized that his friend was the most logical person in whom to confide. In addition to being one of Starfleet's top minds in theoretical chemistry and molecular physics, the excitable researcher also was the person most likely to spread details of Xiong's observations among their colleagues, sparing Xiong from having to share the details more than once.

"I saw a good number of people die at that thing's hands, Gek," he said after a moment, his gaze fixating—for no apparent reason—on one particular data slate sitting atop the stacks of paperwork on his desk. "It's not that easy for me to be so objective about it."

Hesitantly at first and then with greater ease, Xiong described the attack in detail as well as the perpetrator, at one point stifling a chill as he recalled the towering black apparition and the carnage it had wrought. To his surprise, Gek said nothing, obviously trying to restrain himself from prying or pushing for more information than Xiong was willing to give.

"I've never heard of anything like you describe," Gek said, when Xiong paused in his recitation. "Can you recall anything else?"

Xiong shook his head. "Not really, no." Shrugging, he added, "There just wasn't much to it, but I remember every detail of what I saw. It's not something I'm likely to forget."

"No, that's all right," Gek said, his smile forced in an obvious attempt to conceal his disappointment at the lack of detail in Xiong's description. "I imagine it was quite the frightening experience."

"Yes," Xiong replied, offering a slow nod, "it was. I was sure I was going to die."

His expression displaying frank discomfort at the open admission, Gek stammered, "I'm . . . well, we're . . . glad you didn't, Lieutenant."

The Tellarite's uneasiness was not difficult to understand, Xiong knew. Neither of them had ever shown a propensity for talking to one another—or anyone else, for that matter—about subjects outside the scope of their official duties. The lieutenant had always viewed such a separation as being important, a perspective he believed had served him well on this assignment in particular.

Following the events on Erilon, and the continuing need he felt to talk to someone, anyone, about what had happened, Xiong decided his earlier stance now required reexamination.

Gek, as if sensing that the time might be right for a change of subject, rose from his chair. "Anyway, Lieutenant, when you're . . . well . . . ready, we've been collating the new information transmitted to us from the research team on Erilon." His voice faltering as he spoke the last word, the Tellarite cleared his throat once more. "That is, before we stopped receiving their feeds. We've been running various tests between their findings and those from Ravanar IV, and our preliminary results might interest you."

"Really?" Xiong asked, his interest piqued.

He followed Gek to one of the conference niches, the main table of which was festooned with several slates and data cards of assorted colors as well as a tri-sided tabletop display monitor and a workstation interface. Waiting until the doctor settled himself at the computer station, he watched as Gek's puffy hands played over the rows of switches, activating the tabletop monitors.

"As you can see," Gek said as he pointed to the viewer, "we've created a comprehensive mapping of the genetic sequence found in the samples collected on Ravanar IV."

Though he had seen computer-generated images of metagenome samples countless times since being assigned to this project, as he studied the image arrayed on the viewer, Xiong once again found himself drawn in by the unparalleled complexity of what he was seeing. Determined to possess more than three million nucleotide subunits, the genetic information encoded within the DNA samples found on Ravanar IV far outstripped the ability of the human mind to comprehend. Equally staggering, he knew, was the potential the meta-genome possessed to alter the fundamental understanding of life itself.

What we could do with that knowledge, he thought, not for the first time.

"We've only just gotten started on doing the same for samples found on Erilon," Gek continued. "It takes a great deal of time, as you know. We've had to develop entirely new coding schemes just to keep track of it all. Still, we've made enough progress to make some early comparisons." Adjusting several controls on the computer interface, Gek brought up another image on the viewer, which he aligned next to the original picture. "At first we thought we had a match to the Ravanar sample, but we also found a few new proteins, which we believe act as a sort of containment scheme designed to hold the base DNA." Looking up at Xiong, he added, "Then, things get interesting."

The image on the viewer shifted, and Gek pointed to the new graphic. "We found several distinct check sequences, which appear designed to protect against any errors during the replication process, and from that point the two samples are nothing alike."

His eyes narrowing as he studied the data, Xiong said, "I'm not seeing anything here that might act to initiate the replication process." Though more complex than the samples found on Ravanar, the Erilon specimen still seemed to be lacking key components.

"Despite the differences," Gek continued, "it's the same basic story with both specimens. The core genetic structures appear to be identical, but after that, nothing is the same."

"Meaning?" Xiong asked.

Gek leaned back in his chair. "Only a fraction of the total information within any one sample appears to be necessary for the generation of life-forms, so why include the rest of it?" He shrugged in answer to his own question. "To me, it's obvious. This genetic material was artificially engineered. The designers created a basic template—ostensibly for use in a virtually unlimited number of ways, most of which are far outside anything we might possibly imagine. What we've found on Ravanar and Erilon is but the merest scratching of the surface."

Frowning at the melodramatic climax to the doctor's report, Xiong shook his head. "So what you're saying is that while we've learned a lot from Erilon . . ."

"We've posed more questions than we've managed to answer," Gek replied, his expression grim.

Xiong nodded. "So, we keep digging," he said. "We've plenty more to review, thanks to the *Endeavour*'s sensors and a few other items we brought back." His voice trailed off, his mood darkening as he envisioned the body of his friend, Bohanon, lying atop a table in the station's morgue and awaiting examination.

Looking to the computer interface's chronometer display, the lieutenant released a tired sigh. "Unfortunately, you'll have to carry on without me for a while. I'm scheduled for debriefing in half an hour." According to orders received even before the *Endeavour* made port, Xiong was to report to Commodore Reyes before meeting with a member of Captain Desai's JAG staff. He was not looking forward to either meeting, knowing that secrecy would be the order of the day, as it always was when it came to his mission and how he interacted with almost everyone on the station. It was an aspect of his assignment which he loathed, even though he understood—to a degree—the necessity behind it.

Taking his leave of Dr. Gek and heading for the Vault's exit, Xiong longed for the day when secrets, military or otherwise, would no longer be necessary, while also admitting that such a day was unlikely to come in his lifetime, if ever.

23

"I must admit, Your Excellency," Sovik said as he entered the main meeting room of Jetanien's suite of offices, "that serving in the Federation Diplomatic Corps never ceases to offer a conduit for . . . unique experiences."

"Perhaps you would care to elaborate for us, Mr. Sovik?" Jetanien asked, indicating the rest of the meeting's participants as they each took seats around the room's polished conference table. Moving toward his *glenget*, the backless "chair" that allowed the Chelon to kneel in repose, he slurped heartily from his bowl of chilled Javathian oyster broth before setting it down on the table.

The Vulcan envoy remained expressionless. "I did not believe that a Tholian was capable of emitting sardonic laughter." Pausing a beat, he punctuated his observation with a slight raising of his right eyebrow. "Until today."

Jetanien allowed a smirk to cross his leathery features, but one that likely would be discerned more by his fellow beak-mouthed Chelons than his staff. "Well," he said as he surveyed the room from his seat at the head of the table, "I'm reasonably certain that the Tholian to whom you refer . . ."

"Ambassador Sesrene," Sovik clarified.

"Ah, yes, *Ambassador* Sesrene," Jetanien amended, "would be pleased in his own way to know that the nuance of his inflection was not lost upon his audience, particularly in light of the fact that Vulcans seldom appreciate sarcasm." He chuckled at that, which came out as a halting series of clicks and chirps.

Sovik offered nothing more as he took a seat next to Akeylah

Karumé, the colorfully attired diplomatic envoy assigned to Ambassador Lugok of the station's Klingon delegation.

Situated across from Karumé, who seemed to sneer over the rim of her steaming cup of coffee, was a tired-eyed Dietrich Meyer, whose apparent inability to manage himself with the Klingons recently cost him his posting as Lugok's point of contact to Jetanien—to say nothing of nearly losing his life via the business end of the Klingon ambassador's *d'k tahg.*

Seated next to Meyer was Anna Sandesjo. In contrast to Meyer's slouched and disheveled appearance, the young aide sat ramrod straight in her chair, prepared as always to carry out her plethora of duties as Jetanien's trusted senior attaché. Observing her, a woman whom he could appreciate as being physically appealing among humanoids, Jetanien unconsciously straightened himself on his chair. While he did not doubt that his presence carried with it an air of respect among his staff, he nevertheless suffered from an occasional bout of preoccupation as to how he appeared before them.

Part of being in control is looking in control, he reminded himself for perhaps the hundredth time this month.

"Despite whatever our estimable Tholian colleague may have communicated to Mr. Sovik," Jetanien said as he regarded his staff, "we are preparing for him and his delegation to join us here with Ambassador Lugok as quickly as possible. While there are sure to be many specifics offered for superficial discussion, our intent is to root out the truth underlying their people's escalating conflict here in the Taurus Reach, and then lead them to an accord that will settle this situation before it embroils us all."

Meyer turned toward Sandesjo and mumbled something under his breath, which prompted barely a glance from the woman. Jetanien expected no less from Meyer, but nevertheless felt compelled not to let it pass without comment. "While I am one to appreciate your fumbled attempts at lightheartedness on occasion, Mr. Meyer, even you should be able to grasp the importance of timing to the art of comedy. This, sir, is hardly the time."

Meyer cleared his throat and offered a sheepish expression. "Excuse me, Your Excellency."

"I would excuse you from this meeting," Jetanien said, "as well as from these particular proceedings and from the Diplomatic Corps completely, Mr. Meyer, were I not for some reason laboring under the impression that you have something to contribute to this process. Is my belief misplaced?"

His words seemed to have a sobering effect on Meyer, who widened his eyes and pushed himself up in his seat. "No, Your Excellency. It isn't."

"Then comport yourself accordingly," Jetanien said before turning to Karumé. "May I presume, Ms. Karumé, that the invitation you extended to Ambassador Lugok was accepted with a dash more civility?"

"Um, as *you* might define it?" Karumé asked. "Or as Lugok would?"

"I would settle for either," Jetanien said as he reached for his broth.

Leaning back in her seat, the envoy nodded. "Then, yes, he very politely accepted our invitation to meet with the Tholians, and followed his acceptance with an offer to let me watch as he pulverized Sesrene into the ambassador's 'orthorhombic component structures,' as he put it." Shrugging, she added, "Frankly, I was a bit surprised to hear that Lugok knew that much about crystallography."

Allowing a moment for Meyer's bout of laughter in reaction to Karumé's deadpan observation, Jetanien said, "I'd hardly recommend you start trusting the ambassador's prowess in the sciences, though it does offer us some insight as to Ambassador Sesrene's reticence to attend our summit, now does it not?"

Turning in her seat so she could face him, Sandesjo replied, "That's hardly surprising, Your Excellency. Given that our intelligence suggests the Tholians have been the aggressors in every recent confrontation with the Klingons we've been able to document, they're likely itching for a fight. Further, their tactics of sneak attack and retreat are probably adding insult to injury. That's certainly not what a Klingon would view as—"

"Honorable conduct," Jetanien said, anticipating what his aide was about to say. "Yes, of course. One day soon, I shall undertake a comprehensive course of study as to what precisely constitutes Klingon honor. I assume such things are written down, on sacred parchment or stone tablets or some such thing. I further gather that such sacrosanct documents must be viewed by very few Klingons, given their propensity for redefining their notions of honor more often than I don fresh undergarments."

A chorus of polite laughter echoed in the meeting room for a moment, before Meyer leaned forward in his chair and rested his elbows atop the conference table. "Isn't it safe to say that their actions might enrage anyone, Anna, Klingon or not? Even with Lugok not at the table, what makes us think that Sesrene would be any more forthcoming to us as to the Tholians' motives lately?"

It was Sovik who replied, "The Federation has held to its declaration that no armed action would be taken against the Tholian Assembly in the wake of the *Bombay*'s destruction. That should have earned us a modicum of trust with Ambassador Sesrene by now." Clasping his hands before him and interlocking his fingers in what Jetanien recognized as a Vulcan meditative posture, the envoy added, "The Tholian delegation may be more inclined to a series of discussions apart from the Klingons. While more lengthy, such an approach may prove more fruitful."

"Not acceptable," Jetanien said, slapping his webbed manus on the table. "We do not have that kind of time, Mr. Sovik. With that in mind, how do we proceed in getting the ambassadors face to face?"

Sandesjo frowned. "Short of lying to them?"

Shrugging, the ambassador replied, "Let's hold that strategy in reserve as a final option." His remark brought a sly smile to his attaché's face, a gesture that he returned as best he was able given his lack of malleable facial features.

"It's more of a function of getting the Tholians here," Karumé said. "As I mentioned, Lugok is more than interested in sitting down."

His brow furrowing in obvious concern, Meyer asked, "But will he stay down?"

"That may depend," she answered, looking into the envoy's bleary eyes, "on whether you can keep your comments about his family to yourself."

As Meyer opened his mouth to respond, Jetanien rose from his *glenget*. "It's enough that I have to prepare myself for such bickering between the diplomatic delegations," he said in a loud voice, bringing Karumé and Meyer to pause. "This summit is too important to the Federation to jeopardize with posturing and pettiness amongst my staff. Am I clear?"

What he did not say, however, and what burned within him was his heartfelt belief in the importance of the summit's success to *himself.* This was an unprecedented opportunity which had been handed to him, and he was well aware of the necessity to craft a positive, lasting resolution that would benefit not only the Federation but also its interstellar neighbors for decades to come. He was acutely aware of the situation in which he found himself, and that he—as well as any decisions he made here—might very well be judged in historical texts and classrooms long after he had departed this mortal plane.

I came to the Diplomatic Corps to make a difference, to leave a legacy of some sort, he thought as he looked around the table to see each envoy nod in response to his harsh question. *Nothing I have done until now is as vital as what I must do here. I must not fail, nor can I allow my staff to fail me.*

"Mr. Sovik," Jetanien said after a moment and as he returned to his perch, his usual calm demeanor once again reflected in his voice, "we've each had our dealings with Ambassador Sesrene, and I'm sure you'll agree that he's a very guarded being. However, what is the one thing that even Sesrene cannot shield from us during our conversations with him?"

The Vulcan nodded, obviously understanding the track the conversation was taking. "His desire for information, Your Excellency, particularly pertaining to the motives of anyone with interests in the Taurus Reach."

"Correct," Jetanien said, capping the word with a few satisfied clicks before looking once more to the rest of his staff. "Therefore, as part of our effort to make this summit more enticing to its participants, we tell the Klingons that the Tholian delegation intends to offer an explanation for their aggressive strikes against the empire . . ."

Smiling, Karumé finished the thought for him. "While a well-placed suggestion to the Tholians that the Klingons are coming to the table with a willingness to reveal details of *their* plans for the Reach just might prove tempting enough that they would attend if only to learn something new."

"As they say," added Meyer as he offered an approving nod, "you're more likely to draw flies with honey than with vinegar."

"Are you trying to make me hungry, Mr. Meyer?" Jetanien asked, releasing a deep basso laugh as Meyer returned a sour expression. "A lesson in appropriate comedic timing as well as in diplomacy. You're doing quite well today." To the rest of the group, he said, "Now, let us try again to persuade our respective delegations that there is something to be gained for all of us by sitting down and settling these matters of conflict. I expect reports from each of you as soon as you've succeeded in establishing a meeting time and agenda. Dismissed."

Lingering as her colleagues rose from their seats and filed out of the room on their way to attend to their respective tasks, Sandesjo approached Jetanien as he finished his broth. "If I may, Your Excellency," she said with a hint of a grin, "shall I presume that our final option turned out to be . . . ?"

"The best choice?" Jetanien said, rising again to his feet. "No, you should not. I view this course of persuasion as less of a lie and more a case of wishful thinking. I'd hope that our guests, once we gather in an atmosphere of cooperation and goodwill, might rise above their reactive natures and come to an objective understanding that the Taurus Reach has room enough for us all."

Frowning, Sandesjo replied, "That is a lofty expectation, Your Excellency."

"Well, I should expect no less of them than I do of myself, yes?"

No, I should not. I will not risk what might be the foundation for a new chapter in the Taurus Reach—one written by me.

Hurrying from Jetanien's offices toward the privacy of her own quarters, Sandesjo imagined that word of the impending summit meeting and the possibilities it afforded the Klingon Empire might make it back to Ambassador Lugok in time for him to exploit the situation in his favor.

If Lugok knows ahead of time that the Tholians are expecting to hear something about Klingon activity, she thought, *he has the chance to play them directly into the empire's hands. Now, I just need to get to Turag. . . .*

Her head bowed, her legs striding forward purposefully, she made her way down a corridor that emptied into a station for the tram tube that encircled Starbase 47's terrestrial enclosure within its disk-shaped primary hull. As she came upon the crowd of passengers who had just exited the tram, her reverie was broken as she heard someone calling her name.

"Anna? *Anna!* Hello!"

She looked up to see the station's archaeology and anthropology officer—*What was his name again? Xiong, yes*—tentatively waving with one hand over the scattering of people between them as she started to enter the tram.

"Hello!" she replied in greeting, trying to sound enthusiastic about seeing him. "I'm sorry, I'd wait for the next one, but I'm already late for an appointment," she lied as she stepped across the threshold of the tram car.

"It's okay," Xiong said, lowering his hand as well as his gaze. "Maybe I'll see you before the *Endeavour* ships out again."

The Endeavour, she remembered, *of course.* Sandesjo was aware that Xiong had returned to the station with the starship the previous day, and she also had seen the notice regarding the memorial service for the vessel's well-regarded captain as well as other Starfleet personnel, who had lost their lives while the ship was on assignment somewhere in the Gonmog Sector.

Sandesjo turned to face the young lieutenant from where she stood just inside the tram's doors. "I'm not going anywhere," she said, offering a small, wistful smile and arching her eyebrows suggestively as the doors began to close. Xiong perked up at that, and Sandesjo found herself considering—if only for a moment—any possible merits of seeing the young lieutenant in a social context.

Mildly attractive, for a human, I suppose, she decided, and while the lieutenant appeared to display a satisfactory level of fitness for a member of his species, she worried about his ability to withstand any sort of physical activity that might result from a more intimate encounter. *Such bruising and broken bones would be difficult to explain to a superior officer, after all.*

Not that it mattered, of course. For all the lieutenant's qualities, he was simply not T'Prynn.

Taking a seat along the tram's port-side bulkhead, Sandesjo closed her eyes and put the irksome if harmless Xiong out of her mind. Her commute home would take only a few moments, yet she seized the opportunity for a brief respite, knowing that her next task was to communicate this latest plan of Jetanien's to Turag. It would be difficult to convince her handler of the merits of having Lugok meet with the Tholians, particularly given the current state of animosity that existed between them and the empire.

Still, if Lugok were to take care with regard to the information he provided Ambassador Sesrene, working with the High Council to offer what the Tholian delegation wanted to hear, a few carefully dropped hints and suggestions might lead the Tholian *plaQta'* right where the empire wanted them to go.

After that, matters could proceed toward satisfactory resolution in a much more straightforward manner.

And where would that leave her? Once her assignment here was complete, what would she do? Her initial feeling was that she would at last be able to return home—finally able to shed her human identity and once again embrace the comfort of her natural visage as well as the culture from which she had been separated for far too long.

But, what of T'Prynn?

A reckoning was coming, of that Sandesjo was certain. The bond she had forged with the alluring Vulcan who inhabited her waking thoughts as well as her dreams already was at odds with her duty. What would happen when her feelings for T'Prynn collided head-on with what she must do here, and a choice had to be made for which path she must follow?

It was a question Sandesjo found herself asking with increasing frequency, and to which she had as yet no satisfactory answer.

24

"Ever see anything quite like this?" Dr. Fisher asked.

"Well," said Dr. Jabilo M'Benga as he stepped closer to the body of the nude Denobulan male lying atop the examination table, "I've seen stabbings, puncture wounds, and impalements, but nothing on this scale." At the center of the Denobulan's chest, where his thoracic cavity and its associated organs were once harbored, only a gaping, circular hole remained. The polished steel of the table was clearly visible on the other side of the ghastly wound.

"Me neither," Fisher replied, reaching to the shelf set against the bulkhead above the examination table to retrieve a fresh pair of sterile surgical gloves. Working his right hand into the first of the gloves, he added, "And after fifty years out here, that's saying something."

The two doctors currently were the only living occupants in Starbase 47's morgue, itself an unassuming area of the station's four-level medical complex. The morgue was housed within the hospital's lowest deck and situated near Vanguard's core and well away from more active sections of the station; its physical placement, Fisher knew, owed much more to the glacial pace of change regarding the traditions of medicine than it did to the facility's function. While twenty-third-century postmortem medical practices had advanced far beyond the need for such archaic conventions as refrigeration and chemical preservatives thanks to the development of stasis fields and other such useful technology, what still remained was the superstitions and general discomfort of the living that seemed to accompany the physical presence of the dead.

Keep the morgue in the basement, Fisher mused. *Can't be giving anyone the creeps now, can we?* As if to hammer home the point, even the temperature in this room seemed to be several degrees cooler than in the rest of the hospital.

As he returned to the subject of his study, however, even Fisher had to agree that the sight of this ill-fated being might be enough to give anyone pause. The Denobulan, stripped of all garments that might have indicated his rank or station in life, lay before them blank-faced and motionless on the examination table extending from one of a bank of stasis units along the rear wall of the morgue.

"I thought you might want to be in on this one, Jabilo," Fisher said, "given that a physician attached to starship duty might run across this sort of thing more often than those of us bound to a mere starbase."

Fisher could not resist the sly remark, which he tempered with inflections of good-natured sarcasm in the hope of couching somewhat the underlying edge of bitterness behind it. He had devoted a good deal of his time these past months preparing M'Benga to assume the role of chief medical officer for Starbase 47, a task to which Fisher attended with the true desire of ensuring that the station—and his dear friend Diego Reyes—was left with a capable physician and surgeon upon his impending retirement.

That desire was dashed, however, when the younger doctor filed a request with Starfleet Medical to transfer to the next available physician's posting on a starship. Fisher had swallowed his disappointment long enough to sign off on M'Benga's request—but had since put little effort into restraining his words on those occasions when his displeasure at the idea made itself known.

If M'Benga was fazed at all by the jab, he did not show it. *Guess his tour of duty in a Vulcan medical ward lends him the occasional stoicism,* Fisher thought, *or simple indifference to my situation, at least.*

"According to his file," M'Benga said, already down to business, "Mr. Bohanon here was part of the research team on Erilon. Was he involved in an accident?"

Fisher shook his head. "He was attacked. At least, that's what

I was told. By what, I don't know." Once more he directed his attention to the massive hole in the Denobulan's chest, which had relieved the victim of his lungs, his heart, and a significant portion of his spine.

Reaching out to trace the outline of the wound with a gloved finger, M'Benga said, "It looks almost surgical in its precision. Whatever did this, it struck him with tremendous force."

"If not for the strength of his rib cage," Fisher replied, "whatever hit him likely would have just torn him in two." Tapping a control set into the wall next to the table, he activated a spotlight, which he then directed to better illuminate the cavity. "See how it tapers inward from front to back? He was stabbed—skewered, really—by something that got wider as it went deeper." Dipping his own gloved hand inside the wound, he gently probed its edges with his fingers. "Its sides are uniform and smooth, but it doesn't seem to be from some sort of heat cauterization."

"What else might cause that?" M'Benga asked.

Shrugging, Fisher replied, "Acid. An alien enzyme, maybe. It could simply be a function of his being transported almost exactly at the time of his injury, and the transporter buffer just . . . tidied things up."

"You're suggesting he was literally beamed right off the object that killed him?" M'Benga frowned at that suggestion. "If that was the case, then why wasn't that object, or even a piece of it, brought up with him?"

Fisher nodded in approval at the observation. "Good question, but you're assuming the deadly force here was inflicted by a physical object. If he was hit—for example—by a shaped antiproton beam, that might explain a few things."

"But wouldn't such an attack leave some residual energy that might be detected at the wound site?" M'Benga asked.

"Not if the stasis field that Mr. Bohanon entered on the *Endeavour* shortly after his death nullified any energy traces we might hope to find." Fisher smiled, noting the younger physician's knit brow as he considered that possibility. "It's a tangled web we attempt to unweave in an autopsy, Dr. M'Benga, but we have one thing going for us."

"And that is?"

"It's pretty obvious how this poor fellow died, which means we get to spend more time trying to discover what was used to kill him."

Fisher reached for a laser scalpel set atop a tray positioned next to the stasis bed. By applying a deft touch with the device, he carved away a sliver of muscle tissue from the surface area of the cavity and placed it in a waiting specimen dish. Handing the sample to M'Benga, he said, "Let's see what a molecular scan can tell us."

The younger doctor led the way across the room to a near-by workstation that offered an array of scanning equipment as well as a standard computer interface terminal. Fisher watched as M'Benga placed the tray under the sensor array and entered a series of instructions into the small keypad set into the worktable. The sample dish was bathed in a soft blue light, the forensic scanner sending its findings to the computer for further processing and analysis. Within seconds, data began to coalesce on the workstation's display monitor.

And Fisher's eyebrows rose.

"What the hell is that?" he asked as he studied the information being put out by the computer. "Anabolic activity? These cells are *alive*?" He leaned closer to better scrutinize the computer monitor, but the data displayed upon it did not change.

"That's impossible," M'Benga said. "Something must have contaminated the site."

"They look like new metabolic pathways," Fisher said. Watching the computer-enhanced image of the cell sample, the doctor could plainly see that some as-yet-unidentified substance had come into contact with the exposed areas of the open wound, and even now was slowly but surely working to break down the Denobulan's cells, only to rearrange them into something resembling a crystalline structure. "Whatever it is, it's mineralizing the muscle cells somehow."

But what the hell for?

Beside him, M'Benga asked, "Could it be a form of viral infection native to Erilon that was arrested when the body was placed into stasis, and only became active once it was exposed to an atmosphere?"

"The *Endeavour*'s CMO scanned the body for infection, but found nothing," Fisher replied.

M'Benga nodded toward the screen. "Shouldn't he have found this?"

"He wasn't allowed to autopsy the body," Fisher said. Frowning as he said that, he nevertheless kept his thoughts on that decision, as well as who had made it and issued the appropriate orders, to himself. "Besides, if there was any kind of contamination, our autocontainment procedures would already have kicked in and sealed this place off. We're not looking at any kind of contagion." Turning away from the workstation and moving back to where Bohanon's body still lay, he called over his shoulder, "Get a portable scanner."

It took only a moment to survey the rest of the ghastly wound in the Denobulan's chest and confirm Fisher's suspicions. Holding the scanner up so that he could see its collected data, M'Benga said, "The same readings. Every exposed area of internal tissue is in the process of gradually being altered at the cellular level."

"Putting him in stasis halted the process," Fisher said. He indicated the control panel on M'Benga's side of the table. "Jabilo, put him back in. I want to study this, and we need to preserve what we've got as long as we can."

"Yes, Doctor," M'Benga replied, pressing the control that retracted the examination table and its current occupant back into its storage drawer. The door hissed shut and a gentle hum exuded from the bulkhead as the small chamber's stasis field activated.

"Have you detected a rate of progress?" he asked as he rejoined Fisher at the computer workstation.

Pointing to the monitor, Fisher replied, "Already plotting one out." The screen displayed a small graph inset atop the main image of the ongoing cellular metamorphosis. "Not that it's going to help us much. The process is tapering off. At this rate, it'll neutralize completely before it extends more than a millimeter or two into the surrounding tissue."

"The process might need more of its catalyst in order to continue," M'Benga said. "Maybe something native to the planet?"

Fisher offered a small grunt of affirmation. "Could be, but maybe all it needs is more living tissue." Turning back to the workstation, he began to key in a series of instructions. "We've got everything we need to try a computer model. Let's see what kind of luck we have with that."

In response to his requests, the computer screen generated a new graph. Fisher watched as the function graph did not slope toward the zero baseline but instead spiked quickly.

M'Benga, who was watching the computer's progress along with him, drew in a loud breath. "If he'd been alive, he'd have been fully compromised by the process."

"In a matter of minutes," Fisher clarified, "and depending on the size or location of the wound, I'm guessing it wouldn't have been a pleasant experience."

The sound of a pneumatic hiss from behind them caused both men to snap toward the morgue's doorway as Rana Desai entered the room.

"Did I scare you gentlemen?" she asked, her tone suggesting that she hoped she had.

"You didn't, no," Fisher said, looking at M'Benga, "but we've got a case of the willies all the same. How can we help you, Captain?"

"Well, I'm not looking to interrupt," Desai said, glancing at M'Benga a moment before returning her gaze to Fisher.

After a moment in silence, the younger physician nodded. "I ought to excuse myself, anyway," he said. Looking to Fisher, he added, "I'd be very interested in hearing about any . . . developments, Doctor."

"I'll keep you posted," Fisher replied, waiting until his colleague had left the morgue before turning to Desai and offering a sly smile. "I'm beginning to think you like hanging out in the basement."

Desai shrugged in mock defensiveness. "Okay, so the occasional investigation happens to bring me down here once in a while, but maybe it's not the morgue that I like so much as your charming company."

"Uh-huh," Fisher said, feeling more than a little unconvinced. "Well, if you're down here, I'm guessing the *Endeavour* incident's still on the fast track."

"In a fashion, yes," the captain said, pulling a chair closer to Fisher's workstation and settling herself into it. "We've gotten some preliminary reports from those who survived the attack. Everyone's accounts line up. The whole thing amounts to an expedition and a landing party that ran into something unanticipated and overwhelming. Based on their interviews, there's just nothing that anyone could have done differently. This all seems . . . well, routine, for lack of a better word." She released a tired sigh before adding, "Damn, I know that makes me sound cold, but how else do I say it?"

"How about 'Accidental in the line of duty'?" Fisher offered. "You're saying no one's to blame."

"Not every investigation in our office is launched with the hope of being able to turn up a mistake or a scapegoat," Desai said, her defensiveness this time sounding genuine.

"You don't need to tell me that, Rana," Fisher said.

"Well, I have to tell Diego," she shot back. "Every time."

A tone from the computer terminal echoed in the morgue, and the doctor smiled. "Well, I guess you'll have some good news for the commodore today." Indicating for Desai to join him, he turned the monitor so that she could see the information displayed upon it.

"What are we looking at?" Desai asked.

Fisher did not reply at first, his attention instead riveted on the results generated by his computer model. "Oh, my," he finally said, trying to absorb as much of the detailed report as he could at once.

"Oh, my, what?" Desai said, reminding him that he had an audience.

"I don't rightly know," he answered, ignoring the twinge of excitement he felt in his gut and the sensation of feeling his pulse increase. He even felt goose bumps rising along his arms. "I've never seen anything like this."

He stared at the whirling virtual representation of a DNA

strand from Bohanon's compromised cells—realizing as he did so that "strand" seemed a wholly insufficient term to describe what he was seeing. It was a genome, yes, but wondrously complex, encoded with far more raw biological data than he ever had seen in one place . . . more than he even imagined might be possible.

"Fish, talk to me."

The physician let Desai's plea hang unanswered, so intent was he on what he was seeing. The genetic structure dwarfed a typical human DNA strand and—according to the computer's own messages, at least—appeared to baffle even the vast storehouse of knowledge available to him via Starfleet Medical. He entered a rapid-fire string of search requests, each one coming back unanswered or not understood by computer or the massive database with which it was communicating.

This is incredible.

Somewhere in the middle of that convoluted web of genetic code, Fisher imagined he saw the keys to uncounted medical and scientific advances, be they cures for disease, repairs to genetic defects, even enhancements to the human genome itself. There was no end to the speculation of what this might signify for the future of all known races in the universe.

Assuming somebody can figure the damn thing out.

"Doctor," Desai said, more forcefully this time, "does this have anything to do with what happened on Erilon?"

Without looking up from his viewer, Fisher said, "I wish I could tell you."

That the strange biochemical residue in Bohanon's corpse was capable of crystallizing tissue was one thing, but to detect within that substance and the affected cells a genomic structure on the scale he was seeing—Fisher knew the implications were staggering.

And to think I could have retired before seeing something like this.

"Fish," Desai said, her expression now one of concern, "what the hell is this about?"

Stroking his silvered goatee, the doctor replied, "Well, it looks like we'll both have something to share with our friend the commodore."

"Well, then, my timing is perfect."

Reyes's voice rang through the morgue, loudly enough that it startled Fisher and visibly shook Desai. The doctor looked up to see the station's commander striding their way. "But here I am without an invitation to the party—again."

Fisher crossed his arms, smiled wryly at Reyes. "And as usual, you don't have a problem assuming that it wasn't intentional."

Desai quickly chimed in. "It's not as much fun down here as you might think."

"It never is," said Reyes, letting the words hang in the air for several seconds before turning to Fisher. "Zeke, we need to talk."

"Yes, we do," the doctor replied, instinct telling him that the commodore's timely arrival was more than simple coincidence.

"Is this about the Erilon incident?" Desai asked. "If so, then my team's finished their preliminary report, and . . ."

"I'm sorry, Captain," Reyes said, cutting her off. Fisher noted the almost apologetic look in his friend's eyes as he regarded Desai. "But I'm afraid this is a security matter. Stop by my office in an hour, and I'll take your report then. That'll be all for now."

Desai's eyes went wide, and the doctor noted the tightening of her jaw, but she only nodded in response to the sudden turn of the situation. "Aye, sir," she said, glancing toward Fisher before turning and making her way out of the morgue, leaving a grim-faced and even tired-looking Reyes standing before him.

"Something tells me this is going to be pretty interesting," Fisher said.

25

"I've seen ships after they've suffered massive combat damage," Commander Jon Cooper said as he stood next to Reyes on the observation platform overlooking docking bay four, "and I've seen them after they've had all but the stuffing beaten out of them by an ion storm. Hell, I was once on a recovery operation for a starship after it crashed into a moon." For emphasis, he pointed through the transparasteel window that protected those inside the observation area from the vacuum currently engulfing the docking bay. "Commodore, not a one of them ever looked as bad as that heap of junk."

Reyes said nothing to his executive officer, offering only a tired yet still amused smile as he and Cooper watched the *U.S.S. Lovell* cross the threshold of the massive space doors that separated the ravages of open space from the protective embrace of Vanguard's docking bay. He felt a rumbling in the deck beneath his boots as the generators powering the spacedock's tractor beams guided the *Daedalus*-class vessel into its parking slip.

Maintenance lights played across the battered and beaten hull of the aged vessel as it was maneuvered into position by the station's navigational control systems. The harsh illumination served only to highlight the numerous flaws in the *Lovell*'s exterior. Reyes shook his head as he once again beheld pockmarked and dented hull plates—many of them only bare duranium, while others sported paint that contrasted with the ship's overall gunmetal gray paint scheme. Visible weld lines joined a few of the plates, evidence of repair work conducted without the comfort and features of a well-equipped ship-maintenance facility.

Not that odd, Reyes reminded himself, *considering the entire crew is composed of engineers.*

Far from a pristine vessel and possessing absolutely nothing akin to the aesthetic beauty Reyes likened to more modern starships, the *Lovell* nevertheless was a testament to an engineering philosophy and quality of design that had proven its worth to Starfleet and the Federation for more than a century. Its spherical primary hull leading a stocky, cylindrical engineering section and ribbed warp nacelles certainly lacked the streamlined grace of a more modern *Constitution*-class ship, but Reyes also could see the resolve and tenacity of the era from which it had been born echoed in its rougher, coarser lines.

Among the first model of vessels produced in large numbers following the founding of the Federation more than a century earlier, *Daedalus*-class starships had proven their worth as instruments of both deep-space exploration and defense as the fledgling cooperative of united worlds made their first joint forays into the vast unknown reaches of the galaxy.

Easily constructed and maintained, the ships made up for their bland appearance and lack of creature comforts found on other vessels of the period with a rugged durability. Though the last of them had been removed from active Starfleet use near the end of the last century, a few *Daedalus* ships had survived to enjoy extended life in the hands of civilian shipmasters.

Then, there was the *Lovell.*

Before his initial encounter with the ship and its crew of engineering specialists, Reyes had not even known that any *Daedalus*-class vessels were being used by Starfleet in any capacity. It therefore had come as somewhat of a surprise when the *Lovell* arrived at Vanguard months ago to assist in the final system installation and adjustments necessary to bring the station to full operational capability in accordance with its accelerated schedule. His amazement only deepened upon learning that the aged yet still reliable workhorse was one of three currently in service to Starfleet's Corps of Engineers.

"For the love of all that's good and holy in the universe," Cooper said a moment later as the decrepit-looking ship slowed to a stop within the confines of its parking slip, "will someone please tell me what the hell is keeping that beast from exploding all over the docking bay?"

Standing behind the exec and Reyes, Lieutenant Isaiah Farber unleashed one of his trademark wide, toothy smiles as he replied, "Strategic placement of forcefields, Commander, along with thermoconcrete and what I assume is the kindness of at least three different benevolent deities."

Turning from the window, Reyes regarded the brawny, imposing officer, whose layered muscles seemed perpetually ready to rip the seams of his red Starfleet uniform tunic. Though Reyes himself was no small man, even his broad-shouldered physique was no match for the two-time Starfleet weight-lifting champion. "Feeling a bit nostalgic, Lieutenant?" he asked with a slight grin.

Farber shrugged. "I'd be lying if I said I wasn't, Commodore." Lifting his chin as a means of indicating the direction of the *Lovell,* he said, "She may not be much to look at, but she's got a heart of cast rodinium. She's made it through some tough scrapes, and that's just while she's been a Corps of Engineers ship. Say what you will about her, but they don't make ships like that anymore."

"Thank God," Cooper said, though he too was smiling, reassuring the lieutenant that he spoke in jest.

Formerly assigned to the *Lovell,* Farber had come to Vanguard during the ship's first visit to the station, a few months earlier, when the vessel's accomplished—if unpolished and unorthodox—complement of engineering specialists had assisted in finalizing the station's readiness for full operation. So enamored was the lieutenant with the facility and its state-of-the-art technology, not to mention its mission of support for Federation expansion into the Taurus Reach, that he had applied for a transfer. Likewise impressed with the role Farber had played in solving the mystery behind the station's difficulties, a concession of which was the tragic loss of the station's previous chief engineer, Reyes and the *Lovell*'s captain, Daniel Okagawa, had agreed to the request, resulting in Farber's eventual assignment as Vanguard's senior engineering officer.

"If you're really that heartsick, Mr. Farber," Reyes said, "I can have you back aboard before her engines cool down."

Chuckling, Farber shook his head. "That won't be necessary, sir. I'm quite happy here on Vanguard."

"Glad to hear it," Reyes said. "Of course, if you're going to change your mind, I'd suggest you not waste a lot of time doing it. The *Lovell* won't be here that long."

Making an exaggerated and still joking show of rolling his eyes, Cooper added, "One can only hope." To Reyes he said, "Any word from Starfleet on a permanent replacement for the *Bombay*, Commodore?"

Reyes shrugged. "The fleet's spread pretty thin right now. Along with the new exploration push, there've also been reports of increased activity along the Klingon border. Starfleet Intelligence thinks they may be planning some kind of big offensive."

Given the demands—both scientific and military—currently placed on Starfleet's resources, the result was a shortage of vessels that met the specific needs of Vanguard and its mission. According to the last report Reyes had received, it would be a minimum of two months before another *Miranda*-class starship or something in the same capability range could be assigned permanently to the station.

"Of all the ships Starfleet could have sent us," Cooper said, "they decided on a boatload of engineers." The exec shook his head. "Far be it from me to question the wisdom of my superiors, but what the hell were they thinking?"

Reyes allowed the comment. After all, there was no way for the commander to know the real reasons for choosing the *Lovell* as a substitute vessel to support Vanguard. Considering the nature of the station's true mission, security was of paramount importance. Even though the crews of the base's other tenant vessels, the *Endeavour* and the *Sagittarius,* were oblivious of the mystery surrounding the Taurus Reach, they knew enough to be able to carry out their duties without the need to ask questions that—for the time being, at least—lacked answers. Such would have to be the case with any new vessel brought in to support the station. Starfleet had provided the commodore with a short list of ships that were available on an interim basis, none of which had impressed him in the slightest.

Faced with that dilemma, Reyes instead had opted to go another route.

"They kill two birds with one stone," he said. "The *Lovell* has adequate cargo storage space, even if it's less than a *Miranda,* and its crew has tweaked and bribed its warp engines so much that it actually makes better speed than a ship half its age." He said that last part while casting a respectful nod to Farber. "Add to that the fact that their engineers are already familiar with our systems. The lieutenant here will have more help than he can handle for a month or two. By the time they're finished, this place'll probably have its own warp drive. At the very least, the food slot in my office won't give me any more trouble."

Of course, Reyes's true motivation for selecting the *Lovell* was far simpler. While his assessment of the ship's capabilities was accurate, there was also the matter of its crew's awareness—albeit in an abstract sense—of the anomaly which had caused the station's rash of malfunctions prior to becoming operational. The commodore would be able to assign the vessel to investigate anything related to that still-unexplained carrier wave with the comfort that the *Lovell*'s crew would have at least some of the necessary perspective to make their efforts worthwhile to the overall exploration of the Taurus Reach, all while presenting a minimum risk to operational security.

Now that things had become even more complicated with the loss of Zhao Sheng, Reyes needed another shipmaster that he could trust implicitly, particularly in light of some of the decisions he was about to make.

For the moment, that person—whether or not he wanted that responsibility—was Captain Daniel Okagawa.

I wonder what he'll have to say about that?

"With all due respect, sir," the *Lovell*'s captain said as he stood next to Reyes outside the Vault, which they had just exited, "what the hell am I doing here?"

Compared with the commodore, Okagawa was a small man.

Still, he possessed a stocky, toned physique, the set of his shoulders and their proportion to his waist suggesting that the captain's preferred method of exercise might be swimming or perhaps gymnastics. Though he was comparable in age to Reyes, his close-cropped black hair featured a liberal peppering of pale gray, which when coupled with the wrinkles around his eyes and across his forehead only served to enhance his air of dignity and grace.

Reyes offered the captain a tired smile. *Not exactly what I was expecting, but close enough.* He said nothing as the section of bulkhead slid back into place, concealing the innocuous pair of red doors and the room behind them and restoring the otherwise nondescript office—located in the depths of the station's cargo decks—to an illusion of normalcy. Once more, the Vault and its reclusive denizens were tucked away, safe from any prying eyes.

"I'll be honest with you, Dan," Reyes said as he took a seat behind the empty gray desk that was the office's most prominent piece of furniture. He gestured for Okagawa to take the room's only other chair. "You weren't my first choice. I know your crew isn't suited for this kind of thing, but if I have to bring a vessel in here temporarily for some of the things I need done, I wanted someone who already has an idea of what the hell's going on out here."

After detailing Farber to get with the *Lovell*'s chief engineer and ensure that any supply or maintenance requisitions and wish lists were filled in order to have the ship ready for departure within seventy-two hours, and having Cooper coordinate with its first officer to handle any outstanding personnel issues regarding the vessel's assignment to the station, Reyes was left only with the duty of briefing Okagawa about the role of his ship and crew with respect to Vanguard's mission. While the captain had accepted the need for the range of duties for which the *Lovell* would be responsible during its short-term tenure with the station, it was the additional, covert tasks with which the captain had understandably taken issue.

It had been easy for Reyes to connect the dots between the

handful of planets scattered throughout the Taurus Reach where samples of the meta-genome as well as remnants of the peculiar alien architecture had been discovered. For his part, Okagawa had taken the revelations in stride. A Starfleet veteran for nearly as long as Reyes himself, the man had doubtless been witness to all manner of bizarre phenomena during the decades he had spent in space. Still, that did not prevent the captain from appreciating the scope of the situation.

"I can imagine your frustration, Commodore," Okagawa said as he settled into the chair. "So many questions, so many uncertainties. I'm no geneticist, but even I can grasp the implications of what you've found here. Learning who or what's responsible for the meta-genome might change our understanding of life and evolution at a fundamental level, and if this is the result of some kind of artificial genetic engineering, who knows what else those responsible were capable of."

Reyes nodded, rubbing the bridge of his nose. "The Klingons are already prowling around the Taurus Reach, trying to figure out why the Federation finds this region so interesting. As unhappy as the Tholians are about us being here, they're even more worked up over the Klingons. We're a heartbeat away from interstellar war. The only question left unanswered is who the players will be."

"How in the name of hell does Starfleet expect you to keep a lid on all of this?" Okagawa asked. "You've got a station full of people who think they're supporting colonization and exploration initiatives. Starship crews are running back and forth across space, looking for clues and conducting research with no real idea about what they're looking for. Only a handful of people even know the truth, and most of them are locked away in that dungeon you've constructed." He indicated the Vault, the entrance to which was once again secreted behind its unexceptional bulkhead. "Speaking of which, that Dr. Gek and his gaggle don't strike me as the kind of people who get out much."

Despite himself, Reyes laughed at the captain's observation. "So far as security goes, they're the easiest ones to keep a handle on. I'd have to check access logs to be sure, but I don't think they've come out of there since the station came online."

"Well," Okagawa said, "I suppose there's plenty in there to keep them entertained." His own expression faltered a bit, the small smile he had sported melting away. "What I don't understand is why you told me this much if I'm here for only a short time. Surely you could have assigned me to missions that didn't require me having all of this information." He indicated the wall next to Reyes and the secrets hidden behind it with a wave of his hand. "Given the security surrounding this operation, I'd think Starfleet would have your head for revealing too much to those without a specific need to know."

Reyes shrugged. "Maybe they will, but I don't care." While he agreed in principle with the idea of maintaining strict secrecy of Vanguard's true purpose, the fact was that keeping that secret had already cost far too many lives for the commodore's taste. Though he would continue to observe the security of the mission so far as he was able, he would never again allow that secret to stand in the way of safeguarding the people under his command.

That decision also had extended to including Ezekiel Fisher into the small cadre of people with whom he had entrusted this information. It was an unexpected turn of events, coming after the station's computer had alerted T'Prynn and Reyes to the doctor's research in relation to the autopsy he was performing on the Denobulan scientist brought back from Erilon. The discovery of meta-genome traces within the wound inflicted on the corpse had opened up an entire new arena of investigation, and while Fisher was not the ideal candidate to conduct that investigation, he was the most qualified person at Reyes's disposal, to say nothing of the commodore's utmost trust in his old friend.

Not that it'll stop Starfleet Command from firing a photon torpedo up my ass.

"Don't get me wrong," Reyes continued, "I trust you'll inform only those members of your crew who absolutely need to know the truth, and even then just enough to accomplish the tasks I'll set for you while protecting your people. As for Starfleet"—he waved a hand as if dismissing any concern he might have over defying the strict orders he had been given upon first receiving his assignment as commander of the station—"leave them to me. That's what commodores are for."

Now it was Okagawa's turn to offer a small chuckle. "Okay," he said, "so what is it you want me to do?"

Leaning forward until he could rest his elbows on the top of the barren desk, Reyes replied, "You're going back to Erilon. I want to know what attacked the outpost, and if or how it's connected to what's there." For the sake of official Starfleet inquiries, he already had addressed the deaths of the Corps of Engineers team as well as Captain Zhao and members of the *Endeavour*'s crew—an action that had left a sour taste in his mouth that refused to dissipate—but of course that was not nearly enough.

Whatever the mysterious life-form was that had massacred the research team and the starship's landing party, there was more than enough evidence to suggest that it was somehow connected to the artifacts and meta-genome fragments found on Erilon, Ravanar IV, and other planets in the Taurus Reach. The aspects of the devastating attack both on Erilon's surface and against the *Endeavour* in orbit allowed for precious few other logical explanations.

Lieutenant Xiong had explained his theory with unbridled passion during the otherwise downbeat post-mission briefing. In addition, the A&A officer was certain that the full potential of Erilon as a piece of the massive Taurus Reach puzzle still was waiting to be realized. Reyes had seen the determination in the young officer's eyes, the drive to prove his theory, not just because it was his mission but also as a means of making sure that the losses suffered to this point—the *Bombay,* the engineering team, as well as Captain Zhao and members of his crew—were not in vain.

Reyes was anxious to give Xiong that chance, as a means for the lieutenant to exorcise not only his own demons but perhaps those carried by the commodore as well.

"I want the research station on Erilon restored to full operation," Reyes said after a moment. "The *Endeavour* will be responsible for providing security. No holds barred this time. Your first mission will be to figure out what's behind the planetary defense system and get control of it. I don't want a repeat of what happened to the *Endeavour* brought down on your fellow Corps engineers, but it goes deeper than that. If there's more to this than a single planet, then we could be facing alien weapons technology that's way out of our league."

Okagawa nodded. "In other words, one more thing we have to keep from the Klingons and Tholians."

Already feeling the first hints of a dull ache behind his eyes, he offered a tired smile. "Welcome to my world, Captain."

26

Morqla's eyes snapped open and he sat up on the hard shelf that served as his bed. Every muscle tensed and every sense strained to detect the presence of whatever it was that had disturbed his already fitful slumber.

"What?" he blurted, though of course there was no one in the room to answer the question.

The low rumbling seemed to reverberate through everything around him, emanating from the stone floor and continuing up along the coarse, dark walls that formed the simple, unassuming chamber he had chosen as his private quarters. It was only a slight vibration, and had he not been a habitual light sleeper Morqla might well not have noticed it at all. Had he been aboard ship, the governor would almost certainly have dismissed the subdued murmur as the characteristic drone of powerful warp engines.

Here, however, where the native inhabitants were still centuries away from developing even the most primitive forms of mechanization, the odd thrumming sound was as alien to this planet as he was.

Rising to his feet, Morqla paused long enough to retrieve his disruptor pistol and his *d'k tahg* knife from the small bureau situated next to his sleeping platform. He stepped into the hall, having to duck in order to pass through the doorway designed with the shorter Palgrenai physiology in mind. The low rumble was somewhat louder here, and more evident in the cold stone floor beneath his bare feet. He was satisfied to see that in addition to the sentries posted at each end of the narrow corridor, other officers under his command had exited their own rooms, and he noted his own expression mirrored on the other eight faces, each of his men regarding him and one another with puzzlement.

"Where is that coming from?" Morqla snapped as he tucked the *d'k tahg* into the waistband of the loose-fitting trousers he wore. Securing the knife at the small of his back and tucking the tail of his rough-hewn shirt behind the weapon's handle, he ensured he could reach it without having to fumble with his own clothing.

His second-in-command, Kertral, emerged from his own room with disruptor in hand, shirtless and with his dark, long hair flying wildly about his head and shoulders as he turned to face him. "It feels as though it comes from underneath us," he said. "Has Terath finally succeeded in activating that ancient power generator?"

"At this hour of the night?" Morqla asked, doubt coating every word. While he knew Dr. Terath was dedicated to her pursuit of science, he also had seen her during the evening meal and knew from her own comments that the scientist had planned to retire soon after eating. Her intention had been to rise before dawn so that she and her team could journey some three thousand *qell'qams* to the far side of the continent in order to explore another recently discovered storehouse of centuries-old artifacts, which appeared to be of the same type as those she had been studying these past weeks.

Still, the governor realized, the activation of some ancient power source far beneath the surface of the village made the most sense. All that remained now was to discover who was responsible. Common sense told Morqla it had to be a member of Terath's science contingent. They had tended to work at all hours of the day or night, never bothering to observe the curfew rules enacted for the village. Their casual dismissal of that and other directives he had enacted since the garrison's arrival here had given Morqla cause for annoyance more than once.

"Find Terath," he snapped at Kertral. "Bring her to me." Now fully awake with no hope of returning to sleep before the new day began, Morqla grunted in resignation. The desk in his office was littered with incomplete status reports, supply requisitions, and other administrative detritus that defined the role and life of a planetary governor, the majority of which he had ignored for days already. There seemed to be no compelling reason to put it off any longer now that he had an unexpected window of opportunity to make an attempt at gaining back some of that ground. "And send me K'voq," he added as he turned on his heel and lumbered down the narrow, low-ceilinged passageway. "I'm going to need *rakta-jino.*"

It likely was going to be one of *those* days.

Running footsteps echoing in the stone stairwell preceded the arrival of his aide, K'voq, even his trim form seeming to fill the narrow archway leading to the steps as he dashed into the corridor. He pulled up short at the sudden sight of his superior officer, his eyes wide with unease.

"Governor," he said, holding up a communicator, "we're starting to receive reports of disturbances from several of the neighboring villages."

His brow furrowing in confusion, Morqla's reply was more growl than spoken word. "What?"

"Fires have been set in many buildings that our forces have occupied," the aide continued. "The *jeghpu'wI'* are employing catapults to launch balls of lead coated in a flaming oil. Lieutenant Vekpa reports that the supply depot we established at the *Grap'hwu* province has been destroyed."

Despite the alarming nature of K'voq's report, Morqla actually smiled. "So, it seems the *jeghpu'wI'* have gained a new measure of courage." Taking the proffered communicator from his assistant, he made his way down the stairs and outside the building that had been commandeered for use as officers' billeting. He noted that even at this early hour, the air was still thick and humid in keeping with this hemisphere's near-oppressive summer season.

His attention was drawn to the flames licking the edges of the building at the opposite end of the village's center square. A hole was visible in the thatch material that covered the structure's sloped roof. Groups of Palgrenai had emerged from a few of the surrounding buildings to investigate the source of the commotion. Flickering light cast off from the fire reflected off their leathery skin, momentarily reminding Morqla of one species of particularly fierce reptile he had encountered during his youth while hunting in the jungles of Qo'noS.

As Morqla moved farther into the courtyard he noted from the expressions on some of the villagers' faces that few of the locals appeared to be frightened or surprised by the sudden assault of the otherwise peaceful night. He saw nothing that indicated outright guilt or even complicity, but instinct told the governor that the local populace was not entirely ignorant about what had happened.

"Look out!" a voice shouted from somewhere behind him at the same instant Morqla caught sight of something hurtling through the air to his right. A ball of fire, perhaps the size of a bloodwine barrel, then two more objects of similar size all arced over the trees surrounding the outskirts of the village. The trio of flaming projectiles sailed into the perimeter of the courtyard. Klingons and Palgrenai alike scattered in all directions as two of the fireballs struck the compacted earth while the third plunged through the roof of the building that had been designated as a dining facility for the Klingon garrison. Sparks and pieces of the structure flew into the air from the point of impact.

"*Bekk!*" Morqla heard Kertral shout above the rising din of people yelling and the sound of alert sirens echoing through the courtyard. The governor turned to see his executive officer gathering a cadre of *QuchHa'* as they emerged from the building that served as a barracks for enlisted troops. "Form a search party. I want those cretins found and their heads on pikes before the sun rises!"

Even as his second-in-command issued further orders for the rounding up of Palgrenai villagers, other Klingon soldiers and locals continued to seek shelter from a new barrage of flaming shot raining down from the surrounding forest. Morqla had to admire the audacity of the attack, by far the most intensive act of sedition the *jeghpu'wI'* had attempted since the beginning of the occupation.

"Catapults," he said, as another pair of flaming shots was launched from the trees and into the village square. "Impressive."

Both of the projectiles missed hitting any of the buildings ringing the courtyard, though a few of his soldiers had to scramble to avoid being in the path of one as it plunged back to earth and bored a hole into the dry, dusty soil. Burning globs of whatever flammable substance the *jeghpu'wI'* had used to coat the makeshift cannonballs were flung into the air, some of it landing on a few of his troops, who in turn smacked and swiped at the flaming debris now sticking to them.

For the Palgrenai to have constructed not only the primitive implements but also the strategy to deploy them—apparently in concert with similar attacks taking place at other villages in the region—without their preparations being discovered by members of the Klingon garrison was a surprising feat. It spoke volumes not only of the villagers' abilities to employ secrecy and cunning but also the seeming ineptitude of his own soldiers to monitor the activities of the not-so-helpless primitives over which they presided.

Turning to K'voq, he asked, "Have any casualties been reported?"

His aide shook his head. "None so far, Governor. The buildings that have been targeted to this point have either been designated as storage facilities, or else were unoccupied at this time of night."

Morqla nodded at the report. "Interesting." The number and tenacity of the attacks would seem to have invited at least some casualties, but would not be consistent with what he had learned of the Palgrenai since arriving on this world. While the *jeghpu'wI'* had been content to destroy structures, equipment, and other matériel during their previous acts of insurrection, they had gone out of their way to avoid injuring anyone, Palgrenai or Klingon alike.

It was an approach the governor could not understand, particularly given the fact that a large number of the conquered had died at Klingon hands. Still, he knew the approach would prove futile. So long as the Palgrenai were unable to do everything in their power to secure their liberation, they had no hope of ever shaking off the hand of their oppressors.

Nevertheless, Morqla reminded himself, *this defiance must be crushed. Now.*

"Kertral!" he shouted toward his executive officer, who still was in the process of disseminating orders to subordinates. "Execute Special Occupation Order Two!" It was a choice he made with much reluctance.

His second-in-command offered a terse, formal nod before saluting in response to the directive. "As you command, Excellency."

Releasing a grudging sigh, Morqla shook his head as he watched his troops begin the process of corralling those villagers who still remained in the courtyard. Around the village square, he saw other soldiers kicking or shooting their way through the doors of buildings or using their *bat'leths* to tear through the comparatively thin walls of neighboring dwellings, all in the name of rounding up those *jeghu'wI'* who still remained in the village and carrying out the order he had issued.

The time had come for total suppression of the uprising—merciless punishment not only of those responsible for the revolt but also those who might be complicit in the action. At the moment, Morqla was not concerned that he might be taking into custody parties innocent of any wrongdoing. The priority now was to restore order to the populace and reaffirm with brute force the nature of their status as servants of the empire.

Elsewhere, the telltale pulses of disruptor cannons pierced the night air at the same time as hints of harsh crimson energy illuminated the dark jungle surrounding the village. It seemed that his soldiers had found at least a few of the locations from which the insurgents were attacking and had taken to deploying weapons to deal with the rebels' comparatively archaic and ultimately wasted efforts.

As expected, the increased measures on the part of his soldiers were causing a reaction from the forest. More of the flaming shot sailed through the air, this time crashing through the wooden walls of homes or digging furrows in the stone façades of the larger structures. Fire could be seen scorching the roofs of several of the buildings surrounding the square, and one smaller dwelling at the far end of the courtyard was already being consumed by massive flames and clouds of billowing smoke.

"Reports are coming in from all of the surrounding provinces," K'voq reported, holding out his communicator and running to stand alongside Morqla. "The rebels are attempting counter-attacks, throwing improvised firebombs at our soldiers and trying to damage disruptor cannons with those cursed catapults of theirs. We're starting to take casualties, Excellency."

At last, Morqla mused. It seemed the Palgrenai were indeed still capable of surprising him. Not that it would help them, of course. A line had been crossed, not only by the slaves but by the masters as well, and it was now far too late to turn back. Order demanded that control be restored, by any means necessary.

If that meant killing every *jeghpu'wI'* for hundreds of *qell'qams* in every direction, then so be it.

"Governor! Look out!"

Only the timely warning from his loyal aide and his own battle-honed reflexes allowed Morqla to avoid the ball of fire coming right at him. He threw himself to the right and rolled across the dry, hard ground just as the massive flaming sphere plummeted from the sky and drilled a hole in the dirt less than an arm's length from where he had been standing.

Unfortunately, K'voq was between the projectile and the ground.

The Klingon moved too slowly, and the fiery shot plowed into his chest, driving him to the earth. He was dead even before he came to rest in the parched soil, his loose-fitting and rough-hewn clothing erupting into flames as it was coated by burning oil. The stench of sizzling flesh assailed Morqla's nostrils as he scrambled away from other patches of blazing debris.

More of the projectiles rained down on the village, now coming from points all around the forest perimeter. The steady whines of disruptors and the angered battle cries of his warriors echoed in the humid night as fire painted the settlement in blistering crimson that paled only fleetingly in any feeble moonlight that penetrated the low, heavy cloud cover.

A last gasp, perhaps, Morqla mused with some bitterness as he brushed dust and dirt from himself. *Do what you must to retain what little dignity and honor you still possess. It will make no difference.*

Looking down, he regarded the unrecognizable body of K'voq, now nothing more than a lifeless shell while his warrior's spirit made the journey to *Sto-Vo-Kor*. Rage welled up within him, and Morqla felt his muscles tense, blood rushing in his veins as he drew air into his lungs and released a deep, bellowing howl that rattled every ounce of his being. The *Heghtay* cry echoed off the walls of the surrounding buildings, augmenting the glorious ritual and heightening the warning he issued to the dead that a warrior was about to enter their midst.

His anger refused to abate, however, fueled by the knowledge that there was no honor in dying before an enemy who attacked from the shadows, one too weak or timid to stand on the field of battle and engage an opponent while looking them in the eyes. It was possible that loyal K'voq might yet be denied the ultimate fate promised to all loyal warriors who died in service to the empire.

"Worry not, old friend," Morqla said to the still-burning remnants of his long-trusted aide. "I will see to it that you are greeted in *Sto-Vo-Kor* as you deserve."

Turning away from the gruesome sight, the governor headed into the courtyard and the chaos threatening to consume it. There would be much blood spilled before the sun colored the horizon, he decided, and he wanted to be sure that some of it stained his own blade.

He ran through the narrow streets leading away from the courtyard, toward the sounds of running and screaming coming from the direction of the main entrance to the village. Rounding a corner, he emerged into an open plaza that prior to the occupation had been used by the villagers as a meeting and entertainment venue. Now it was the scene of unchecked carnage as dozens of *jegh-pu'wI'* fell beneath the onslaught of a mobile disruptor cannon. Klingon soldiers added to the unchecked chaos of the scene by firing their own weapons into the scrambling crowd. Others had waded into the mass of villagers, attacking them with blades or with bare hands.

Ruthless bursts of brutal crimson energy sliced through the night air, cutting through wood, stone, and soft flesh with equal impunity. The stench of death filled the plaza, a disjointed chorus of horrific screams and plaintive, vain calls for help or mercy competing with the rhythmic, mechanical cycling of the massive weapon. In the cannon's operator seat, a Klingon soldier sat with his face pressed to the gunner's sight that covered the front portion of his head, focusing his view on the disruptor's computer-generated targeting display. From his own experience as a young officer manning such a weapon, Morqla knew that anyone or anything unfortunate enough to fall within the targeting sights of the cannon's fire-control computer was as good as dead.

Hurried movement from his right caught his attention, and Morqla turned to see an atypically large Palgrenai lunging for him, brandishing what looked to be a shovel. Feeble moonlight reflected off the tool's dulled, rusted blade, and it was obvious to the governor that the villager was attacking out of desperation. Saliva dripped from both sides of its narrow, elongated mouth, and Morqla saw rows of teeth bared in anger and fear as it charged forward, releasing a garbled hiss.

Morqla ducked as the flat side of the shovel swung past his head, taking advantage of the Palgrenai's sudden loss of balance to step forward and deliver a powerful punch to his attacker's head. He felt bone cave beneath his fist as he drove it down into the villager's skull, and the *jeghpu'wI'* dropped to the ground, already dead but its body offering up a final series of spasms as life drained from its dark, leathery carcass.

Now feeling the heat of battle coursing through his veins, Morqla turned away from his first kill of the night and began looking for another.

And then he saw it.

A dark, indistinct blur, it might have been humanoid but it moved with such speed that there was no way to be certain. There was no time to study it, for no sooner had it appeared than it lunged for the Klingon soldier closest to it.

"Defend yourselves!" Morqla shouted, but it was already too late. The creature, whatever it was, towered over the warrior, who saw it only at the last moment and tried to bring his weapon around. His movements were far too slow as the new arrival loomed closer, lashing out with at least two extremities that Morqla was able to distinguish from its fluid, undulating form. They slashed across the soldier, and the governor felt his mouth go slack as he watched his subordinate instantly separated into four lifeless hunks of dismembered flesh, bone, and clothing, each falling to the floor of the plaza and releasing a torrent of blood that stained the dark, dry cobblestones.

Uttering a tortured, enraged battle cry, Morqla raised his disruptor and fired at the creature even as it moved again, the pulsing red energy bolts chewing into the stone of the nearby buildings as the thing moved. Other soldiers were firing at it now, as well, a few of their shots even hitting it, of that Morqla was certain, but their efforts seemed to have no effect.

"What *is* it?" he heard someone yell above the hail of disruptor fire as the creature, all but formless and defying description, moved with deliberate haste, altering its path not the least in reaction to the attack now being directed at it. Instead, it charged other members of his garrison, and blood arced into the air yet again as whatever unholy blades the thing wielded found new targets, and two more of his men fell decapitated to the ground. The appalling scene was repeated twice within the space of seconds, with half a dozen of his soldiers unable to flee the creature's unchecked wrath as it slashed again and again, with Morqla watching helpless as the thing cut through his men with the ease of a fish swimming through water.

Then it changed direction yet again, this time its trajectory bringing it directly at Morqla.

"Come to me, you filthy *ha'DIbah*!" he roared, standing his ground and firing at his nearing opponent, watching as the bolts from his disruptor were swallowed by the creature's body, which reflected none of the light cast off by the cloud-dulled moon or the surrounding fires. Undeterred by the weapon, the thing drew closer, threatening to block out everything with its looming, all-encompassing darkness.

Then the concentrated whine of the disruptor cannon erupted

in the plaza once more, and Morqla saw the creature enveloped by a cocoon of frenzied scarlet energy. A chilling wail of pain echoed off the walls around him, and he watched as the thing crumpled beneath the force of the cannon's blast.

Thankfully, the soldier operating the formidable weapon had the sense to fire again, unleashing another hellish barrage upon the creature. This time the effects were more pronounced, parts of the thing's formless, featureless hide exploding as its molecular structure was decimated by the disruptor cannon. Morqla saw the creature's body start to come apart, finally surrendering to the weapon's vicious fury before collapsing in upon itself in a burst of destabilized molecules that within seconds faded altogether.

The silence enveloping the plaza in the aftermath of the horrendous firefight was all but deafening now, Morqla realized. His soldiers could only stand in silent awe, staring at the patch of scorched stone where only moments before the creature had stood. Even those Palgrenai who had survived the initial wave of attacks by his garrison could only look on, the terror and uncertainty in their wide, dark eyes matching Morqla's own as each of them tried to comprehend the staggering scene they had just witnessed.

"What servant of *Gre'thor* has *Fek'lhr* unleashed upon us now?" he asked aloud, but the night swallowed his question whole.

27

"Report!"

On the bridge of the imperial cruiser *Zin'za,* Captain Kutal snarled the order, shouting to be heard over the dull drone of the alert klaxon. Gripping the armrests of his chair with his massive hands, he felt the deck still heaving beneath his heavy boots as his helmsman fought to bring the ship back under some semblance of control.

Over his right shoulder, sparks erupted from the communications console, sending the officer manning that station stumbling backward with his arms thrown up to protect his face. Acrid smoke tinged the already warm air, and the taste of burned insulation and wiring coated his tongue. All around him, consoles blinked and flickered in concert with the compromised overhead lighting, telling Kutal that the ship's main power systems were suffering in the wake of the massive, unexpected attack on his vessel.

"It is a planet-based weapons system!" was the shouted report from his tactical officer, Lieutenant Tonar. "The attack was launched from four of the locations where we detected the unexplained power readings."

Of course. Kutal cursed his lack of foresight as he studied the green-brown ball that was the lush world of Palgrenax, rotating before him on the bridge's main viewscreen. Tonar had first detected power sources coming online from sixteen separate locations on the planet's largest continent—each of them situated far beneath the surface—less than a *kilaan* before. Each of the locations appeared to be receiving its power via geothermal vents carved from the bowels of the planet and channeled to what Tonar had identified as massive generation and distribution venues. The technology was unlike anything on record, and estimates of the equipment's age placed it as being older than most explored civilizations in this quadrant of the explored galaxy.

And yet, it works, Kutal mused. It was not lost on him that at least seven of the locations corresponded to sites that Dr. Terath determined featured examples of the ancient structures and technology which had so drawn her interest.

"The energy discharged from those locations combined into one beam for a single strike," Tonar continued. "If our shields had been down, we might be crippled now."

And those other twelve power readings might be weapons stations, as well.

"Move the ship to a higher orbit," Kutal ordered his helmsman. "Route power from nonessential systems to the shields." He knew he did not have to elaborate as he spoke the words. The *Zin'za*'s chief engineer would take the directive at face value, channeling energy from every shipboard system save weapons—including life-support—to strengthen the vessel's defenses. Of Tonar, he asked, "What about those other sites? Are they a danger?"

His large hands playing over the tactical console that seemed too small to accommodate his oversized, muscled physique, Tonar consulted an array of status monitors. "I do not believe so, Captain. They are not showing power readings on the same scale as the locations which combined to attack us. However, the original four sites appear to be cycling through their earlier power levels and internal temperatures are rising." Turning to Kutal, he added, "They may be preparing to fire again."

Kutal shook his head in mounting anger. "What has Morqla released from the depths of that cursed rock?"

The governor's harried, fragmented report had offered little in the way of useful information. At first confronted by the brazen, if ultimately futile, series of raids and disruptions set into motion by segments of the planet's native inhabitants, Morqla and his garrison apparently had been forced to direct their efforts and focus to a new, more powerful threat, with numbers of his warriors facing off against mysterious humanoid figures that seemed more like wraiths or apparitions than physical beings. More surprising to Kutal even than this outlandish account were the claims that Morqla's troops were being bested by a mere handful of these creatures, with the unknown assailants taking on and killing dozens of Klingon soldiers.

The very notion is as obscene as it is absurd. Kutal felt his jaw clench and his jagged teeth grind in frustration as the thought coalesced, knowing even as it did so that his brusque dismissal of the notion was incorrect. Morqla, despite his many flaws, was not given to flights of fancy or irrationality. His report, coupled with the happenings beneath the planet's surface and the attack on the *Zin'za,* told Kutal everything he needed to know about just how serious the situation was in danger of becoming.

"Damage reports are coming in now, Captain," said Lieutenant Kreq, his communications officer, who had taken the initiative to transfer the functions of his regular station to one of the smaller, backup consoles at the back of the bridge. "There is a coolant leak in weapons control, and engineering reports that antimatter containment has been weakened. He may have to take the warp engines offline."

Kutal growled in dissatisfaction, shaking his head in disgust as he considered the idiot currently serving as the *Zin'za*'s chief engineer. "Tell him if he does that, I'll personally see to it that he's ground up and fed to the *jeghpu'wI'* on the planet." Had the fool never seen combat? To even suggest that the ship deliberately be deprived of its primary power systems at such a time was ignorance at best, and treasonous at worst.

He made a note to execute the engineer at the earliest possible opportunity. For now, there were other matters to consider.

"So, it seems this planet has more to offer than even the High Command first realized," Kutal said to no one in particular as the annoying, wailing alarm finally was silenced. Illumination on the bridge was now a deep red in keeping with the ship's heightened alert level, and a quick glance to the tactical station along the left bulkhead told him that the *Zin'za*'s deflector shields were still up, though their strength had been weakened by the unexpected attack from the planet's surface.

Naturally, he should have suspected something untoward the moment Tonar reported weapons fire coming from the settlement where Governor Morqla had elected to establish headquarters for his planetary occupation. The activation of the power source—located beneath the same village where Dr. Terath had been concentrating her research since her arrival—seemed to be an additional warning he should have heeded.

Hindsight is a crutch for politicians, he reminded himself, *and warriors unable to adapt to the flow of battle.*

Turning to his tactical officer, Kutal said, "Target those locations and stand by weapons." His brow furrowing, he added, "Was one of the sites beneath Morqla's headquarters?"

The tactical officer shook his head, the gesture causing his long, wild hair to twist about his broad shoulders. "No, Captain."

"A pity," Kutal replied. He possessed little respect for the governor, Terath, or any of her ilk. It might have been nice to eliminate two problems with a single strike. "What caused those power generations? Was it Terath?"

"Unknown," Tonar replied. "I'm not able to establish contact with the research team or Governor Morqla."

It had been several moments since the initial reports of disruptor fire from the surface, and Tonar had reported sensor indications of fires emanating from structures from six different settlements scattered throughout the region where Morqla had centered his occupation. From high above the planet, the scenario appeared easy to describe: The natives of Palgrenax had become discontent with their roles as servants to the empire, and finally had summoned the courage to do something about it.

Kutal respected the Palgrenai's bravery and apparent resolve to stand up to a superior foe and do their best to drive their oppressors from their home, even though the cold reality was that their efforts ultimately would prove pitiful and fruitless. Still, he thought, it might have at least been invigorating to be on the planet's surface right now, participating in the quelling of the uprising.

Not that he lacked his own matters to deal with at present, of course.

His attention was drawn to a series of tones emanating from the tactical station, and he turned to see Tonar looking at him. "Captain, our sensors are registering a low-level communications signal being transmitted between the different underground sites, as well as to whoever is attacking our forces on the ground. It's a scrambled signal, employing an encryption scheme I have never seen before."

"Can the transmissions be jammed?" Kutal asked.

Tonar shook his head. "I have already tried, sir, but there is no effect."

Impressive technology, the *Zin'za*'s captain ceded, particularly given that by all accounts the responsible civilization had been dead for uncounted millennia. "If we cannot squelch it, then we shall remove it altogether. Target the source of those transmissions." Nodding in satisfaction at his own plan, Kutal swiveled his chair back around so that he faced the bridge's main viewer once more. "Helmsman, prepare to alter course. Tactical, stand by for orbital bombardment."

Behind him, he heard Tonar enter several series of commands before announcing, "Targets plotted, Captain."

Whatever had deigned to attack soldiers of the Klingon Empire—to say nothing of one of the emperor's finest battle cruisers—Kutal vowed to demonstrate the foolhardiness of that ill-informed choice.

Pain!

Though not unexpected as they were during the first assault, the all-encompassing waves of agony washed yet again over the Shedai Wanderer as a second of her Sentinels succumbed to the irrepressible power of weapons the *Telinaruul* had brought to bear. The energy from that initial attack had taken her by surprise; so unprepared was she for such an aggressive defense that she nearly failed to sever her connection to the overwhelmed Sentinel.

As it was, only frantic last-instant action had enabled her to withdraw the tendrils extending from her mind and pull them back to the safety of the Conduit. Ensconced within the depths of what had once been a proud monument to her civilization's technological prowess and the alacrity with which they had employed that knowledge to rule this entire region of space, the Wanderer registered the torment exacted upon the guardians she had sent forth as though the wounds were being inflicted on herself. So painstaking in detail and precision was the connection she shared with her servants that every sense was as if experienced firsthand. From the warm breeze that failed to cool her, to the bright lights being shone upon her as her opponents attacked from the predawn shadows, to the shock of tortured nerve endings reacting to the particle beams being directed at those she commanded, the Wanderer was immersed in all of these sensations as though it were her standing on the surface.

And along with the pain came another sensation for which the Wanderer had received no preparation: fear. Never before in her lifetime—before the uncounted generations that had passed since she had first yielded to the long, cold sleep—had she experienced such trepidation, and never when facing lesser beings such as those the Shedai once had ruled.

Refocusing her attention on the third of six Sentinels she had dispatched to disparate locations across the surface of the world above, the Wanderer once again felt the energy of life coursing through her consciousness as she directed the guardian's movements. She sensed yet ignored the impacts of the energy weapons the lesser beings carried, their personal weapons too small and inconsequential to inflict any significant damage to the body she wore. Gravity weighed against it as she directed it to face approaching attackers, and she relished the feel of its stoneglass arms slicing through fragile flesh and bone. So sensitive were the receptors formed into the shell's bioconstruct that the Wanderer even felt the warmth and moisture of *Telinaruul* blood as it splashed across the Sentinel's face.

Upon first dispatching the team of guardians, she had likened her opponents to those she had encountered on the ice-bound planet from which she had come. They certainly were larger, stronger, and even more aggressive than those she had fought on that world, something she had taken into account when choosing to deploy more than one Sentinel on this occasion.

She initially considered that she might have overcompensated as the first of the Sentinels engaged the *Telinaruul* on the planet's surface. Despite their heightened ferocity—something the Wanderer actually had found refreshing—her opponents initially had proven to be little more than the bothersome pests she previously had encountered. As before, the Sentinel now at her command rebuffed the brave yet pitiful attempts at attack, pushing through the *Telinaruul* with the ease of water flowing over rocks in a stream.

Similar scenes were playing out in much the same fashion with the other three Sentinels that shared her consciousness. More of the opponents were coming to the individual battles now, showing none of the fear of those she had encountered on the barren, glaciated planet. If anything, losing comrades in battle seemed to be having the opposite effect, spurring them on to even greater hostility and fury. Likewise, this heightened emotional response did not seem to detract from their tactics or sense of awareness while doing battle. Indeed, even as her Sentinels cut down and slaughtered a growing number of their brethren, the Wanderer surmised that this species of lesser life-form appeared to thrive on the chaos and intensity of combat.

They are a proud people. It is a pity that they must be destroyed, but their meddling cannot be tolerated.

She already had killed those *Telinaruul* whom she found skulking within the winding corridors of the subterranean complex that housed the Conduit anchor point's power-generation and support structures. Those beings had provided nothing in the way of a challenge, certainly nothing like she was experiencing on the surface. It was those engagements that now were giving her cause for concern as, for the first time since unleashing her cadre of guardians to the surface, the Wanderer was feeling the initial pull of fatigue. The demands of directing the Sentinels when coupled with her need to oversee the global defense network as it dealt with the vessel in orbit above the planet were causing a pronounced strain—one the likes of which she had not been required to endure for unknown generations. If the splintered, protracted battles continued, the notion of her opponents gaining a decisive advantage moved from dim hope to potential threat.

She felt another barrage of weapons fire—channeled from another of the Sentinels through the Conduit to her own stressed consciousness as the *Telinaruul* began their assault anew—and directed the guardian to retaliate. Her opponents were so close now that olfactory senses relayed the pungent stench of unwashed bodies and foul breath consistent with a carnivorous diet. One of them released a loud, fierce cry of anger as it and a companion lunged forward, each brandishing a large edged weapon with a curved blade.

The Wanderer was able to admire the attackers' skill as they employed the implements in an almost choreographed series of maneuvers no doubt designed not only to intimidate an enemy but also to celebrate a culture that had long ago embraced ritualized aspects of the combat arts. She could admire such devotion, as the Shedai had long fancied themselves accomplished practitioners of similar martial disciplines. Further, it was that appreciation which allowed her to more quickly and easily detect her oncoming opponents' weaknesses and more appropriately adjust her counterattack.

Her fatigue was greater than she had first surmised, however. It was only as the larger, mobile energy weapon—one similar to those already deployed against her other Sentinels—had finished moving into position that the Wanderer took notice of it. By then it was too late and she felt her entire consciousness gripped in a torrent of shock and pain as the weapon was unleashed on the Sentinel. The connection she shared with the servant body fluctuated and threatened to dissolve altogether, carrying with it the very real risk of leaving her essence trapped within the guardian's mortal shell and at the mercy of the mighty weapon as it fired once more.

Sensing yet another loss, the Wanderer had no choice but to withdraw from the Sentinel, recalling that part of herself back to the Conduit just as her servant body surrendered to the barrage of energy enveloping it. She felt the last vestiges of its life consumed by the weapon's ferocious power even as she struggled to refocus her flagging strength between the three remaining Sentinels and the needs of the global network she was trying to direct.

It was foolish to have overextended herself in this manner, she realized, though there was nothing to be done about correcting her flawed decision, particularly now as the defense system's orbital sensor web informed her that the *Telinaruul* ship in orbit was repositioning itself for what probability algorithms described as an attack profile.

From deep within her own being, the Wanderer saw the scene as if floating in space before the enemy vessel, watching as its weapons ports spouted a series of blazing crimson plumes. Eight elongated spheres of packaged energy raced away from the ship and plummeted toward the planet below, accelerating and superheating as they entered the atmosphere. She watched as they divided into pairs before separating, four double contrails cutting swaths through the still-dark sky and the dense cloud cover.

The first vicious jolt came moments later. Alarm indicators streamed through the Conduit to her, reaching out from points within the planet's global information network. Immediately she felt the loss of connection to one of the defense system's vital hubs, then sensed the decline in her control over the rest of the system. The sensation was repeated twice more in rapid succession as more of the ship's torpedoes found their intended targets and detonated, laying waste to yet more support facilities.

When the fourth volley struck, the Wanderer had no choice but to withdraw from the defense system, leaving it behind in a desperate attempt to preserve herself. Even as she redirected her consciousness to other areas of the thoughtspace, she felt the demise of the protective network, collapsing in on itself as the physical structures and equipment that supported it fell victim to the barrage of fire raining down from space.

Struggling to retain some semblance of focus on what little of this world's Conduit anchor point remained, she observed that only a few of the key systems were available to her. Even her access to her remaining Sentinels had been compromised, her essence now feeling the effects of their disconnection from the Conduit and thusly vulnerable to her aggressors' weapons. She could do nothing about that now, just as she was unable to manufacture and deploy replacements for those guardians which already had been lost. Those areas of the thoughtspace remained unavailable to her, and reestablishing an interface to those channels would take far more time than she believed remained to her.

Once again, the Wanderer felt fear at the realization that she was on the brink of being overcome by these *Telinaruul*. All the Shedai held dear on this world, everything for which they had prepared as part of her people's vision to return to power, might be at stake if left in the hands of these savage interlopers.

Only one option remains.

28

With each strike of the *Zin'za*'s torpedoes, Kutal released a deep, wolfish laugh of unrestrained satisfaction.

"Continue bombardment!" he shouted to Tonar. "I want every one of those sites reduced to burning cinders." A tactical overlay displayed on the main viewer showed him the current assessment of the orbital attack's effectiveness, and he nodded in approval at what he saw. Of the sixteen sites determined to house active power sources which had come online as of their own accord, six of them had apparently been destroyed thanks to Tonar's skilled marksmanship.

Whatever the ancient planetary defense system possessed in raw power, it seemed obvious to Kutal that it appeared to be lacking in something as basic as a means of protecting itself from attack. Perhaps the original designers had believed their offensive capabilities to be so superior as to nullify the ability of an enemy to counterattack. While Kutal could grasp and even admire such audacity, there was a fine line to be drawn between confidence and foolhardiness, and it appeared this world's long-departed original inhabitants had chosen to travel on that divider's wrong side.

Such are the fortunes of battle.

Kutal knew he was taking a risk by releasing the full fury of his vessel's armaments, given the apparent importance the High Council placed on the plethora of ancient structures and artifacts littering the planet, which presumably also would include any weapons technology that might be hidden down there. Still, whoever or whatever now commanded the weaponry being used against his ship as well as the garrison on the surface could not be allowed to escape punishment for their actions. Those on the planet below, or by extension beings native to the Gonmog Sector and unfamiliar with the political realities of neighboring regions, would learn at Kutal's hand the imprudence of daring to challenge the Klingon Empire.

It's long past time we announced our presence in this sector with due authority.

"Adjusting orbit to bring us in line with the next set of targets, sir," Kutal heard his helm officer report, and on the viewer he noted the angle of Palgrenax shift as the *Zin'za* modified its position over the planet. The tactical overlay highlighted sites that already had fallen victim to the battle cruiser's weapons; bright red circles were superimposed on the computer-generated map of the world's natural topography.

"Sensors are continuing to register subterranean power sources," Tonar called out. The tactical officer turned from his console to regard Kutal. "It appears there are redundant systems which are coming online to compensate for the primary targets we're destroying."

His brow furrowing as he rubbed his chin, Kutal nodded at the report. "Perhaps those original designers were not so shortsighted, after all. Factor the new targets into your firing scheme and relay revised coordinates to the helm." To Lieutenant Kreq at the communications station, he asked, "Any contact with Morqla or the garrison?"

Kreq replied, "I'm unable to reach the governor, Captain, but I am continuing to get scattered reports from other officers on the ground. The battles continue, both with *jeghpu'wI'* as well as the new enemy. There are accounts of many casualties, though no reliable estimates as of yet."

The report did nothing to assuage Kutal's growing concerns. What was going on down there? Where had the strange attackers on the surface come from? Did they live underground, somehow shielded from the scrutiny of his vessel's powerful sensors? Had they arrived from elsewhere, perhaps in another ship he somehow had failed to detect? Who controlled the mammoth network of weapons which had been deployed against his own ship? What other capabilities did they possess?

Swearing a particularly vile oath under his breath, Kutal rose from his chair and stalked toward the front of the bridge until he stood before the main viewscreen. He crossed his arms and watched as the *Zin'za*'s orbit shifted to align with the next targets called for by Tonar's bombardment plan. The area of the planet now visible to him was still shrouded in darkness and dominated by dense cloud cover, preventing him from seeing the outlines of the continents or even those areas that now burned in the aftermath of orbital attack. His inability to see his targets only deepened the mystery surrounding the odd battle he now waged.

"New targets selected," Kutal heard Tonar say from behind him. "All weapons are ready. I await your . . ."

When the rest of the customary report did not come, Kutal turned away from the viewer and saw the tactical officer hunched over his console, his face bathed in warm yellow as he peered with intense scrutiny at one of the sensor display monitors.

"Massive spikes in power readings are being detected across the planet," Tonar finally said. "Geothermal activity is rising rapidly."

"Helm, break orbit," Kutal said, feeling the hair on the back of his muscled neck stand up as he considered the report. "Prepare for evasive maneuvering." If their faceless enemy was preparing to unleash yet another weapon against his ship, he wanted to be ready.

Then Tonar whirled away from the tactical station, his eyes wide with terror. "Captain, the planet! We need to move away from it! Now!"

Frowning, Kutal turned back toward the viewer, muscles tensing in anticipation of a renewed attack from the surface. "What?"

Despite himself, the captain felt his mouth fall open in mute shock.

The rim of the planet seemed to glow as the blanket of clouds shrouding his view of the world below began to burn away before his eyes. Was it his imagination, or was he able to discern cracks in the very continents themselves, easily visible even from his vantage point thousands of *qell'qams* overhead? Highlighted in bright orange as magma from deep within the planet's crust was forced to the surface, the fractures appeared to widen and multiply with every passing heartbeat.

"What in the name of Kahless is this?" Kutal asked, though of course he expected no one on the bridge to answer. Whatever was causing the horrific scene before him, common sense told him that it could not possibly be a natural phenomenon. No indications of problems beneath the surface had been detected on any previous sensor scan. The only explanation for what he was seeing—as startling as it was to contemplate—was that it was the result of a deliberate act. Who or what could possess such power?

Ask your questions later! The mental rebuke stung with the force of a physical blow. *Assuming you survive!*

"Get us out of here!" Kutal shouted, pointing to his helm officer even as he pivoted on his heel and lunged for his chair at the center of the bridge. "Full impulse power!" Slamming his fist down on the arm of his chair with such force that he thought he might break the control pad embedded there, he shouted into the intercom, "Engineering! Stand by warp drive!"

"What about our warriors on the planet?" Tonar asked, his expression a mixture of shock and confusion. "We cannot leave them."

"They're already dead!" Kutal said, his attention riveted to the main viewer. The deck plates vibrated and even shifted slightly beneath his boots, the *Zin'za*'s harried maneuvering away from the planet coming so quickly that the ship's inertial-dampening systems struggled to maintain balance for the robust yet still fragile living beings inside it. Below and far behind the bridge, the steady drone of the battle cruiser's impulse engines increased to a whine that was transmitted across every surface of the ship as their power amplified in response to his orders. On the viewscreen, Kutal saw plumes of lava and magma hurled skyward from the surface as the tortured planet slid out of view.

Anyone on the surface, he knew—be they Klingon, *jegh-pu'wI'*, or whatever had put this entire nightmarish scenario into motion—was doomed. If they were fortunate, they already were dead, and would be spared the apocalypse that was to come.

"Reverse angle!" he ordered, feeling the ship complete its rotation as his helm officer aimed its bow for the comparable safety of deep space. The image on the viewer shifted as the impulse drive kicked in and the planet began to recede on the screen.

Then there was nothing for Kutal to do except watch with an odd mixture of horror and fascination as the entirety of Palgrenax collapsed in upon itself.

"Shock wave approaching!" shouted Centurion Darjil from his workstation at the center of the *Bloodied Talon*'s bridge. "Impact in fifteen *ewa!*"

Pointing to the centurion manning the helm console, Commander Sarith ordered, "Evasive! Deactivate the cloak and engage warp drive! Emergency power to the shields!"

With everyone on the bridge scrambling to carry out their tasks, Sarith watched as the planet came apart, splintering into billions of fragments that along with magma from the ill-fated world's molten core were hurled outward in all directions. The core itself, freed from the tremendous tectonic and geothermal pressure at the heart of the planet, vaporized as it surrendered to sudden vacuum, generating a maelstrom of frenzied color and violent energy that served only to punctuate the awesome destructive power which had been unleashed.

None of that mattered to her now, however. The largest threat at this moment was what she could not see.

"Tactical plot!" she ordered, and Centurion N'tovek responded by activating a computer-created digital map outlining the ship's current position in relation to the world referred to by its native inhabitants as Palgrenax. More accurately, it depicted where Palgrenax once had been, along with the trajectory of the Klingon vessel that the *Talon*'s sensors had been observing from behind the curtain of stealth offered by the ship's cloaking device. The battle cruiser was already long gone, having made the jump to warp speed well ahead of the spherical shock wave also displayed on the map. The wave emanated outward from what had been the center of the planet, expanding in all directions with speed far greater than that of the *Talon*.

"Where are my warp engines?" she called out even as she felt the first effects of the wave beginning to wash over the ship. Her bridge crew gripped support struts, consoles, anything that might provide a handhold while bulkheads shook and deck plating rattled. In the depths of the ship, powerful engines attempted to wrestle it from the orbit of the planet at it succumbed to its death throes. Above all of that, she heard the cycling of the cloaking device as it was deactivated and all of the power it required in order to operate was redirected to the warp drive.

Sarith knew her ship. She was intimately familiar with all of its inner workings. She understood its defects as well as its strengths, its idiosyncrasies and the telltale sounds it made. Because of that awareness, she could decipher from the sound of the *Talon*'s engines—groaning as they received power once hoarded by the cloaking device and clamoring for more—that they would not achieve the levels needed to accelerate to warp speed before it was too late.

"Channel all available power to the shields!" she shouted. "Everything including life-support!"

Sarith heard the objecting groans of the *Talon*'s power-distribution system as the emergency changeover went into effect. Lights flickered across the bridge, and on the master systems station she saw computer-simulated representations of energy being redirected from systems that—should this tactic fail—would become irrelevant in short order.

Above it all, the force of the shock wave was becoming more pronounced. Every surface of the bridge vibrated, and a deep rumbling reverberated through the hull. In her mind's eye, Sarith saw the wave coming at her, threatening to envelop her and the *Talon* like a wave crashing over rocks on a distant shoreline.

Beside her, Ineti tapped the control on a wall-mounted communications interface. "All hands, brace for impact." Then there was nothing more for him to do except grab Sarith by the arm and push her toward a nearby bulkhead and the handhold mounted there. She gripped the handle with both hands, muscles tensing as she counted down the *ewa* until . . .

A deafening thunderclap roared through the bridge as Sarith felt herself upended and slammed into the bulkhead. Her handhold slipped from her fingers and she was thrown to the deck as the reverberation of the shock wave playing across the *Talon's* overstressed deflector shields was translated through the hull of the ship. The cacophony all but drowned out the alarm klaxons and cries of fear and distress that came as the lights flickered and died, plunging the command deck into near darkness, with the only illumination coming from the room's array of display monitors and consoles.

Still tumbling without control across the pitching deck, Sarith finally came to a halt as she slammed into the support mounting that housed the central hub workstations. The column's sharp corner caught her in the side just below her rib cage and she felt bone snap, forcing the air from her lungs and making her cry out in pain.

"Emergency power to structural integrity and inertial dampeners!" she called out, each word like a stab to her injured side. She knew there was no way to outrun or outmaneuver the wave, and that their best option for survival was to ensure the continued operation of those shipboard systems which could prevent the crew from being killed simply by being tossed about the vessel's interior.

The effects of the shock wave finally were ebbing, and Sarith felt the ship slowly beginning to calm itself as the dampeners compensated and reestablished normal gravity. Holding her damaged ribs, she gritted her teeth and struggled to sit up amid showers of sparks illuminating the otherwise gloomy bridge. The odor of burned wiring and insulation stung her nostrils and she looked up to see two of the master systems monitors erupt into flame, spewing glass and composite plastics across the deck.

Other muffled explosions echoed across the bridge, followed by a howl of agony from somewhere over her left shoulder that made Sarith flinch. She looked up to see N'tovek falling away from his workstation and landing with a sickening thud as his helmeted head struck the deck. Even in the feeble light she could make out mangled and flash-burned flesh on his hands and face.

No!

"Alert the doctor," Sarith called out above the chaos enveloping the bridge. Clenching her jaw to bite back her own pain, she pulled herself around the central hub to where N'tovek lay unmoving. Ineti beat her there, kneeling down beside the fallen officer and immediately placing his fingers to the side of the other man's neck. Sarith saw the fragments of shrapnel that mutilated the centurion's once-handsome face, and that his eyes were fixed and staring at the ceiling, and knew without doubt that N'tovek was beyond any help the *Talon*'s physician, Ineti, or even she might provide.

"It does not appear that he suffered," Ineti offered as he reached up to close the dead centurion's eyes. "That much is fortunate, at least."

Forcing the gamut of emotions raging inside her to remain beneath the veneer of composure she was fighting to keep in place, Sarith used her free hand to pull herself up, every movement agony as she rose to her feet. All around her, emergency lighting positioned at key points along the bridge's perimeter struggled to activate, their weak attempts doing little to dispel the near total blackness engulfing the cramped chamber.

"Damage reports coming in from all decks," Darjil called out from where he had resumed his duty station. "System overloads and malfunctions are scattered across the ship."

"Give me vital systems status," Sarith ordered, moving her way across the bridge to the chair behind her small yet functional desk. As she slumped into the chair, she noted that the computer terminal was charred black, it too a victim of the rampant overloads plaguing the ship.

Darjil replied, "Life-support is operating on backup power systems, and warp drive is offline." Looking up from his console, he added, "The engineer reports that the antimatter containment sphere was cracked and he was forced to eject the entire assembly."

Sarith looked to Ineti as she absorbed the report, saw her own anxiety mirrored in her friend's eyes. Both of them just as quickly buried their momentary emotional lapse beneath their professional façades for the sake of their subordinates on the bridge, all of whom were now regarding her with varying expressions of fear and uncertainty. There was no need for anyone to say anything more with regard to what Darjil had just conveyed.

To a person, all of them knew what the loss of the antimatter containment system meant. Without it, the *Talon*'s warp drive was useless. Unable to achieve faster-than-light velocities, the ship and its crew were centuries from Romulan space.

They would never see home again.

"What about communications?" she asked Darjil, for the first time noting that dark green blood was streaming down the younger man's face.

"Partially functional," the centurion replied. "Long-range communications are offline, but initial reports are that it can be repaired."

Crossing the deck toward the central hub, Ineti asked, "What about the cloak?"

Darjil nodded. "Still functional, Subcommander."

How propitious, Sarith mused with no small amount of bitterness. *If we die out here, we still can do so with utmost stealth.* Almost as soon as the thought manifested itself, she forced it away. There were always alternatives, even in the most desperate of situations, but unchecked emotion could blind one's judgment and ability to see those options.

"Notify the engineer that communications and life-support are priority," she said, sucking air through gritted teeth as the pain in her ribs began to assert itself with renewed force. She knew she would soon have to see the physician, but now was not the time. With the crisis they faced just becoming clear, her officers needed to see her maintaining her position of leadership and control over the situation.

Such as it is.

As if reading her mind, Ineti added, "Pass on to the crew that we'll need to conserve power as much as possible."

Sarith nodded in approval at the subcommander's initiative.

Without the warp engines to provide primary power, she knew that the additional strain on the impulse drive would force some shipboard systems to rely on battery backups until repairs were complete and power requirements assessed and appropriately redirected.

The bridge's softer secondary illumination, coupled with the thin shroud of smoke hanging in the air, appeared to make the angled bulkheads loom even closer in the feeble, flickering light.

For an insane moment, Sarith was reminded of her childhood aversion to small, confined spaces, which had manifested itself one fateful summer when torrential rains had flooded caves littering the mining quarry near her family's village. Naturally she and her young companions had disregarded parental warnings to stay away from the dangerous mines, a willful decision that exacted a tragic cost. It had taken several *dierha* to reach the surface in the dark, and only after one of her friends and playmates, a young boy whose name escaped her now, had been swept deep into the maze of underground tunnels by the onrushing water. His body was never recovered, and it was the last time Sarith ever would set foot anywhere near the quarry.

If only such a choice were available now.

Looking about the damage-stricken bridge, she could not keep her gaze from finding N'tovek. Even in death, she still could discern some of the same peace and vulnerability she had observed while watching him sleep. Once more she felt a pang of sorrow grip her heart, made all the worse from knowing that she never again would enjoy the pleasure of observing her lover in repose, to say nothing of the other joys the younger man had managed to bring to her otherwise lonely, duty-bound life.

"What happened?" she finally asked after a moment, looking to Ineti for guidance and answers. "Only massive tectonic stress could have destroyed a planet like that, but our sensors detected nothing? That's ludicrous. How could Darjil or . . ." She shook her head as a sudden lump formed in her throat, and she swallowed it before continuing. "How could he or N'tovek miss something like that?"

"They didn't," Ineti said, moving around from the far side of the central hub, taking a moment to offer a paternal pat to Darjil's shoulder before continuing over to her. "No sensor scans detected anything unusual about this planet, save for the Klingon presence. It's only been in the last *dierha* that we received indications of anything untoward occurring down there."

Sarith nodded. The power readings, while significant and emanating from multiple points around the planet, had come as something of a surprise, particularly given Darjil's original report, which showed the indigenous population as being a preindustrial society. The only technology in existence had belonged to the Klingon garrison that had usurped the native civilization, though that in itself also was a mystery.

While her initial assessment had been that the Klingons perhaps had claimed this planet to act as a base to support ship operations within the sector, even casual scrutiny revealed the problems with that theory. The *Talon*'s sensors had detected no hints of ship maintenance facilities, for instance, not so much as a lone orbital drydock. Likewise, there were no indications of planet-based refining or manufacturing installations.

"Those power readings," Sarith said after a moment. "They were far above anything the Klingons could have generated with the equipment of theirs that we detected. Could they have found something else? Something unknown even to the local population?"

Pausing to consider the idea, Ineti nodded. "I suppose it's possible." Then he shrugged. "We'll never know for certain, though."

Tempted to chastise her friend for stating the obvious, Sarith instead grunted an acknowledgment of the subcommander's observation before turning back toward the rest of the bridge. The ache in her ribs was announcing its presence with relish now, but she ignored it. Ineti must have seen the wince she could not hold in check, however, and leaned forward.

"Let me call the physician," he said, concern swathing every word. "You do not look well."

Sarith waved away the suggestion. "Later," she replied as she saw Darjil turn from his station and look to her with what appeared to be an expression of puzzlement clouding his bloody, soiled features. "We have much to see to first." To the centurion, she asked, "What is it?"

"Commander," Darjil said, "before the planet exploded, our sensors were operating in both passive and active modes, at least so far as the cloak would allow. I missed it before, but it seems that the sensors registered a low-level energy signature connecting the different sites on the planet where we detected the unexplained power readings."

Her brow furrowing in confusion, Sarith shook her head. "They were connected? Like a network?"

The centurion nodded. "Correct, Commander."

Sarith's eyes widened in disbelief. "A global, interconnected weapons system?" If true, it was an impressive achievement, unlike anything she had ever seen before. No race encountered by the Romulans had ever displayed technology on such a scale.

Releasing a tired sigh, Ineti said, "So, was a similar weapon used to destroy the planet, or was it merely a colossal, tragic accident?"

"Even if it was misfortune, the potential for such power to be weaponized cannot be ignored, particularly if it's in the hands of an enemy." If a civilization located in the Taurus Reach possessed or was developing weapons technology capable of destroying entire planets, then prudence demanded that their potential threat to the security of the Romulan people be investigated with all due haste.

Unfortunately, Sarith reminded herself, the only Romulans in a position to report this prospective hazard were here, with her, aboard a wounded and dying ship stranded several lifetimes away from home.

29

In the privacy of her quarters aboard the *Endeavour*, Atish Khatami stared at herself in the mirror as she tugged at the hem of her new tunic, pulling it more tightly against her body. The wraparound-style top was tinted in a light green that struck her as a little less harsh against her brownish skin than did her former yellow uniform, while offering a nice contrast to the black trousers she had opted to wear. She smoothed her fingers against the flap of fabric running from the tunic's V-neck and cutting diagonally across her chest. Just for a moment, she wondered whether the design seemed more provocative than professional.

Then, using the back of her hand, she brushed her thick black hair to one side and revealed a set of gold braids sewn in sweeping arrowheads into the tunic's shoulders.

You're not ready for this, Tish.

Upon the ship's arrival at Starbase 47, Khatami had presumed that word about a new captain would be forthcoming from Starfleet Command—that the starship might be routed away from the Taurus Reach on orders to pick up its new commanding officer before returning to Erilon.

Those orders never came.

Instead, Commodore Reyes had simply appeared on the bridge the morning of the *Endeavour*'s departure, ordering the communications officer on duty to open the ship's intercom so that he might address the entire crew. Standing before the main viewer, his voice carrying forward the authority he seemed to wear with the comfort of a favored shirt, the commodore without preamble read aloud from the folder he had brought with him the orders from Starfleet Command promoting Khatami to the rank of captain as well as assigning her as commanding officer of the *Endeavour*.

Certain that the color had drained from her face even as her fellow bridge officers slowly broke into a round of what she perceived as stunned, polite applause, Khatami had stood unmoving while Reyes offered her a narrow-eyed, tight-lipped grin.

He outfoxed me.

Following her interview with members of the station's JAG contingent regarding the incident on Erilon—a process that, based on the questions she was asked, seemed to her to be little more than an attempt to assess any possible negligence that might have contributed to Captain Zhao's death—Khatami had been summoned to Reyes's office for what she thought would be her official briefing on the future of the *Endeavour*'s command. Instead, she had found herself reviewing his greatly expedited repair schedule for the ship, the majority of it executed by station personnel while her crew rested, only then to slip into nearly an hour's worth of swapping humorous and admiring tales regarding the career and achievements of their mutual friend Zhao Sheng. She had been dismissed from the meeting with the question of Zhao's successor—and her role with regards to that person—still unanswered.

He knew exactly what he was doing. He was sure I'd turn it down if given the chance. Maybe I would have.

Maybe I should *have.*

Khatami knew that she possessed the skills and the intellect to perform the duties required of a starship captain. Indeed, her entire career to this point had unfolded in anticipation of this moment. So, why now was she grappling with insecurity even as the *Endeavour* made its way back to Erilon? Why was she plagued by an inner demon that ate away her self-confidence, tormenting her thoughts and emotions, telling her that the trust of those around her in her ability to lead was misplaced? Each time Khatami watched one officer lean over and whisper to another, she wondered if they saw through the façade of calm and control she to this point had managed to affect, exposing her for the fraud her inner voice told her she was.

What will you do next time, "Captain"? Who will you leave behind? Of course there'll be a next time. There's always a next time.

The ping of the door chime startled Khatami, and she glanced at her desk chronometer on her desk to see that she had been standing before her mirror for almost ten minutes. "Time to pull yourself together, Captain," she said to herself, running her hands down the sides of her tunic to smooth it into place one final time before calling toward the door, "Come in."

In response to her command the door slid aside to reveal Mog, all but filling the entryway.

"Well," the burly Tellarite remarked with no small amount of enthusiasm as he stepped into the room, "command colors and braid appear to suit you, Captain. Though I have to say, I miss the skirt."

Khatami smiled at the remark, one that only a close friend such as Mog even would attempt in the first place. "Captain's prerogative. I always liked the pants, anyway." Moving toward her desk, she indicated for the engineer to do the same. "I take it that's your report?" she asked, noting the data slate in his meaty right hand with a nod.

"Indeed it is," Mog replied, "and it's even filed early, I might add." He dropped his considerable frame into the chair situated in front of her desk. "Everything is green across the board, thanks to the Vanguard maintenance crews. We're maintaining warp six point five." Shrugging his brawny shoulders, he added, "I'd push us a bit faster, but between you and me, I don't think our escort ship would be able to keep up."

"The *Lovell*?" Khatami shook her head as she thought of the deceptively decrepit-looking *Daedalus*-class vessel accompanying them back to Erilon. "From what I've read, you shouldn't underestimate those Corps of Engineers ships or their crews. Engineers with lots of time to tinker, rewire, reroute, and rebuild? If Captain Okagawa says he can keep pace with us even at warp seven or better, I'm not betting against him." Nodding her head toward the bulkhead and, presumably, in the direction where the *Lovell* was traveling somewhere to stern, she added, "Besides, I don't think Lieutenant Xiong would have gotten aboard that thing if she were going to shake apart on the way."

Mog laughed. "You're probably right. In any event, we've got two days before we get to Erilon, but we're ready to go right now. We'll hit the ground running for sure."

Khatami nodded in approval. The assignment handed to the *Endeavour* and the *Lovell* was not an easy one: reestablish the research outpost wrecked by the mysterious being which had attacked Captain Zhao and the landing party, while at the same time searching for answers about why the assault had occurred in the first place—preferably without triggering another such incident. While the orders as delivered by Commodore Reyes also included instructions on attempting to find and make peaceful contact with the mysterious alien entity should the opportunity arise, his actual words on the subject had been quite clear: Take whatever action necessary to protect the ships and their crews.

"Lieutenant Xiong and the engineering group have been analyzing the data we collected from . . . the last time we were here," Mog said. "Whatever happens this time, we'll be ready, Captain."

Releasing a long sigh, Khatami affected what she knew to be a weak smile. "Hopefully, we'll *all* be ready."

The Tellarite paused a moment, and she noted how his expression seemed to turn sour in response to the remark. His features softened after a moment and he shifted in his chair, and Khatami sensed he might try to change the subject, a suspicion confirmed the instant Mog opened his mouth.

"You know, those were some very nice words that Commodore Reyes shared with the crew yesterday."

"Yes, they were," Khatami replied. "He and Captain Zhao were friends for a long time."

"I *meant*," Mog interrupted, "what he said about *you*."

Khatami swallowed a lump that materialized in her throat. "I suppose those were nice, too."

Leaning closer, the engineer locked eyes with her. "Your promotion wasn't someone's idea of a grand joke, Atish, and it wasn't a mistake. I don't know Commodore Reyes that well, but I've seen enough to figure he's not one to make stupid or ill-informed decisions. He had to have pushed for your promotion in order for it to go through as fast as it did. Would he have done that if he didn't think you were suited to the job, and that you deserved a chance to prove it to any and all doubters?"

"I didn't deserve it this way," Khatami said, shaking her head. "Not at the expense of a good man's life."

"You need to stop that kind of thinking right now." Reaching across the desk, Mog took her hand in his much larger one. "Atish, for your own sake, and the rest of the crew's, you need to quit agonizing over your last decision and start worrying about your next one, and the ones after that."

Comforted by her friend's forthright demeanor, Khatami squeezed the Tellarite's hand in reassurance. "Thank you, Mog." Tilting her head as she regarded him, she said, "Actually, it's my next decision I wanted to talk to you about. I still need to select a first officer, you know."

"Excellent," Mog said, his smile revealing a mouth of uneven teeth. "Who do you have in mind?" As the highest-ranking member of the crew after her, he had been serving in that capacity on a temporary basis, but she knew that the added responsibility was taking him away from his primary duties. A decision needed to be made one way or another, in order to best serve the needs of the ship and her crew.

Khatami said nothing, allowing her own smile to communicate her answer, and she watched as the Tellarite's robust features melted and realization took hold.

"Not me," he said, his voice containing more than a bit of pleading. "I already have a job."

"You've already shown me you can do it, Mog," Khatami replied. "This isn't the time for transitioning in someone new. I need somebody I can trust without question, who knows me and what I expect, particularly now."

"But I'm not on the command track," the engineer replied, "never have been. I'm not even remotely qualified to do this full time." Shaking his head, he added, "Besides, all you'd be getting is a mediocre babysitter, and losing a damn fine engineer."

"If you do say so yourself," Khatami said.

Mog nodded. "Of course I say so, myself," he snapped, his Tellarite ire coming to the fore. Relaxing a bit, his eyes narrowed as he offered another playful smile. "Besides, I look better in red."

Despite the teasing nature of the comment, Khatami could not help but feel the genuine sting of rejection the words carried.

Even he wants to keep some distance from you, the demon whispered.

Apparently realizing that his words might have carried the wrong sentiment, Mog held his hands out in a gesture of entreaty. "Atish, as your chief engineer, I can give you the best-running ship in the fleet, and you know I'm always here if you need support or a confidant. But I'm not suited to command, and we both know that." Grunting, he replied, "Can you imagine me trying to be nice to admirals and ambassadors? I'd probably end up starting a war."

Khatami allowed herself a small chuckle at the comment. "Well then, what do you suggest I do, my confidant and supporter?"

"You need someone you can trust to second-guess you and tell you where you might be heading down the wrong path," Mog replied. "Someone who'll get in your face a bit if that's what it takes. In other words, someone like me, though not an engineer. I wouldn't bet on finding someone as handsome as me, either." Making a show of examining his fingernails, he added, "You have a number of capable officers under your command. Something tells me you might find what you're looking for in one."

Weighing her friend's counsel, Khatami nodded after a moment. "You may be right. My main concern is how this change will affect the crew. I respected Sheng, and part of me really liked him, Mog, but I know that I don't want to command like he did. I can't match up to any comparisons between us, and I don't even want to try."

His eyes gleaming with barely contained mischief, the engineer replied, "Have you stopped to consider there may be plenty of people on this ship hoping and praying that you are *not* like Captain Zhao?"

Khatami laughed again in spite of herself. "Still, everything is so . . . different now, Mog. Sometimes, there's no way of putting a finger on it, and other times it just slaps me in the face." Her brow furrowing, she held out an open hand. "Like just now, and I hope this doesn't sound odd, but when you talk about him, you don't just say 'the captain' anymore. You say his name. Have you noticed that?"

"Of course, Atish," Mog said as he rose from his chair. "That's because *you're* 'the captain' now, and if there's nothing else, Captain, I will take my leave."

Nodding, Khatami reached for the data slate he had brought for her. "That'll be all, Mog." She looked up at him. "Thanks, for everything, and that includes not taking me up on my offer."

The engineer shrugged. "So long as you're screening candidates, there's always Dr. Leone."

She offered a mock grimace. "Please. You might start a war, but I'm pretty sure putting the good doctor in a position of command is a recipe for universal entropy."

Roast beef sandwich. Vegetable soup. That's all I want, and it shouldn't be too much to ask from that damned contraption.

The thought continued to reverberate in Leone's mind as he entered the officers' mess. He regarded himself as a capable and intelligent man who felt completely comfortable with all manner of technology, be it a computer or a piece of equipment being field-tested by some young idealist stationed at Starfleet Medical. He even considered himself to be a shuttlecraft pilot of reasonable talent and skill.

The *Endeavour*'s food synthesizers, however, were his nemesis.

Gritting his teeth and forcing a smile onto his lean, nearly gaunt features, Leone nodded politely to an ensign he passed on his way to the bank of slots positioned along the dining facility's rear bulkhead. Choosing one of the stations at random, the doctor inserted the menu selection card he had brought along from sickbay into the reader above the food slot's main door and keyed its activation sequence. He rolled his eyes at the lyrical series of beeps and tones emitted by the unit until, seconds later, the door slid up to reveal his lunch.

A roast beef sandwich and a bowl of steaming soup.

"I don't believe it," he said to no one. "Somebody contact the FNS. Better yet, somebody check my pulse."

Allowing a pinched grin of satisfaction, Leone retrieved his tray from the slot and made his way to an empty table next to one occupied by a trio of human officers. With a sigh of anticipation as he regarded his well-earned feast, he picked up his spoon and dipped it into his soup. Noting what his movements were stirring up within the bowl, Leone's brow furrowed in confusion. That bewilderment turned to suspicion as he raised the spoon to his lips—before devolving into defeat as he took a tentative sip.

Plomeek *soup,* he thought, a sneer curling his upper lip. *Figures.*

Trading his spoon for his sandwich, Leone raised it to his mouth and took a bite, savoring the taste of roast beef cooked almost to perfection—until his tongue registered a spicy burning sensation at the same instant a piquant odor assailed his nostrils.

"Gah," Leone exclaimed, grimacing around his wad of chewed sandwich. *Horseradish.* He drew a sharp breath through sinuses now opened at the mercy of the pungent root. *When in the hell will we be able to just tell those damned things what we want to eat?*

"I'm telling you," said one of the officers at the next table, just loud enough for Leone to hear, "if things don't change soon, we're going to be in big trouble."

The doctor cocked his head at that, interested in where the conversation might be going while at the same time dreading that he already knew the destination. Taking his sandwich apart, Leone grabbed up his spoon to scrape the offending condiment from his roast beef while trying to listen to the discussion at the next table without appearing too obvious.

"C'mon, Muller," said another man, who Leone saw in his peripheral vision wore a blue jumpsuit. "You can't be serious."

Without turning his head, the doctor was able to see the first man, who wore a gold uniform tunic, lean closer to his two comrades. "It was her indecision that got Captain Zhao killed, and now we're heading back to the scene of the crime. What are we looking for? Another fight? You ask me, this ship isn't safe with Khatami in charge."

Leone dropped his spoon onto his tray, his appetite having disappeared now. Rising from his seat, he took his tray and made his way toward the row of recycling slots, walking slower than usual in order to continue listening to the conversation which went on as the three officers at the next table also concluded their meals and rose from their seats.

"What," said the third man, dressed in a red tunic and whom Leone recognized as a member of the *Endeavour*'s security force, "because she's a woman?"

"Oh, give me some credit, please," Muller said as he fell in line behind Leone. "Species, gender, age, whatever. Incompetence knows no boundaries. She may have been fine making duty rosters and supervising landing parties, but Khatami doesn't belong in the center seat. Period."

Tossing his tray into the nearest recycler slot, Leone pivoted on his heel until he was facing Muller, who had to come to an abrupt stop to avoid running into the doctor. "Excuse me, Lieutenant," he said, his eyes locking with those of the younger man. "I'd like a word with you out in the corridor."

To his credit, Muller said nothing until both men exited the dining hall. Once in the passageway, Leone folded his arms across his chest as he glared at the other man.

"As an officer, Mr. Muller," he said, "you have an obligation to lead by example. That means presenting a professional demeanor when in the presence of subordinates, and keeping to yourself any unfavorable opinions you might have regarding this ship's chain of command."

"I'm not saying anything that other people haven't said," Muller replied, his tone growing more defensive with each word. "She could have gotten us all killed during that attack. You know that."

Feeling his ire rising even as he regarded Muller through narrowing eyes, Leone snapped, "The fact that you're alive to run your mouth about what happened obviously means she did something right. Now tell me, Lieutenant, do I look like the type of person who enjoys quoting rules and regulations? All they do is piss me off. Therefore, I *suggest* you reevaluate your comments, particularly when you're in a public setting among the rest of the crew."

His own expression growing cold, Muller leaned forward, and when he replied his voice took on what Leone imagined the other man thought to be menace. "Frankly, Doctor," he said, his chest puffing out a bit, "until I see a reason to believe differently, I'm going to hold to my opinion, and I'll share it with whom I please. *Captain* Khatami is a disaster waiting to happen."

Leone sighed as he noted the arrival of Muller's dining companions, both of whom were taking an interest in the conversation. "That's where you and I have a problem, Lieutenant. You see, as the ship's doctor, it's part of my job to ensure that the crew's morale remains high at all times. Your bad-mouthing Captain Khatami erodes that morale. That's a problem for me."

"You don't say?" asked Muller.

"In fact," Leone said, his voice raising in volume, "it looks like it might be a problem for you, too." He made a show of squinting as he stared down the other man. "Come to think of it, you're looking a bit worn right now. Maybe you ought to excuse yourself to your quarters. You know, relax, get some rest."

"Forget it, Doctor," Muller said, offering a smug grin. "I feel just fi—"

The rest of his sentence was lost, shoved back into his mouth as Leone's fist impacted with the lieutenant's jaw. Muller's head snapped back and he fell like a limp doll, unconscious even before he hit the deck.

Leone turned, fire in his eyes, to stare at Muller's two friends, who still stood nearby. "Mr. Muller's condition looks contagious," he said. "How do you gentlemen feel?"

"Uh, I feel great, sir," the ensign in security red replied, his head nodding so fast Leone thought it might break loose from his neck. Looking to his companion, he asked, "You okay, Brad?"

The crewman in the jumpsuit simply nodded.

"I'm thrilled to hear it," Leone said, nodding to each of them. He indicated the insensate Muller with a wave of his hand. "I suggest the two of you help spread the word about this . . . disease I've just treated. Mr. Muller here just might be Patient Zero if we're not careful. You think?"

The two men mumbled something which to Leone's ears sounded like acquiescence. Offering a curt nod, the doctor turned and marched up the corridor toward the turbolift, ignoring the stares of baffled onlookers. No doubt word would make its way with undue haste to Captain Khatami, who was sure to address the issue with a rich, verbose dressing-down.

He ignored that thought for now, though. Waiting until he was well around a bend in the passageway and out of sight of the milling of officers near the mess hall, he lifted his aching right hand and flexed his fingers, already noting the discolorations on his knuckles, which appeared to be well on their way to becoming full-blown bruises.

Damn, that hurts worse than the horseradish.

30

He knew it was his imagination, of course, but the longer Reyes studied the star chart as displayed on the viewscreen in his office, the more he believed that he could see the hole in the galaxy where the planet Palgrenax once had been.

"What do we know?" he asked, his attention remaining focused on the computer-generated representation of the Taurus Reach. The map had been redrawn several times during the past months, regularly updated with new territorial borders, lines representing patrol routes, points of interest, and potential hazards in accordance with the increased presence not only of Federation colonies and ships but also those of the Klingon Empire.

Standing to the left of the screen, her hands clasped behind her back, T'Prynn replied, "According to telemetry received from long-range sensors, the planet exploded at 2247 hours, station time."

Reyes turned from the viewer and crossed the office to his desk. Dropping into his chair, he reached for his cup of coffee, his second since being roused from a fitful sleep less than thirty minutes previously. As he drank generously from the warm brew and despite every fiber of his being telling him to look elsewhere, the commodore could not help but glance at the chronometer situated at the base of his desktop computer terminal: 0342 hours.

The start of another beautiful day.

"To say that speculation is running rampant would be an understatement of epic proportion," Ambassador Jetanien offered from where he stood before Reyes's desk. The commodore was gratified to note that the towering Chelon apparently had chosen to forgo imbibing the hateful beverage he normally consumed in great quantities and the odor of which usually sent Reyes looking for something in which to vomit.

Taking a generous sip from his coffee cup, Reyes said, "But they don't know what we know." He looked to T'Prynn. "Do they, Commander?"

The Vulcan shook her head. "Correct, sir. The Klingon vessel that was in orbit of the planet until the moment of its destruction reported significant power readings emanating from multiple subterranean sources, all of which were working in concert to introduce massive tectonic destabilization. Prior to that, no geological anomalies which might account for such an event were detected."

"And these power readings," Jetanien said, "they were the same as those observed by the *Endeavour* at Erilon?"

"The indications are that technology similar to that discovered on Erilon was in use on Palgrenax, though on a much greater scale, of course."

Frowning as he considered the information for the tenth time since being roused at this unholy hour, Reyes asked, "You're saying that whoever built those structures on Palgrenax included what was basically a planetary self-destruct?"

Pausing a moment as if to consider the notion, T'Prynn then offered a curt nod. "That is essentially correct, sir."

"Any chance the Klingons did this to themselves?" Reyes asked. "An accident of some kind while investigating something on or beneath the surface?"

T'Prynn replied, "That is a possibility, of course, though nothing in any of the communications we have been able to decipher to this point provides any such indication."

"Perhaps the Tholians found a way to trigger the event," Jetanien said. "Though I suspect you would have found something in their communications to that effect."

"Much of it has defied our attempts at decryption," T'Prynn said, "but we have translated enough to know that the Tholians are blaming the Klingons, accusing them of unleashing some form of heretofore unknown superweapon on the planet. As expected, the

Klingons are leveling similar allegations toward the Tholians, claiming the Assembly is exacting vengeance for the isolated encounters that have already taken place."

Rubbing the bridge of his nose, Reyes released a small sigh. "So, everybody thinks someone else did it, but nobody knows who, to say nothing of why."

That latter question burned in the commodore's mind, even more so than wanting to know the identity of whoever might have carried out such a calamitous action. There was more to consider here than conflict between the Klingons and the Tholians, he knew. Whoever or whatever had destroyed Palgrenax, they had done so without any apparent regard for the race of intelligent beings that had sprung up on that world. It suggested that the responsible party had an agenda which did not include the fate of innocents as a priority.

Not for the first time, Reyes felt the pull of regret as he considered the consequences of the Federation's movements into the Taurus Reach on those civilizations native to the region. While Starfleet had taken great pains to avoid contact with local species—especially those that had not yet progressed to warp flight—the Klingons of course had felt no such compelling need. Seven planets had fallen under the empire's banner, four of them inhabited.

Could Starfleet and the Federation have done more to prevent that unchecked expansion? The question had nagged at Reyes more times than he had bothered to count. While it could be argued that the Klingons might eventually have ventured into this region of space on their own, planting their flag on various worlds in the same manner in which they already had done so, Reyes also believed that it was an argument put forth by weaker men.

They're here because of us. Everything that happens here is our fault.

While he acknowledged the need to tread with care through the political and military minefield that the Taurus Reach represented in order to avoid inciting an interstellar incident—with the Klingons or the Tholians—Reyes had no intention of allowing that reasoning to cloud or gloss over the simple fact that innocent parties would suffer because of the Federation's encroachment into this part of the galaxy.

Whatever we end up finding out here, it better damned well be worth it.

"If it was an accident," he said after a moment, "they might well have simply activated the wrong piece of equipment." A chill wormed its way down his spine at the thought of the eager Lieutenant Xiong committing a similar tragic mistake. Reyes made a note to ensure that a full report of this incident was transmitted to the lieutenant within the hour, well before the *Endeavour* and the *Lovell* reached Erilon.

"However," he continued, "if it was a deliberate act, then why? Were the Klingons the target? Are we talking about something like what happened at Erilon?" Even as he spoke the words, he felt a twinge of remorse at the thought of what had happened to Captain Zhao and the research team on that ice-bound world.

"None of the communications transmitted from the Klingon ship to their base suggested any contact with unknown alien entities," T'Prynn said as she stepped away from the viewer. "That does not rule out such a possibility, of course."

As she crossed the room to stand before the commodore's desk, her hands still clasped behind her back, Reyes for the first time noted what he thought to be hints of fatigue in the commander's eyes. He knew that Vulcans did not require sleep with the same frequency as humans, just as he also was aware that they could be quite stubborn when it came to seeing to their own basic health needs.

She's a big girl, he reminded himself. *She can take care of herself.*

"Perhaps the Klingons destroyed the planet to protect the secret of what they'd found," Jetanien said. "However, a scenario worth considering is that whatever attacked our people on Erilon staged a similar assault on Palgrenax, only this time they felt the need to initiate more drastic measures."

Despite himself, Reyes felt his eyes widen as he digested the ambassador's theory. "That's a hell of a leap to make, Your Excellency. On what are you basing this?"

"Logic," the Chelon said. Turning to T'Prynn, he added, "My apologies for stepping into your realm of expertise, Commander, but Captain Zhao and his people were attacked after discovering and activating components of the ancient alien technology discovered on Erilon. Based on the Klingons' sensor readings, we can conclude that similar technology was found on Palgrenax, after which it was apparently used as an instrument to destroy that planet." Rolling his massive shoulders, he released a burst of clicks before saying, "To employ one of your people's idioms, Commodore, someone or some thing does not want anyone playing with their toys."

"You're suggesting someone has interests on both of these planets," Reyes said, making no effort to hide his skepticism, "light-years apart, and with no detectable mode of transportation between those two points? Who? Why?"

The ambassador shook his head. "I am not in possession of all the relevant facts. I merely posit a theory based on what information is available at this time."

Just what I need, Reyes thought. *Another mystery.*

As if reading his mind, Jetanien said, "Given our current situation, however, we cannot afford to waste time with idle speculation. Both the Klingons and the Tholians are ratcheting up the rhetoric after this incident, Commodore. Anger and posturing are—as you can imagine—laced with fear, given that each side is now worried that they can be obliterated by the other. For the moment, they seem content to simply point accusatory fingers at one another, but we can be sure that will not last."

Releasing a heavy sigh as he leaned back in his chair, giving in only slightly to the protests his body was staging in reaction to his lack of sleep, Reyes said, "Tell me about it." He reached for one of several data slates littering his desk and held it up for emphasis. "Have you seen this report from the *Sagittarius*? Captain Nassir broke up what was about to become a fistfight between a Tholian patrol ship and a Klingon D-5 battle cruiser."

"An impressive feat," T'Prynn said, bowing her head in appreciation, "considering the limitations of his ship."

"It's only limited if your enemy knows that," Reyes replied, allowing a wry grin to creep onto his face. The *Sagittarius,* an *Archer*-class scout ship, was not equipped or armed for combat—particularly when outnumbered. Still, that had not stopped her captain from stepping into the line of fire, a decision which had yielded quite a lively after-action report. Nassir's chief engineer had devised a "fake-out" whereby the small scout had appeared on the aged Klingon vessel's sensors as a larger and far more intimidating *Constitution*-class starship. The tactic had proven effective to the point that the Klingon cruiser broke off its attack and retreated at high warp.

"Remind me to buy Master Chief Ilucci a drink when they get back," Reyes said as he tossed the data slate onto his desk. "Unfortunately, head fakes and other cute tricks aren't going to be enough for the long haul. We're getting other reports of scuffles between Klingon and Tholian ships. So far it's just isolated, limited engagements, probably because neither side has any appreciable ability to project force into the region, but you can bet that won't last long." He looked to Jetanien. "We need a permanent fix, and fast, Your Excellency. Any progress on the diplomatic front?"

The ambassador shook his head, the blunt beak of his mouth clicking in what Reyes had come to recognize as an expression of dissatisfaction. "To this point our overtures to the Klingon and Tholian delegations have been most disappointing." Indicating the viewscreen with a nod of his oversized head, he added, "However, this incident may well have provided us with a unique opportunity. I have already been in contact with my esteemed counterparts, and both seem at least somewhat eager to explore some form of peaceful solution. Both the Klingons and the Tholians have agreed to send envoys to meet with me."

"And this is supposed to make me happy?" Reyes asked, shaking his head at the thought of three headstrong ambassadors locked in a room for however long it took to broker a diplomatic solution to the touchy political situation they all faced.

Or kill each other—whichever comes first.

"There may be no better time to seize this initiative," Jetanien said. "Further, if there is another, larger threat to consider, then it would seem to be a threat to all of us. Perhaps we might join forces against a common foe."

It sounded good in theory, Reyes admitted, though his gut told him the reality of the situation would likely resist the ambassador's good intentions. Regardless, he was confident Jetanien could handle whatever the Klingon and Tholian delegates threw at him. Besides, whatever he dropped, Lieutenant Jackson and the rest of the station's security contingent would be there to catch. Reyes would see to that himself.

"Well, you're going to have your hands full, there's no doubting that," Reyes said as he rose from his chair and made his way around his desk and crossed his office until he was standing once more before the viewscreen. Again his attention was focused on the computer-generated star chart depicting the solar system which once had been home to Palgrenax. "But, so are the rest of us, I think."

"You are concerned that the ambassador's theory might be correct," T'Prynn said as she moved to stand next to him.

"That something else might be out there, and that it seems to be mad at everybody?" Reyes asked. "You're damned right, I'm worried. It seems like for every rock we turn over out here, five more show up, and I end up not liking what I find under three of those."

"Under at least one of those rocks lay the answers we seek, Commodore," Jetanien said. "There can be no turning back now. Simply too much is at stake."

Releasing a tired, humorless chuckle as he cast a knowing glance toward T'Prynn, Reyes turned from the screen. "I have to tell you, Ambassador, the more I hear that, the more I want to find out who said it first and beat them with a lead pipe."

"You can be certain it was a politician," Jetanien replied, offering the Chelon equivalent of a broad grin.

Reyes nodded. "I rest my case."

The conversation was interrupted by the sound of the intercom on his desk emitting its telltale tone. Looking toward the row of status lights embedded at the base of the small gray rectangular module which housed the comm unit, Reyes noted that the red

light on the far left was blinking. He reached for the control pad
set into his desk, entering a sequence of coded commands. "Computer, activate security encryption algorithm Sierra Delta-Six."

There was a delay as his request was processed, after which
the female voice that characterized Starfleet computer systems
replied, "Security protocol enabled."

Satisfied that the communication now was sheltered under an
umbrella of protection, the commodore activated the channel.
"Reyes here."

"*Commodore, this is Dr. Gek,*" said the nasally voice of the
Tellarite scientist, the effect only enhanced from being filtered
through the comm speaker. "*I've discovered something that's
most interesting, sir. Something you should know about.*"

Exchanging intrigued glances with Jetanien and T'Prynn,
Reyes leaned closer to the comm unit. "What is it, Doctor?"

Gek cleared his throat before answering, a sound that Reyes
likened to a Grenthemen water hopper stalling after having its
clutch popped. "*Sir, we have been going over the sensor data
gathered by the* Endeavour *during the incident at Erilon. According to our findings, the power signatures emanating from the subterranean weapons emplacements appear to have at least a
passing resemblance to Tholian technology.*"

The silence that descended upon Reyes's office was total, to
the point that after several seconds, Gek felt compelled to ask,
"*Hello? Is this unit functioning?*"

"Fascinating," T'Prynn said, her right eyebrow ascending
nearly to her hairline.

Jetanien clicked and chirped before nodding. "Well, this seems
to have become a new thing altogether. It should make the coming
summit that much more interesting."

Resting his head in his hands so as to better rub his now throbbing temples, Reyes said, "As always, Your Excellency, your gift
for understatement knows no bounds."

31

"Hands on the switch, newsboy," Quinn said, sounding remarkably sober to Pennington as the pilot maneuvered the *Rocinante* around for yet another pass at retrieving their target. "We're pressed for time, here."

"Now, *why* are we doing this again?" Pennington asked, turning to look at Quinn in the pilot's seat. Between pinpointing the location of the Klingon sensor drone T'Prynn had tasked the trader with obtaining and cocking up their previous attempts to snare the device, they had been jockeying about the thing for the better part of an hour.

"Because you screwed it up the first two times," Quinn shot back, his attention focused on his helm console. "So keep your eye on the targeting scanner and quit looking at me."

Clenching his jaw as he forced down his mounting frustration, Pennington said, "What I meant was, why do we have to bring the bloody thing aboard? Can't you just scan it for whatever it is you need?" Of course, he knew that given the age and condition of the *Rocinante*'s sensor suite, they were lucky to be able to scan for entire planets.

"I need to access the hardware directly," Quinn said through gritted teeth.

"Then why not go out in an envirosuit?" Pennington's suggestion was an attempt to rankle his traveling companion more than anything else. During the days it had taken to travel from Yerad III to the probe rendezvous point, his efforts to goad Quinn into exasperation or frustrated silence had become his favorite pastime.

"That's actually an excellent idea," said Sakud Armnoj from where he sat on a fold-down jump seat situated just aft of the

Rocinante's cramped cockpit, "because you know he's just going to miss again."

Oddly, and despite the sadistic fun he himself had been having at Quinn's expense, Pennington found the fussy Zakdorn's relentless complaints and bickering—most of it aimed at the pilot—not nearly as amusing. In fact, the accountant's constant needling annoyed him as much as it did their shared whipping boy.

Maybe we should have brought his snotty beast with us just to shut him up. Thankfully, they had not. After regaining consciousness following his encounter with Quinn's stun pistol—and after much wailing and complaining as he gathered his accounting files and other materials for Ganz—Armnoj finally had relented and seen to it that his prized pet was placed in the care of a trusted neighbor before the Zakdorn was whisked away to the *Rocinante*.

Pennington tried to tune out the newest volley of Armnoj's bleating voice. "If you had a tractor beam on this worthless excuse of a ship instead of an antiquated grappling hook, you'd have been done by now."

"Stifle your hole before I weld it shut!" Quinn shouted, not even bothering to turn from the helm console.

"As amazing as this sounds," Pennington said, affecting mock sincerity, "I think I might actually agree with him this time."

Grunting something unintelligible, the pilot regarded him with a wan smile. "Well, hell, maybe I'll just stuff you both in the cargo hold for the next week, seeing as how you're so agreeable and all." He waggled his eyebrows suggestively before returning to the business at hand. "We're in range," he said, indicating a status gauge on the helm console which had begun flashing green. "Lock on target."

"Even if he manages to hit it," Armnoj said, "the take-up reel will just jam like it did last time, when he *missed*!"

"Shut up!" Quinn and Pennington yelled in unison.

Maneuvering the grappling hook's targeting controls with his right hand, Pennington watched as an indicator light turned from dark blue to amber. He felt his finger tighten against the grappler's firing trigger.

"Hurry, dammit, before we drift too close!" Quinn shouted.

"Almost got it," Pennington replied, watching the targeting screen as the sights moved to line up with the computer-generated image of the man-sized sensor drone. Then the crosshairs illuminated as bright yellow at the same time the target lock indicator glowed red. "That's it!"

He uttered the exclamation at the precise instant a pair of maneuvering thrusters on the drone's hull fired. Pennington pressed the grappler's firing control, but he was too slow. The drone moved out of the target lock and angled away from the *Rocinante,* leaving the grappling magnet and its length of flexible duranium cable to sail harmlessly through space.

"Oh, for crying out!" Quinn shouted.

"He missed again," Armnoj said with no small amount of superior satisfaction. "I knew it."

Muttering what Pennington recognized as a string of particularly vile Rigelian oaths, Quinn pounded several of the helm controls in a frenetic sequence that Pennington found difficult to follow. "Damn proximity sensors," he said. In response to his commands, the *Rocinante* pitched to starboard as Quinn once again set about giving chase after the sensor drone. Rising from his seat, he prompted Pennington to vacate the copilot's chair by hooking a thumb over his shoulder. "You're fired. Sit over there and don't touch anything. I've programmed the autopilot to maneuver us to the limit of the grappler's range. Hopefully that'll leave enough distance to avoid setting off the drone's collision avoidance software."

"Sorry, Quinn," Pennington said with a measure of sincerity. Glancing toward Armnoj, who was studying them both with his customary air of condescension, he leaned closer to the pilot and asked in a low voice, "You think we've been here too long?"

"Dunno," Quinn replied. "The damn thing's probably sent some kind of distress call by now. Whether the Klingons actually answer it is another matter. Let's hope that doesn't mean it's already transmitted its sensor logs and purged its data storage core." He adjusted the grappler's targeting scanner and set about resetting the device for another attempt.

It took only moments for the *Rocinante*'s autopiloting system to maneuver the dilapidated Mancharan starhopper into position. Pennington watched as Quinn manipulated the grappler's controls with ease. The audible signal of the target scanner locking its crosshairs on the drone had only just begun to sound when the pilot pressed the trigger, and Pennington saw on one display monitor the image of the drone as the grappler slammed into the unmanned probe, locking on and holding against the device's weathered, beaten hull.

"Nice shooting," Pennington offered with genuine admiration.

Ignoring the compliment, Quinn instead keyed another set of switches on the grappler's control console. "Now, we bring it into the hold and get this over with," he said. "That is, assuming its thrusters don't fire again."

Pennington frowned, renewed concern edging into his voice. "You think they will?"

"Sure," Quinn replied, shrugging. Glancing back toward Armnoj and speaking loud enough for the Zakdorn to hear, he added, "It'll probably drag us into the nearest star, where we'll blow up real good."

"*What?*" came the shocked reply from just outside the cockpit, evoking a satisfied smile from the pilot.

After locking Armnoj inside the one part of the ship where he was likely to cause the least trouble—the shower stall—Quinn and Pennington made their way to the *Rocinante*'s hold, where, thanks to Quinn's skilled marksmanship with the grappler, the now inert Klingon sensor drone lay in the center of the small cargo bay's dull, scuffed deck.

"Don't worry," Quinn said as he paced a circle around the probe. "The grappler's electromagnets were strong enough to jam any outgoing comm signals. There's no way it got off any kind of distress signal."

"If it didn't send one during our first three tries to nab the bloody thing," Pennington replied as he scrutinized the drone. Essentially a cylinder lying on the deck, it measured two meters in length, its outer shell a series of rectangular plates. The seams be-

tween the hull sections were visible, and he even noted a few that
had been creased, breaking their seal. Had the grappler caused
that?

"According to T'Prynn," Quinn said as he walked over to a
nearby worktable and retrieved a piece of equipment Pennington
did not recognize from a worn leather satchel, "this little gizmo
should take care of the hard part." The device, whatever it was,
looked to be slightly larger than a Starfleet-issue tricorder. Rectangular and sporting a silver finish, it possessed a flap that Quinn
opened as he walked back to the probe.

"What is it?" Pennington asked.

Quinn replied, "Some kind of scanner thingamabob. If I set it
up right, it'll download the drone's data, then replace it with some
mumbo jumbo T'Prynn made up." Shrugging, he added, "She explained the basics, but I was nursing a warp-five hangover at the
time. The salient details may have eluded me."

"Fancy that," Pennington replied, rolling his eyes before
returning his attention to the sensor probe. "I wonder what this
thing has that T'Prynn wants so badly." He frowned, remembering what Quinn had told him of the assignment the intelligence officer had given him. "If it works the way you told me,
then whatever data it was set to transmit had to have been collected from that system it passed through most recently." Did
the Jinoteur system harbor some value to Starfleet, particularly with regards to the presence of Starbase 47 in the Taurus
Reach? Might it have any connection to why the Tholians
were so agitated by the Federation's encroachment into the
region?

Is there a connection to what happened to the Bombay? *To*
Oriana?

"That's what she told me," Quinn replied as he tapped a few
controls into the keypad set into the top of the scanner. "I don't get
paid to overthink these things, you know?" The unit began to emit
a series of tones, which increased in pitch and intensity as he
moved closer to the drone. Kneeling next to the drone, Quinn held
the scanner against the burnished metal hull plating, and Pennington heard a metallic click as the unit attached to the probe's hous-

ing. That accomplished, the pilot looked up. "Not sure how long this is supposed to take."

By way of reply, a surge of blue energy crackled across the scanner's faceplate. Quinn, one hand still on the unit, was thrown back by the shock to land heavily on the deck. Pennington saw smoke belch from the unit at the same instant its keypad and miniaturized display exploded.

"Quinn!" he shouted as he crossed the deck to the fallen pilot, who already was pulling himself to a sitting position. "Are you all right?"

"Yeah," Quinn replied, rubbing the back of his head with one hand. Allowing Pennington to help him to his feet, he added, "Damn. I forgot about the built-in anti-tampering system."

Pennington walked over to the probe, noting the burned-out husk of what only moments ago had been T'Prynn's mysterious scanner. "Well, it looks like you've got another problem here, mate." He pointed to the ruined device. "As my grandfather used to say, this furshlugginer veeblefetzer's gone all potrzebie."

Squeezing his eyes shut, Quinn shook his head in evident disgust. "T'Prynn's going to have my hide." He nodded toward the sensor probe. "Want to bet it managed to pop off a distress call that time?"

Pennington sighed in exasperation. "We're *never* going to make it to Boam II, are we?"

"We are if you let me figure this out," Quinn slurred, still shaking off the effects of the shock to which he had been subjected. Muttering another string of noteworthy profanities—which Pennington recognized as originating on Argelius—Quinn moved to a storage locker on the cargo bay's far bulkhead. He returned a moment later carrying a dented toolbox. Setting it down on the deck next to the probe, he removed from it a laser torch and a pair of goggles.

"That ought to make for an undetectable infiltration," Pennington remarked.

Quinn grunted. "We're past our deadline for 'undetectable,' I think." Donning the goggles, he activated the laser torch and went to work on what Pennington recognized as the only hull plate along the drone's exterior which featured an access panel.

What is this idiot doing? Pennington raised a hand to shield his eyes from the glare of the torch as it began to slice through the probe's thick hide. "How is this helping us?" he shouted over the cutting tool's dull whine.

"I'm trying to remove the memory core before this thing starts transmitting and wipes it clean," Quinn replied, his attention focused on his task.

Clearing his throat, Pennington said, "You're just going to cut it out?"

"Looks that way, huh?" the pilot replied. The air of the cargo bay was now tinged with the smell of heated metal, an aroma Pennington found only slightly less offensive than Quinn himself.

"Not to be a nag," he said, "but what about the data you're supposed to replace it with?"

Setting the cutter down next to his feet, Quinn reached into the toolbox and retrieved a palm-sized device featuring a magnetic base. Affixing it to the center of the hull section he had just cut, Quinn pulled the section away, revealing the drone's interior.

"I'm thinking that plan's pretty much down the toilet," the pilot said as he dropped the section of hull plate to the deck, its clatter echoing across the cargo bay. Stepping closer so he could examine the probe's now-exposed innards, Pennington could see what looked to be a black rectangle, from which protruded a tangled collection of multicolored wires and glowing filaments. He watched as Quinn removed his goggles before pulling a sonic screwdriver from the toolbox and proceeded to disconnect the object from the surrounding wiring.

"There," he said a moment later as he pulled the device from its mounting. "One data core."

"Very deft touch you've got there, Quinn," Pennington remarked. "And are you as delicate with the ladies?"

Quinn glowered at him. "Never had any complaints."

Pennington nodded toward the object in Quinn's hands. "Is it okay?"

"Yeah," Quinn replied as he rose from his kneeling position, "the data's still intact." Frowning, he added, "At least, I think it is. I'm sure T'Prynn'll forgive me for screwing up the rest of this little operation."

Not with the luck we've been having, Pennington mused. "Okay, now what?"

"Now," Quinn said, "we dump this piece of Klingon scrap before someone . . ."

The rest of his sentence was cut off by the sound of an alarm siren wailing through the cargo bay, bouncing off the bulkheads and driving like a spike directly into Pennington's skull.

"What the hell is that about?"

Quinn was already running for the corridor. "Sensors," he yelled over his shoulder. "Something's heading our way."

Uh-oh. Pennington felt his heart jump into his throat as he set out after Quinn. It seemed their luck, already questionable to this point, was about to take a further turn for the worse.

Both men ignored the muffled wailings of Armnoj on their way to the cockpit. By the time Pennington got there, Quinn was in his seat, his hands moving over the control console.

"We're being hailed," he said as his fingers moved to the communications interface. He tapped a series of switches, and Pennington flinched as a voice boomed through the speakers set into the cockpit's angled bulkheads.

". . . *power down your engines and prepare to be boarded. Surrender your vessel or you will be destroyed.*"

"Who is it?" Pennington asked, feeling his pulse beginning to race. Was it the Klingons? He did not think so. According to what he had read, Klingons did not typically take prisoners.

Quinn shook his head. "Beats the hell out of me." The next instant, the entire ship seemed to shake and rattle around them. The pilot grimaced in realization. "Tractor beam." Looking up at Pennington, he said, "Well, I've got some bad news for you."

"Bad?" Pennington asked, regarding Quinn with confusion. "You mean, worse than this?"

Quinn nodded. "Yep. Looks like we're not going to make Boam II after all."

So far as Pennington was concerned, the room in which he, Quinn, and Armnoj found themselves made the interior of the *Rocinante* seem sterile by comparison.

"They don't have to kill us," Pennington said as he paced the length of the squalid chamber, which to him resembled a cargo hold not that dissimilar to the one aboard Quinn's ship. "We stay put long enough, we'll probably die from exposure to whatever fungus is growing in here."

The hold, like the other areas of the ship they had seen after Quinn's vessel was pulled aboard via tractor beam, was filthy. Discarded cargo containers, packing crates, and waste-storage units lay scattered about the room. From the smell permeating the air, Pennington guessed the waste containers were in need of emptying, or cleaning at the least. Dust clung to everything, including a layer coating the deck plates which featured hundreds of footprints—what looked to be human footwear as well as tracks made by species he did not recognize.

"I'm guessing this isn't a hospital ship," Quinn said. He sat reclined atop a cargo container, resting with his back against the near bulkhead. "Just a hunch I've got, mind you."

"Pirates," Armnoj replied from where he stood near the center of the room and in no danger of brushing or rubbing up against any of the hold's grimy contents. "They run in packs near the Yerad system, and I've heard they're spreading out into the Taurus Reach. There's nothing to stop them, after all."

Their hijacking had possessed at least some of the hallmarks associated with piracy, Pennington decided. Within moments of the *Rocinante*'s becoming trapped in its tractor beam, the attacking vessel had pulled the smaller starhopper into a cargo bay that the journalist had observed was even more cluttered than the room they currently occupied. Rather than risk damage to his ship during what surely would prove to be a futile standoff, Quinn had allowed their assailants to step aboard, just as he had permitted his own capture as well as that of Pennington and Armnoj.

The trio was marched out of the vessel and watched for several minutes as a motley assortment of individuals, dressed in worn and soiled clothing and each armed with at least one disruptor pistol as well as varying numbers and styles of edged weapons, began ransacking Quinn's ship. Among the first things taken was Armnoj's attaché, and the Zakdorn had become agitated and even enraged at that sight. Likewise, Quinn's anxiety level—and Pennington's, for that matter—ratcheted up several degrees upon seeing the accountant's briefcase as well as the data core he had retrieved from the sensor drone. He was helpless to watch the scene unfold as those items, as well as an assortment of replacement engine components and various other stuff, were removed from his ship by the pirates. The wholesale looting continued even as the three wayward travelers were marched from the cargo bay and dumped without ceremony into the filthy room they now occupied.

"I don't get it," Quinn said after a moment. "Why aren't we dead?"

"A fortunate oversight, perhaps?" Pennington snapped, every word dripping with sarcasm. "I'm sure if you're feeling cheated, our hosts can bloody well oblige you."

Quinn offered a dismissive wave. "What I mean is, something's not right here. Every pirate I ever heard about would just as soon kill the crew of whatever ship they hijack as keep them prisoner. No need to worry about locking them up or keeping an eye on them, that way."

"Even pirates must operate under some kind of ethics or rules," Armnoj countered. "Maybe this group chooses to refrain from killing unless no other option presents itself."

"Well, out here in the real galaxy," Quinn said as he swung his feet off the cargo crate and toward the floor, "that's usually more of a guideline than an actual rule. If we're still alive, it means we're of some value, at least for the moment." Frowning, he added, "Problem with that is, I have no damned idea what we have that they might want." He pointed a finger at Armnoj. "Besides you, that is."

"Me?" the Zakdorn asked. "The only thing I have of any value is Mr. Ganz's accounting records."

The notion made perfect sense to Pennington. "Exactly. No doubt your knowledge of Ganz's finances makes you an attractive target for his enemies." He glanced in Quinn's direction. "I say we trade him for us."

"I beg your pardon?" Armnoj's eyes had gone wide in response to Pennington's suggestion. "You wouldn't dare."

"I'd do it in an Arcturian minute," Quinn replied. "Unfortunately, that leaves me with the prospect of a painful death at the hands of Ganz's men if I don't bring you in. I hate you, Armnoj, but I hate the idea of dying more."

Their conversation was interrupted by the sound of the hold's far hatch cycling open. The trio turned to see two men, humans, enter the chamber, each carrying a disruptor rifle which he wasted no time aiming on the hostages.

"Here we go," Pennington whispered, feeling his pulse beginning to race and a knot forming in his gut. They were going to die here, of that he was certain. While the idea of death frightened him, that sense of dread also was highlighted by the disillusionment at knowing he would meet his end in this fetid sewer of a cargo hold, cut down while in the company of such unsavory characters as Cervantes Quinn and the ever-irritating Sarkud Armnoj.

Fate, you surely are a cruel bastard.

The two new arrivals stepped to either side of the open door, keeping their weapons at the ready as another man stepped into the room. He was burly and scruffy, with greasy brown hair that hung past his broad shoulders and a round, chubby face sporting several days' worth of beard stubble. A long dark coat hung over his large frame, partially concealing what Pennington recognized as a gun belt with a holster strapped to the man's right hip. All that was missing, the journalist decided, was an eye patch in order to complete the illusion that the man indeed was a pirate.

"Looks like our luck's changing for the better," Quinn said.

Pennington cast a hopeful glance at the pilot. "Really?"

"No."

The third man, obviously in charge, strode across the cargo hold, offering a smile wide enough that Pennington could see the uneven rows of dull, discolored teeth. "Quinn," the man said, "good to see you again." His voice was low and rough, sounding as though he was talking around a mouthful of rocks.

"Broon," Quinn said by way of greeting. "I'll be damned."

Still smiling, Broon asked, "Surprised to see me?"

"Flabbergasted is more like it. How does somebody who can't find his own ass with a star chart and a flashlight manage to track me down in the middle of nowhere?"

The pirate's smile faded. "I'd watch that mouth of yours, Quinn. You don't have any snipers to bail you out this time."

"You two know each other?" Pennington asked, looking once more over to Quinn.

The pilot nodded. "That's one way of putting it. We've run into each other a time or two in the past."

"You cost me a lot of money the last time our paths crossed," Broon said. "Now, one has to wonder about that Klingon probe we found aboard your ship. Are you in the espionage business now, Quinn?"

"Yeah, because I'm prime spy material," the pilot replied. He shrugged, and Pennington could tell he was trying to affect an air of someone in control of the current situation. "Some of its internal components are worth big money on the black market. I was trying to score some fast cash."

"Good to know," Broon replied. "I'll be happy to add that to the bill you owe me." He pointed to Armnoj. "But I'm really here for you. Ganz wants you, and the faster I get you there, the bigger my fee."

"I already have an abductor," the Zakdorn countered with measured disdain.

"Your fee?" Quinn asked, aghast. "What the hell are you talking about?" He took a step forward, a move that engendered the immediately refocused attention of Broon's two thugs and their nasty-looking disruptor rifles. Fear gripped Pennington and he felt his heart trying to beat its way through his chest in anticipation of seeing the pilot gunned down before his eyes.

Broon said, "All I know is what was communicated to me when I took the job. That sneaky enforcer bastard of Ganz's, Zett, contacted me, told me where to go, who to get, what to bring back, and when to get it there. He didn't say anything about running into you." He smiled once more. "Guess he figured I'd appreciate the surprise."

"That son of a bitch," Quinn said.

"What?" Pennington asked.

Ignoring the question, Quinn pointed to the pirate. "Broon, he set me up. Hell, he set us both up, if you think about it."

"What are you talking about?" Broon asked, a heavy crease forming over his brow.

"You can't kill me," Quinn replied. "If Ganz wanted me dead, he'd have taken care of it weeks ago. He needs me alive because I do favors for him." He hooked a thumb in Armnoj's direction. "Like going to pick up this idiot."

Broon shook his head. "That's a pretty weak lie, even coming from you. Sorry to disappoint you, but Zett paid half my fee up front. I get the other half as soon as I plop the accountant down in front of Ganz, with a bonus for each hour I get him there ahead of schedule."

"What about us?" Pennington asked.

"No instructions," Broon replied as he nodded toward Quinn, "except to say that he didn't want to see them on the station or Ganz's ship ever again." Regarding the journalist, the pirate shrugged. "Didn't mention you, though. Guess you're a bonus, too," he said, his malevolent smile returning.

Wonderful, Pennington thought.

"You're not taking me anywhere."

The comment, loud and forceful, surprised everyone, coming from Armnoj as it had. The Zakdorn seemed to have grown a few centimeters in height, his back ramrod straight as he glowered at Broon with his dark, narrowed eyes.

"What did you say?" the pirate asked.

Armnoj shook his head. "I said I'm not going with you. The only way I'm of any value to you is if I bring my accounting records to Mr. Ganz."

"Considering we have those," Broon replied, "I don't see this as an issue."

"That's why you're a fool," the accountant said, his voice rising in volume and pitch with each word. "Those files are encoded with a multi-quad encryption algorithm capable of thwarting any attempt at unauthorized access. I designed the software myself, including . . ."

"Shut up!" Quinn said, an action that earned him disbelieving stares from Pennington as well as everyone else in the room. Glowering at Armnoj, he added, "Do you *want* him to kill us? Who cares about all of that?"

The Zakdorn matched the stare with a scathing one of his own. "You should, for one," he said before returning his attention to Broon. "As should you. Part of the security measures for my files is a mechanism designed to erase them from the portable computer in my briefcase unless I enter the correct response to one of two hundred password prompts, which it selects at random every one hundred and eight minutes."

His expression darkening as he absorbed the implications of this new development, Broon growled in growing annoyance. "You're bluffing."

"We'll find out," Armnoj replied as he consulted a chronometer he wore on his left wrist, "in forty minutes and thirty-seven seconds."

Pennington imagined he almost could see the wheels turning behind Broon's eyes as the man tried to think his way out of the quandary the accountant had presented him. There was only one way to deal with such an ultimatum, of course, and the journalist felt his stomach tightening up as his mind began to lay out new imagery to support that notion.

"Go get the briefcase," Broon said to the thug standing to his right, "and get Divad up here. She can probably crack the encryption on that thing with her eyes closed."

Armnoj sniffed the air haughtily. "I'm the only one who can countermand the protective measures. It's tamper-resistant and will delete everything if anyone tries to defeat the locks."

Releasing a low growl from the back of his throat, Broon fixed the Zakdorn with a look that Pennington believed capable of re-crystallizing dilithium. "Mr. Armnoj, you can either fix it so those files are safe now, or you can spend the next forty minutes wishing you had. However, I'm betting it won't take that long to get you to change your mind."

"He's no good to you dead," Quinn said. Pennington noted the slight trembling in the other man's voice even though he attempted to present a brave façade.

"But you are," Broon replied, offering a renewed smile of satisfaction before motioning toward his men. "Bring the bookworm his briefcase, but before you do that, show these two the way out."

As the henchmen indicated for Quinn and Pennington to move toward the hatch, Quinn called out, "Come on, Broon! You hate Zett as much as I do. There has to be something you want from me that'll make this work out for all of us."

To Pennington's fading hope, the pirate appeared to consider the notion for a moment before nodding.

"The only thing I want from you," Broon said, "is to see the look on your face when I blow you out the airlock." He looked to Pennington, and the journalist watched as the brawny man shrugged. "As for you, what can I say? You should have picked better friends."

Casting a hateful glare at Quinn, Pennington could only nod in meek agreement. "Bloody story of my life."

32

At some point during the initial period of his formal education—he could not exactly remember when—Ambassador Jetanien received a piece of advice that had remained with him to this day: Whenever you schedule a meeting, ensure you are the last to arrive.

For most of his early career and while his normal duties required him to be at the beck and call of more senior diplomats, Jetanien had disliked that notion. It always had irritated him to be kept waiting by someone else, a vexation for which his tolerance all but evaporated upon earning the title of ambassador. As part of his daily routine aboard Starbase 47, he made it an inviolable directive that all meetings start and end on schedule, and that all participants—himself included—were present at the appointed time. Leadership was best employed if demonstrated by example, after all. To the Chelon, whether tardiness was as a result of laziness, forgetfulness, or arrogance mattered not. Regardless of the cause, he always addressed such lapses as well as the responsible party without mercy. The harshness of his redress increased in direct proportion to the rank and position of the person committing the blunder.

Despite his well-known feelings on the subject, however, Jetanien knew that there were rare occasions when employing such a loathsome tactic had its advantages.

Now, for instance.

Moving with no undue haste toward the conference chambers which were the centerpiece of the offices and other facilities designated for use by the station's diplomatic contingents, Jetanien glanced toward a chronometer mounted high along one bulkhead near the entrance to the section's formal dining hall. Its digital display told him that he was arriving slightly less than eleven standard minutes after the summit's scheduled start time. Just enough of an interval, he surmised, to inform those already seated inside the meeting room just who was running the show today.

A pair of bright red doors marked the entrance to the conference chamber, their vivid hue part of the standard Starfleet color scheme and which Jetanien had forgotten to order replaced with something more soothing. The doors were flanked by a pair of Starfleet security officers, one a human female and the other an Andorian *thaan*. Both were dressed in red uniform tunics and dark trousers—a practical choice on the part of the woman, he decided—and their sleeves each sported the gold braid denoting their respective ranks of lieutenant. The guards came to attention at his approach, the woman nodding to him as he stepped closer.

"Good morning, Your Excellency. The other parties have been seated and are awaiting your arrival."

"Of that I am certain, Lieutenant," Jetanien replied, offering a knowing laugh. The officers apparently understood his meaning, as he noted each attempting to hide their own smiles of approval. "What is it you humans are fond of saying? Let's get this show on the road."

The doors parted and he strolled into the room, noting with satisfaction that—as he had requested—both the Klingon and Tholian ambassadors as well as their respective attachés already were at their places on opposite sides of the polished black conference table. The Tholians, of course, being even less suited anatomically to sitting than Jetanien was, eschewed the chairs on their side of the table. At the far end of the room sat his own envoys, Sovik and Akeylah Karumé, flanking the as-yet-unoccupied space at the head of the table. Everyone in the chamber turned at his arrival, their expressions ranging from expectation to confusion and even to utter disdain.

Once more unto the breach, Jetanien mused.

"Good afternoon, gentlebeings," the ambassador offered by way of greeting as he made his way toward the table. Behind him, the doors slid closed and locked in accordance with his prearranged instructions. Now they were able to be opened only by use of the keypad set into the wall next to the entrance or by command from one of the security officers stationed just outside.

"On behalf of the United Federation of Planets," he continued, "I extend to you greetings and our sincere thanks at your decision to gather here today, particularly in light of current events." Stopping before his *glenget*, he turned to face the assembled audience. "Simply coming here is a gesture of faith and hope, my friends. Let us all do our best to ensure your efforts are not wasted."

"*tojo'Qa*," spat Ambassador Lugok, a response mirrored by his attaché, Kulor. "How dare you force me to sit here with nothing better to do than stare at these *taHqeq*." The Klingon waved a large, gloved hand across the table, indicating the Tholian delegation.

Well, Jetanien thought, *that didn't take long.*

"Please excuse my tardiness, Ambassadors," he said, extending his hands in a gesture of supplication. "I was unavoidably detained." With that, he lowered himself down upon the perch that had been constructed to accommodate his ungainly physique.

"*You present no excuse*," replied the voice of the room's universal translator, offering a clipped rendering of Ambassador Sesrene's words amid the muted but still audible screeches issuing from within the Tholian's silken envirosuit. "*Such disrespectful behavior is unacceptable.*"

Knowing that his tactics played against the Tholians' near-obsessive penchant for punctuality, Jetanien chose his next words with care. "Not an excuse, Ambassador, but instead a reason that I hope you both will find satisfactory. I have been meeting with Commodore Reyes to review the latest information regarding the destruction of the planet we know as Palgrenax." What he did not mention was that the meeting had concluded several hours earlier, and that he had spent the interim secreted in his private office, refining his strategy.

Besides, the longer you two sit in silence and allow your anger to fester, the more likely you are to forget any rehearsed stories and react honestly to what I have to say.

"Bah!" Lugok barked. "What can you tell me that I do not already know? That planet was claimed by the empire, in the same way that we have established ourselves on other worlds in the Gonmog Sector. The Tholians take issue with our actions and attack us without honor!"

"Cowardly *toDSaH*."

Though Kulor had uttered the words under his breath, Jetanien nevertheless had heard him. Grunting loud enough to catch the assistant's attention, the Chelon hoped the glare he leveled at the Klingon was enough to forestall any such further comments.

"And now," Lugok continued, his voice louder and more intense now, "they have created a weapon capable of destroying a planet and have unleashed it against us!"

"Unfounded accusations do not become you, Ambassador," Jetanien said, almost besting the Klingon in tone and volume. "Do you have evidence to substantiate these claims?"

Lugok glared at the Chelon, his eyes seething. "I challenge the Tholians to offer evidence to the contrary," he said, the words hissed from between gritted teeth.

Occupying the position at the table opposite the Klingon diplomat, Ambassador Sesrene reached out with silk-sheathed appendages toward both of his attachés, his gesture mirrored by his companions in what Jetanien knew was the precursor to the activation of their habitual touch-telepathy link.

As he witnessed the communing, Jetanien once more wished for a better understanding of the Tholians not merely as politicians but as individuals. Not even the Federation's leading xenobiologists and sociologists could lay claim to any real insight into the acutely secretive race, their very nature isolating them from introspection by other species. He had known upon taking the assignment to Starbase 47 that doing so would provide him with an unequaled opportunity to study what he considered to be one of the most fascinating societies he ever had encountered.

If I can't find a Tholian expert, I'll simply become one myself. Jetanien was certain that someone somewhere would find such a distinction useful. After that, who knew where such unparalleled knowledge and expertise might lead?

Sesrene folded his arms back against his body, turning his oversized head until Jetanien could make out the yellow slits cut into the helmet of the Tholian's envirosuit.

"We do not have any offensive weapon such as the Klingon describes. It is they who destroyed the planet, likely as an example to other worlds that do not bow down before them. If left unchecked, the Klingons will continue to unleash havoc upon all who oppose them. Their reign of violence and terror must be halted immediately."

"Ambassador," Jetanien began as he looked at the Tholian.

Rising from his seat, Lugok stabbed a finger in Sesrene's direction. "The empire has made no moves against any world inhabited by your kind, and yet your vessels attack ours without provocation. It is obvious you seek to do battle."

"We have acted only in self-defense," Sesrene replied. *"We are well aware of the Klingon Empire's thirst for power and conquest. It will not be tolerated. Go back from whence you came and war can be avoided."*

Both hands placed flat atop the conference table, his lips pulling back to reveal uneven rows of sharpened teeth, Lugok glowered at the Tholian diplomat. "Are you claiming the Gonmog Sector as your own? By what right do you assert that authority?"

"Fellow sentients," Jetanien called out, acutely aware that he was in danger of losing control of the meeting, "this is hardly the sort of constructive dialogue which will lead us to mutual understanding of the issues and how they affect us all. Might I . . ."

"He is like the rest of his kind," Kulor said, pointing at Sesrene. "Liars, all of them. The galaxy would do well to see itself rid of their . . . infestation."

Before Jetanien could react, Karumé rose from her seat at the ambassador's left hand and strode with undeniable purpose toward the Klingon attaché. Kulor looked up and offered a wolfish grin, but Karumé ignored it, instead stepping forward until she was able to deliver a vicious punch to his face that almost made Jetanien flinch.

"Still your profane tongue, *tu'HomIraH,*" she growled even as Kulor's right hand moved toward the *d'k tahg* knife at his side.

The action did not go unnoticed, as Sesrene's attachés each reacted by maneuvering back from the conference table, their rear legs tapping in frenzied rhythms loud enough to be heard even on the room's thick carpeting.

"That is enough!"

The words exploded from Jetanien's mouth, accompanied by the slamming of his hand against the top of the conference table. Everyone in the room fell silent, all eyes now locked once more upon him, each person now regarding him with an expression of unqualified shock.

Of those surprised by the outburst, none were more so than Jetanien himself.

"This bickering is pointless," he said, the words delivered in a measured cadence designed to convey that he would tolerate no interruptions. "It is obvious that we have much work ahead of us if we are to forge any sort of understanding here. Lies, half-truths, exaggerations, and hyperbole serve only to undermine our efforts, and they cannot be tolerated."

Turning to face the Chelon, Kulor began, "You accuse us . . ."

"I accuse no one," Jetanien said, cutting off what he sensed was another imminent diatribe. "The simple facts are enough to illustrate the issues we face. Even while your governments send envoys here to meet in peace, acts of aggression continue in the Taurus Reach. Tholians attack Klingons, Klingons attack Tholians, and Tholians attack the Federation." As he uttered those last words, his gaze fell upon Ambassador Sesrene. He knew a reminder of the tragedy that had befallen the *U.S.S. Bombay* was necessary, but still he drew satisfaction from seeing the Tholian diplomat shift his stance as if discomfited by the remarks.

Yes, he decided, *now is the time to act.*

With a confidence he had not felt even at the start of the proceedings, Jetanien rose from his *glenget*. "The only way we will succeed," he continued, beginning to pace toward the front of the room, "is if we all commit ourselves to the notion that there are other, better alternatives than aggression to solve these issues. We must resist the temptation to fall back upon the timeworn distraction of partisan brinksmanship." As he reached the doors leading from the conference room, he turned once more to face the delegation. "In order to serve that end, I propose we remove those things which lend themselves to such diversion."

With that, he turned to the door and pressed a control on the wall-mounted keypad. The doors slid aside to reveal the pair of security guards still standing at their assigned posts.

"Lieutenant Beyer," Jetanien said to the female officer, "kindly step in." To the rest of his assemblage, he leveled a stern gaze. "Mr. Sovik, Ms. Karumé, please resume your normal duties. I will call on you if I have need of your assistance."

Sovik's immediate reaction was to raise his right eyebrow. "I beg your pardon, Your Excellency?"

"You heard me, Mr. Sovik. I have the situation well in hand. Surely there are other matters requiring your attention?"

Karumé could only stare at him in openmouthed shock for several seconds. Then, with everyone facing Jetanien and thus unable to see her expression, she offered him a knowing smile. "As you wish."

Excellent, the Chelon thought. *She understands.* Though Sovik's expression was of course as implacable as ever, Jetanien imagined he saw comprehension in the Vulcan's eyes, as well.

"As for the Klingon and Tholian delegations," he continued, "with the exception of Ambassadors Lugok and Sesrene, the rest of you may return to your respective embassies. Lieutenant Beyer and her staff will provide escort, to ensure you encounter no trouble along the way."

"What is the meaning of this?" Kulor asked.

Jetanien shrugged. "I should think my meaning is plain. Get out." He nodded to Beyer. "Lieutenant, if you please."

The process of removing the ambassadors' envoys from the room took nearly a full minute, during which both Kulor and the Tholians made every effort to protest short of physically resisting overtures from the Starfleet security officers to direct them from the meeting chambers. As the doors slid closed behind Beyer, Jetanien turned once more to the keypad and tapped out a sequence.

"Computer, this is Ambassador Jetanien. On voice command, you will engage security protocols for this room until further notice. No one is to be allowed access or exit without my personal authorization. Voice command: Initiate security protocol."

"What are you doing?" Lugok shouted, rising once more from his chair.

"*Working,*" the monotone, female voice of the station's computer said. "*Voice command verified. Security protocol is now in effect.*"

Nodding in satisfaction, Jetanien turned back to Lugok, who by now was all but apoplectic. "This is an outrage," the Klingon said, his hands tightening into fists, though he remained where he stood.

"*Unacceptable,*" added Sesrene, his leg tapping against the floor once again as though offering a visible demonstration of his disapproval.

Jetanien nodded. "It is indeed an outrage, and it may well be unacceptable. You are free to lodge a formal complaint to the Federation Council once our business here is complete."

"You're *kidnapping* us?" Lugok asked, his expression one of disbelief.

" 'Kidnapping' is such an ugly word, Ambassador," the Chelon replied as he made his way back to his seat at the head of the table. "I prefer to think of this as a unilateral yet temporary rearrangement of your calendar. I've always felt that it's best to pursue a single goal at any one time, lest one's focus and attention be diluted to the point where effort is wasted. The more imperative the objective—such as the one confronting all of us here and now—the more important it is to observe such deliberation."

"What are you blathering about, Chelon?" Lugok asked, making no effort to hide or soften his evident disgust at the turn the meeting had taken.

Moving his shrouded body about in agitation, Sesrene added, "*What exactly are you proposing, Ambassador Jetanien?*"

As he lowered himself into his *glenget,* Jetanien eased into the curved cushion designed to support his barrel chest and clasped his hands together on the edge of the conference table, effecting what he hoped conveyed the relaxed posture of one who was in total control of the situation. "My proposal is simple: We cannot afford to part company without first reaching a consensus on how to address our respective issues regarding the Taurus Reach, preferably without dissolving into full-scale war. To that end, none of us will leave this room until such an accord is forged."

He delivered the words with practiced conviction, having rehearsed the oratory a dozen times prior to arriving at the meeting chamber. Looking back and forth across the table to his fellow diplomats, Jetanien could tell that his words had invoked their intended effect. His fellow ambassadors glowered at him, but they remained at the table.

It was a start.

Even as he regarded his colleagues, Jetanien could not help considering the promise this room now held. In centuries to come, history might well cast a favorable eye on the events of this day, to say nothing of their architect.

Or, it may well damn me.

33

If hell ever does freeze over, it'll look a lot like this, Xiong decided, watching his breath fog before his face as he entered the subterranean control room that until a week ago had been the focal point of his research on the planet Erilon—the subterranean chamber ensconced within the alien structure which he hoped would at last begin to provide answers to his many questions.

Thankfully, a landing party from the *Endeavour* had been sent in ahead of him, tasked with removing from the scene the remains of his former comrades, all of whom obviously had been killed by the nightmarish creature which had attacked them—and which also had been responsible for the deaths of Captain Zhao and members of his security detail. With that grisly duty completed, the control room was on its way toward being as he remembered it, though of course there were many new elements.

Instead of his research team, a contingent of engineering specialists from the *U.S.S. Lovell* now moved about the chamber, though their attention was not focused on studying and appreciating the structure's design and potential, or attempting to discern the motivations of those who had built it. Instead, they simply were concentrating on functionality alone. The air of discovery and delight which once had permeated this place was gone, wiped away and replaced with one of efficiency and purpose.

Other repair crews, both from the *Endeavour* and the *Lovell,* were at this moment working overtime to bring the research outpost back to full operational capability so that Xiong and a new team might continue the work he had been forced to leave behind. Given the earlier incident here, to say nothing of the mind-numbing events that had transpired in the

Palgrenax system, the artifacts and structures discovered on Erilon remained Starfleet's first and best hope of gaining some measure of understanding about the mysteries that seemed to define the Taurus Reach.

That included Xiong's current mission: acquiring some means of accessing the ancient technology buried beneath Erilon's surface—primarily in order to ensure that whatever destroyed Palgrenax did not happen here. The engineering team from the *Lovell* was also bringing their exceptional range of talents to the table, working from the premise that the creature that had attacked the research team had to have been in some form of contact with the ancient weapons technology brought to bear against the *Endeavour*. With that in mind, the engineers were attempting to develop a means of counteracting or at least interfering with that link.

It was an assignment Xiong had accepted with no small measure of uncertainty, given the need to return to the scene of so much wanton violence and death. Shouted orders and cries for help, phaser fire, and the strange tingling that irritated his exposed skin every time he looked up in muted horror to see the approach of the . . .

"Ming?" A calm voice intruded on his tortured thoughts. "Ming? Anybody home in there?"

Blinking rapidly as his mind returned to the present and the matter at hand, Xiong looked up from his tabletop scanner to see Lieutenant Mahmud al-Khaled, wearing a Starfleet-issue dark blue parka with the hood pushed back and regarding him with an expression of confusion and concern.

"Yes, of course," Xiong replied, offering what he hoped would appear as a nod of reassurance to the other man.

An engineer and leader of the Corps of Engineers team assigned to the *Lovell*, al-Khaled already had proven himself months ago, when he and his crew of engineers had visited Vanguard with the task of resolving the rash of unexplained technical issues plaguing Starbase 47's onboard systems in the weeks leading up to its coming into service. Indeed, it was al-Khaled who led the effort to identify the source of the problems, and now the young engineer was assisting here in the control chamber, where his skill and talents hopefully would aid Xiong in carrying out their latest demanding assignment.

"This place is incredible," al-Khaled said, running a hand through his dark, unkempt hair, which Xiong noted appeared to be slightly longer than Starfleet regulations typically allowed. With a wave of his right hand the engineer indicated one wall with its banks of consoles that according to Xiong's tests had lain idle for millennia. "No metal or plastic composites, just polycrystalline lattices fused together in specific configurations. What did you make of this during your initial investigations?"

Xiong said, "My first theory is that it must be organic. I've found no other means of explaining the construction method used here."

Unzipping his parka, al-Khaled shrugged. "I'm no geologist, but it seems to me that the only way this sort of crystalline configuration could route power is in a manner similar to the way light is channeled through a prism; refracting across the various interior surfaces from its origin point until it reaches its destination."

"Or perhaps something akin to electrical impulses moving through our brains," Xiong offered.

Al-Khaled frowned. "You're suggesting this material is sentient?"

"Not at all," Xiong replied. "Only that it possesses some degree of biological components, though of course it would have to be a form of life we've not yet encountered. Perhaps a biomechanical combination? Living cells fused within a crystalline structure?" Releasing a frustrated sigh, the lieutenant added, "Of course, it's just a theory."

"Well," al-Khaled said as he shook his head, "it's not like anything I've ever seen before, believe me."

Of course you haven't, Xiong thought, *just as you've probably never taken a xenobiology course to study Tholians. If you only knew what I knew . . .*

Once again, Xiong felt the weight of secrecy pressing down upon his shoulders, the supposed need for security preventing him from sharing all of his knowledge with al-Khaled. As always, he was baffled by Starfleet's reluctance to engage its brightest minds—such as those belonging to al-Khaled here as well as to any number of scientists and engineers scattered throughout the Federation—in a bid to piece together the puzzle harbored by this region of the galaxy.

Instead, he could only sit and hold his tongue, listening as al-Khaled spoke aloud many of the same thoughts, ideas, and theories Xiong himself had put forth during the first days of his investigation, hoping that even without the assistance and information Starfleet already had accumulated here, the engineer might through his own skill and perspective provide some fresh avenue of insight, a new way of approaching the seemingly inexhaustible list of questions Xiong's own efforts continued to accumulate.

"So," Xiong said after a moment, "any ideas on how to interface our equipment?" He suspected he might be able to anticipate al-Khaled's answer, given his team's previous attempts.

Confirming his suspicions, the engineer replied, "We might try fitting a portable generator with a dynamic mode converter. Adjusting the converter's polarity to account for the lack of a physical conduit with which to connect might give us an idea of how power flows through these circuits." Frowning, he added, "If that's what you want to call them, that is."

Xiong nodded, pretending he was hearing the notion for the first time instead of already having seen the idea tested and proven successful several times. "Worth a shot, I suppose, though I have to wonder how effective it would be. We might be able to stimulate some of these . . . circuits . . . but I can't see how that would give us any real interface to the technology."

"It won't," al-Khaled replied as he moved back to the table where he had been working alongside Xiong. "It'd be like pressing our foreheads to a console aboard ship and trying to access the library computer through the electrical impulses in our minds. We're not compatible." He tapped his fingers atop the table, considering the problem for a moment. "What we're missing is a piece of connective technology to bridge the gap between equipment and user."

Xiong found himself impressed with the engineer's capacity for deductive reasoning. For the past several days he had deliberated the theory that a form of biometric "key" might be required in order to gain access to the storehouse of ancient technology. Considering the sensor readings recorded by the *Endeavour* during the previous incident here and factoring those readings in with the remarkable discovery made by Dr. Fisher during his examination of Xiong's ill-fated friend Bohanon, the lieutenant now believed that the meta-genome almost certainly had to be a crucial component of such an interface.

Bioneural impulses channeled through a complex polycrystalline lattice, he mused. *Makes the Tholian connection all that much more interesting, doesn't it?*

The discovery by Dr. Gek and his team that the subterranean power signatures detected both on Erilon and Palgrenax bore a distant and all-but-indistinguishable similarity to Tholian technology had thrown a spanner into the research data collected by Xiong and the Erilon research team. Such a parallel, no matter how superficial, brought with it the potential for a staggering change in the way he—and Starfleet—viewed their approach to learning the truth about the Taurus Reach.

That the enigma of the genome might somehow play a part in acquiring the means to understand this place and all it harbored was a hypothesis Xiong had shared with no one. Listening to al-Khaled begin to formulate a similar theory—a task he could never complete without possession of the knowledge he was denied thanks to the secrecy enveloping the meta-genome's very existence—only added credence to his belief that there must be some substance to his own conjecture.

"Mahmud," Xiong said, choosing his words with care, "we know it's possible for a living organism to generate neural impulses that an artificial construct can interpret and react to. We have prosthetic limbs, devices to aid with visual impairments, and so on." He indicated the row of inert control consoles along the chamber's far wall. "What kind of connection would be required in order to tie into equipment like this?"

Al-Khaled rubbed his chin as he pondered the question.

"Something akin to a keypad or even a fingerprint or retinal scan. A bioneural interface of some sort."

"What if the artificial and biological components were bonded at the genetic level?" Xiong suggested.

"That'd be a neat trick," al-Khaled replied. "Biology was one of those subjects I skipped in order to spend more time taking things apart and figuring out why they work. I'm an engineer, though, so that means I'm not above the occasional juicy rationalization." Moving from the worktable, he crossed the chamber until he was able to run his hand across the surface of the dormant control consoles. "Still, it's not hard to figure out that if we're really looking at the kind of biomechanical fusion you're talking about, it would be genetic engineering on a scale that's way, way beyond anything we understand. Forget all about bionic prosthetics and the Eugenics Wars and cloning. This is a whole new ball game, Ming."

Xiong nodded in approval at the engineer's reasoning. Everything they had discussed fit with his theory as well as matched up with what he knew must have happened here during the incident with the *Endeavour*. According to what he and his team had learned to this point and in order for the power generators and other systems tied into the weapons unleashed against the starship to have been activated, an interface such as the one he and al-Khaled were theorizing would have to be involved.

The thing that attacked us—it must have contained the metagenome. That has to be the answer. The more Xiong thought about it, the more excited he became at the notion. He was here, on the cusp of grasping a fundamental thread that weaved through the very fabric of the Taurus Reach mystery.

All that was needed was a substantive sample of the creature's DNA.

Not the easiest task to complete, he mused with no small amount of frustration.

Feeling confined inside his insulated parka, Xiong unzipped the garment and allowed some of the chilled air permeating the chamber to cool him. "So," he said, fighting to keep his mounting excitement in check, "how do we rig an interface for us, without subjecting ourselves to some bizarre and as yet incomprehensible form of genetic manipulation?"

Al-Khaled chuckled. "Off the top of my head? Develop something like a universal translator, though one capable of transmitting signals or impulses through an organic means." Frowning, he added, "We'd have to devise a method to regulate the power flow—enough to communicate basic commands until we get a better grasp of whatever it uses for software, and not so much that we overload the control panel's lattice the first time we use it."

Xiong nodded as he considered the engineer's off-the-cuff concept. Listening to it laid out in such straightforward terms lent all sorts of credence to his own theory about the meta-genome's involvement in the use of the technology around them.

Everything we've been looking for could be right here, but where?

Feeling stuffy, he stood up in order to shrug out of his parka, and saw al-Khaled doing the same thing.

"Mahmud," he asked, "have your people installed an enviro-control system down here?" He was unaware of any such task on the list of assignments that had been given to the *Lovell*'s team.

A frown creased al-Khaled's olive complexion. "Not that I know of."

Wiping his brow, Xiong was surprised to find a bead of perspiration wetting his fingertip. "It's getting warmer in here."

34

Throughout her time as a ship commander, Sarith always had regarded her quarters as a refuge, a place of solace from which she could—if only temporarily—escape the myriad burdens of leadership. The few precious hours she spent here when not on duty, be it sleeping or immersed in a treasured book or listening to favorite music, always had been vital to her well-being and peace of mind, in her opinion even more so than the exercise and diet regimen dictated to her by the *Bloodied Talon*'s physician.

Now, however, her sanctuary seemed more like a prison.

Without the faint yet omnipresent hum of the *Talon*'s warp engines channeling through the hull, it seemed to Sarith that much of the life had been removed not only from her quarters but also from the entire ship. A languid pall seemed draped over the room like a stifling blanket, even the air she breathed feeling heavy and stale in her lungs. Due to power conservation requirements enacted by the ship's engineer, primary lighting throughout the ship had been reduced save for the most critical of uses. A single light source situated over her desk pierced the darkness of Sarith's quarters, its feeble illumination managing only to chase the shadows to the corners of the room and offering the sensation that the bulkheads might be trying to close in on her when she was not looking.

Enough with that foolishness. You are not a child.

The reprimand seemed to echo within the confines of her sleep-deprived mind even as Sarith looked down at herself and allowed a small laugh to escape. For the first time she realized that she was sitting in her favorite overstuffed chair with her legs held close to her chest, her arms wrapped around her knees and pulling them tight to her. It was a pose she had adopted often as a young girl, sitting before the firepit in her family home and listening as her grandfather read aloud from a book of treasured stories, his nightly gift to his grandchildren before it was time to sleep. Sometimes the stories were frightening and young Sarith would be frightened, tuck her body into a ball in an attempt to ward off the monsters described in the pages of the storybook.

"If only it were that simple," she said, though there was no one else in the room to hear her.

A gentle knock echoed on her door, a substitute for the intercom tone that sounded whenever one of her guards notified her of a visitor. Power consumption aboard ship had been reallocated to the point that even such small indulgences as a door chime were viewed as wasteful.

"Enter," Sarith called out, loud enough to be heard in the corridor beyond her quarters. A few seconds passed as the centurion outside used a manual release lever to open the door, and she smiled as she beheld Ineti standing before the threshold.

"May I come in, Commander?" he asked, his wizened features warmed by an almost paternal smile.

Rising from her chair, Sarith motioned her second-in-command to enter. She waited for the guard to close the door before stepping forward and throwing her arms around her lifelong friend, ignoring the resulting pain in her side. Ineti said nothing, merely wrapping his own arms around her and allowing her the time to extract as much comfort from the gesture as she needed.

"My trusted friend . . . for as long as I can remember," she said after a moment, patting his chest before pulling herself away and using her hands to smooth the wrinkles from her uniform. "You've always known how much I look to you for strength and guidance, and never have you considered it a weakness, just as you've never asked anything in return. If we are to die, I can think of no better way to do so than with you at my side."

Ineti's eyebrows rose. "You'll forgive me, Commander, if I refuse to look ahead to that tragic event with any great enthusiasm." Looking toward the ceiling of her quarters as if contemplating the stars that lay beyond the hull of the ship, he added, "We are not finished yet, Sarith. So long as we draw breath, we are not yet defeated."

"Save that for the crew," Sarith countered as she turned toward a small bureau positioned near her desk and retrieved a half-consumed bottle of ale along with two glasses. Motioning Ineti to be seated in the chair situated near her desk, she poured generous portions of the radiant blue liquid into the glasses before offering one to her companion. "What's our current status?" she asked as she returned to her recliner, attempting to reassert herself at least somewhat into a command mind-set.

If Ineti was bothered by her dismissive comment, he chose not to indicate it. "The warp drive is a hopeless cause, of course. Even if the physical damage was repaired, the lack of an antimatter containment assembly renders the entire point moot."

Sarith nodded in acknowledgment. Even if the engineer were able to manufacture a replacement, the original containment sphere had taken with it the *Talon's* entire supply of antimatter. Without that vital ingredient, the ship's warp engines were nothing more than vital organs which already had surrendered to a disease ravaging a dying body.

"We are operating on partial impulse power only," Ineti continued. "Life-support is currently our most demanding power requirement, though other essential systems are being supported via battery backups, but without the warp engines to recharge them their usefulness will be exhausted in eighty-six *dierha*. The engineer is attempting to configure a means for replenishing the batteries from the impulse drive, but it is a risky procedure."

"Compared to what?" Sarith asked, drinking liberally from her glass and savoring the warmth of the ale as she swallowed it. "Allow him whatever latitude he requires. We are far past playing it safe, I think." If the *Talon* was to survive long enough to be rescued, it would do so through effort and ingenuity—at the same high level now displayed by her crew.

Steadfast and loyal to the end, she mused as she took another sip from her glass. *Perhaps they will survive long enough to see the Praetor recognize their fidelity.*

She doubted that, of course.

Taking a moment to sip from his own drink, Ineti regarded the sparkling cobalt ale in his glass before continuing his report. "Our supplies are also an issue. A significant portion of our food stores has been contaminated by coolant leaks. I've already imposed a rationing schedule to extend our remaining provisions as long as possible." He offered a small smile. "You did say you wanted to take your diet more seriously, did you not?"

Though she knew the situation did not warrant it, Sarith allowed herself a mild laugh at the gallows humor. She sobered almost immediately, though, as her mind turned to her next question, the most grave of those she needed to ask.

"What about casualties?"

Reclaiming his own typically staid composure, Ineti replied, "The physician has finalized his casualty report. There were four deaths in all. Two from engineering were killed by a collapsing bulkhead, one died in weapons control due to a coolant leak, and Centurion N'tovek, of course."

Sarith nodded at the report. Power constraints being what they were, it was impractical to utilize stasis chambers to preserve the bodies, and jettisoning them carried the risk of detection. She therefore had given the order for the remains to be disintegrated with hand disruptors following an interval for the crew to pay their appropriate final respects to their comrades.

"Perhaps they were the fortunate ones," she said as she sipped from her glass. "They at least will be spared whatever fate awaits the rest of us."

Turning in his seat, Ineti regarded her with a hard expression that Sarith frankly found intimidating. "It is unlike you to embrace such a negative attitude, even in private."

Sarith nodded, feeling more than a bit ashamed. "Forgive me," she offered, hoping the words sounded more convincing to her friend than they did to her own ears. "Fatigue appears to have gripped my tongue, as well."

"When was the last time you slept?" Ineti asked.

Grunting in what she knew was inappropriate amusement, Sarith replied, "Probably the same time you did." Glancing toward her sleeping area, the commander felt a new weight press down upon her as she regarded her still-rumpled bed. She had attempted a few *dierha* worth of rest earlier in the evening, but that had proven to be a futile exercise. N'tovek's familiar musky scent lingered within the sheets, mute testimony to the final ardent night of lovemaking they had shared. Those memories, and the knowledge that she never again would enjoy his presence and passion, had chased away any chance at sleep.

She suspected that Ineti understood what troubled her, but as usual he reserved his comments only to what was necessary to convey his concerns. "You cannot afford the luxury of allowing yourself to wallow in remorse or even loneliness. All of that must be left behind, buried, incinerated . . . now."

He leaned forward in his chair until his face was less than an arm's length from her. "More than ever, the crew requires you to be their commander and see them through this crisis." Pausing, he cast his eyes down toward the floor before adding, "No matter how it is to end. If you cannot do that, then we may as well destroy the ship now, for without your leadership we are surely doomed."

Despite the gravity she sensed behind her friend's words, Sarith could not help but smile. "I can always count on you to offer a straightforward perspective, Ineti." Such unfiltered counsel was one of the many qualities she treasured in him, not only as her second-in-command but also as her confidant and even as a means of seeking her own moral focus.

"Very well," she said, draining her ale before rising from her chair to refill her glass. "Let us talk about our next steps. First, I want to dispatch a status message to Romulus in three *dierha*. Can we afford the power to generate the necessary signal strength?"

Ineti nodded. "We can, but there are other issues to consider. Without warp drive, we are unable to travel an appreciable distance from our point of transmission. We therefore risk detection in the event our communications are intercepted."

You should have remembered that, Sarith scolded herself. As part of the procedures designed to maintain the *Talon*'s stealth while traveling through the Taurus Reach, communications were limited to encrypted burst transmissions executed at irregular intervals. Protocol called for the messages to be sent while in the proximity of a star, using solar radiation as a means of masking the signal's origin point. Afterward, Sarith would order a high-warp route away from that location, minimizing the risk of detection by other ships that might be within sensor range.

Her vessel's compromised and weakened condition made following that procedure impossible, of course.

Knowing the risk, she nevertheless had ordered a short message dispatched soon after the *Talon* had sustained its damage in order to alert Command to the ship's dire situation. It was too soon to know if the message had been received, and Sarith knew that the likelihood of receiving a response was minimal at best. Bearing that in mind, she and Ineti already had decided that once the appropriate time had passed—assuming they were still alive, of course—she would simply inform the crew that a rescue operation was under way. It was one of the few ways she could hope to maintain her people's flagging morale.

There was also duty to consider, of course.

"We have no choice," she said as she returned to her seat. "The Praetor must be alerted to the possible danger posed by forces in this region of the galaxy." There was no denying that her government must be made aware of the potential threat posed by whatever as-yet-unidentified race that wielded the power to obliterate Palgrenax. Only with warning and ample time to devise strategy could the security of the empire be protected.

"That said," she added after a moment, "our first priority is preserving our stealth, no matter the cost. The Federation must not be allowed to learn that we have struck out beyond our borders, not before the Praetor is ready to announce our presence with the proper authority."

Rising from his chair, Ineti nodded. "Worry not, Commander. If and when the time comes, the crew and I will follow you wherever duty demands we go."

Sarith smiled, confident in her friend's loyalty as well as that of her crew.

The only question lingering in her mind was whether she was worthy of that allegiance.

35

"I will tolerate no more of this!"

Pushing out of his chair, his eyes wide with storied Klingon ire, Lugok lunged across the conference table, hands grasping for whichever part of Ambassador Sesrene around which he could wrap his fingers. The Tholian dodged the attack, his legs moving with uncanny speed as he skittered to his left and toward Jetanien's end of the table.

Fearful that any damage to Sesrene's envirosuit might compromise the delicate balance of gases comprising the ambassador's internal atmosphere, to say nothing of exposing him and Lugok to the same, Jetanien jumped to his feet and rushed to position himself between the enraged Lugok and his quarry.

So much for progress, he mused as he leveled a withering gaze at the Klingon ambassador. After nearly thirteen hours confined within the meeting chambers, Jetanien for the first time was beginning to fear that his hopes for facilitating peace among the parties vying for interest in the Taurus Reach might well have been premature after all.

On the other hand, he seemed to be well on his way to inciting an interstellar incident the likes of which might remain unmatched throughout the remainder of his life.

"And *you*," Lugok snarled, raising a massive gloved fist toward Jetanien. "You've done nothing but talk for hours on end, but you've yet to say anything I've found of value."

Well, he admitted to himself, *circumlocution* is *one of my stronger suits.*

Growling, Lugok bared his teeth as he stepped closer. "Since our first meeting, you've said nothing of the Federation's plans in this sector. Do you truly expect us to believe that your sole interest in this region is colonization?" Waving a dismissive hand in Jetanien's face, the Klingon turned to return to his seat. "Nothing you have said here today has changed any of that. How are we supposed to trust you when you operate behind a veil of secrecy?"

"*This farce has gone on far too long already,*" came the Tholian's translated vocal oscillations. "*Release us.*"

"Or . . . defend yourself," Lugok added, his *d'k tahg* appearing in his hand as if materializing from thin air.

Jetanien forced himself to remain composed in the face of the ambassador's threat, which was to say it was an effort to refrain from laughing.

"You do not want to threaten me, Your Excellency," he said firmly, maintaining his bearing while attempting to strike an imposing enough figure to match Lugok's bluster. Klingons responded more favorably to confidence and even outright arrogance than to placation. It would require a deft hand in order to move past this interruption and get the meeting back on track.

"Tell me, Ambassador," he said after a moment, "before accepting the honorable mantle you now bear, I assume you spent some time in service with the Klingon Defense Force?"

His chest swelling with pride, Lugok nodded. "Of course I did, fool. I fought in many campaigns, including battling Starfleet at Donatu V. It was a glorious victory for the empire."

"Indeed," Jetanien said. Knowing that the battle between Federation and Klingon forces had been fought to a virtual standstill, he nevertheless was pleased to see that his rudimentary attempts to deflect Lugok's anger already were beginning to have an effect. "And in your storied career, have you ever battled a member of my species?"

The ambassador regarded him as a hunter might study a potential quarry before offering a leering smile. "There's always a first time."

"I fear it would also be your last," Jetanien replied. "When attacked, Rigelian Chelons have an autonomic defense mechanism which manifests itself as a deadly toxin secreted from our skin."

Lowering his blade, if only slightly, Lugok scoffed. "Poison is a coward's weapon."

Jetanien nodded. "I'd never argue a point of honor with a Klingon, Ambassador, but there is little I can do to prevent it. Within hours of exposure, you would suffer a quite agonizing and inglorious demise, and then where would we be?"

"It is a ruse," Lugok said, turning to face Sesrene. "The Chelon is nothing but bluster."

"*Feel free to test your assertion, Ambassador,*" the Tholian replied. "*I would await the outcome with interest.*"

Growling in irritation, Lugok returned his blade to the sheath on his left hip. "I do not dance on the request of my enemies." He turned his attention back to Jetanien. "Not that his suggestion is an unsound one."

Jetanien raised his hands, open and away from his body to demonstrate to Lugok that he had no intention of initiating hostilities. "Friends," he said, sensing that he may have found a clumsy yet effective way to navigate this latest obstacle, "we have not been asked to serve our respective peoples because we are the best at squabbling. We are the best at negotiating, and at agreeably reaching clear-minded concessions so we all can exist in harmony. We have an obligation to carry out our sworn duty. May we proceed?"

To his surprise, Lugok turned and moved back to his seat, though he did so only after offering a parting snarl. Sesrene likewise returned to his position at the table, uttering an indecipherable series of chirps and clicks.

Perhaps all hope is not lost after all, Jetanien mused as he also moved to his place at the head of the table.

"Shall we revisit the point yet again?" Lugok asked as he settled into his chair. "How much longer are we to argue over who has the right to assume control over *unclaimed* space? The Tholians have staked no claims in the Gonmog Sector, and yet they block our every move to do so for ourselves."

Sesrene clicked his appendages on the floor before responding. "*As I have already stated, our motivations are our own.*"

"And as I have already demanded repeatedly," Lugok countered, "explain yourselves!"

Jetanien rapped his webbed digits on the table. "One might argue that the Tholians are within their right to protect the indigenous races of this region from being exploited by unwanted and aggressive interlopers."

"So," the Klingon sneered, "the Federation supports this policy? Allow the Tholians to dirty their hands, or their . . . whatever they have, while you prop yourself up with your vaunted standard of non-interference."

"The Federation does not dictate our actions," Sesrene said. *"My people have no intentions of establishing control over the territory in question."*

Jetanien schooled his features to offer no visible reaction to the Tholian's comments. *How curious he would admit that now, at the very time when it appears his people may have more at stake here than any of us.*

"Once more, you offer lies," Lugok said, his eyes narrowing in renewed suspicion. "Your people have always asserted territorial control whenever and wherever it suits you. Why is the Gonmog Sector to be any different?"

Tapping one of his appendages on the table for emphasis, Sesrene replied, *"I offer truth and facts. Our presence in this region and our actions against your expansion efforts reflect only our desire to leave this space undisturbed."*

"And so you all but declare war on the Klingon Empire?" Lugok roared.

"Ambassador, please," Jetanien pleaded, fearful that Lugok's ever-present invective would only serve to send Sesrene back into his figurative shell, particularly now that it appeared the Tholian might be prepared to offer details about the odd actions his people had taken in recent weeks. Turning to Sesrene, he said, "Your Excellency, if you could elaborate, I think it would be most helpful for all of us. The Federation wants only to understand the Tholian people's motivations so that we might better respect your concerns here."

Sesrene did not answer at first, and Jetanien wondered if the ambassador might be once more communing with his envoys. *"I . . . cannot comply,"* he said after a moment. *"This place is . . ."*

There was another pause, and Jetanien thought that perhaps the conference room's universal translator might be having trouble interpreting some heretofore unencountered aspect of Tholian speech.

When Sesrene spoke again, Jetanien was sure the translator was broken, with the ambassador's vocalizations sounding more like metal grinding on metal. When a translation finally was offered, it provided the Chelon with more questions than answers.

"This place is . . . Shedai."

Frowning, Jetanien shook his head. "I'm afraid I do not understand, Your Excellency. This place is taboo? Quarantined? Forbidden?"

"From long ago," Sesrene said, *"our people have avoided this place. It is believed the unspeakable occurred here. Of all places, this is where we are not to be."*

Lugok released a hearty laugh, one Jetanien recognized as derisive. "Folk tales," he said. "Stories to frighten the meek and mewling. These Tholians truly are cowards."

Jetanien, however, found himself listening with intent to Sesrene's words. Could this supposed fable have a foundation in ancient fact? Might the ambassador's seemingly ingrained fear of this space possess roots to a danger so dreadful and frightening as to leave an impression lasting millennia?

What if they fear whatever it is we're looking for? What if the very builders of the artifacts—the originators of the meta-genome—have struck millennia of terror in the Tholian people? All of this is connected. It simply has to be.

It has to be.

So focused was the ambassador on this new train of thought that the sound of the conference chamber's doors unlocking and parting all but startled him out of his chair. All three diplomats jerked their heads in that direction to see Commodore Reyes entering the room with powerful strides and a grim expression darkening his human features.

"Commodore!" Jetanien blurted, caught off guard by the untimely interruption. "I ordered this room sealed. How did you get in here?"

Stopping at the opposite end of the table, Reyes replied, "It is *my* station, Your Excellency." He looked first to Lugok and then to Sesrene before speaking again. "I'm here to inform you that this summit and all further discussions between the three delegations are hereby terminated."

"I beg your pardon," Jetanien said. *How can this be happening? Why now, when I might be so close to our first true breakthrough?*

Reyes shook his head. "I'm sorry, Ambassador, but this comes directly from the Federation Council. We've just received word that earlier today, a Klingon task force attacked and destroyed the Tholian military outpost on Zenstala II."

"Excellent," Lugok said, his voice low and menacing.

"And the Tholians retaliated in like fashion against Klingon holdings at Dorala and Korinar."

"*A suitable response to Klingon aggression,*" Sesrene offered.

Already knowing what the impact of the new developments would be, Jetanien forced himself to remain impassive as he asked, "What does this mean, Commodore?"

His expression one of disappointment, Reyes replied, "Both the Tholian Assembly and the Klingon Empire have called for the withdrawal of all peace delegations, including those serving within the United Federation of Planets and specifically Starbase 47." To Lugok and Sesrene, he said, "Further, any delay in having these directives carried out will be seen by your governments as interference by the Federation and acted upon 'accordingly.' Therefore, I'm declaring an end to these proceedings, effective immediately. My instructions are to have you off the station no later than 1200 hours local time tomorrow."

"That's outrageous," Jetanien said, forcing himself to remain in his *glenget* and to keep his tone of voice level. "We have only just begun to make significant progress here." He looked to Sesrene, hopeful that the revelations of the past few minutes might result in a show of support for his protest.

Instead, the Tholian ambassador stepped away from the conference table and headed toward the doors without so much as an acknowledgment of his diplomatic colleagues or even Reyes as he strode from the room.

"It is just as well," Lugok said as he rose from his chair. "The Tholians are without honor. We will never agree, on anything. So far as the empire is concerned, they are nothing more than *jeghpu'wI'*. They simply do not know it yet." Offering another contemptuous scowl to Jetanien, the Klingon marched from the chambers without another word.

As the doors slid shut behind the ambassador, Reyes turned to Jetanien. "I'm truly sorry, Your Excellency. It seems our friends aren't yet ready to take such a bold step forward, after all."

"I am not so sure, Commodore," Jetanien replied. "There was some progress made here today, though not of a type I was expecting." Reviewing what he had learned from Sesrene in the closing moments of the meeting, the Chelon decided that it was not yet the appropriate time to convey this new information to Reyes. There was no way to know at this point if what Sesrene had conveyed was fact or myth. Considering the stakes, this was no time to proceed with uncertainty.

"It's going to be a hard road going forward," Reyes said after a moment. "Starfleet Command thinks war between the Klingons and the Tholians could come at any time." He shook his head. "And here we are, with ringside seats."

"All the better to continue our mission, Commodore," Jetanien said after a moment. "I refuse to surrender, not while an iota of hope remains. We will prevail."

Afraid to make eye contact with his friend, the ambassador wondered if the commodore sensed the false optimism, for even as he spoke them, the words and the confidence they carried rang hollow in Jetanien's ears.

36

Even Pennington winced when the second of Broon's men landed a vicious punch to Quinn's stomach. The privateer sagged to the deck of the cargo hold, releasing another bout of violent coughing as he tried without success to keep from falling onto his face.

"That one's going to leave a mark," Quinn said between ragged breaths. Blood streamed from a cut over his left eye, compliments of the first hit he had taken from one of Broon's thugs. He reached up to wipe his face, but his arm was pulled away as two of the men yanked him to his feet, only to hold him steady as yet another member of the gang slammed his fist into the pilot's gut.

"Is this really necessary?" Pennington shouted, making no attempt to hide his indignation at being forced to watch Quinn suffer.

Standing a few meters away near a table where Armnoj had been planted along with his briefcase, Broon regarded the journalist with a leering smile made all the more sinister thanks to his yellow, crooked teeth. "No, but it's fun." He indicated Quinn with a wave of his hand. "Your pal there gave me a lot of grief on Kessik IV last month. He was supposed to die there, you know. Ganz contracted me to kill him. Things didn't work out, obviously, thanks to some friends he brought along. What I don't get is why Ganz didn't kill me afterward. He's not usually so forgiving."

Pennington remembered Quinn mentioning something about Kessik IV during one of his frequent stupors. To hear him tell the tale, Quinn had been the benefactor of action on T'Prynn's part. The specifics were lost amid the pilot's inebriated slurring, but

Pennington had gotten the gist: Vanguard's senior intelligence officer had a need for Quinn—for the short term, at any rate—and Ganz was smart enough not to get in the way of that.

Evidently, Broon lacked similar comprehension of the situation.

Turning to where Armnoj sat at the table fiddling with his still-closed briefcase, the pirate smacked the Zakdorn across the back of the head. "Why isn't that thing open yet?"

Armnoj reached up to rub where he had been struck. "It takes time to disengage the security measures protecting the contents," he said, his voice even more high-pitched and nasally than usual. "Do you want me to destroy everything because you rushed me?"

Looking to Pennington, Broon sneered. "I'm amazed you didn't kill him days ago."

"The thought crossed our minds," Pennington replied, looking in the direction of the Rigelian currently training a disruptor pistol on him. The thug was dividing his attention between him and Armnoj while also listening to his boss.

A yell of pain caught his attention and Pennington turned to see that one of the four men taking turns beating Quinn had landed another blow to his face. Quinn reeled from the blow, falling backward and dropping to one knee where, thankfully, he remained. His attackers, apparently possessing at least a modicum of decency, refrained from further action and instead waited for him to regain his feet.

They're going to kill him, and even if they don't, we're both dead anyway.

Looking about the cargo room, a different and much cleaner one than where he, Quinn, and Armnoj had been held after being brought aboard Broon's ship, Pennington's eyes fell upon the open hatch leading into the airlock, which according to Broon would be the gateway to oblivion so far as he and Quinn were concerned. Fear, anger, indignation, and helplessness all fought for control of the journalist as he stared at that hatch. The thought of waiting inside the cramped vestibule for the harsh, unforgiving vacuum of space to claim them terrified Pennington. It was no way to die, not for any being, even the vilest of criminals.

His gaze wandered to the airlock—and fixed upon the control panel mounted to the bulkhead next to it. In that instant Pennington's conflicting emotions resolved themselves into a single, unwavering moment of conviction.

If I'm going out, I'm taking these bastards with me.

Lunging forward, Pennington slapped his hand down upon the large switch on one end of the control panel. The Rigelian guarding him was startled by his sudden action, his slow response further hindered when an alarm blared through the cargo hold.

"What the hell?" Broon turned, his eyes wide even as one beefy hand reached beneath his coat for the disruptor strapped to his hip. Imagining the crosshairs on his back, Pennington ignored him and instead smacked his hand down upon another control, which was answered by the sudden roar of venting atmosphere.

Here's hoping I didn't just open the bloody door!

Other reactions quickly followed as the men thrashing Quinn turned toward the hatch, their expressions equally terrified as they realized what was happening. Pennington disregarded all of that, too, his focus instead on the Rigelian who was backpedaling away from the airlock. The henchman's attention was more on getting to safety and therefore he was unprepared when Pennington slammed him into a bulkhead. The journalist wrapped his left hand around the barrel of the Rigelian's disruptor pistol and jerked it up and away, at the same time lashing out with his right fist and connecting with the thug's temple.

Orange energy whined past his ear and Pennington ducked as a disruptor bolt struck the wall next to his head. He pushed to his left, taking the dazed Rigelian with him even as he landed another punch to the guard's head. Now holding the disruptor, he brought the weapon up as he spun to face the center of the room, firing it indiscriminately at Broon and the others. He hit nothing, of course, but it was enough to cause the pirate and his crewmen to scatter in search of cover. Pennington dashed away from the airlock, disruptor bolts tearing into the walls and deck around him as he sought refuge behind a nearby cargo crate. Once under cover, he turned and aimed the weapon toward the control panel for the airlock. He pressed the firing stud and the disruptor spat energy yet again.

The control panel erupted in a wash of sparks and small flames, followed immediately by a shrieking alarm beginning to wail within the confines of the room. Pennington heard the now very pronounced hiss of escaping air. If his guess was right, with the control panel destroyed, there was now no way to stop the airlock and—thanks to its open inner hatch—the rest of the cargo hold from completely depressurizing.

Thankfully, Pennington saw that the airlock's outer hatch remained closed. *Small favors, I suppose.*

"You fool!" Pennington heard Broon cry from wherever the pirate was hiding. "You'll kill us all!" More disruptor fire rang out through the room, as though emphasizing the quickly escalating problem.

Suppose that means my guess was right, Pennington mused. While Pennington figured the action likely would be arrested by one of Broon's men from elsewhere on the ship, perhaps the immediate chaos his tactic had generated would be enough to allow him, Quinn, and Armnoj a chance to escape.

From the corner of his eye Pennington saw Quinn lumbering across the deck, body slamming one of the men who had been beating on him. The two men stumbled into the nearby wall and Quinn drove the top of his skull into the other man's jaw. It was enough to drop the man to his knees, giving Quinn the opening he needed to punch him again as he grabbed the thug's disruptor. The pilot all but fell to the deck as an energy bolt hit the wall next to him, firing his own weapon as he scrambled for something behind which to hide.

"Tim!" Pennington heard Quinn shout. "The door!"

Understanding what the other man meant—at least, he hoped he did—Pennington looked to his left to see the hatch leading from the cargo bay into the adjoining corridor. The only way from the chamber that did not involve explosive decompression and immediate death, the hatch was still closed. If Broon or any of his men got to it before he did, he, Quinn, and Armnoj would be trapped here. Of course, if he could not get the door open, he and everyone else in here were going to asphyxiate, anyway.

And what if more of his men come through *the door?*

A disruptor bolt chewing into the side of the cargo container behind which he was crouching pushed away the unhelpful thought. Ducking to his left, Pennington saw one of Broon's men leaning around the side of a storage locker, lining up for another shot. The journalist tried to bring up his own weapon but he was too slow. Another energy discharge rang out across the cargo hold, this one catching the other man and slamming him into the locker he used for cover. Pennington looked to see Quinn firing his own captured disruptor again, this time using the weapon to pin down another of Broon's thugs as he moved from his place of concealment toward the hatch.

"Quinn!" Pennington heard Broon shout, the hefty man's booming voice sounding even more ominous than what he had previously heard. The pirate rose from where had sought protection, aiming his disruptor in Quinn's direction. Quinn did not react to the shout, instead firing at another of the henchmen who had made the mistake of exposing themselves from behind a cargo container. The energy burst struck the man in the chest, driving him backward; he slammed against a support strut before falling to the floor.

Sensing his breaths coming with more difficulty now that the balance of the oxygen had been released from the room, Pennington detected movement to his left and turned to see the fifth of Broon's thugs trying to sneak around a group of smaller crates haphazardly stacked along the hold's far bulkhead. He released an involuntary yelp of surprise, swinging his disruptor to aim at the approaching assailant. The other man found himself caught out in the open as Pennington pressed the weapon's firing stud.

The first shot went wide to his right and the second sailed too far to the left, but his third attempt found its mark, striking the man in the left thigh. He fell to the deck, dropping his disruptor in order to clutch his wounded leg. Pennington fired again, this time hitting the man in the chest. The pirate slumped unconscious to the floor.

"Get Armnoj!" Quinn shouted as he dodged Broon's disruptor fire, throwing himself behind another cargo container. He fired back toward the pirate's hiding place, both men now doing their utmost to pin down the other.

Ignoring the firefight unfolding on the other side of the cargo hold, Pennington lurched from his own place of protection across the deck toward Armnoj. The sounds of continued depressurization did not drown out the cries of terror the Zakdorn emitted from where the reporter saw he now cowered beneath the worktable, his briefcase clutched to his chest. With each new disruptor bolt he uttered a fresh shriek and tried to hide even farther under the table.

"Come on!" the reporter shouted, reaching beneath the table and grabbing the accountant's collar to pull him from his hiding place. Armnoj stumbled to his feet, still clasping his ubiquitous briefcase to his body.

"Get me out of here!" he whined, struggling for breath in the oxygen-depleted air of the cargo hold and grasping Pennington's free arm as though it were a lifeline.

Pennington grimaced in irritation but could not shake himself free. "Let's go," he hissed through gritted teeth, flinching as more disruptor fire echoed through the room. Hugging the wall, Pennington guided Armnoj toward the door leading from the cargo bay. Passing the airlock, he reached out to hit the control panel, halting the depressurization and beginning the process of restoring the atmosphere to the air-depleted room. The action served an additional purpose, as he knew the hatch leading to the corridor would not open so long as there was a threat of compromising the rest of the ship's atmosphere.

Another disruptor bolt hit the wall in front of him and Pennington recoiled, feeling the heat from the energy blast as he fell backward. More disruptor fire illuminated the cargo hold and he looked for its source to see Broon ducking behind a trio of storage drums. Pennington fired in that direction, hoping to make the pirate keep his head down.

"Move, damn you!" he shouted, his lungs aching as he shoved Armnoj in the direction of the door. To his right he saw Broon sticking his head up from behind one of the storage drums, realizing too late as he stared at the barrel of the brigand's disruptor pistol that the bastard now had him dead to rights. The son of a bitch even was smiling.

Then Pennington heard another pulse of energy and saw the blast hit Broon in the chest. The outlaw convulsed as the disruptor bolt washed over him before he fell limp to the deck, disappearing from sight behind the storage cylinders.

Thank God. Pennington breathed a sigh of relief, realizing that all of the potential threats inside the cargo bay appeared to have been neutralized.

"Don't get comfortable," Quinn said as he made his way, somewhat slowly and in what Pennington realized was a marginal amount of pain, across the room to where Broon's prone form lay prostrate on the deck. "No telling how many more goons he's got aboard." As the reporter watched, Quinn knelt down next to the unconscious pirate and delved through the pockets of his jacket. It took him only a moment to retrieve what he had been seeking: the data core from the Klingon sensor drone.

"What are we supposed to do now?" Armnoj asked, his eyes wide with fear. He appeared even to be trembling, still gripped by the intensity of the past few minutes.

Quinn shrugged. "Get the hell out of here," he said as he tucked the data core into his jacket pocket. Moving to a row of lockers lined up along a nearby bulkhead, he began rummaging through the different storage compartments.

"Won't Broon's men have something to say about that?" Pennington asked.

"Probably." Reaching into one of the lockers, Quinn extracted what appeared to be a civilian model of tricorder. "Would you rather stay?" he asked, turning to regard Pennington as he headed for the door.

The reporter shook his head. "Lead the way, mate."

Broon employed at least two more men, both of whom were waiting as Quinn led Pennington and Armnoj to the cargo bay holding the *Rocinante*.

The first shot came as Quinn stepped through the hatch leading

into the bay, striking the wall to his left. It was followed by another
shot of equally poor aim that tore into the deck in front of him.
Pennington followed the trajectory of the energy pulse up to see
one of Broon's thugs crouching atop a catwalk and aiming a disruptor rifle in their direction.

"Up high!" Pennington shouted, raising his weapon to fire at
the would-be sniper. Though he missed, the man scrambled from
his perch in search of cover.

From where he knelt near a tool locker, Quinn motioned for
Pennington to keep moving. "Get that idiot to the ship!" he
shouted before firing toward the first shooter, driving the assailant
deeper into the cargo bay.

The decrepit starhopper never had looked as good to Pennington as it did at that moment. Grabbing Armnoj by the arm, Pennington propelled him in the direction of the boarding ramp
leading into the *Rocinante*'s cargo hold. Disruptor fire flashed
around him, coming from two different directions, though thankfully Broon's crew seemed to view marksmanship with the same
importance they did sanitation and hygiene.

Reaching the bottom of the ramp, Pennington pushed
Armnoj ahead of him, only to have the Zakdorn stop so suddenly that the reporter nearly ran into him. "What the bloody
hell is wrong with you?"

Then the shadow fell across the ramp and Pennington looked
up to see another of Broon's men standing at the entrance to the
ship, disruptor pistol in hand. Armnoj emitted another cry of
panic, attempting to backpedal away from the new threat. The
thug at the top of the ramp brought his weapon up, sighting down
the barrel toward the Zakdorn.

Pennington was faster, aiming his disruptor and firing. The energy burst struck the man in the gut, throwing him against the
open hatch before he fell to the deck.

"Get inside!" Pennington shouted, pushing Armnoj up the
ramp. He turned at the sound of approaching footsteps and saw
Quinn running with a limp across the open deck of the cargo bay
toward a freestanding control console. Taking a few seconds to
study the bank of switches and status indicators, Quinn punched

several buttons. An instant later, a warbling alarm began to sound, echoing the length of the hold.

"What are you doing?" Pennington shouted to be heard above the siren.

Quinn took a step backward before aiming his disruptor at the console and firing. Bristling orange energy tore into the control station, obliterating it. Leaving behind his handiwork, he turned and headed for the ramp.

"Time to go," the pilot said between ragged breaths as he scrambled up the ramp, grunting with the exertion. "I started the depressurization sequence and keyed the hatch. It should be open in a minute or so."

For the first time since their escape had begun, Pennington saw the extent of Quinn's injuries from the beating he had suffered. He was favoring the ribs on his right side, and he was sporting a large discolored bruise on his right cheek. A nasty bruise over his left eye already was beginning to swell, and dried blood stuck to skin and hair on the left side of his head.

"Are you all right?" Pennington asked.

"I'll live," Quinn said. He nodded toward Broon's unconscious goon. "Get rid of him, and watch the ramp." As Pennington enlisted Armnoj's assistance to remove the fallen man from the ship, Quinn busied himself with the Klingon sensor drone, which still lay on the floor of the *Rocinante*'s cargo hold. He pulled the tricorder taken from the other cargo hold and activated it, running it over the inert probe.

"What are you doing?" Armnoj asked, his voice now reaching a level of nasally buzzing that Pennington was sure might be useful as a weapon to ward off wolves.

"Shut up," Quinn said.

From where he stood near the top of the boarding ramp, Pennington glanced over his shoulder to see Quinn making adjustments to the tricorder. The device emitted a series of beeps and tones that seemed to satisfy him, and the pilot reached into the opening he earlier had cut into the hull probe's hull plating.

"Now what?" Pennington asked.

"Calling for help," Quinn replied. Rising to his feet, he lurched his way over to a nearby storage locker and flung open its door. From inside he extracted a portable antigravity maneuvering unit, which he quickly attached to the side of the sensor drone.

An energy burst struck the left support strut for the landing ramp and Pennington ducked away from the hatch. "Well, hurry the hell up about it!"

Using the antigrav unit to move the sensor probe toward the hatch, Quinn gave the weight-neutralized drone a kick that sent it down the boarding ramp before slapping the control pad next to the door. "That ought to piss some people off," he muttered as he stumbled his way toward the *Rocinante*'s cockpit.

"Are you going to explain what that was about?" Armnoj asked as he followed after the pilot.

"Sit down and stay quiet," Quinn growled, "or I'll kick your ass down the ramp, too." He pushed the accountant into his customary jump seat just outside the cockpit before proceeding on to his seat, his hands moving across the helm console as he went through the startup sequence to bring the ship's engines to life.

Dropping into the copilot's chair, Pennington stared through the cockpit canopy at the cargo hold outside the ship. He saw the two thugs who had been shooting at them running for the bay's exit, trying to get out ahead of the depressurization currently laying claim to the atmosphere inside the chamber.

The rumble of the *Rocinante*'s engines shook the deck beneath Pennington's feet as Quinn continued the power-up sequence. "Get us out of here, Quinn, before they override the door."

"Working on it, newsboy," Quinn replied without looking away from the helm console. He tapped the controls for the ship's maneuvering thrusters and Pennington felt the ship lurch, rotating to its right as it lifted from the deck of the cargo bay. He saw the bulkhead in front of the ship slide past as the starhopper maneuvered toward the hold's massive space doors, which Pennington was relieved to see beginning to cycle open. Quinn nudged the thrusters a bit more and the *Rocinante* jumped forward. "Here we go."

Pennington held his breath as the gap between them and the doors shrank. Then the hull of Broon's pirate vessel gave way to open space and he was pressed back in his seat as Quinn keyed the impulse drive.

"Get on the sensors," Quinn said, "tell me if they're coming after us."

Leaning forward in his seat, Pennington entered the commands to activate the ship's sorry excuse for scanners, taking a moment to scrutinize the readings before shaking his head. "Not yet, anyway."

"I'm plotting our course for warp speed now," Quinn said. "Another minute and we'll be in the clear."

Pennington nodded. "What was with the drone?" He could not understand why Quinn would waste time fooling with the device.

"I activated its transceiver relay," Quinn replied. "It's sending a distress call right now." Looking up, he offered a sly smile which appeared crooked thanks to the bruising on his right cheek. "With luck, the Klingons will be on the way and Broon can explain to them what he's doing with a piece of their hardware."

Despite himself, Pennington could not help returning the smile. "Grand."

"I thought so," Quinn said, chuckling. "Nice moves back there, by the way. Tripping that airlock was pretty smart thinking. Saved our hides, mine in particular." Glancing sideways toward Pennington, he nodded. "I owe you one, Tim."

"No charge, mate," the reporter replied, taken somewhat off guard by Quinn's sudden display of gratitude. It was most out of character for the trader, though not at all unwelcome.

Their sense of amused self-satisfaction was short-lived, however, as Armnoj rose from his seat and stuck his head into the cockpit.

"Is this how you protect Mr. Ganz's valuable property?" the Zakdorn opined, looming over Quinn's shoulder with his briefcase. "I could have died back there."

"You can die right here, if you don't shut up," Quinn replied without looking up from his console.

Sniffing the air in his usual self-aggrandizing manner, Armnoj made a sound which to Pennington sounded like a rapacious cat readying to pounce on a wayward mouse. "Rest assured I'll be making a full report to Mr. Ganz immediately upon our . . ."

Pennington slugged him, his fist connecting with the accountant's jaw and sending him staggering out of the cockpit, tripping over his own feet and landing with a heavy thud on the deck.

"Thanks. Now I owe you two," Quinn said as he keyed a series of controls and the *Rocinante* jumped to warp speed.

37

Sitting in the center seat on the bridge of the *Endeavour*, Atish Khatami once more was gripped by the nagging sensation that the chair and the responsibilities which came with it were too much for her to bear.

"Detecting seven power sources coming online, Captain," Ensign Klisiewicz reported from the science station. "Same locations as before, including the one directly beneath the site where the landing party and research teams are working."

Khatami noted the nervousness in the young man's voice, certain that everyone around them shared his anxiety. The memories from the *Endeavour*'s last visit here—and what it had cost them—still were fresh, though her people of course were manning their posts and seeing to their assigned duties with the air of aplomb and professionalism Captain Zhao always had demanded. Still, she sensed none of the uncertainty or discomfort she knew had plagued members of the crew in the days following her promotion.

Maybe Leone's cure for that particular malady is starting to spread.

Emboldened by that thought—as juvenile as it might seem—and despite the tension she knew permeated the bridge, Khatami felt herself sit up just a bit straighter in the command chair.

"Captain," Klisiewicz called out, turning in his seat, "temperatures at those locations are rising, but they're doing so faster than before."

"What?" Mog said, looking up from the engineering station. "Faster?"

Klisiewicz nodded. "Yes, sir. The rate of increase is almost double what we experienced . . . the last time."

"Somebody's been busy while we were away," Khatami said. Faster temperature increase meant that the lag between attacks from the planetary defense system they had faced during their last encounter would be cut almost in half, and said nothing about any increase in accuracy or power that the massive weapons may have received. "Red alert, all hands to battle stations," she ordered before glancing over her shoulder to the officer seated at the communications station. "Ensign, get me Captain Okagawa on the *Lovell.*"

It took only a moment for the frequency to be set up, and the image on the main viewer shifted to display the anxious face of the other ship's commanding officer, his face creased with worry lines as he sat on the somewhat smaller yet still vibrant bridge of his own vessel.

"*I take it you've picked up the power readings?*" Okagawa asked by way of introduction.

Khatami nodded. "Yes. Their rate of increase is faster this time around. Captain, I don't think your shields will be enough to protect you. We had enough trouble ourselves during our first run-in. I suggest you orbit out to maximum transporter range and wait."

She could tell by the look on his face that Okagawa was not pleased with that notion, and could sympathize. Like her, he had people on the surface and had no desire to leave them unprotected. That worry had to be waging with his obligation to follow her instructions, as she was the on-site commander of the current operation.

"*Very well,*" he said after a moment, his expression belying his apparent willingness to concede to her judgment. "*My people are continuing to study those power readings. Now that we've got some fresh information to work with, they might be able to tell us more about this supposed link between the different locations.*"

"Keep on that, Daniel," Khatami answered before offering what she hoped was a reassuring smile. "We'll take care of the nasty stuff if necessary."

A warning alarm from the science station made her turn her

head in time to see Klisiewicz rising from his chair and moving to peer into the console's hooded sensor viewer. "Captain," he said without looking away from the viewer, "power readings are approaching pre-firing temperatures."

"Reroute power from nonessential systems to the shields," Khatami ordered. "Plot firing solutions on those locations and stand by photon torpedoes."

The previous attack had come with such speed and fury that there had been time to do nothing save tuck tail and scamper for safety. That would not happen this time, Khatami vowed, not while she still had people in harm's way down on the planet's surface. She would leave no one behind, not now, not ever again.

"I think we're in trouble."

The temperature inside the control chamber was now almost on par with the standard environment aboard ship. Xiong had long since abandoned his parka and sweat ran down the sides of his face as he and al-Khaled worked. Holding a tricorder, the lieutenant adjusted the device's settings while using it to scan their surroundings. "Power levels are increasing," he reported after a moment. It had been a simple matter to detect the activation of the mysterious power source buried somewhere deep beneath their present location. Even though the tricorder had picked up power signatures activating at scattered points throughout the ancient structure, none of the consoles in this chamber had been affected by this new development, much to Xiong's disappointment.

He turned at the sound of al-Khaled's communicator beeping for attention, and he looked over as the engineer retrieved the device from his belt and with a flick of his wrist flipped the unit's cover open. "Al-Khaled here."

"*This is Commander zh'Rhun,*" said the voice of the *Lovell's* first officer, who at the moment was overseeing the reconstruction of the outpost's main camp. "*Power readings from the other sites of those weapons emplacements are coming online, Lieutenant. I want your location evacuated and everyone transported up on the double.*"

Al-Khaled already had informed the commander upon Xiong's

detection of the sudden activation of power sources deep beneath their own location. Zh'Rhun had allowed them to stay on site despite her misgivings over the new development, but Xiong knew that their grace period now had expired.

"We have to stay," Xiong protested anyway, waving his arms to indicate the banks of dormant control consoles. "Our defensive measures are in place, and this could be our only chance to see this equipment in operation."

Members of al-Khaled's Corps of Engineers team were at this moment working less than thirty meters from where he stood, farther down the corridor that—like this chamber—had been carved with mathematical precision from the solid rock. In addition to the forcefield generators they already were in the process of deploying, the engineers also were setting up emitters for what they hoped would be a power generator capable of producing a dampening field to disrupt any communications signals detected between this location and other points across the planet. Sooner or later, Xiong surmised, they would have to test that equipment, and despite the fear gnawing at his gut as he remembered what happened here the last time he faced attack, he knew that now was as good a time as any.

"*I'm not ready to try those forcefields with live test subjects, Lieutenant,*" zh'Rhun replied, her tone terse, "*and we have no way of knowing if the dampening field will have any effect at all.*" Though he had met the Andorian officer for the first time only during the *Lovell*'s transit to Erilon from Vanguard, that initial encounter was enough to tell him that the commander was unaccustomed to having her orders questioned. "*Get to the surface and call for beam-out. I want everyone out of there right now.*"

Xiong was tempted to argue the point but never got the chance as al-Khaled replied, "Understood, Commander. We're leaving now. Al-Khaled out." Closing the communicator and returning it to his belt, he regarded Xiong with a resigned expression. "You heard the boss, Ming. Let's get our people."

Whatever dissatisfaction Xiong harbored vanished, however, at the sound of his still-active tricorder emitting an alert tone. Holding up the device to inspect its miniaturized display, his eyes widened even as he felt his pulse quicken.

"I've got something new here," he said. "Proximity sensors have detected three unidentified life-forms. They weren't there a minute ago."

"Transporter?" al-Khaled asked.

Xiong shook his head. "No transporter signature. One second nothing, the next there they are. Two are on the surface, heading for the base camp."

The engineer frowned. "Where's the third?" he asked, his right hand drifting to rest atop the Type-II phaser he wore on his hip.

"Fifty-seven meters below us," Xiong replied, his jaw clamping in confusion at what the tricorder was telling him. "This doesn't make any sense. According to these readings, that should be solid rock."

"Or something designed to present the appearance of solid rock," al-Khaled said, turning to run from the chamber into the corridor beyond. "Come on!"

Xiong followed after his companion as al-Khaled sprinted into the underground passageway to where two members of his engineering team, a Denobulan female and a human male, crouched near a piece of bulky equipment. Xiong recognized it as the main component for a portable forcefield emitter, one side panel of which lay open to expose its internal mechanisms. The Denobulan—an ensign named Ghrex, according to the nametag embossed over the right breast of her red utility jumpsuit—looked up at al-Khaled's approach.

"Are the forcefields ready to go?" he called out.

Ghrex nodded. "We know," she said as she returned her attention to her task. "We picked up the life-form."

"We need thirty seconds," added the other engineer, whose nametag identified him as Ensign O'Halloran.

As if in reply, the corridor around them rumbled as though gripped in a single intense, monotonous drone. The vibrations ran through everything—the walls, the equipment, even the tricorder Xiong still carried in his left hand.

"That can't be good," al-Khaled said.

Running footsteps echoed through the passageway behind them, and Xiong turned to see Lieutenant Jessica Diamond, the *Lovell*'s weapons officer, jogging toward them accompanied by two members of her security team, each of them carrying a phaser rifle. She was still wearing her open parka, and Xiong noted how the perspiration on her face matted to her forehead the bangs of her shoulder-length brown hair.

"Time to go, people," Diamond called out as she approached them. Unlike her two subordinates', her breathing seemed unaffected by her exertion, even though Xiong knew the trio had to have run the hundred or so meters from the entrance to the underground compound.

Studying his tricorder, Xiong once more felt his heart beginning to pound in his chest. "Too late for that, Lieutenant. I'm picking up a life-form—not one of our people—heading this way."

Then the rumbling returned, and this time all of them in the corridor nearly were thrown off their feet. It continued for several seconds and, in a fit of panic, Xiong stared wild-eyed at the ceiling of the passageway, searching for signs that the stone tunnel might cave in on them.

"What the hell is that?" he cried, shouting to be heard above the din.

Khatami had only time to grip the armrests of her command chair.

The energy blast slammed into the *Endeavour*'s forward shields, overflow from the point of impact bleeding through the protective screens and lashing out against the hull of the ship itself. Khatami felt the force of the attack transferred through the innards of the starship, the deck shuddering beneath her feet even as the starship lurched to starboard, throwing her against her chair.

Overhead lighting flickered as alarms rang out across the bridge. All around her, people held on to anything that might provide support, be it the railing around the command well or their own workstations. Only Mog failed to anchor himself in time, his robust frame tumbling from his chair to the deck near the turbolift alcove. Even over the alert klaxons Khatami heard the engineer grunt in pain from the force of his fall.

"Mog!" she shouted as she swiveled her chair in his direction. "Are you all right?"

The Tellarite rolled to a sitting position even as Lieutenant Neelakanta wrestled the helm console to bring the *Endeavour* back under his control. "I'm fine," he called out, pulling himself to his feet and stumbling back to the engineering station.

"Damage reports," Khatami ordered, ignoring the dull ache in her side from where she had struck her chair.

"Shields at seventy-three percent and holding," Mog replied after a moment. "All systems functional."

Nodding at the report, Khatami swung her chair back to her right until she could see the science station. "Ensign, is the *Lovell* under attack?"

Klisiewicz shook his head. "No, Captain. They seem to be out of range."

"Let's keep them out there," Khatami replied. "Where are we with the weapons emplacements?" she asked even as she saw the younger man returning his attention to his sensor displays.

"Power stations are recharging," Klisiewicz said a moment later. "Estimating next barrage in fifteen . . . *mark*!"

"Get us some maneuvering room, helm," Khatami ordered. "Do we have targets plotted yet?"

Seated next to the Arcturian, Lieutenant McCormack turned from the navigator's console and nodded. "We can launch strikes at three targets from our present position, Captain," she said. "We'll have to shift orbit to take runs at the others."

One step at a time, Khatami reminded herself.

Her first attempt to order torpedo bombardment was interrupted as Klisiewicz announced another volley of incoming fire. Again the sequence was repeated, with the *Endeavour*'s shields bearing the brunt of the attack while the excess pushed past, reaching out to hammer against the ship's comparatively weaker hull. Renewed alarms wailed across the bridge and the lights flickered again before dying out altogether, leaving the command center in momentary darkness before backup illumination activated.

"Localized overloads, Captain," Mog called out from his station. "Engineering is rerouting main power to the bridge now. Shields at fifty-eight percent and holding, but we're taking a beating. Another round might be too much for the generators."

Ignoring the damage report, Khatami leaned forward in her chair. "Fire on designated targets," she ordered. "Full spread."

Once more the lighting wavered as the ship's defensive systems drew power from wherever it could be found, and Khatami watched as six photon torpedoes—one after another and each encased in a writhing orange ball of unfettered energy—darted away from the ship and arced toward the planet's surface.

"Picking up photon detonations, Captain," Klisiewicz reported several seconds later while still peering into the viewer. "Two direct hits, the others missed." After a moment, he shook his head. "All locations still registering power readings."

Damn!

"Helm, bring us about," she said. "Mog, route power from secondary systems to the shields."

From the corner of her eye she saw the Tellarite turning in his seat. "Captain, the shield generators are already showing signs of strain. We might lose them altogether if we get hit again."

"We get hit without the shields and we're dead," Khatami countered. "Let's make sure that doesn't happen."

From over her right shoulder, the ensign at communications said, "Captain, we're being hailed by the landing party. They're picking up intruders on the surface and are requesting emergency beam-out."

Before Khatami could reply, Klisiewicz cut her off. "Incoming!"

Even as she gave the order for evasive action, Khatami's eyes were drawn to the image on the main viewer. Rising up from the frigid surface of Erilon, seven streaks of crackling yellow light converged on one another to form a larger, more intense ball of energy that continued to race outward from the atmosphere on a collision course with her ship.

"All hands!" she shouted. "Brace for impact!"

38

Lieutenant Jeanne La Sala was the first to see them coming.

"Activate the forcefields!" she shouted to her companion, Ensign Roderick, even as she dropped down behind the stack of crates containing supplied transported to the surface from the *Endeavour*. Other than shelters and other small buildings—all constructed from thermoconcrete—radiating outward in a haphazard formation from the center of the research outpost's base camp, the groupings of cargo containers and other equipment scattered about the compound were the only protection available.

Seconds later and in response to her command La Sala heard the telltale hum of power generators activating from somewhere behind her. A low droning sound filled the air, and she directed her gaze toward the forcefield positioned ten meters to her left. Essentially a metallic shaft rising three meters out of the frozen earth, it was adorned with an indicator light positioned atop the pole. The bulb flared to life, a blazing crimson that seemed as out of place on this barren, lifeless plain as she or her companions. The emitter, like the twenty-nine other such devices deployed around the base camp's perimeter, were now acting like a blanket for the outpost, protecting it not from the harsh elements of this inhospitable world but rather whatever demons it seemed to have spawned.

"Forcefield activated," Roderick called out from where he was crouched behind another cargo container to her left. Holding up his tricorder for emphasis, he added, "All emitters functioning."

Showtime, La Sala mused, pulling the hood of her parka up onto her head in an attempt to ward off the chilling effects of the breeze blowing across the open ground. An involuntary shudder ran down her body, a stark reminder not only of the harsh environment in which she found herself but also what had happened the last time she had found herself in such a situation.

Forcing the unwelcome thought to a dark corner of her mind, La Sala peered through the sights of her phaser rifle, focusing on the pair of dark figures approaching from across the snow-covered plain. They moved with phenomenal speed, kicking up a wake of snow and dirt that plumed into the frosty air behind them. Other than being able to tell that their upper extremities appeared to taper into sharpened points rather than anything resembling hands—it was difficult to make out any details from this distance—so far as La Sala could tell the newcomers were identical to the one they had previously encountered.

Watching their approach, La Sala recalled the mission briefing as delivered by Captain Khatami, who in turn had relayed Commodore Reyes's instructions on attempting to communicate with the creatures. As a Starfleet officer, La Sala understood and valued the need to make such overtures. The Federation's philosophy of peaceful expansion and the seeking of mutual friendship and cooperation with other species throughout the galaxy was worthless if it was not embodied by every single person, like her, who swore an oath to defend those lofty principles.

Did that apply to situations when the other party appeared incapable or unwilling to listen to such reason? Not so far as La Sala was concerned. If the creatures—be they intelligent beings or mindless animals—attacked again as they appeared to be preparing to do, she and her people had the right to defend themselves.

Assuming we survive, she mused, *we can try talking afterward.*

"Here they come," she called into her communicator, which lay open near her left elbow and tuned to the frequency she had established for all members of the landing party working in the base camp. "Everyone hold their positions."

If the looming apparitions noticed or cared about the forcefield now insulating the base camp, it was not indicated by their actions. As they approached, La Sala saw them split up, veering to her right and left even as they continued their advance toward the outpost. She kept her attention on the one which appeared to be coming in her general direction, tracking its movements through her phaser rifle sights. The distance between it and the forcefield shrank with every beat of her heart; it grew larger in her sights with every step, and still it defied all her efforts to make out any sort of identifying characteristic. It was nothing more than a featureless obsidian humanoid, moving with deadly grace over the snow-covered terrain.

Without slowing so much as a single step, it plunged headlong into the invisible barrier.

An unrestrained fury of energy charged the air as the creature made contact with the forcefield. La Sala winced at the piercing sound elicited by the miniature maelstrom, sensing the effects of the violently released discharge playing across her own exposed skin. She watched spasms and convulsions rack the thing's body, yellow radiance reflecting off its dark, featureless hide with the same intensity that sunlight might be refracted through a prism and—for a moment, anyway—giving the creature an odd crystalline appearance. Then the effect was over as the creature stepped back from the forcefield. It stood motionless, less than fifty meters in front of her, appearing to stare straight ahead as though pondering its next action. Its elongated, pointed upper extremities hung still and useless at its sides.

La Sala could not shake the sensation that it was looking directly at—if not through—*her*.

"Good god!" Roderick exclaimed, his attention split between the sight before him and his tricorder. "The power drain on the field generators was enormous!"

As if to punctuate his report, another bout of unleashed chaos lit up the dull gray sky to their left, and La Sala turned to see that—in the distance—the other creature was attempting a similar assault at another point along the perimeter. The result was the same, with the thing moving away from the charged boundary only to stand, unmoving, mere paces from where its approach had been rebuffed.

"*Lieutenant La Sala,*" said a composed voice filtering through her communicator, "*this is Ensign Sulok. We are detecting im-*

mense strain on the forcefield perimeter in response to the creature's attacks."

Recognizing the voice of the Vulcan engineer sent down from the *Lovell*, La Sala picked up her communicator even as she kept her attention focused on the motionless humanoid before her. "We're seeing that, too, Ensign. You S.C.E. types have any ideas?"

"Not at this time, Lieutenant. We are examining our options, but thought you should be aware of the potential for the barrier to be breached."

La Sala opened her mouth to reply but the action was stifled as the creature lunged forward, impacting against the forcefield once more and eliciting the same vicious, cacophonous response.

They're going to get in.

It was only a matter of time now.

"Get to the control room!"

Xiong heard Diamond's order over the dissonant howl of unleashed energy as the thing—identical to the creature he had seen kill Captain Zhao—for the second time threw itself against the forcefield now blocking this section of the underground corridor. He could not be sure but he imagined he heard the nightmarish, featureless humanoid crying out in pain as it was subjected to the hellish discharge of energy feeding the protective barrier.

He saw Diamond motioning for her security detail and the other members of al-Khaled's team to get moving even as she held her ground, her phaser rifle aimed at the creature which stood before the still-humming forcefield—as frozen as the earth from which it had come. Xiong's eyes were drawn to the menacing lances at the ends of its arms, imagining them piercing the fragile bodies of Captain Zhao and Bohanon just as he had witnessed during the earlier attack. Dread gripped him, holding him frozen in its grasp while it waited for its servant to penetrate the barricade separating it from its prey.

"It won't stop until it gets to us," he said, feeling his fingers tighten around the handgrip of his phaser.

"We're not finished yet," al-Khaled replied from where he and Ensign Ghrex crouched next to a piece of ungainly equipment, both engineers wielding tools and scanners and working at a rapid pace.

"Can you get that thing running or not?" Diamond called out, backpedaling until she stood abreast of her shipmates.

"Almost there," al-Khaled replied without looking up as he fused one end of a length of optical cable to what Xiong recognized as a power-distribution node—a very *old* model of power-distribution node.

Xiong could not even be sure he understood how the engineers were proceeding with their admittedly outlandish scheme. After studying the power signatures recorded by the *Endeavour*'s sensors during the ship's previous visit to Erilon, al-Khaled and his engineers had set about building a device to counteract the host of communications signals detected between various points around the planet.

Whereas he had expected to see some form of state-of-the-art technology resulting from that effort, a sterling example of twenty-third-century engineering prowess, what Xiong instead found himself looking upon appeared to be cobbled together from a host of surplus detritus scrounged from a salvage yard. Optical cabling and tools littered the ground at their feet as the engineers worked, seemingly oblivious of the scene unfolding around them.

We're all going to die.

Xiong flinched at the flare of energy created by the creature choosing that moment to once more slam into the forcefield. Shadows fled from the corridor as multihued tendrils arced between the pair of emitters positioned on opposite sides of the passageway, playing across the humanoid's opaque, austere form.

Then the light died and the omnipresent hum of the emitters faded, and the creature stepped forward.

The whine of weapons fire echoed across the open ground and La Sala felt the tingle of discharged phaser energy washing across her skin, but she ignored it. Her focus now was the haunting vision of hell that had just broken through the forcefield and that was at this instant moving toward her.

"Back! Everybody back!" she shouted before firing again. The beam struck the creature high near the right shoulder, its skin seeming to absorb the energy while leaving no trace of her attack. As it continued to advance, La Sala pushed the phaser rifle's intensity setting forward as far as it would go, adjusting the weapon's power level to maximum. She fired once more, the rifle's high-pitched howl playing across her ears and causing her to wince from the discomfort.

Though the creature staggered in the face of the barrage, it did not stop.

"Dammit!" she shouted in frustration as the creature moved in lurching steps to its left, angling toward where Roderick huddled behind the cargo container and trained his own weapon on the approaching intruder. "Roderick! Get out of there!"

The ensign rose from his crouch and began to retreat, continuing to fire at the oncoming attacker. He tripped on a coil of cable lying near one of the other cargo containers, stumbling backward but maintaining his balance. Still, it was enough to make him lower his weapon in an attempt to keep from falling to the ground.

"Look out!" La Sala cried, continuing to fire her ineffective weapon after the horrific attacker in their midst.

It was all the opportunity the creature needed. Falling forward more than lunging, the thing lashed out with one of its immense arms, skewering Roderick through the chest. The ensign's eyes went wide with terror and surprise, his body going limp within seconds as life drained out of his body from the massive wound inflicted upon him. Withdrawing its blood-slickened arm from Roderick's chest, the creature did not wait for the now dead man even to fall to the frozen ground before turning in search of its next target.

Trembling from the raw horror of what she had witnessed, La Sala was already moving, scrambling around the side of the cargo container in search of even momentary concealment. "This is La Sala! I need help here!" she shouted into her communicator, knowing even as she made the plea that others around the camp would never reach her in time. The creature seemed to be regaining its earlier flagging strength, picking up its pace as it trudged through the snow toward her.

"Son of a bitch," she hissed, laying her phaser rifle atop the cargo crate and centering the intruder in her sights. At the rate she had been firing the weapon, experience told her that its power cell was almost exhausted. This stand, however pitiful it might be, would be her last.

Less than twenty meters from her, the creature lurched to an abrupt stop, its joints appearing to lock up in midstride even as momentum carried it forward until it tumbled face first into the snow. No sooner did it strike the ground than its body collapsed, slumping to the earth and remaining still.

Rising from her meager place of protection, La Sala regarded the now immobile creature lying on the ground. "What the hell just happened?" she asked, though no one was around to offer an answer.

Xiong could only watch in rapt fascination as the creature jerked to a stop, its entire body shuddering as if being subjected to an intense electrical shock. It staggered backward several steps, convulsing as though gripped by extreme pain, though of course it uttered no audible sounds.

"It's working!" al-Khaled shouted from where he and Ensign Ghrex still knelt next to the dampening field generator. Xiong looked to see that the unit's array of status indicators were glowing a steady hue of pulsating colors, accompanied by a vibrant hum denoting the power it was channeling.

Diamond dropped her drained phaser rifle to the ground, reaching inside her parka to extract the type-2 phaser from her belt and aiming the smaller weapon at the creature. The thing appeared not to care; its spasms now had ceased. It stood motionless for several seconds, during which Xiong wondered why neither Diamond nor anyone else in the corridor—including him—seemed to possess the presence of mind to open fire.

"We have to kill it," Diamond whispered, aiming her phaser to fire once more.

Then, the creature turned and ran back up the corridor from whence it came.

Xiong exchanged looks with Diamond, figuring that the dumbfounded expression on her face must mirror his own.

"I'll be damned if I understand any of that," Diamond said. "Where's it going?"

Shaking his head, Xiong pointed down the corridor. "Back down to whatever chamber it appeared in earlier? There's no way to know without following it."

"Thanks," Diamond replied. "But, no."

"The dampening field's working," al-Khaled reported as he pulled himself to his feet. Holding up his tricorder, he added, "It's only about five kilometers in diameter, but it seems to be enough to cause a localized disruption in most communications signals within its radius, with the exception of two frequencies I was able to screen out so we could contact the *Lovell* or the *Endeavour*."

"So," Xiong said, "we've not neutralized the technology at other points around the planet?"

Moving to stand next to al-Khaled, Ghrex shook her head. "No, sir, though we've blocked the ability for anything to interface with those sites so long as they remain within the dampening field's perimeter."

"Great work, you two," Diamond said, wiping sweat from her forehead. "I owe you dinner when we get back to the station."

"A real dinner from one of the restaurants?" Ghrex asked. A wide, long smile brightened the Denobulan's features. "Deal."

From where it was situated in an upper pocket of his parka, Xiong's communicator chirped. Extracting the device and flipping open its antenna grid, the lieutenant said, "Xiong here."

"*This is Captain Khatami,*" replied the voice of the *Endeavour*'s commanding officer. "*Our sensors are registering the presence of the dampening field at your location, Lieutenant. It seems to have had the effect of disrupting the weapons taking shots at us. We show the other sites as still being active and in contact with each other, but all contact with your location appears to be severed.*"

Everyone in the corridor released cries of relief and victory at Khatami's words, and even Xiong felt the irrepressible need to smile at the welcome news. "It's had other effects down here, as well, Captain," he said, eager to share the landing party's own discovery. "That same signal seemed to affect the creatures attacking us. When the switch was thrown, the one coming after us tucked tail and ran."

"*I suggest we not push our luck, Lieutenant,*" Khatami said. "*Get to the surface and stand by for beam-out. We're already transporting the people at the base camp. I don't want anyone down there until the situation is secure.*"

Behind him, Xiong heard a brisk series of beeps and tones and turned to see al-Khaled consulting his tricorder. Xiong started to ask what was going on but the words died in his throat as he became aware of a low, ominous rumbling coming from . . . somewhere. "What is that?"

"Massive power buildup," al-Khaled replied. Everyone in the corridor regarded him with nearly identical expressions of confusion and worry as he consulted his tricorder. "Whatever it is, it's huge. This is more power than . . ."

Even as the engineer stopped talking, realization chose that moment to smack Xiong across the face.

"Oh, damn," Diamond whispered.

"Don't tell me," Xiong said, already knowing what al-Khaled would say.

The engineer nodded. "It's like Palgrenax. Something's initiating an immense geothermal buildup. If left unchecked, it'll blow a hole in this planet half a continent wide, with us at the center of the whole thing."

39

The Shedai Wanderer had failed.

Her mind still racked with a pain she could never before have imagined, she raced away from the *Telinaruul* who tormented her, her consciousness guiding the movements of the Sentinel to carry her deeper into the temple, away from those whose suppression should have been child's play but instead had proven themselves to be a devious adversary, if not a worthy one.

She had been weakened by the need to divide herself among three Sentinels, and the pain that had washed over her had come as if from nowhere, nearly driving her consciousness into the void which existed beyond the safety of the Conduit. It had taken all of her remaining strength to withdraw the tendrils of her mind from two of the servants she had pressed into service. Only with supreme effort had she been able to retain control of the lone remaining Sentinel, driven as she was by her obligation to protect the Conduit and the temple at all costs.

The lesser beings had somehow managed to sever her mental link with the rest of the planet's assets as well as her ability to commune with the Conduit. No longer could she access the global defense system—which she had spent a great deal of time improving after the last encounter with the *Telinaruul* vessel. She did not comprehend how such a feat might be possible, nor could she spare the time or energy to investigate. The Wanderer could do nothing so long as she was trapped within the confines of this physical shell. She required direct access to the Conduit.

There was little time, she knew. Her connection to this shell was fading, and her consciousness was at risk of becoming completely disassociated for eternity—from the Sentinel as well as the

Conduit—if she could not find a means of escape. Also, the *Telinaruul*, no doubt emboldened by their limited success, would be coming. Consumed by the desire to possess what was not rightfully theirs, they would follow her, their goal one of greed, or of lust. It mattered not what propelled the interlopers, for it would not be enough to protect them from the final defensive option at the Wanderer's disposal.

Entering the Conduit and attempting to access various points around the planet's information network told her that the efforts of the *Telinaruul* had been more comprehensive than first surmised. Only assets at her location were available to her, though much of those connections also had been compromised. Sending forth tendrils of purpose and determination, the Wanderer activated the final protocol, the only option remaining to her that might safeguard at least some of the secrets of the Shedai.

Interfacing with the Conduit via physical contact was a sensation that existed only in her earliest memories. It was a rudimentary approach, typically useful only in teaching children the fundamentals of navigating the thoughtspace until such time as a Shedai's latent abilities manifested themselves.

Now, it was the only option the Wanderer possessed.

Her joy at carrying out her duty was short-lived, as she felt the drain upon her consciousness. The assets she required floated in and out of her grasp, her capacity to control them limited by her impeded ability to extend herself through the Conduit. Her strength and life ebbing with each passing moment, the Wanderer felt the momentary glow of energy pouring forth from the belly of the planet, racing upward and outward to do her bidding, but the next instant it was lost, fading into nothingness as though it never had existed.

Protecting the interests of her people was no longer within her power. Reaching out with one of the few surviving tendrils available to her, she sensed the approach of the *Telinaruul*. Capture was unthinkable, though she suspected she would not survive even if she allowed such a repulsive action to take place.

No, the Wanderer decided. There was but a single course to follow. She must survive in order to continue the fight. The

Telinaruul might celebrate their victory here today, but such triumph—in keeping with their simple existence—ultimately was fleeting. The Shedai had waited uncounted generations for their chance to return to their rightful station as rulers of all that was known.

They could wait a while longer.

40

Diamond was the first to enter the chamber, stepping over pieces of fallen rock and through the ragged hole in the stone wall, the phaser rifle she had taken from one of her security officers leading the way. Xiong followed on her heels, his hand phaser also out and aimed ahead of him. Carrying his tricorder in his free hand, he studied the unit's display screen once more before tapping Diamond on the shoulder. He pointed toward an archway carved out of the stone wall, from which filtered feeble, wavering lighting.

"That way."

Upon realizing that the region of Erilon on which they stood was not, apparently, in any danger of blowing up, and pausing momentarily to offer up a measure of thanks—to those deity or deities who might be listening for the stroke of immense good fortune they had chosen to visit upon the landing party—Xiong immediately had convinced Captain Khatami to allow a search party to remain on the surface.

"Are you tempting fate, Lieutenant?" Khatami had asked, finally relenting to the request after retrieving the balance of the landing party. Though the captain might not possess all of the knowledge pertaining to the Taurus Reach, she knew enough to understand that whatever risk might be involved, the stakes warranted it—particularly given the appalling costs that already had been incurred.

Sensors had registered new power readings emanating from another location far beneath the ancient structure's long-dead control room—the same spot that he had detected earlier. Xiong at first was confused how such a reading could be possible, given his understanding that nothing but solid rock existed beneath the chamber, which had been the focal point of his research on this planet since his initial exploration of the alien artifact.

"Like I said before," the engineer offered as the trio followed the readings from Xiong's tricorder deeper into the millennia-old ruins, "appearances can be deceiving."

Following the path of the retreating creature into the depths of the artifact with the only illumination provided by handheld lights to guide them, the Starfleet officers could not admit surprise when they came across the hole leading through the rock wall of the passageway. Obviously not created in the same meticulous manner that characterized the corridors and chambers throughout the artifact, this opening appeared to have been blasted from whatever lay beyond. Evidence of the unrefined work lay all around them, fragmented chunks of stone and dirt littering the floor.

With al-Khaled following behind them, Diamond led Xiong toward the illuminated entryway. Drawing closer, Xiong could make out a low, droning hum coming from the chamber, the source of whatever was generating the power readings he tracked with his tricorder.

I can't believe it. We're finally here. At last, he and his companions were about to come face-to-face with what he had sought since first discovering the vast storehouse of mind-numbing technology.

"Faint life signs," he whispered, reaching up to adjust one of the tricorder's controls. "I'm barely picking it up, and it's fading fast."

"Dying?" Diamond asked, her expression itself posing the same question.

Xiong nodded. "I think so."

Motioning for him and al-Khaled to hug the wall behind her, Diamond inched toward the entryway. She aimed the barrel of her phaser rifle through the opening, slowly sweeping the room before exposing herself to possible attack. A moment later Xiong watched as her body stiffened and she even recoiled a step before turning to him. "Look at this."

She entered the doorway, and Xiong and al-Khaled followed. Xiong stopped as his eyes took in the sight before him.

"Oh, my," was all he could whisper as he beheld what at first appeared to be the mirror image of the control room far above them. What distinguished this chamber from that other room was, of course, the buzz of activity and life permeating the atmosphere here. The chamber's far wall was dominated by an array of control consoles all but identical to the ones Xiong had studied for weeks, save for the fact that the equipment here was functioning. Status monitors depicted graphics and text in a language the lieutenant had no hope of understanding. Rows of multicolored indicators flashed in irregular sequences and at varying frequencies, offering no clue as to their function.

Standing before all of it was the creature.

Instinct brought Xiong's weapon hand up, the phaser training on the dark, stationary figure, but he did not fire. Only then did he realize that the thing was not so much standing before the collection of control mechanisms as it was sagging against it.

"Let's end this," Diamond said, stepping forward and pulling the stock of her phaser rifle to her shoulder.

Placing a hand on her arm, Xiong called out, "Wait!" Even as he offered the plea, his attention turned back to where the creature had remained since their arrival, offering no hint that it even was aware of their presence.

"What's it doing?" al-Khaled asked, and Xiong noticed that the engineer had exchanged his own phaser for the tricorder slung over his shoulder. "I'm picking up massive power readings. Not just here but even farther down below us."

"The self-destruct?" Diamond asked, her voice holding an anxious edge.

Al-Khaled shook his head. "No, this is new, and different. I've never seen anything like this. It's as though . . ."

His remaining words were consumed by an intense rumbling that seemed to come from the walls, the floor and ceiling—everywhere. The illumination offered by dozens of indirect sources embedded into the stone walls flickered as if in response to an immense energy drain, though it did not seem to affect the chamber's banks of computer screens and consoles.

"What the hell is happening?" Diamond asked, her words a

hoarse whisper as she—like Xiong—watched the scene unfold with ever-widening eyes.

The lieutenant's communicator beeped and he retrieved it from his belt to flip it open. "Xiong here." He had to hold the unit close to his ear in order to hear the reply.

"*Khatami here, Lieutenant. We're picking up new power surges from your location. What's going on?*"

"I wish I could tell you, Captain," Xiong replied, shouting to be heard over the rising din. "We're watching it happen."

Standing motionless before the rows of consoles, its arms resting atop two panels, the creature seemed unaffected by anything as the crescendo continued to increase with each passing second. Many of the graphic displays accelerated their scroll of vibrant colors and alien text into a turbulent, unrestrained frenzy. Xiong's efforts to cover his ears and muffle the disharmonious wail were futile as the noise storm rising up around him began to induce actual discomfort.

Then, as he and the others watched, the creature fell away from the consoles. The instant it broke contact with the smooth, featureless surface, everything stopped, stilled as though a simple switch had been flipped. The only sound in the chamber was the clatter of the humanoid figure as it crashed to the stone floor, collapsing into a lifeless heap.

The silence was so sudden, so encompassing, that Xiong all but staggered back a step at the abrupt shift. "My god," he said as he stared, openmouthed, at the unmoving form. Activating his tricorder, he held it before him in order to capture detailed readings from the motionless figure. "It's dead." Frowning, he added, "At least, I think it is."

"It did this," al-Khaled said, holding his arms open to indicate the entire room. "Everything we saw, everything used to attack us. That thing controlled it all from here."

"One life-form, controlling everything on this entire planet?" Diamond asked. "Including the attack on the *Endeavour*? That seems pretty far-fetched." Turning to look around the room for a moment, however, she nodded. "Of course, far-fetched seems to be the order of the day around here."

Al-Khaled nodded. "The dampening field. It's possible that it cut off access to the other power sources. We might even have cut it off from whatever it was using to initiate the self-destruct procedure." Looking around, he exhaled a sigh of profound relief. "Whatever happened, we got damned lucky."

"Lucky?" Diamond asked. "I didn't think engineers believed in luck."

"I do today," al-Khaled replied.

His focus riveted on his tricorder and the corpse of the alien lying before him, Xiong ignored the banter. According to the readings he was getting, the creature's physiology was as much crystalline composites as it was living tissue, with one mutual component working to blend the two disparate substances into a seamless, balanced whole.

The meta-genome.

As with the samples he had studied both here and on Vanguard, Xiong easily identified the primary sequence of genetic data common to every sample of the magnificent DNA. Beyond that, his tricorder was registering hundreds of thousands of new components, orders of magnitude more complex than anything they had yet encountered.

It's all here—waiting.

The force of the revelation was such that it took every ounce of strength and discipline to maintain his composure, lest he offer too much information to al-Khaled and Diamond about his true reason for being here. If his guess was right, if his theory about biometric interfaces being necessary for access to the artifact's collection of ancient technology had any merit, then the evidence to prove that hypothesis was right here, having been all but dropped into his lap.

With the alien dead, however, validating the idea would still prove a challenge—if indeed it was possible at all.

Xiong could not wait to find out.

41

All things considered, Reyes decided that Desai was reacting well to what she had just been told.

"You son of a bitch," the captain repeated for the second time, rising from her chair in front of Reyes's desk and beginning to pace the width of his office. "I can't believe you've been keeping this from me all this time."

"I had my orders, Rana," Reyes said, slouching back in his own chair. "You know how that is."

Waving her hands to indicate the office and—by extension— the rest of the station, Desai said, "So, all of this is nothing more than a sham? That's why we're here, to put on a show for curious onlookers? We keep everyone's attention focused elsewhere while you send out ships to look for who the hell knows what? And what about the *Bombay*? Did the Tholians destroy it because we were trespassing into their territory?"

"No," Reyes countered, holding up his right hand and pointing upward for emphasis. "Everything about this station and its role to support new colonization and exploration efforts is absolutely legitimate. The *Bombay* was delivering supplies to the Ravanar IV outpost when it was attacked without provocation. That's the truth." Of course, it was not the entire truth, but Reyes had already decided that while he needed Desai to know certain facts in order to effectively do her job without making his own responsibilities more difficult, that did not mean he was prepared to lay out every single detail for her. Not today, at least.

Desai stopped her pacing, turning to glare at Reyes as she placed her hands on her hips. "Of course it is. The more truth you mix in with the lie, the easier it is to tell the lie. What's worse is

that I'm part of that lie. Officially, I discontinued the *Bombay* inquiry because it was determined that the Tholians' attack was pre-
meditated, but we both know it wasn't unprovoked. They attacked
that ship because they felt threatened by its presence near that
planet, and now you seem to be telling me that their actions may
well have been justified."

"It's not that simple, Rana," Reyes said, his voice coming off
louder and harsher than he had intended. Pausing a moment to
clear his throat, he continued, "We don't know what it is we've
found here, who's responsible for it or what other technology they
might have created. If what Xiong and his team have managed to
figure out is any indication, the possible impacts to science as we
understand it are staggering. It should also go without saying that
whoever's behind it all, assuming they're still around, has the potential to upset the status quo of this part of the galaxy." If Xiong's
latest report from Erilon was any indication, that statement had
taken on an enormous new meaning.

"You're talking like a soldier again," Desai said, her hard
expression unchanging.

"Because it's the kind of talking that's required right now,"
Reyes countered. Leaning forward, he locked eyes with her.
"Rana, you've seen what Fisher discovered in the lab. Now, imagine if that level of sophistication were applied toward the creation
of some kind of weapon. If that sort of technology is lying around
out there, just waiting for someone to find it, would you rather it
be us, or the Klingons, or perhaps someone worse?"

Desai released a sigh of exasperation. "I don't know, Diego.
It's all a bit much to wrap my head around just this minute." She
closed her eyes, reaching up with her right hand to pinch the
bridge of her nose as if fighting back a headache. After a moment
she raised her head to regard him once more. "You said you think
there's a connection between the Tholians and this . . . thing . . .
you've been chasing. Do you think they might be protecting
this—ancient technology?"

Reyes shook his head. "Xiong doesn't seem to think so, but we
have no way to be certain right now." The revelation that the
energy signatures from the ancient power generators on Erilon

bore some connection to current technology employed by the Tholians—if only on a most basic level—made for a compelling reason as to why the Tholians had reacted in the manner they had toward the *Bombay*. Despite that, the commodore's gut told him things simply did not add up that cleanly.

For one thing, it still did not explain the initial incident on Erilon that had claimed Captain Zhao and his party as well as the Corps of Engineers team there, nor did it offer any insight into what the *Endeavour* and the *Lovell* had experienced during their return visit to the planet. So far, the only thing that seemed to lend credence to any sort of shared heritage between the Tholians and whatever might be responsible for the meta-genome was what Dr. Fisher had found during his autopsy of the Denobulan victim brought back from Erilon.

Crystallizing that poor bastard's DNA? Why?

It made no sense for the oddly xenophobic race to be doing anything that might bring them into prolonged contact with other species, but as Fisher had reminded him on more occasions than Reyes could count, science did not lie. It might misspeak due to lack of information or offer answers to questions as yet unasked, but it never offered untruths. Reyes knew that eventually science—perhaps with the aid of no small amount of luck—would provide understanding for those answers.

What he did not know was if he could afford to wait that long.

"Maybe that corpse recovered on Erilon will shed some light," Desai said after a moment.

"Hopefully on a lot of things," Reyes countered. It was a test of will to keep from marching down to the morgue this minute and watching over Fisher's shoulder while he and Lieutenant Xiong conducted their examination. What secrets did the body of that unknown alien hold?

In addition, Dr. Gek and his research team down in the Vault were poring over the new collection of data collected from the planet, in the hopes of learning more about the newly discovered technology storehouse. Would they find some concrete link between Erilon and Palgrenax, and perhaps even Ravanar IV and any number of other planets throughout the region? For the first time since they had begun this extended scavenger hunt, Reyes felt that his people might just be on the cusp of unlocking at least one new door that led deeper into the maze of mystery the Taurus Reach seemed to represent.

Desai said nothing for several moments, folding her arms across her chest and allowing her gaze to drop to the carpet. Her thoughts elsewhere, she seemed oblivious as Reyes watched her jaw clench, recognizing the expression as one she adopted whenever she was trying to work out a problem while weighing the need to handle things herself rather than ask for help. It was a rare instance that she appeared vulnerable to any degree and, then as now, she appeared absolutely radiant.

Finally, she looked back up to him. "Diego, why now?"

"Why what now?"

Her eyes narrowing, Desai replied, "Why tell me all of this now, after everything that's happened?"

"Because of *everything* that's happened," Reyes replied, rising from his chair. "After what you've seen and heard, you can't be expected to do your job if you're still in the dark about various important details." Stepping around his desk, he moved to stand within a few paces of her. "A lot's going on in the name of duty and security, Rana, a lot of it unpleasant and some of it questionable: morally, ethically, legally. I need someone I can trust to guide me through some of the rough spots I know are coming."

"What about Jetanien and T'Prynn?" Desai asked. "T'Prynn can give you all the logic you'll ever need, and if there's someone better qualified than Jetanien to counsel you on the military and political minefield you're crossing, I've never heard of them."

Reyes shook his head. "This is different. I need someone I can *talk* to," he continued, "who'll let me work things out while giving me perspectives I might be overlooking."

"You mean like the colonies you try to draft as Starfleet supply depots?" Desai asked.

Despite himself, he released a tired chuckle that did much to ease the pressure he had been feeling of late. "Exactly," he said, extending his arms toward her. "Somebody who's not afraid to tell me when I'm wandering off course." While it was true that Jetanien already had proven to be an invaluable source of insight into how best to deal with the Klingons and the Tholians, and T'Prynn's particular talents were also of enormous benefit—despite the questionable methods she had employed to date—neither of them seemed suited to provide the sort of moral compass he had decided was necessary if he was to be successful going forward.

Holding her ground, Desai cocked her head as she regarded him. "Have you told me everything there is to know?"

"No," Reyes answered without hesitation, dropping his arms back to his sides.

While it was true that they both shared deep respect for ethics and justice, Reyes knew that Desai simply would not accept as defensible some of the actions that had been taken to preserve the security of Vanguard's true mission. If she were to learn of such things, she would be legally and ethically obligated to conduct an investigation and report her findings to higher authority—no matter what the consequences might be to the secret he and his handful of trusted confidants were laboring to protect.

That's why you need her, Reyes reminded himself. *The end has to justify the means, otherwise, what the hell are you doing here? She'll help you see it through.*

"There are also some things I probably won't ever tell you," he said. "I'm sorry, but that's just the way it has to be. I can't promise you that it won't happen again going forward, either. There's simply too much at stake, and for now some secrets are necessary. I won't lie to you, or feed you disinformation, but there will be times when I can't tell you something. You're just going to have to trust that I'm doing it for the right reasons."

"I do trust you, Diego," Desai said, "which is why I terminated the *Bombay* inquiry. I felt it was the right decision at the time, based on what had been revealed about the attack and because I believed you hadn't done anything negligent or illegal." Cocking her head to the left, she glared at him. "That was before the whole mess with Tim Pennington fell out. At first, I thought he was an incredibly crafty son of a bitch who just got overeager and didn't check his facts, but I think we both know it didn't happen that way. He was deliberately set up to take that fall, and there's only a handful of people on this station who could have made that happen. In fact, I'd wager there's only one person who could've done it."

Reyes said nothing.

Holding up a hand, Desai continued, "I understand operational security, Diego, but even that requires accountability. If I thought I could prove T'Prynn broke regulations, I'd have already hoisted her from the nearest yardarm. You need to know that I'm not done looking for that proof, either." She pointed a finger at his chest. "Don't put me in the position of having to file false reports or participating in any further cover-ups. I know you need some leeway here, but that doesn't mean I'm willing to violate the law."

Reyes kept his expression fixed. "You're sexy when you take a stand, you know that?"

The joke had its intended effect, as he noted the ghost of a smile play across her lips before she clamped down, driving it away. "I mean it, Diego."

Nodding, Reyes replied, "I know you do, and frankly I expect no less from a Starfleet captain. I won't prevent you from doing your job or following your orders, but you need to know that I've got my orders, too, and one of them is that operational security here has to be maintained." Looking down at his feet, he released a sigh. "If there's going to be any lying or covering up, I'll be the one to do it."

There was a moment of uncomfortable silence, both of them looking at each other and contemplating the ramifications of his words. Reyes saw in Desai's eyes the burden of what she had learned here today.

"Don't let me catch you," Desai said, her voice softer now as she stepped closer. "I'd hate to have you court-martialed." She moved to where she could lay her head against his chest, and Reyes felt her arms wrap around his back, pulling him tight against her. He returned the embrace, resting his chin atop her head and reaching up to stroke her dark hair with his hand.

Holding her, Reyes could feel the tension in her body. He imagined he could sense a struggle already beginning within her, as though her unflinching devotion to the rule of law and her ability to understand the need for latitude when dealing with the unknown already were taking up arms against one another. Those forces were readying for battle, preparing for the day when, inevitably, Desai's convictions would be put to the test as a consequence of what she now knew.

He could sympathize, given that the same war waged within him.

That such a conflict would visit Rana Desai, Reyes was certain. What he did not know was—when that time came—how it would affect her actions and feelings toward him. Would she be an enemy or an ally?

It was a question—like countless others that continued to plague him—for which Reyes had no answer.

42

As always, it was one big party on the gambling deck of the *Omari-Ekon* and, as usual, Cervantes Quinn was not on the invite list.

Walking behind Sakud Armnoj and preceding Zett Nilric, Quinn made his way through the room and tried to ignore the atmosphere of merriment surrounding him. Music provided a festive backdrop, blending with the voices and laughter of patrons all around the room. Money in assorted currencies and denominations changed hands; a layer of smoke lingered about the gaming parlor, along with a mixture of odors generated by the plethora of substances various beings were inhaling into their lungs—or what might pass for lungs in nonhumanoid species; more than one patron moved about the room with a drink of some kind, reminding Quinn that it had been some time since he last had partaken of his favorite beverage.

Lucky bastards, he thought, thinking again of how fortunate Tim Pennington was at the moment. Upon the *Rocinante*'s return to Vanguard and still upset over the string of events that had unseated his plans to visit the colonists on Boam II, the journalist had declined Quinn's offer to accompany him to see Ganz, opting instead for a visit to Tom Walker's place and, as he had put it, "Life."

"I've counted fourteen health and safety code violations since we boarded," Armnoj said, holding close to his chest the black briefcase which seemed more like an extension of his own body and doing his best to avoid coming into contact with anyone he passed. "This place is a hive of disease and pestilence, to say nothing of its utter moral depravity."

"Shut up," Quinn said, the Zakdorn's perpetually squeaky

voice once more threatening to give him a headache to go with his bruised ribs and his sore jaw. Five minutes, he figured. Five minutes, and this putrid, annoying excuse for a sentient being would finally be out of his life.

As they passed one of the roulette tables, Quinn was forced to step to his left in order to avoid one guest who even by his standards seemed to have enjoyed far too much of the apparently free-flowing spirits. His movement nearly made him brush up against a sultry Orion woman, one of several employed by Ganz as part of his ship's "entertainment staff," who in turn smiled at him as she gave him a frank visual once-over from head to toe. She apparently was unaffected by the bandage over his left eye or the swelling along the right side of his jaw—souveniers from his short visit with Broon. Despite himself, Quinn nodded his head in greeting.

"Stop gawking, Quinn," Zett said from behind him, his low menacing voice somehow managing to carry over the bustle of the gambling deck. "You know Mr. Ganz doesn't like to be kept waiting."

It was the first thing the Nalori had said to him since meeting him at the *Ekon*'s entry ramp. Quinn had been tempted to bring up the whole mess with Broon, but figured the assassin already had received a report from his hired minion. He had half-expected Zett to gut him like a fish the moment he stepped through the airlock, but was reassured by the fact that—for the moment, anyway—Ganz still had need of his services.

Let's hope my luck isn't running out.

Quinn offered a sidelong glance toward the Nalori, noting that his dark, dapper suit served only to make his obsidian complexion seem even more sinister than normal. "It's not like you to wear black this early in the day. The regular *maitre d'* call in sick?" Though Zett said nothing in reply, Quinn could tell by the narrowing of his eyes that the comment had achieved its intended goal. The trader smiled in satisfaction, saying nothing else as he followed Armnoj up the stairs from the gambling deck to Ganz's private balcony.

The Orion merchant prince awaited him, lying in repose atop

the cushions and pillows that adorned the raised dais dominating the upper tier of the gambling deck. Dressed in a maroon toga that complemented his emerald green skin, Ganz propped himself up on his left elbow while holding a silver goblet in his enormous right hand. An Andorian *zhen,* wearing only a thin wrap of gold fabric that left to the imagination precious little of her otherwise nude figure, lay next to him, feeding Ganz small pieces of exotic-looking fruit.

Quinn's stomach chose that moment to remind him he had yet to eat today.

He knew enough to hang back, standing just in front of Zett and waiting his turn for an audience with Ganz. Experience had taught him that if the crime boss was anything, he was a stickler for his particular brand of protocol. Putting his hands in his pockets, Quinn looked over to see Morikmol, one of the Orion's associates, regarding him with his customary expression of annoyance and repressed disgust.

The thug stepped forward at their approach, indicating for Armnoj to stand between the pair of black obelisks situated before Ganz. The Zakdorn hastened to comply, his usual bluster all but gone now as he stood in front of his employer.

"Mr. Ganz," Armnoj said, holding his right hand out in greeting while using his left to clutch his briefcase close to his chest, "I can't tell you what a privilege it is for me to meet with you. It truly has been too long." The words came so fast that Quinn was sure the accountant would keel over from oxygen deprivation.

Ganz said nothing for several moments, instead taking a long pull from whatever beverage filled his goblet. When he did speak, it was with his usual low, rumbling tenor, though his expression denoted that already he was bored with this particular interaction. "Armnoj, I have to admit, you never cease to amaze me. How is it you've been able to survive out there on the fringes after all this time?"

His posture straightening, Armnoj's chest seemed to swell with pride as he replied, "Well, I have to tell you, it's been no easy feat, and there was no small amount of obstacles in our way just getting here. Why, just the—"

"It was a rhetorical question," Ganz said. "Did you bring your records?"

Nodding, the Zakdorn held up his briefcase. "Right here. As you know, all of my files are encoded with a multi-quad encryption algorithm that will thwart any attempts at unauthorized access. I designed the software myself, including a self-regenerating cipher that allows for—"

"Nobody cares." Ganz's expression was morphing from disinterest to annoyance. "Just unlock the files, please."

Armnoj cleared his throat, straightening his posture in an attempt to shrug off having his figurative knees taken out from under him. "Yes, of course." Looking around, he asked, "Might I be provided with a place to work?"

Indicating where the Zakdorn was standing before taking another drink from his cup, Ganz replied, "You've got it."

The accountant offered a haughty sniff, displeased with the way he was being treated. It took physical effort on Quinn's part not to laugh, and a quick glance to his left told him that a smile even tugged at the corners of the irrepressible Zett's mouth.

"It will just take a moment," Armnoj said as he cradled the briefcase in his left arm while using his free hand to tap an eighteen-digit combination into the small keypad molded into the case's handle. A few seconds later, he opened the case and Quinn got his first look at its contents. It contained what looked to be a nondescript gray portable computer interface, with a display monitor installed inside the case's lid.

Taking a square yellow data card from a small pocket to the right of the monitor, the accountant entered another long string of commands and the screen activated. As everyone watched, Armnoj replaced the data card with a red one and repeated the process of tapping instructions into the computer.

Ganz's sigh was audible across the deck. "Stars are dying out, Mr. Armnoj."

The bookkeeper did not reply for several seconds, until a rhythmic series of beeps emitted from the briefcase. "There we are," he said, his face brightening into the Zakdorn equivalent of a smile. From where he stood, Quinn could now see that the computer monitor was displaying a rolling screen of data, orderly columns and rows depicting text and numbers in varying colors, whatever pattern they might be employing far beyond his ability to decipher.

"This is everything?" Ganz asked. "I'm sure you won't mind if my staff here verifies your figures."

Armnoj nodded. "Well, why certainly. I think you'll find everything to be in order, down to the last credit, including a comprehensive ledger detailing every transaction I've made on your behalf since you first employed me. The cross-reference database should prove most helpful, as it includes journal entries with locations, dates and times, transaction origin and destination information, all meticulously organized and capable of being displayed via any extract criteria you might—"

"Thank you." Looking to Morikmol, Ganz indicated for his henchman to take the case from the accountant. As Armnoj surrendered the unit, the Orion added, "I think we're done here."

Clearing his throat again, the Zakdorn nodded rapidly several times. "Very well. What would you like me to do now?"

"Disappear," Ganz said, and Quinn saw the look he exchanged with Zett as the Nalori reached beneath his jacket and extracted a stout silver cylinder with a single red button set into it. Without aplomb, Zett pressed the button.

Quinn's eyes widened in realization. *Holy . . .*

The air hummed and crackled as the obelisks flanking Armnoj glowed to life. Searing white energy spat forth from each of the obsidian stanchions to wash over the Zakdorn. His body was obscured by the blinding flash of light for an instant, allowing the accountant one final befuddled look before his form dissolved. Then the light was gone, and with it Sarkud Armnoj.

"What the hell?" Quinn blurted, a faint lingering scent of ozone the only residue of the bookkeeper's passing. Stepping forward, but taking care not to move between the obelisks, he directed a stunned look at Ganz. "I don't get it. You told me he was valuable!"

His expression remaining neutral, the Orion replied, "Actually, what I said was that his information was valuable. As for him? He was whiny and self-important, like most Zakdorns. Why do you think I had him banished to that backwater mudball? He was more trouble than he was worth." His brow furrowing, he asked, "Didn't you notice?"

Relieved to at last be free of the irritating accountant but feeling more than a bit put off by the harsh and arguably unnecessary method used to expedite his departure, Quinn's main concern at the moment was that he might be joining Armnoj sometime in the next few minutes. A quick glance told him that Zett still was holding the small control device in his right hand.

As if reading his mind, Ganz actually released a chuckle, though to Quinn it sounded more like the sound a predator might make upon finding its next meal. "Relax, Quinn. You at least still have some use to me."

"Glad to hear it," Quinn replied. As relief washed over him, the pilot was caught by a sudden, unexpected thought: *I wonder if Sniffy gets everything in the will.*

The Orion held up his glass. "Other men might have tried to take advantage of the situation I placed you in, maybe taken a shot at learning where some of my money was stored; you might have helped yourself to whatever you could cram into that pitiful excuse for a ship you fly. You didn't. That goes a long way with me." He offered a mock salute with the goblet before taking another long pull from its still mysterious contents.

Holding his hands out, Quinn affected his best smile. "Mama raised no fools, Ganz."

"That's good," the merchant prince replied. "Then you'll know when you're threatening to overstay your welcome." Nodding in dismissal, the Orion added, "But don't go too far. I might need you sooner than you think."

I can't wait.

Quinn said nothing as he preceded Zett down the stairs and back across the gambling deck. This time he ignored the gaming, drinking, and carousing taking place all around him, focusing instead on the fact that he still needed to deliver the data core from the Klingon sensor drone to T'Prynn, and the possibility that Zett might kill him before he made it back to the boarding ramp.

"I suppose you've figured out by now that Broon blew it," Quinn said over his shoulder. "You always were the smartest one on Ganz's payroll."

Unsurprisingly, Zett offered no reply.

Quinn stopped, turning on his heel to face the Nalori. Regarding the assassin's seemingly bottomless black eyes, the privateer did his best to hide his nervousness, knowing without doubt that his counterpart could kill him six different ways inside of ten seconds. If he was still alive right now, it was only because the normally unflappable Zett was still afraid of angering his employer.

"You could have told Ganz," Zett said, his lips curving upward to offer a sinister smile while revealing a mouthful of gleaming, sharp teeth. "Why didn't you?"

"I'm no snitch," Quinn snapped. "This is between you and me."

"Between you and me," Zett repeated, "you were fortunate this time, Mr. Quinn." His tone and expression betrayed nothing. "That won't be the case forever."

Though the contention between them had until this point been limited to verbal jousts, Zett had taken things to a new level. Despite that, neither of them would take their squabble to Ganz, to preserve their pride if nothing else. Quinn knew that the situation between him and the Nalori was far from over, and would likely remain unresolved until one of them was dead.

Maybe I can find someplace nice and peaceful to settle down and hide, Quinn thought. *Like the Klingon homeworld.*

43

"Do you people think I'm a physician or a geologist?"

On the all-too-frequent occasions throughout his career when he found himself faced with an autopsy, Ezekiel Fisher always harbored a single question: How had death come to claim the unfortunate soul whose remains were placed in his care?

Standing once more in the station's morgue—his second time in as many weeks—and as he looked upon the body of yet another being whose life had ended amid the frozen wastes of Erilon, Fisher was confronted not only with the challenge of understanding how his latest patient had died, but also how it had lived, as well as what it had been in the first place.

"Well, *I'm* sure not the geologist," Xiong said, glancing up and offering a supportive smile to his newest colleague as they both regarded the body lying atop the examination table that was as much mineral as it was flesh.

This isn't some kind of joke, is it?

Unlike the cold, polished metal of the table itself, the body's dark shell—that was how Fisher thought of it, anyway—seemed to absorb the room's ambient light. His attention once more was drawn to the head and face, which were devoid of features, and the conical limbs, which tapered to points rather than digits.

Xiong finally spoke. "What did the commodore tell you about this?"

"Just the basics," Fisher replied, recounting in broad strokes the information Reyes had provided to him about the creature's presence on Erilon and how it was believed to have been the same assailant that had decimated the original research team as well as

Captain Zhao and his landing party from the *Endeavour*. His first look at the thing upon entering the morgue was enough to tell the doctor that it or its apparent twin—whatever the hell it might be—had killed the Denobulan, Bohanon, whose body he had examined the previous week.

Initial scans of the lifeless form lying atop the table also had proved interesting, revealing a startling absence of internal organs. Instead, the thing's crystalline structure appeared more as an endoskeleton of some kind, sheathed in the obsidian dermal layer, which, according to the reports from the Erilon landing parties, had resisted even the most intensive phaser fire.

"Anything you want to tell me?" he asked, knowing that Xiong was probably under orders to provide only that information which was relevant to Fisher's current needs as a medical examiner.

"We think it somehow telepathically communicated with various equipment across the planet," the lieutenant replied, "including the weapons used against the *Endeavour*. I also saw it directly interfacing with computer consoles we found in ruins beneath the surface, something we've not been able to do."

Stroking his beard as he listened, Fisher asked, "Any ideas how it might have done that?"

"Well, I have a thought," Xiong said, "but it's somewhat radical."

"I have a high tolerance for 'radical,' son," Fisher replied, offering a paternal smile. "Humor an old man, why don't you?"

Drawing what the doctor presumed was a bolstering breath, Xiong said, "In short, I want to know whether this creature is able to establish a physical and mental connection with a crystalline lattice."

"Oh," Fisher replied, his eyebrows rising. "Is that all?"

Unfazed by the comment, the young officer continued, "Obviously we can't learn that here, but if we can verify that this thing's physiological structure lends itself to the controlled sending and receipt of electrical pulses beyond its body, then I'll have something to work with."

Considering that for a moment, Fisher nodded. "That's a pretty tall order, but I suppose we can poke around and see what we see."

At least I don't have to worry about triggering any security alarms this time around, or worry about saying the wrong thing to the wrong people.

Unlike Dr. M'Benga, whom Reyes had not permitted to be briefed into the project, Xiong was certain to provide a storehouse of knowledge Fisher would find useful during his examination.

"Okay, then," Xiong said. "What do we do now?"

Fisher shrugged as he turned to the instrument tray which he had positioned next to the examination table. "For starters, let's see what it takes to get a look inside our friend here."

Retrieving a laser scalpel from the instrument tray and adjusting it to its highest setting, Fisher trained the tool's beam in a tight focus on the surface of the corpse's torso. An immediate trail of thin smoke wafted from the site of incision as the beam bored without resistance into the dark, inflexible surface. The smoke held a bitter, metallic smell that lodged within his nostrils.

"Watch out," he warned, jerking his head to the right to avoid the stream of viscous, dark gray fluid that sprayed from the opening he had created. The first spurt arced over the table and splattered onto the floor, though the flow's pressure eased the next moment, finally ebbing to a slow but steady trickle that continued to ooze from the wound. Reaching to the tray for an emesis basin, the doctor placed it next to the wound and began collecting a sample of the fluid, which did not appear to be caustic—at least not immediately so.

"I don't understand," Xiong said, his brow creased in confusion. "This thing withstood phaser rifles set to maximum. Why is it so fragile now?" Taking the tray from Fisher, the lieutenant picked up a hand scanner from the nearby tray and waved it over the specimen. "It's saturated with lyotropic nanostructures," he said a moment later. "This stuff is liquid crystal."

"Is it safe?" Fisher asked.

Xiong nodded. "It appears to be."

"Fabulous," the doctor said as he retrieved a grafting laser from the tray and used it to suture the wound he had created. "Interesting if this thing used it for blood."

Waving the scanner over the prostrate form, Xiong nodded. "The liquid flows between the different components of its internal crystalline structure." Looking up from the scanner, his expression was one of confusion. "Could the organs have decomposed into liquid form after death?"

Fisher retrieved the basin from Xiong, ever mindful not to spill any of the charcoal-colored liquid as he crossed the room to the computer workstation. Taking a sample of the fluid and placing it in a specimen tube, the doctor inserted it into a port at the base of the dynoscanner and activated the unit. He tapped a series of commands into the computer interface. Thanks to the work he already had performed on samples taken from the Denobulan, it did not take the computer long to complete its first, rudimentary scan.

"And there you are," he said as the results he anticipated were displayed on the computer screen, "you crafty little meta-genome, you."

Leaning closer, Xiong smiled. "Amazing, isn't it? I never get tired of looking at it. It's mesmerizing." Clearing his throat, he stepped back from the workstation. "I guess that sounds rather foolish to you, Doctor."

"Not at all, Lieutenant," Fisher replied, smiling again. "Now, while the scanner is chewing on what we fed it, let's take a look at getting an answer to your question." He toggled a control on the computer interface and the viewer's image shifted to that of a spectroscopic view of the fluid.

Pointing to the screen, Xiong said, "Look at that. There's no electrical resistivity at all. The entire organism looks as though it could be a classical superconductor at room temperature."

Fisher eyed the lieutenant. "Am I supposed to understand any of that?"

"Sorry, Doctor," Xiong replied. "Ancient forms of power generation and regulation. Believe it or not, I've learned more than I ever wanted to on the subject while researching my theory." Indicating the screen with a nod, he added, "If this is right, it's an incredible find. What if electrical impulses channeled through this stuff resulted in a form of . . . I don't know . . . fortifying or hardening of the skeleton? That might account for its resistance to phaser fire."

"Well, that'll be an interesting addition to our report," Fisher said. "Now, given what Commodore Reyes has told me about the work being done by your friends down in the belly of this place, there's something else I want to check." Turning back to the computer interface, he flipped a series of switches and entered a pass code to give him access to the classified repository of information collected by Xiong and his team of research specialists.

"What are you doing?" the lieutenant asked, watching Fisher work.

"Cross-referencing our findings with the Vault's databanks." As he entered a final set of commands and initiated the search, it took only moments to match the DNA sample of his autopsy subject to another entry in the database.

Tholian. The simple word made the hairs on the back of his neck stand up.

"I'll be damned," Xiong said, his voice little more than a hoarse whisper.

The connection might well have been imperceptible to the unschooled eye; it may even have escaped a trained xenogeneticist at a passing glance. However, there was no denying the computer's representation of the unmistakable similarities between the DNA of the mysterious alien and the Tholian sample from the database.

"Some sort of ancestral link," Fisher said, wondering aloud. "Maybe going back millennia. A mutation of some kind, followed by thousands of years of evolution."

"Or something more deliberate," Xiong countered. "Genetic engineering. Eugenics, or something similar."

Fisher considered the idea. "As good as anything I've got." The question facing them now was whether or not this link between the Tholians and this newly discovered race had any bearing on the present situation with the Assembly and their current antagonistic attitude. Were the Tholians even aware of the connection?

It'd explain one helluva lot, Fisher conceded.

The computer beeped once more, and the doctor looked up to see that his search query had yielded an additional result. "What have we here?" he asked as he reviewed the data now scrolling across the screen.

"I don't believe it," Xiong said, leaning in closer in order to get a better look at the display.

Frowning, Fisher regarded the lieutenant. "Don't believe what?"

Xiong pointed to the viewer. "The computer has identified similarities between part of the DNA coding from this new sample and a string of data from the carier wave that gave the station so much trouble months ago."

Fisher stroked his beard as he absorbed that. He of course had been aboard the station when the odd alien transmission had wreaked havoc with so many of Vanguard's sensitive systems, and Reyes had explained the nature of the signal—as much as was known, anyway—while briefing him about various other aspects of the station's clandestine mission here in the Taurus Reach. Despite the limited amount of information which had been gleaned from the signal in the months since it had stopped transmitting, one thing that seemed to be accepted was that the carrier wave was in fact a type of communications protocol from a race never before encountered.

According to the data on the screen before him, however, Fisher could see that at least the station's computer thought it might also be something more.

"That signal wasn't transmitting DNA information," he said. "We would have caught that early on."

Xiong shrugged. "Maybe, maybe not. We only had the original meta-genome samples from Ravanar at the time the signal was being studied, which are different in several respects from those we obtained from Erilon." He paused, examining the data on the screen once more before continuing. "On the other hand," he said, pointing to one column of information, "that string from the Erilon sample has some commonalities with the Ravanar specimens."

Already seeing where the lieutenant was heading, Fisher

keyed a new query to the workstation. "Let's see what happens when we broaden the search parameters a bit." Both men said nothing as they waited for the computer to process the request, though the doctor felt his pulse beginning to quicken in anticipation. *You know what it's going to say.*

Then the screen displayed the results.

"Both sets of samples share traits with the carrier wave?" Xiong said, his eyes wide with astonishment. "How did we miss that?"

"You didn't," Fisher said, tapping the screen. "The similarities are so remote that the computer needed a third set of data to help with triangulating anything. It's not so much that the samples themselves are similar. The carrier wave is the key to both." Sighing, he shook his head. "Of course, I have no idea why that is."

"It's still a huge step forward," Xiong said, a broad grin brightening his features. "Don't you understand? The carrier wave might be the very cipher we've been looking for: the biometric key that can help us understand how that thing we fought on Erilon was able to interface with the technology there." Xiong's smile seemed to widen. "You may just have found a very important piece to this puzzle, Doctor."

And how about that, Fisher mused, unable to resist returning the smile. *Still a few tricks in this old dog yet.* "The question now," he said, "is what do we do about it?"

Both men looked up to the sound of a bosun's whistle—rather, the computer-generated version of one, anyway—filtering through the intercom system.

"*Desai to Dr. Fisher.*"

Reaching to the workstation's comm unit, the doctor opened the frequency. "Fisher here. What can I do for you, Captain?" His eyes widening in realization, he looked toward the chronometer mounted on the nearby bulkhead. "Did I miss our lunch? I just need twenty min—"

"*No, that's not it,*" Desai interrupted. "*Actually, I'm calling to cancel. I need some time . . . to myself. I've got some . . . stuff to process.*" Fisher frowned as he listened to the tone of his friend's voice. He imagined Desai sitting in the solitude of her office, slumped in her chair with her head in her hands.

He looked over to Xiong, and the lieutenant merely nodded as he stepped away from the workstation. "I can get started reviewing this new material," he offered in a low voice. "I'll be in my lab if you need me." Excusing himself, he gathered his belongings before exiting the morgue. Fisher smiled as he watched the younger man go, part of him envious that Xiong would now get to spend an inordinate amount of time pursuing the puzzle they had only just begun to pursue together.

Lucky bastard.

"Rana," he said as the doors slid shut, leaving him alone in the room, "something you want to talk about?" He considered terminating the conversation and going to her. If she indeed had something troubling she wanted to talk about, it would be better for her to do so face-to-face with someone she could trust.

"*No*," she said, her response coming almost too fast. A moment later, she added, "*Zeke, I talked to Diego.*"

Zeke? Then this is *serious.*

"I see," he said, leaning back in his chair. Folding his arms across his chest, he reached up to stroke his beard. "Not to pry," he said, "but are you all right?"

"*It's nothing like that*," Desai replied. "*It's just, well, work stuff. Diego told me . . . told me about some things he thought I should know. It's a little . . . overwhelming.*"

"Ah," Fisher offered in return.

Reyes had briefed her into the project, he realized. While he was sure the commodore had told her only those aspects of the station's true mission which were necessary to keep her from compromising the security of that assignment—a measure he also had taken with the doctor himself—Fisher knew that even such a limited amount of information was in all likelihood more than Desai would ever *want* to know.

"If it helps," he said after a moment, "I felt the same way when he told me. Don't worry about lunch. We can always reschedule. Open invitation, and all that."

"*First chance I get, Fish*," Desai said, and Fisher already could hear a lift in her voice. *"I promise. I just need to do some mental filing today, is all."*

Hating the distance imposed by the impersonal communications system, Fisher sighed. "Absolutely, Rana," he said, hoping his words offered the support he wanted to convey. "And, for what it's worth?"

"Yes?"

"What happens with the commodore stays with the commodore," he said. "No obligations to share with me, know what I mean?"

"Only if you make the same promise," Desai countered, and Fisher imagined he could see her smiling on the other end of the channel.

"No problem. You know me. We'll leave shop talk in our offices and just bad-mouth your boyfriend. Deal?"

The genuine laughter filtering through the intercom made him smile in satisfaction. *"Agreed. Desai out."*

As the connection was severed, Fisher actually felt relieved that Reyes finally had brought Desai into the fold, in a manner of speaking. In the doctor's opinion, the commodore needed a confidant, someone he could trust with the very human moments of indecision and struggle that he could never reveal to his staff. That Desai was that counsel and not Fisher himself did nothing to bruise his perceived standing with his friend. After five decades in service to Starfleet and knowing Reyes as long as he had, the doctor had carried more than his share of confidences; he certainly felt no need to gather any more.

He knew also that Desai would at times be troubled by the things she surely would discover as Vanguard's mission in the Taurus Reach continued. Such anxiety no doubt would be exacerbated by the fact that Reyes would have ordered her to keep much of what she learned to herself.

Welcome to the club, Rana, Fisher mused. *Diego's giving me plenty that I can't share with you, either.*

44

"The Jinoteur system," T'Prynn said as she regarded Commodore Reyes, Lieutenant Xiong, and Ambassador Jetanien in what was becoming something of a ritual—a clandestine meeting within the secured confines of Reyes's quarters. "So named as part of Federation long-range stellar-cartography missions conducted two years ago during our preliminary investigations of the Taurus Reach. Except for unmanned probes, this system remains unexplored."

T'Prynn.

She kept her hands clasped behind her, hoping none of the others would see how nails dug into her palms, the sole physical manifestation of the struggle she found herself pursuing even as she endeavored to maintain her composure and carry out her present duties.

Leave me, her mind implored.

Submit, Sten responded, the simple command embodying her long-dead lover's *katra,* fighting as always to push aside her own thoughts in a bid to assert its dominance over her.

Forcing away the summons, T'Prynn turned back to the viewscreen situated just to her left. Depicted upon it was a standard computer-generated representation of a solar system. At the center of the image was a large white sun, and orbiting it were five planets, situated on different planes and describing orbits at varying angles around the star, with those tracks further depicted in a different color.

"As you know," she said, "this is the origin point for the carrier wave we discovered interfering with the station's systems several months ago." She indicated Xiong with a nod of her head. "The lieutenant and his team did an admirable job tracking the source of the signal, and the sensor data I've since obtained offers us insight into this system that I believe you will find most intriguing." She tapped a command sequence into the keypad next to the viewscreen, and the image shifted to zoom in on the first planet. The blue circle illustrating its orbit vanished as the picture was enlarged and enhanced to display the planet's two moons.

"Three of the five planets each possess two natural satellites," she said, "while one of the others has three moons and the other four. While the sensor data presently available to us shows that none of the planets appear to be inhabited, there are indications of a civilization that might once have existed on the fourth planet."

"Correct me if I am wrong, Commander," Jetanien said from where he stood before Reyes's desk, "but it is my understanding that save for a single long-range probe assigned to star-mapping duties in that sector two years ago, we have little to no information on this area of the Taurus Reach."

"You are not wrong, Your Excellency," T'Prynn replied. "This information was delivered to us via different means."

The ambassador let loose with his version of a laugh, which to the Vulcan sounded more like the low rumbling of an avalanche on a rocky slope. "I take it from your lack of clarification that you'd rather not divulge your source?"

Her right eyebrow raising a notch, T'Prynn nodded once. "That is correct, sir. This data was obtained from a Klingon sensor drone, though the particular aspects of how it came to be in our possession are classified." Looking to Reyes, she asked, "Would you not agree, Commodore?"

"Don't let me stop you, Commander," Reyes replied, his words laced with sarcasm. "I'm assuming you were able to obtain this information in a manner that won't put us at war with the Klingon Empire, at least not before dinner?" There was no mistaking the expression of dissatisfaction on her superior officer's face.

While T'Prynn was aware of Reyes's penchant for delegating authority rather than hovering over his subordinates' shoulders while they carried out their duties, she knew also that he did not like being kept out of the information loop, nor did he appreciate being caught by unexpected turns of events or—as humans referred to them—surprises. She had learned that much while dispatching the problem with the journalist, Pennington, the previous month.

Despite that and given the immense security concerns surrounding Vanguard's primary task, there were some aspects of her assignment which required insulation even from Reyes, for the good of the mission as well as the commodore himself. The less he knew about certain actions undertaken by her, the less he had to consider imparting to others who might not share the same outlook with regard to security. Lieutenant Xiong, for example.

Captain Desai, for another.

Submit, Sten demanded.

Be silent, she responded.

"Rest assured, sir," T'Prynn said, "that this information was obtained through methods which cannot be traced back to Starfleet." While Quinn's destruction of the drone while making his escape from the pirate vessel was unfortunate, the Vulcan had weighed the risk of that development and considered it to be minimal. It would be weeks before the empire concluded that the probe was lost, after which they likely would assume that the drone had fallen victim to malfunction or—at worst—piracy.

Not so far from the truth, after all.

Considering her answer, Reyes frowned. "I feel more relaxed already." Indicating the viewscreen with a nod of his head, he asked, "So, what's so special about this system that it required going to such an effort to get info on it?"

T'Prynn keyed the control pad again, causing the image on the viewer to zoom in closer to one of the moons. "The sensor data reveals an interesting trait shared by all of the natural satellites in this system. Each of the moons follows an orbital path that never places them between their host planets and the system's star."

"Interesting?" Jetanien said. "I would characterize that description of yours as an understatement, Commander."

"Is that even possible?" Reyes asked, his brow furrowing. "I've never heard of anything like that."

T'Prynn nodded. "I verified the data myself, Commodore. It is conclusive."

"And it gets better," Xiong said from where he sat in one of the two chairs situated before Reyes's desk. "While the moons exhibit rotation, they do so in concert with their orbits so that one hemisphere always faces outward, away from the center of the system. Further, the sensor data Commander T'Prynn obtained indicates the presence of artificial structures in those outward-facing hemispheres."

"The signal originated from one of the moons orbiting the fourth planet," T'Prynn said. "According to the sensor data, the power readings emanating from that point match those we already have recorded on Erilon and Palgrenax."

"Now why did I see that one coming?" Reyes said as he leaned forward in his chair. Rubbing his chin with the back of his right hand, he asked, "So, the signal. Was it intended to link with either or both of those planets? What about other locations?"

You belong to me, Sten prodded.

Never.

Shaking her head, T'Prynn replied, "We do not know yet, sir. The facts currently available to us could be used to support several theories, sir, though I am reluctant to engage in speculation until we have had an opportunity to gather more information."

"Well, that's never stopped me." Reyes said. Standing up, he moved across the office to stand before the viewscreen. He touched the keypad, changing the image to again depict the first planet along with its two moons. Pointing to one of the moons, he said, "If these are always facing outward, that means their orbits around their planets, coupled with the planets' own revolution around the sun, might provide a means of monitoring the system's outer perimeter."

"An early-warning network?" Jetanien offered.

Reyes nodded. "Think about it. Our outposts along the Neutral Zone are covered with sensors and monitoring devices that all point into Romulan space, monitoring for signs of activity on the other side of the border. It's the same basic concept."

"Such a deployment of similar assets would presuppose something of extreme value or importance located within the system," Xiong said.

"Something important enough to control the orbits of thirteen moons?" Reyes asked. "Yeah, I think that might be a possibility, Lieutenant." Frowning, he turned to T'Prynn. "What about the carrier wave? We already think it was some kind of warning signal. This would fit in with what I'm proposing."

"Assuming your theory has any basis in reality," the Vulcan replied, "the signal we intercepted would be a form of communication, either between the planets or something intended for other locations."

"Something automated," Xiong said, "perhaps designed to be triggered in reaction to a specific event or set of events." Looking to the others, he added, "We are talking about a race of beings able to change the course of astral bodies and who apparently were genetic engineers of the first order. What precisely would they have to fear? It would have to be something rather uncommon, and therefore rare in occurrence."

Reyes shrugged. "Maybe the warning, if that's even what it was, is just one kind of signal. Seems to me if they'd gone to the trouble to communicate between distant points in space, they'd want to do it for all sorts of reasons."

"An interesting theory," T'Prynn said. If Reyes's hypothesis was correct, it presupposed a race of beings possessing technology and power beyond that of any species ever encountered, even more advanced than what already was theorized just based on what she and her companions knew of the meta-genome. Logic suggested that the originators of all that had been found by Lieutenant Xiong and his teams to this point were long dead, which meant that their vast storehouse of superior knowledge remained hidden, concealed deep within the Taurus Reach, waiting for someone to find it.

Submit!

The force behind the directive caught her off guard, Sten's *katra* asserting itself once more and all but drowning out the question Reyes put to Jetanien. She did not hear the commodore's words, instead marshaling all of her mental disciplines to beat back the essence of her long-dead fiancé.

Leave me alone!

The command pressed into the dark, distant corners of her mind even as T'Prynn forced herself to remain standing as she was, schooling her features to offer no clue to the others in the room that anything was amiss. A quick glance to her companions showed that her efforts had been successful, as Reyes and the ambassador were continuing their conversation while Lieutenant Xiong watched and listened.

"The Tholians must know something," Jetanien was saying. "It's the only logical explanation for their actions to this point. That said, I do not believe they are aware of their own apparent connection to what we've found." He rolled his shoulders while emitting a new string of clicks. "Based on my contacts with them to date, if they do know more than they are revealing to us, then they are by far the most consummate actors it has ever been my privilege to watch perform."

Folding his arms across his chest, Reyes said, "Well, I think we can agree that they've got some of the best poker faces at the table." He smiled at his own poor joke before beginning to pace the length of his office. "Mr. Xiong, I suppose you know what your next assignment is going to be?"

The lieutenant nodded. "Yes, sir. A visit to the Jinoteur system."

"Eventually," Reyes countered. "I want that place given a complete once-over before we send you and your team in. Whatever's making use of the technology we're finding on these planets, they've been a step ahead of us for weeks, and that has to change. We got lucky on Erilon, but we can't count on that happening again."

"Our efforts should be on learning how to access that technology ourselves," T'Prynn added. "Mr. Xiong has already provided us with valuable insight in that regard. It is my opinion that his talents can best be utilized to continue that investigation."

"Absolutely," Jetanien said. "I would also add that determining the identity of our mysterious interloper from Erilon would also be of benefit. If there are others like him, it's crucial we find them before our enemies do."

"There's that gift for understatement again," Reyes said as he made his way back behind his desk. "Well, I think we've got more than enough to chew on for one day. If there are no objections, I'd like to go to my quarters and slip into a coma."

Following Jetanien out of the commodore's office, T'Prynn was careful to keep her hands clasped behind her back, hoping as she passed Xiong that the lieutenant would not notice any traces of green blood she was certain seeped from between her fingers.

You are mine.

I would rather die.

Death will not free you.

"Commander," Xiong said from behind her. "Are you all right?"

Turning to face the younger officer, T'Prynn regarded him with as stoic an expression as she could muster. "I beg your pardon?"

Xiong seemed overcome by a bout of nervousness, no doubt owing to his inexperience in dealing with members of the opposite gender, she decided. "You seem . . . unwell."

Her posture stiffening, T'Prynn replied, "I am fine. If you will excuse me, I must return to my duties."

"Yes, of course," Xiong replied, nodding. "I meant no offense."

"Offense is a human emotion, Lieutenant," she replied. Seeing the expression on his face and realizing the words had been delivered with more of an edge than she had intended, she added, "That said, your inquiry is appreciated. Good evening."

She watched him depart, waiting until she was alone and none of the other personnel on duty in the operations center appeared to be looking in her direction before finally bringing her hands around so that she could see them.

Other than the impressions made by her manicured nails, there were no visible injuries or blemishes.

Submit, Sten goaded again, his *katra* feeling like a physical weight pressing down upon her mind.

Meditation, T'Prynn decided as she turned on her heel and marched toward the turbolift. That was what she required now. Once more she called upon the mental exercises taught to her by the Adepts. Fatigue and the need to constantly focus on her myriad and demanding duties had caused her to lose the focus that was vital to keeping her fiancé contained within the cage she had erected for him within the depths of her mind. Her lapse had allowed Sten to escape that prison, and it was now time to pummel him back into it.

You will never know peace, so long as you resist me, he said.

Then I shall never know peace.

T'Prynn opened her eyes, only to discover that she no longer was in the operations center. Looking around, she was alarmed to find herself standing in what she recognized as a corridor within the apartment complex located in Stars Landing, Vanguard's civilian residential and commercial area. The carpeted deck, the walls painted in muted colors, and the irregular placement of plants and artwork lent the passageway an air distinctly different from that of the passageways connecting the quarters assigned to the station's Starfleet contingent.

She held no memory of the turbolift ride down from operations, or of how she had come to be here, either on foot or via the subshuttle tube encircling Fontana Meadow.

Fascinating.

Of equal interest to her was her exact location. Stepping closer to the door before her—its duranium surface coated with a synthetic polymer designed to simulate the dark wood of a native Earth tree—T'Prynn reached out and with her fingers caressed the small black plate etched with white lettering that denoted the apartment number. It took only an instant to search her memory and recall the identity of the resident assigned to these quarters.

Timothy D. Pennington.

Of all the places on the station to which she might have come, why here? The reporter was not a friend of hers, or even a casual acquaintance, their only interaction coming as a result of his bothersome investigations into the *Bombay* incident and the steps she had taken to neutralize the threat his efforts represented.

Perhaps regret has guided you here, or even guilt.

T'Prynn could not determine if the voice taunting her was Sten's or a product of her own turbulent thoughts. Regardless, she refused to accept the notion. Diffusing the credibility of the story Pennington had submitted regarding the loss of the *Bombay* and the Tholians' culpability in the incident had served a valuable purpose, of that she was certain. That the journalist had endured both professional and personal difficulty as a result of her actions was an unfortunate yet necessary collateral consequence. While one life had been disrupted, to be sure, countless others that would have been at risk in the face of a Federation-Tholian conflict had instead been safeguarded.

Logic demanded no other course.

Is it truly that simple?

"Enough."

The word, spoken aloud, startled T'Prynn, and she looked around to see if anyone might have overheard her. She was relieved to see that the corridor remained empty, but it would not stay that way. It would be prudent to depart before her presence here engendered questions from passersby that best were left unasked.

Still, returning to her quarters was not an option she welcomed. While she knew meditation would ease her current mental turmoil, the truth was that fatigue was tugging at the edges of her consciousness. Attempting to meditate in such a state would be problematic at best.

Alone in the corridor, T'Prynn allowed the ghost of a smile to tug at the corners of her mouth. No, she decided as she turned and headed for the row of turbolifts servicing this area of the apartment complex, another means of relaxation would be better.

45

Silence engulfed the bridge of the *Bloodied Talon,* acutely palpable and yet seeming so vulnerable that Sarith feared any movement or hint of sound might destroy not only the envelope of quiet but also any chance for survival remaining to her and her crew.

"Distance three thousand *mat'drih,*" Darjil said, his voice low. "Approaching from astern, Commander."

Sarith heard the mounting tension in the centurion's voice despite his best efforts to maintain his bearing. Hearing the younger officer provide the report from sensors that normally would have been delivered by N'tovek was like an abrasive pad rubbed against an open and raw wound. She ignored her personal grief, pushing it aside as duty demanded, and instead returned her focus to the Klingon battle cruiser depicted on the main viewscreen.

Sensors had first detected the vessel near the end of the previous duty shift. The ship's presence followed that of an automated sensor probe, also of Klingon design, which had passed within three light-years of the *Talon* two days earlier. Analysis of the cruiser's course showed that it was mirroring that of the drone, perhaps searching for signs of Tholian activity in the vicinity of the Palgrenax system.

"It seems someone knows we are here," Ineti said from where he stood beside her.

Nodding, Sarith replied, "They know something is here, that much is certain." Stepping toward the central hub, she leaned closer to Darjil in order to see his workstation's sensor display. Recognizing the standard search pattern the Klingon ship was effecting, she shook her head. "I suppose it was only a matter of time."

The portent of unfortunate things to come had arrived in the form of a systems status report delivered by her chief engineering officer, Jacius, during the early hours of the previous day. One of the distribution nodes channeling power to the *Talon*'s cloaking device had failed and, according to Jacius, there were no replacements.

All options to manufacture a substitute using available materials had also been explored and exhausted, the result being that while the cloak still functioned to maintain the ship's practical invisibility, the concealment of its power emissions no longer was total. Though the odds were fair that a passing vessel might not register the wounded ship's presence, if someone were to take the time to examine sensor readings for anomalies, they might find sufficient reason to arouse suspicion.

The destruction of a planet surely was enough to heighten someone's vigilance, Sarith mused.

With that in mind, she had ordered a circuitous route out of the Taurus Reach, plotting a course that would not offer any clues that the ship, if discovered, was making an attempt to travel toward Romulan space. It was a simple plan, though one she hoped would at least avoid providing any additional clues as to their identity should they be detected.

Studying the sensor data, Sarith frowned as she weighed the situation. "They are sweeping the area with full sensors," she said. "Their weapons are armed, but their shields are down." She shook her head. "Typical Klingon arrogance."

"You expected something else?" Ineti asked, offering a small smile. "So far as the Klingons know, they possess the most formidable vessels in this area of space. The Tholians certainly have nothing to stand against them."

It was a logical assessment, Sarith agreed, even though it did not take into account the capabilities of whatever ships the Federation might have deployed into the region. While spies had smuggled information on Starfleet's current and proposed starship designs back to Romulus over the years—information that Sarith had read and absorbed prior to departing on this mission—that was altogether different from seeing such a vessel firsthand.

Once more, she felt momentary regret that she would not have such an opportunity, a sensation she had experienced several times since misfortune had fallen upon the *Talon*. Facing off with a Starfleet vessel was something to which many Romulan ship commanders aspired, all of whom had been raised on stories of the war the empire had waged and failed to win against Earth and its allies.

Sarith would not achieve that goal, just as she knew she had failed to accomplish her primary mission here. The Federation's motivations for venturing into the Taurus Reach, and why that expansion had triggered such vociferous reactions not only from the Klingons but the Tholians as well, would remain a mystery to the Romulan people for a while longer.

"Sixteen hundred *mat'drih* and closing, Commander," Darjil reported, looking away from his station to regard her with an expression of heightening anxiety. Sarith understood the centurion's cause for concern. The enemy ship was mere moments from being able to detect her own wounded vessel.

"Are they in contact with anyone?" she asked.

Darjil shook his head. "No, Commander. They have not established communications frequencies or dispatched any messages since entering sensor range."

"That means they still do not know for what they search," Ineti said, stepping closer to the central workstations. "If we are going to act, Commander, then now is the time."

"Agreed," Sarith said, knowing without the need for clarification what her trusted friend was implying. What she did not tell him was that it was not the action he had implicitly proposed but merely his concerns with which she concurred. He was right to suggest what he had, of course, as it was the one option that would ensure her ship was not discovered and captured by the approaching enemy vessel.

As she considered the measure, her eyes drifted to the control console situated along one side of the bridge's central hub,

the single station that was coded for access only by herself and
Ineti. She regarded the set of switches positioned there, her
mind recalling the proper sequence needed to set the protocol
into motion. It would take only seconds, and when it was over,
there would be nothing left of her ship for an enemy to
recover.

Duty demanded Sarith take that action—now.

She felt her jaw clench at the notion as she regarded the Klingon ship on the screen. The idea that she must commit suicide because of the chance wanderings of pitiful dregs such as those
crewing the approaching vessel made her want to vomit. *No,* she
decided, *there is another way.*

At the sensor console, Darjil called out, "Enemy vessel has altered its course, Commander, heading directly toward us. Eight
hundred *mat'drih* and closing."

Straightening her posture, Sarith turned to Jacius, who had
come to the bridge to monitor shipboard systems from here rather
than dwell in the depths of the ship's engineering section. "Can
we arm weapons without being detected?"

Jacius nodded. "Yes, though our power signature will become
more noticeable if the Klingon ship comes any closer."

"Let it be noticeable, then," Sarith replied as she locked eyes
with Ineti. "With the exception of the cloak, reroute all power to
the weapons. On my command, channel that power to forward
disruptors, as well."

Ineti smiled. "One last triumphant battle for the Praetor?" he
asked.

Unable to return the expression, Sarith nodded before turning
her attention to the expectant faces of her officers. As one, they all
looked to her, loyal to the end, ready to carry out whatever orders
she gave them in service to the empire.

Then her eyes fell on the battle cruiser now dominating the
viewer, its bulbous primary hull looming as though preparing
to burst through the screen. She imagined she could almost see
the faces of Klingons looking out through the ports peppering
the hull, unprepared for what was to come next.

"One last duty to perform," Sarith said after a moment, her

reply punctuated by the proximity alert signal emitted by the sensor console, notifying everyone on the bridge that the Klingon ship had closed to prime weapons range and telling her it was time to issue her final order as commander of the *Bloodied Talon*, servant and protector of the Romulan Star Empire.

"Execute."

46

Even with the added quiet, given the absence of the steady thrum of the *Endeavour*'s warp engines, which were deactivated while the ship was cradled in the embrace of Vanguard's docking bay three, Khatami found that the solitude and serenity of her quarters did little to enable her concentration on the task at hand. Despite hours spent at her desk, perusing file after file from the ship's personnel database, she seemed unable to make what was turning out to be one of the most difficult decisions of her still young captaincy.

"Captain's Personal Log, supplemental," she spoke to the computer. "So the question remains: Who's my first officer?"

Once more—she had long since lost count of how many times she had repeated this process during the evening—her eyes scanned her desktop viewer, reviewing and comparing the service records of her top three candidates. She had stalled the decision long enough, she knew, waiting until after returning from Erilon, part of her feeling as though she still occupied the post herself. It could be delayed no longer.

"Lieutenant Commander Norton does a fine job leading beta shift," she said. "He has experience and his record clearly makes him the strongest candidate, but he's prickly and overly officious." Shrugging to herself, she added, "There's Lieutenant Stano from gamma shift. She's very capable and very respected by her team, but she's not the most efficient person in Starfleet. And I know she's on the sciences track, but I can see some real leadership qualities in Lieutenant T'Pes. . . ."

Khatami let her voice trail off as she wondered whether she

would be able to build a quick confidence and rapport with any one of them, as she had done with Ensign Klisiewicz. Through their shared need to immerse themselves in the secret information about the meta-genome, they had begun to forge a bond of trust, and it was one she appreciated more than he might realize. Other than herself, there was no one on board who understood more about the meta-genome and Starfleet's greater mission in the Taurus Reach than he did.

She had made a point soon after the *Endeavour*'s departure from Erilon to meet with the young ensign and express her thanks; not only for the assistance he had lent her on the bridge during that mind-numbing first attack, but also for his willingness to step quickly into a role of research and responsibility. He surely must be viewing his posting on the starship as a much greater job than he ever imagined, she remembered asking. And she knew she never would forget his reply.

"I'm only following your lead, Captain," she heard Klisiewicz's voice repeating in her thoughts. *"We're in the same boat, you know? And if you're not getting out, neither am I."*

"Think Starfleet would approve a field promotion from ensign to lieutenant commander?" She smiled at the thought, ridiculous as it may have been. Khatami already had put in a request to promote Klisiewicz to full lieutenant, a rank commensurate with the level of responsibilities he currently held. While Starfleet had not yet responded to the request, she figured there was no need to push her luck. Releasing an amused sigh, she said, "Computer, delete that last remark."

"Deleted," the monotone, feminine voice replied.

Khatami regarded the follow-up mission to Erilon as a success save for the unfortunate loss of three more members of her crew, serving as a small measure of emotional closure for her transition to command and stating in no uncertain terms that it was time to move on. While Commodore Reyes had said as much during her post-mission debriefing even as the *Endeavour* warped back to the station, Khatami herself still harbored no small amount of insecurity about her abilities, particularly as they stacked up to the challenges she knew lay ahead.

You got lucky this time, Tish. The next time won't be so easy.

The tone of her door chime sounded, pulling her from her reverie and the pool of doubt into which she felt herself plunging. "Computer, end recording," she said, relieved by the welcome distraction. "Please, come right in!"

Dr. Leone was standing at the threshold as the door slid aside, his hands clasped behind his back and his eyes crushed into his characteristic squint. "Captain," he said, his expression communicating his discomfort, "I was just passing by and I, well, didn't know whether you'd had dinner yet."

Shaking her head, Khatami replied, "Not yet, no." She waited to see if the doctor would venture into the room on his own accord, and when he did not, she gestured to him with a smile. "You're welcome to join me if you like."

Leone nodded several times in quick succession as he entered, his lips pursed in a tight grin. "Well, I hadn't had a chance to check in since we returned to Vanguard," he said, hovering over the empty seat near her desk. "CMO protocol being what it is and all, it's good form to check on the commanding officer's emotional well-being from time to time, particularly after a stressful assignment. You know, make sure the burdens of command aren't weighing too heavily, that sort of thing."

Suppressing the urge to giggle, Khatami replied, "I understand."

"So, things seem okay then?"

Khatami found herself flattered by Leone's awkward display. Though public expression of friendship or support was by no means the doctor's strong suit, there was no mistaking his genuine concern for her. At the same time, she understood that he was not seeking emotional reciprocity.

"I think so," she replied. "I was just finalizing my decision to appoint my new first officer."

"Well, it's quite an honor to even be considered, Captain. I accept," Leone said as he sat down in the chair opposite hers. His expression remained neutral for several seconds before he added, "By the way, if I ever say that again, feel free to have me locked up for psychological evaluation, and if you thought I was serious, even for a second, then make sure you book yourself into the padded room next to mine."

Now she did laugh, welcoming the rush of warmth that came with it. Though others might take exception to his sardonic personality, in his own way, Leone always had been able to put her at ease.

"So," she said after a moment, "tell me about this mysterious outbreak you contained down in the mess hall the other day." Feeling a hint of mischief taking hold as she noted Leone's worried expression, she fought to school her own features. "I seem to have misplaced your official report on the incident."

Clearing his throat and appearing as though he would rather be somewhere—anywhere—else, the doctor shifted his position in his seat. He even raised a hand in an animated attempt to respond, but as soon as he opened his mouth, she saw comprehension dawn. "It was a minor outbreak, Captain, nothing too serious. I was able to . . . initiate quarantine procedures and keep the reaction from spreading, if that's what you mean. I've stayed on top of the situation, but it appears my single application of the treatment regimen is proving effective. I don't expect there will be any new flare-ups." He squirmed in his seat again, the expression on his face indicative of someone who might just have sat upon an unexploded photon torpedo.

"Ah," Khatami said, folding her arms across her chest and nodding as she listened to the rambling report. "Well, while I appreciate your initiative, Doctor, it's my opinion that you pursue other 'treatments' from now on." When she finally did smile, she leaned across the desk toward him. "I'm sure the idiot deserved it, but I know I'll need time to earn the crew's respect. I also know I need to earn it on my own."

Leone nodded. "Understood, Captain," he replied. "And . . . may I speak freely?"

"You've been doing that for as long as I've known you, Tony," Khatami said, laughing again. "Permission retroactively granted."

"For what it's worth," the doctor offered, "I think you've done a hell of a job. Captain Zhao's a hard act to follow, and I know it takes time to figure out your own way, but I think you'll do just fine."

Khatami smiled. "This isn't just another prescription morale booster, is it?"

Shrugging, Leone replied, "When it rains, it pours."

The door chime sounded again, and when Khatami gave permission for the caller to enter, she turned to see Mog standing in the doorway.

"I'm sorry, Captain," the burly engineer said by way of greeting. "Am I interrupting?"

"Not at all," Khatami replied, gesturing for him to enter. "Dr. Leone and I were discussing a few things before I take him up on his dinner invitation."

Turning to stare at the doctor, Mog affected a mock expression of shock. "You? By Kera and Phinda, I've finally lived long enough to have seen it all." His eyes narrowing, he asked, "Are you feeling well? I hear there's something going around on the lower decks." Leone's reply was limited to a pained grimace, more than enough to elicit a bellowing laugh from the husky Tellarite. To Khatami, he said, "So, is there room for one more in this party?"

"Only if you eat something that doesn't smell like it's been rooted out of a silage pile," Leone said as he rose from his seat, shaking his head. "Sometimes I think Tellarite cuisine was developed as the result of an elaborate dare."

"That doesn't stop you from enjoying my *bojnoggi* in the mornings," Mog noted.

"I'm having it scanned for addictive substances before I drink another drop," the doctor replied, wincing as he headed for the door.

Khatami turned to follow him when she felt Mog's hand on her arm. Waiting for Leone to walk out of earshot, the engineer looked to her. "From the looks of things," he said in a low voice, "the doctor beat me to it, but I'll say it anyway. Captain Zhao would be proud of you."

The words, soft and sincere, embraced Khatami with the warmth and comfort of a favored blanket. While she knew that

Mog's support and loyalty to her was absolute, it still felt good to receive affirmation from one of her closest and most trusted friends. "Thank you, Mog. I appreciate that."

"Hey," Leone said from the corridor, poking his head through the door. "You coming or not? I'm hungry."

Mog chuckled as the doctor's head disappeared again. Nodding toward the door, the engineer said, "I don't think he ever visited Captain Zhao. That has to be a good sign."

Feeling her inner demon recede somewhat in the face of her friend's observation, Khatami nodded with a conviction she had not felt in some time. "I'll take all the good signs I can get."

47

Basking under lamps designed to simulate the warmth generated by the sun of his homeworld, Jetanien lay disrobed and belly-down atop the stone slab that was the dominating piece of furniture in the bedroom of his private quarters. Though the heat expelled by the lamps was far above the tolerance and even safety margins of most humanoid species, for a Chelon the effects were soothing, relaxing and reinvigorating muscles fatigued by the stresses of his position and the anxieties they evoked.

Despite the sun lamps' calming effects, Jetanien was unable to shake entirely the frustration and despair that continued to gnaw at him even here in his otherwise comforting refuge. At this moment, both the Klingon and Tholian delegations were on their way to their homeworlds, having departed the station at the decree of their respective governments.

Though the summit had been tumultuous, Jetanien admitted, he felt also that the first signs of real, measurable progress had taken hold when the meeting met with untimely interruption. Events far beyond his influence had conspired to pull apart the tenuous links he was sure were on the verge of sending the Federation, Klingons, and Tholians down a path of mutual understanding and perhaps even cooperation. Once again, the three interstellar bodies eyed one another as players on different sides of a game board, each waiting for the other to initiate play. No, Jetanien decided, a better analogy was one of warriors in centuries past, who gazed upon each other across ancient battlefields in the moments prior to the first sword being drawn.

In essence, he mused, *I have accomplished nothing.*

In particular, Jetanien regretted the opportunity he had lost with Ambassador Sesrene. The Tholian diplomat had only just begun to offer substantive clues as to the reasons for his people's bizarre, unexplained reactions to the Klingon and Federation presence in the Taurus Reach. That Jetanien might have come so close to answering so many lingering questions before his efforts were thwarted was as disheartening as it was frustrating.

Might a better diplomat have gotten those answers? Would he or she have made a more effective facilitator, rather than wasting precious time trying to regain control of a situation he or she should never have lost in the first place?

As they had from the moment Commodore Reyes suspended the summit, those questions tormented Jetanien. What could he have done differently, or more efficiently? What mistakes had he made, and which now demanded attention and correction in order to avoid repeating them? Would there be an opportunity to redeem himself?

What if it already was too late? Had he squandered his one chance to make a difference here, where steady, lucid leadership and gifted foresight were necessary if the unthinkable was to be avoided?

His thoughts were broken by the sound of his door chime. Rising from his sleeping tablet, Jetanien reached for a robe to cover his considerable bulk before answering the summons.

"Enter." From beyond his bedroom he heard the sound of the door to his quarters opening, followed by the gentle, rhythmic footfalls of someone walking in his direction.

"Ambassador?" called out a female voice, one he recognized. A moment later, Akeylah Karumé appeared in his doorway, wearing one of her customary multicolored robes replete with its dazzling array of abstract designs. The tall, brown woman appraised him with an expression of alarm.

"I apologize for disturbing you, Your Excellency," she said, glancing away in obvious embarrassment.

"Not at all," Jetanien replied, clicking his beak as he stood up and ushered her into the room. "What can I do for you?"

Clearing her throat, Karumé said, "We've just received this parcel addressed to you." She produced what he recognized as a standard-issue green diplomatic pouch of a type used by members of the Federation Council when in session on Earth.

"Indeed," the ambassador said, considering this unexpected delivery. "From one of my esteemed colleagues, no doubt." Experiencing a pang of optimism, he asked, "Might it have come from Sesrene?"

Karumé shook her head. "Actually, it's from Lugok."

Making no attempt to stifle his surprise, Jetanien released a disbelieving snort. "You're joking. Did you have it scanned for explosives?" he asked even as he extended one of his thick webbed hands to take the proffered pouch from her.

"And biotoxins," Karumé replied. "Though any self-respecting Klingon will tell you that to attack one's enemies in such an underhanded manner is dishonorable."

"Only if anyone were to find out," Jetanien countered as he opened the pouch. Its contents consisted of a single green data cartridge, the squared variety used as secondary storage in Federation computer systems.

"Is there anything else, Your Excellency?" Karumé asked after a moment.

Shaking his head, Jetanien moved toward the doorway leading from his bedroom to his office. "No, my dear. Thank you for delivering this. Enjoy the rest of your evening." He walked to his desk, lowering himself onto the stool situated there before turning and holding up the data cartridge so that Karumé could see it. "If there's anything here of note, I'll be sure to call you immediately."

Karumé took her leave of him, and Jetanien waited until the doors closed behind her before inserting the cartridge into his desktop computer interface and activating the unit. A moment later, the display screen flared to life and the image coalesced into view to show an almost genteel-looking Lugok.

"*Ambassador Jetanien,*" the recorded image of the Klingon began, "*I apologize if this message disturbs you at an inconvenient hour.*"

Never trust a polite Klingon, Jetanien mused as he considered Lugok's expression.

"*Your Excellency,*" the ambassador continued, "*as you cer-*

tainly can appreciate, the demeanor of conflict a diplomat might project in a group setting is different than the one he might choose to show an individual in a more private discussion. Politics, as you well know, is as much a game of positioning and perception as it is power and progress."

"I wonder, do I sound this way when I talk?" Jetanien asked aloud, the question of course being heard by no one.

On the screen, Lugok said, *"Despite the impasse at which our respective governments find themselves, I am . . . hopeful that you and I might find a way to continue the dialogue we began before the termination of the summit. It would be unfortunate if our superiors' shortsightedness prevented us from realizing the potential you seem to believe awaits us all. I look forward to your response, so that we might discuss how best to proceed. Qapla', Your Excellency."*

Jetanien was already stunned into silence as he watched the recording. His surprise was only compounded as Lugok's expression melted into something that—loosely defined, of course— resembled a warm, welcoming smile. Then the image faded as the recorded message ended.

"Well," Jetanien said to no one, "that certainly was unexpected."

Naturally, the ambassador was suspicious. What could be motivating Lugok to act in this manner? Jetanien's instincts told him the Klingon's motives were far from noble, but what if he was wrong? Was it possible that Lugok had been visited by a realization that so far seemed to elude his superiors on the Klingon High Council? Might he truly be inspired to forge a lasting peace here in the Taurus Reach?

There is only one way to answer those questions.

Tapping one of his claws against his broad beak, Jetanien grunted in growing anticipation as he considered his options in responding to Lugok's intriguing proposition. How should he proceed? What risks lay ahead, and were they worth incurring?

It seemed he would have to call Karumé after all.

48

Still damp from her shower, Anna Sandesjo stepped from her bathroom and wrapped a robe around her cooling body. Crossing her quarters to her desk while using the towel she still carried to complete the task of drying her hair, she paused, smiling to herself as she realized that T'Prynn's scent still lingered among the other aromas permeating the room. It, the disheveled bedsheets, and the various articles of her discarded clothing scattered with abandon about the room all conspired, along with her own still fresh memory, to reconstruct the scene of vigorous passion that had unfolded here.

T'Prynn's appearance at her door had been unexpected though not unwelcome, and Sandesjo could see that she was distracted, even upset—by Vulcan standards, anyway. At first she had been worried by T'Prynn's unexpected visit, but it had quickly become apparent that her lover had come for a single purpose. Surprised to find herself in the unfamiliar role of caretaker, Sandesjo had asked what was troubling the Vulcan, but her questions had gone unanswered. Then the need for words had passed, replaced by other, more urgent desires, after which T'Prynn had left as abruptly as she had arrived, offering as an excuse a need to return to her duties.

Just as well, Sandesjo mused, *considering that I have duties of my own.*

Opening her briefcase to extract the hidden subspace transceiver, she proceeded quickly through the steps to activate it and send its clandestine hailing message. Engaging in yet another unscheduled communication carried a risk, particularly now, during the time observed aboard the station as "late night." Though most civilian businesses—with the exception of the various taverns scattered across Stars Landing—were closed until morning, Starfleet operations continued around the clock. Her transceiver was programmed to camouflage its signal amid the plethora of communications coming and going from Starbase 47, of course, but there was always the chance that a bored ensign working the late shift might through fortunate happenstance stumble across her clandestine frequency while searching for something more interesting with which to pass the time.

A tone sounded from the unit's interface panel, signifying that the transceiver had completed the connection process. Sandesjo released a sigh of resignation, knowing that the elation she had enjoyed during the past few hours was about to evaporate in the face of the reality that was her duty.

"*What?*" Turag asked as his face came into focus on the transceiver's display monitor. His eyes were wide and bloodshot, and his long hair seemed to fan out in all directions at once. "*Why have you disturbed me? What could possibly be so important at this time of night?*"

Sandesjo could tell by his heavy eyelids and slurred words that while Turag might indeed have been sleeping, he had received assistance from a generous helping of bloodwine or whatever swill her contact chose to imbibe. Opening her mouth to offer her report, she was interrupted by Turag discharging a profound belch that echoed across her quarters. She flinched as something, spittle or perhaps a fragment of whatever he had eaten for dinner, launched from his mouth and landed on the visual pickup of his own transceiver. It clung there, partially obscuring her view of the drunk, disgusting Klingon.

An improvement, actually, she decided.

Holding his head in his hands, Turag regarded her through bleary eyes. "*The Jinoteur system?*" he asked after listening to Sandesjo relay to him her most recent intelligence acquisition. "*We've not sent any ships to chart that region, so far as I'm aware.*"

Sandesjo forced herself to maintain her composed expression.

"As I already said, only unmanned probes have been dispatched to that region. A Klingon probe was intercepted after charting the Jinoteur system and its information stolen by Starfleet spies." It was not entirely true, of course, but she knew that should the High Council forward any formal accusation to the Federation, such a charge would bear only a passing resemblance to the facts she provided.

Her job here and now was to ensure that did not happen.

"*An outrage!*" Turag bellowed, after which he squeezed his eyes shut and rubbed his temples, the alcohol coursing through his veins obviously wreaking havoc with his head. "*Those dishonorable cretins will pay for their insolence. This is an affront to the entire Klingon Empire. I will see to it . . .*"

"You can do no such thing," Sandesjo snapped, cutting him off. "Only a limited number of people know of this, and all of them currently reside on this station. If the High Council attempts to contest this, it will become apparent to anyone with a functioning brain stem that a spy must be at work here."

Turag growled in frustration, more from his inebriation and being roused from sleep, Sandesjo gathered, than from any real frustration with what she had said. Leaning closer to the monitor so that whatever still remained stuck to the visual pickup now appeared as a massive blemish on his nose, Turag asked, "*Then what exactly do you expect me to do, Lurqal?*"

Fool! Would she have to explain everything down to the most minuscule detail? How much of this conversation would he even remember in the morning? Would she have to repeat the entire exchange tomorrow?

"Obviously," Sandesjo said, grappling to maintain her composure, "Starfleet feels this system is of some value, or they would not have gone to the trouble not only to secure the information from our sensor drone, but also to ensure we did not obtain it." Reaching to the transceiver's keypad, she tapped a command string. "Fortunately, I have a copy of that data. I will dispatch it to our contact off-station." In his present state, there was no way she could trust Turag not to misplace or delete the potentially valuable sensor information, assuming he even could refrain from sending it to Starbase 47's general-purpose broadcast network so that it could be read by every computer terminal on the station.

Turag's drunkenness seemed to disappear, perhaps as a consequence of him realizing that Sandesjo was in fact removing him from the decision-making loop. To his credit, the idiot appeared also to comprehend that there was precious little he could do about it at the moment.

His eyes narrowing, he asked, "*How did you come by this? Surely this isn't something Ambassador Jetanien leaves lying about in a desk drawer or an unguarded computer file.*" His lopsided smile grew into a broad, toothy grin. "*Did you perchance bed that whelp of a human who seems so taken with you? No doubt he carries no small amount of useful information, and it would be child's play for you to pry it out of him.*"

"It would," Sandesjo replied, "just as if I were to employ any number of other tactics. How I came to possess the data is not your concern. What matters now is what we do with what we have learned."

Considering the precariousness of her current position, the less Turag—or anyone else, for that matter—knew of her methods, contacts, and other resources at her disposal, the better. For all intents and purposes, she now was on her own and in need of every advantage she could marshal—including maintaining her web of secrecy even from those she supposedly could trust.

In truth, she was apprehensive about the usefulness of the sensor data without more knowledge of the Jinoteur system. Given its remote location near the far border of the Gonmog Sector, why did Starfleet consider it a location of interest? The information contained within the sensor logs was intriguing, certainly. While she was no scientist, even Sandesjo could understand how planets with moons acting in such a manner as attributed to those scanned by the unmanned drone would garner interest.

Was it a naturally occurring phenomenon, or something artificial? If it was the latter, then who was responsible? How did they wield such power, and what other capabilities did they possess? Despite her best efforts to glean any sort of clarifying information, Sandesjo had so far been unable to penetrate the cloak of secrecy surrounding the Federation's motives. Whatever mystery lay in wait in this region of the galaxy, it surely must be of immense value to incite Starfleet to such brazen action while undertaking significant risk.

For her to be successful in discovering those motives—particularly in time for the empire to beat the Federation to reaping any as-yet-unknown benefits—Sandesjo knew she would soon have to invite similar risk. Even with the limited amount of information at her disposal, it was easy for her to comprehend that whatever secrets the Gonmog Sector harbored, the Klingon Empire was compelled to find them first.

"Alert the Chancellor and the High Council," she said. "A strategy must be put into motion that allows our ships to investigate this region without making it appear we learned of its value from the Federation."

"*And what are they to look for?*" Turag asked.

Sandesjo shook her head. "I have no idea, but time is of the essence. I will continue my efforts to learn more, but you must not dawdle with this, Turag. We cannot afford for this to be lost amid one of your nightly repasts of drinking and whoring or whatever it is you do."

"*I know my duty, Lurqal,*" Turag said, his tone reflecting his dissatisfaction at her answers and general attitude. "*You, however, would do well to remember your place.*" Leaning closer to the visual pickup once more, any trace of humor vanished from his features. "*Yours is a dangerous profession, after all. Peril waits beyond every turn, and accidents do happen. It would be a shame for such a tragedy to befall you, particularly before you find your way to my bed.*"

Without waiting for a reply, he reached forward and the transceiver's display screen went dark as he severed the communication from his end, leaving Sandesjo to stare at the inert monitor and her own muted reflection.

Dismissing the idiot Klingon from her thoughts, if only momentarily, she keyed a new command sequence into the transceiver's control keypad. A moment later, the screen flared once more to life as the new frequency was established.

"It's done," Sandesjo said without preamble. "Turag has the information, though I have no idea what he'll do with it." Frowning as she regarded the image on the compact viewscreen, she added, "I also have no idea what purpose it serves to tell him in the first place."

"Your duties do not require you to possess that information at this time," said T'Prynn, from where she sat in the dimmed illumination of her own quarters. *"When it is appropriate, I will provide you with further instructions."*

She had changed from her uniform into a robe, though it was not a typical meditation robe as Sandesjo had seen worn by other Vulcan females. This one appeared to be woven from silk, maroon in color and highlighted by gold stitching as well as an ornate floral pattern rendered in a darker shade of burgundy. Bare skin below her throat was visible at the point the robe wrapped across her chest, and Sandesjo felt her pulse jump as she remembered her own lips pressed to that very spot earlier in the evening.

"Assuming Turag is cognizant in the morning and manages to relay the information I gave him," she said, "the Klingons will certainly send ships to the Jinoteur system to investigate. Why is that advisable?"

"All in good time," T'Prynn replied, her right eyebrow arching. *"For now, carry on with your normal duties. Maintain your cover, especially with respect to Turag. His judgment is lacking, but that only makes him more dangerous."* She paused, and Sandesjo was sure she detected the faintest hint of a smile on the Vulcan's lips. *"I will be in contact soon."* The image faded, leaving Sandesjo to stare once more at the now-inactive viewscreen.

Though she remained at her desk and contemplated the vague nature of T'Prynn's responses to questions, Sandesjo could not comprehend what was to be gained by alerting the Klingons. Of course, she had undertaken several actions in similar fashion since being assigned to T'Prynn; it was the nature of any covert operative to obey the instructions of his or her overseer even if one did not possess complete understanding of the situation's salient details. Often, such insulation was necessary for security reasons in the event the operative was discovered or even captured, a possibility Sandesjo knew she faced every day while working as a double agent.

With that thought, however, came reawakened doubts about the precarious circumstances in which Sandesjo now found herself, how she had come to be the tool of not one but two clandestine intelligence-gathering organizations. It was not a simple story; there was no single incident that had led her down her present path. T'Prynn had played a major role in that odd confluence of events, certainly, and Sandesjo often wondered if the Vulcan regarded their relationship merely as an affiliation of convenience while she carried out whatever larger scheme she was perpetrating. Instinct told Sandesjo that it was true—in the beginning, certainly, and continued even now to some extent. But there were also those moments when the emotions Vulcans guarded with such care could be glimpsed, and she felt she was seeing T'Prynn's true self, the one Sandesjo had been unable—no, unwilling—to resist. Where the line separating love and duty was drawn, and how muddled it had become, was something she suspected she soon would have to confront once and for all.

Still, she was correct about one thing. Turag was a liability, and it was only a matter of time before his fragile pride or inability to stifle his wine-loosened tongue became a detriment to her cover. Despite the inherent risk, Sandesjo knew that removing him as a source of potential trouble was something which must be performed with all haste.

That it also would bring personal pleasure was merely a tangential benefit.

49

For the first time in a long while, Tim Pennington was once again beginning to feel like a reporter.

His second night back on the station and occupying a corner booth in Tom Walker's place while nursing a cup of hot tea—watching Quinn slosh his way through life had made him reconsider his own alcohol intake—Pennington sat back and surveyed the room's various demonstrations of humanoid interaction. Resting his head against the wall behind his seat, he listened to snippets of different conversations, content to allow others to provide the words for a time. For the moment, he had exhausted his own supply following an hours-long frenzy of composition and editing to polish his latest submissions to the Federation News Service.

Writing with passion he had not felt in some time, Pennington drew inspiration from—of all things—his recent excursion with Quinn. The entire ludicrous journey to Yerad III and the lunacy that had followed when faced with execution at the hands of the hapless privateer's professional rivals had sparked a zeal he had not experienced since the loss of his lover, Oriana D'Amato. While part of him missed the lost opportunity to interview colonists on Boam II, he knew that whatever comments and perspective he might have gathered on that backwater colony would not have energized him as had his experiences of the past few days.

He at first had questioned the logic behind expending his time and energy in such a manner. None of his former editors—even those who owed him a few personal favors—had so much as acknowledged his previous two dozen efforts. With sobriety, Pennington seemed to have found some of what he had been missing these past weeks, shades of his former, tenacious self. Optimism as well as hints of his once reliable news sense seemed to be moving slowly from the shadows into the light.

It probably doesn't hurt that I've got nothing else to which I might devote my attention.

The lingering, bitter thought was fleeting and he gave himself a mental kick to send it on its way. Yes, he conceded, his personal life lay in ruins, by his own hand as much as, if not more than, the actions of anyone else. Even his wife, Lora, who had dealt the most recent and vicious—if not unjustified—blow, could not be blamed for the mistakes he had made. Pennington's only option, he knew, was to knuckle down, square his jaw, and forge ahead. No other choice was acceptable, or even thinkable.

It was that resolve which had guided him to Tom Walker's, though not to drown his sorrows in drink. Instead, he started to write, not allowing himself to leave the booth at the back of the bar until he had composed a story for transmission to FNS.

By the time he was finished, he had completed two.

While his former editors had purchased some of his pieces since his disastrous flameout with the *Bombay* story last month, they had not so much as acknowledged his accompanying communiqués with a cursory reply indicating receipt of the stories. Pennington shrugged off their attitude. So long as they were paying him and—more importantly—publishing his work, he could handle the cold shoulders offered by onetime colleagues and friends. If he could keep at least one foot in the proverbial door, there was still a chance that when he finally did report a major news story—one that truly would shake the foundations of the Federation itself—his words would once again engender the trust they currently lacked. Only then would he be able to salvage and perhaps even rebuild the career he had lost—partly through his own admitted recklessness, but also at the hands of those pursuing an agenda and who wished their actions to remain unobserved.

Good luck with that, he thought as he sipped his tea and thought of T'Prynn, the chief architect of his downfall. At least, he believed her to be responsible, as he of course possessed no evidence to substantiate his claims. Further, his instincts told him that she was the key—or one key, at least—to all of the strange activities taking place on the station and indeed Starfleet's actions within the Taurus Reach. T'Prynn held the answers, of that Pennington was sure.

His odd relationship with the commander also had taken a surprising turn after his return to the station. After catching sight of her while walking through Stars Landing and taking note of the odd, almost distracted look on her face, Pennington had decided to follow her along with his reporter's nose. What he had not expected to see was her heading with evident purpose directly for *his* apartment.

Taking care to avoid being seen—a tactic seemingly wasted given T'Prynn's apparently single-minded focus—Pennington had watched as the commander stood outside his door for several moments, appearing to weigh some kind of decision. Had she come to leverage her hold over him as part of some unknown agenda? Given how she already had treated him, it would seem to be the next logical step.

That line of thought went into the recycler, however, as he watched her hesitate at his door before turning and walking away. Had she lost her nerve? Pennington of course found that unlikely. In fact, as he observed her, he could not help thinking that were T'Prynn human, her strange actions might well have been born from guilt.

She certainly did not seem to display such feelings a few hours earlier. Knowing that T'Prynn also had Quinn under her thumb, Pennington had followed the hapless rogue to his meeting with her, watching as Quinn surrendered the Klingon data core. What information did it contain that might justify the clandestine yet overt actions she had put in motion to obtain it? How did it tie into the larger picture?

Perhaps there even was a connection to the events which had transpired on Erilon. Though he had reviewed the official Starfleet releases on the incident and even had used some of that information in crafting one of his latest stories, Pennington's instincts told him there was more there than met the eye. While the information as presented in the reports might be the literal truth, his instincts told him that it was but one layer of truth—the only one that had been allowed to see light while other and perhaps more damaging aspects of that same truth remained cloaked in shadow.

Much like the shadow that fell across his table.

"Mr. Pennington, am I interrupting?"

Startled, the reporter looked up to see Commodore Reyes, standing tall in an ever crisp and immaculately tailored Starfleet uniform. His normally cold, craggy features were warmed somewhat by the suggestion of a smile.

"Commodore," Pennington said, straightening in his seat. Clearing his throat, he added, "No, not at all. Just enjoying a spot of tea."

Nodding, Reyes moved without invitation to lower himself onto the cushioned bench seat opposite Pennington's. For his part, the journalist hoped his expression did not convey nervousness or uncertainty at the other man's presence, though he guessed his efforts were wasted. Based on his past encounters with the commodore, he knew Reyes to be a remarkably observant man.

"I've just finished some interesting reading," the station commander said, leaning against the bench's backrest while leaving his forearms on the table, interlocking his fingers. He said nothing else, though Pennington noted that the man's smile widened—ever so slightly.

When no further clues seemed to be forthcoming, Pennington asked, "Something I ought to read myself, Commodore?"

"Something you wrote yourself," Reyes clarified. "Your dispatches for the FNS. I thought it was excellent work, and wanted to tell you so."

Pennington's eyebrows rose in surprise. "Already?" He had transmitted the pieces less than two hours ago. Only on rare occasions had he received such expedient turnaround on one of his submissions, and that was when he was still in good favor. "I can't believe they posted that. Any of it, for that matter."

"Your perspective on colony life in the Taurus Reach was rather insightful," Reyes said. "It's nice to be able to put a face on the personal struggles colonists have amid the political circus we're holding out here. Getting Ambassador Jetanien to chime in was a nice touch, though I have to admit I'm surprised you were able to pin him down for a statement."

"My inbred tenacity, I guess," Pennington replied, basking in satisfaction. That the Chelon ambassador had agreed to the exclusive interview, during which he had spoken quite candidly about the challenge of colonizing space that also was of interest to the Klingons and the Tholians, was a coup. The journalist had strived to keep his writing sincere rather than sensational, refusing to pick apart gaps in veracity and instead telling what he hoped was a story that might enlighten rather than incite a reader.

"The piece about the accident on Erilon was also very well done," Reyes continued. "Very respectful, particularly toward Captain Zhao and those of his crew who were lost. I wanted to say I appreciated that."

I wonder if he's feeling all right, Pennington mused as he took in the compliments. Writing what he had hoped was a poignant tribute to the latest Starfleet personnel to pay the ultimate price for the Federation's presence in the Taurus Reach, he had—uncharacteristically—waxed heroic on the leadership of Captain Zhao Sheng of the *Endeavour* as well as the entire group of colonists who had so valiantly struggled against the elements on distant Erilon, only to be killed in the crippling earthquake and subsequent reactor explosion that had wiped the nascent settlement from the face of the planet. Creating the piece had been difficult at first, given his natural inclination to distrust any sort of official Starfleet statement. Nevertheless, reading the report on the accident had nearly moved him to tears, after which words seemed to flow without effort.

Wait just a damned minute.

Something about this was not right, Pennington decided. Even if his former editor had seen fit to publish one of his stories, there was no way she would have done so without first checking, cross-checking, and—because it came from Pennington—triple-checking before committing to publication.

Reaching into his satchel for his data slate, Pennington activated it and keyed it to tie into the current FNS news feed. He glanced up at Reyes while he waited for the connection to complete, noting with rising alarm that the commodore's expression remained irritatingly placid.

By the time the tablet emitted a tone, announcing that the most current update from the data feed was complete, Pennington was not surprised to see neither of his stories listed among the recent headlines. "They haven't published anything of mine."

Reyes shrugged. "Well, not yet, anyway. I'm hoping they will."

His eyes narrowing in growing suspicion and even a hint of dread, Pennington said, "I don't understand."

"I screen your mail."

Such was the blunt, casual manner in which Reyes offered the caveat that it took an additional second for the reporter to comprehend it. When realization dawned, he felt heat rise to his face. With restraint that almost failed him, Pennington remained with his back against his seat, even as he glared at the commodore. "You . . . what?" He blinked several times, processing the statement again before finally shaking his head in disbelief. "That's . . . *bollocks*!" he said, clenching his jaw in an effort to keep his voice down. The last thing he wanted was to cause a scene in a public place.

Reyes, for his part, shrugged. "I don't make any secret of it, Mr. Pennington. All communiqués to and from the station are scanned by the computer for security reasons. Anything that matches certain parameters is brought to my attention."

"But my stories were legitimate," Pennington protested. "There was nothing in there that was a breach of any bloody security."

"I agree," Reyes replied. "In the case of journalists, it's standard procedure to verify anything intended for the news outlets."

"That's censorship!" Pennington shouted, feeling the heat rising in his cheeks but no longer caring about the reactions his outburst might provoke. While numerous heads turned in his direction, Reyes did not so much as blink.

Though he had suspected that the commodore had at least passively sanctioned the actions taken against him by T'Prynn, Pennington of course had possessed no evidence to prove his theories.

Here and now, however, Reyes was all but admitting not only complicity in that earlier violation, but that it was in fact simply one act in an ongoing campaign to quash not only his professional voice but his civil liberties as well.

"Do you think for one minute I can't find a way around your 'security measures'?" Pennington asked, his voice low and cold as he spat the words through gritted teeth. "I will be heard, Commodore, one way or another."

"Of that I have no doubt," Reyes said, his voice and demeanor remaining composed even as his eyes bored into Pennington's, "just as you should have no doubts about my not tolerating anything which undermines the safety and security of this station, whether that disruption is caused by someone wielding a sword *or* a pen."

Swallowing a lump which had formed in his throat, the reporter nodded. "Well, I suppose I should appreciate your being forthright about the situation."

"Then we have an understanding," Reyes said, adopting a wistful expression. "Life is so much easier with a few understandings, don't you think?"

Seething, Pennington only nodded.

The commodore leaned forward, adopting a lower tone. "Listen, I know you see things, hear things. You have your 'sources,' and I know that when you've poked around here, sometimes you've gotten two from me and two from Starfleet Command, and it's added up to five in your book. Am I right?"

Intrigued at where the discussion might be heading, Pennington also leaned toward the table. "You have my attention, Commodore."

"Maybe things even added up to five while you were writing about Erilon. Your gut was probably giving you signals, and you thought that, with a little digging, you might even score that story you're hoping will resurrect your career. You'll be back in the good graces of your editors. Your readers would believe you again. Your wife . . ."

"Lora is gone," Pennington said, cutting off Reyes.

Pausing a moment, the commodore nodded. "Sorry."

"I said she's gone," Pennington repeated, his voice harsher and louder this time as he relived the scene that had greeted him upon entering his apartment after returning to the station with Quinn. During his absence, Lora had returned and stripped his living quarters clean. Not a single piece of furniture, clothing, or even food remained.

The only thing left to greet him was the single sheet of paper, pinned to one bare wall, announcing to all who read it that Lora Brummer sought divorce from her husband, Timothy.

"She even took the lighting elements from the fixtures," Pennington said, only now realizing that he had recounted the entire depressing scene aloud. "What kind of twisted individual takes the bloody *lighting* elements?" he asked, anguish enveloping the words as he regarded Reyes.

The commodore studied him a moment before replying. "I said I was sorry, Mr. Pennington, as in 'I'm sorry, and I understand,' not 'I'm sorry, please feel free to discuss it at length with me.'"

Embarrassed at having divulged the disheartening turn his personal life had taken, Pennington cleared his throat, reaching for his now quite cold tea. "My apologies, sir."

Shaking his head as if to clear it of the sudden detour in the conversation, Reyes said, "What I'm trying to say is that I know you could have made this a huge pain in my ass, but you didn't, for whatever reason. My guess is that you're probably waiting for bigger fish to fry. Regardless, I appreciate the restraint you showed, and the respect you paid to those who died on Erilon. I'm here to say thank you, and to tell you that this is something I'll be keeping in mind for next time."

"Next time?" Pennington asked.

"Sooner or later," Reyes said, "you're going to want to talk to me about something important. Maybe it'll be something you learn about before I do." His expression hardening, he added, "Though I doubt it. Anyway, at some point, you're going to need something from me. If I can trust you to do what's right—for *everyone* involved—then I'll be more inclined to help you."

"If you're proposing some sort of partnership," Pennington

said, "then I'll need more from you and your people than what I've gotten to this point, the sort of in-depth information to produce a credible, objective account of what's going on out here. You promise me that, and I'll promise you'll never get sucker-punched by anything I write."

Saying nothing for several seconds, Reyes nodded. "That requires a level of trust you'll have to earn. You're a journalist, Mr. Pennington, and a damned good one. It's second nature to dig for the great story. What assurances do I have that you won't run with every juicy little tidbit you get your hands on?"

Pennington shrugged. "I haven't told anyone you're sleeping with Captain Desai."

Even as he uttered the words, he imagined the ambient noise of Tom Walker's place abruptly dropping to total silence, as every person in the bar turned to face him and regard him with matching expressions that all conveyed the same question now sprinting through his mind: *Are you insane?*

That did not happen, of course, though neither did Reyes say anything, his expression no more malleable than the bulkhead behind him. Then, a broad grin materialized as if by transporter. "Point taken."

Feeling relief wash over him at the realization that the commodore was not—for the moment, at least—going to kick his ass all over the bar, Pennington returned the smile. "So, we have an agreement, then?"

The grin vanished.

"We'll talk later," Reyes said, rising from his seat and marching toward the bar without another word.

Watching the commodore leave, no doubt returning to the station's operations center and the plethora of responsibilities that came with his rank and station, Pennington reached for his tea. The beverage might be cold, he decided, but it did nothing to quell the fire of curiosity and resolve heating up in the core of his being and beginning to spread outward with growing intensity.

I think this place just got a whole lot more interesting.

ELSEWHERE

50

No matter how many times he entered the hallowed chamber of the Romulan Senate, Praetor Vrax never once failed to appreciate the sensation of near-reverence he experienced. Regardless of the situation at hand and despite whatever mental burden plagued him on any given day, he always paused for a moment to reflect upon the history and power emanating from this room.

For what it lacked in size, the Senate Chamber more than compensated with its grandiose appointments, furnishings, and perhaps even the arrogance that had embodied its construction. Situated at the geographic center of Dartha, the capital city of Romulus, the circular hall remained largely unchanged from the first time Vrax had entered its storied confines as a junior senator more than a century earlier. Pairs of polished marble columns positioned equidistantly around the chamber's perimeter supported its high, domed ceiling. Ornate tapestries decorated the walls, and granite tiles dominated the room's open debate floor, upon which had been painted an artist's rendition of a star map depicting the expanse of the Romulan Star Empire as well as the border it shared with the United Federation of Planets.

What Vrax also never failed to notice upon his entry into the Senate Chamber was that the map had remained unaltered for nearly as long as he had been coming to this revered place.

In due time, and with good fortune on our side, that will change, he reminded himself.

The proconsul, Sret, brought the chamber to order as Vrax stepped farther into the room. Various conversations taking place between senators and onlookers extinguished as everyone rose in deference to his arrival. Relying on his cane while eschewing his aide's offer of assistance to reach his chair at the center of the dais situated along the chamber's northern wall, Vrax nodded to several of the senators he passed as he took his place. Before lowering his aged body into his seat, he paused to regard the audience of politicians gathered here this evening. The audience seating area, which consisted of four rows of seats positioned opposite the senatorial stage, was empty on this day, in keeping with the private nature of this closed session.

"Greetings, Praetor," Proconsul Sret said, offering a formal nod that Vrax knew to be no more genuine than the majority of military and political accomplishments with which the younger man chose to embellish his official biography. "Thank you for agreeing to meet with us at this late hour."

"The business and interests of the Romulan people do not usually confine themselves to anything resembling a normal schedule," Vrax replied, the ghost of a smile teasing the edges of his mouth. "As such, we'll forgo your execution for another time." The comment elicited mild laughter from the senators seated around him, despite what he suspected were serious reasons for convening this session.

Any sense of informality was lost, however, with Sret's next words.

"We have lost contact with the *Bloodied Talon,* Praetor," the proconsul said, his voice appropriately subdued and grave. "Based on the last report received from Commander Sarith, we have reason to believe she may have been left with no recourse but to destroy her vessel in order to prevent detection."

"Are you certain?" Vrax asked, his intellect already providing him with the answer he did not want to hear before Sret could even reply. He could not help but glance to where his vice-proconsul, Toqel, stood silent and unmoving near the rows of empty seats composing the audience's viewing area. The uniform of her office was as immaculate as always and her dark hair cropped closer to her scalp in a style even more severe than that preferred by many veteran male military officers, but Vrax saw the resolute set to her narrow jaw and the dark circles seeming to add years to her age.

Her expression was that of stone, belying the turmoil of emotions she must surely be keeping in check.

Again, Sret bowed his head. "As certain as we can be under the circumstances, my praetor. Commander Sarith was maintaining strict communications containment protocols in order to avoid detection, submitting her reports only at the directed intervals and frequencies."

Stepping forward until she stood next to the proconsul, Toqel said, "According to the commander's last transmission, her vessel was in danger of being detected by vessels traversing the region."

Vrax already was familiar with the circumstances surrounding the *Talon*'s impaired condition, having read with no small amount of incredulity Commander Sarith's report of the apparent destruction of an entire planet in what the Federation was calling the Palgrenax system, as well as the horrific experience of being caught in the midst of the resulting shock wave and debris storm. Even more unsettling was the commander's assertion that it appeared to have been caused by a weapon of indescribable force, at least if the sensor data she had sent along to corroborate her report was any indication, and the fact that the possessors of such a weapon remained a mystery.

Who or what has the Federation angered in the Taurus Reach?

Toqel had paused in her report, and Vrax watched as the woman's otherwise impeccable bearing was marred—if only for an instant—while she cleared her throat. He nodded to her, appreciating the vice-proconsul's efforts to maintain her composure. He could only imagine how difficult it must be for her now, having to carry out this most unpleasant of duties, all while mourning the death of her only child.

"I grieve for your loss, Toqel," he said, saddened even further by the fact that Commander Sarith's final heroic act would be all but ignored by the pages of history. For the sake of security, all knowledge of the *Bloodied Talon*'s doomed last mission would have to be buried and forgotten, lest it be discovered by spies— either Federation or working for another government—and trigger a hunt for the dozens of other ships like the *Talon* which were at this moment conducting invaluable covert surveillance on the empire's myriad potential enemies.

The vice-proconsul, sworn to lifelong duty and loyalty, knew this, of course. "She and her crew served the Praetor. That alone makes their sacrifice a noble one."

To Vrax's left and seated at one of the desks reserved for the senators, D'tran leaned forward in his chair, gathering his dark robes about him as he asked, "Did Commander Sarith destroy her ship as a precaution, or did she engage an enemy?" His voice, low and raspy, was a sign of his own advanced age; he was older than even Vrax himself.

Sret shook his head. "We are not certain, Senator, but we believe the *Talon* may have been trying to avoid detection by a Klingon battle cruiser."

Troubled murmurs echoed through the Senate Chamber at the mention of the empire's longtime enemy. Though there had been no direct hostilities with the Klingons in many years, Vrax had known at the time of the *Bloodied Talon*'s departure for the distant Taurus Reach that the possibility existed for the vessel to encounter battleships in service to the Romulan people's storied foe. Indeed, the report he had read of the ship's earlier close call with a Klingon warship was still fresh in his memory.

By Vrax's recollection, it had been decades since the last known encounter with the Klingon Empire. There had been a brief conflict in the years following the protracted war against Earth and her allies, as Romulus attempted to expand away from the region of space claimed by the then-fledgling United Federation of Planets. The Klingons, always on the hunt for new worlds to conquer owing to their ceaseless need for resources that were unavailable within their own territorial borders, had attempted to establish footholds within Romulan space, perhaps thinking Romulan forces depleted in the aftermath of the protracted conflict with the humans.

And our forces, weak though they may have been, certainly showed our enemies the errors of such thinking.

"It seems," Vrax said after a moment, "that we are not the only ones with thoughts of expansion. In addition to the humans, our old adversaries from the Klingon Empire seem to have been gripped by a similar desire." He knew also that hostilities would almost certainly be an inevitable consequence of this action, particularly in instances of newly claimed territory being disputed.

"All things being equal, Praetor, I would agree," replied D'tran, the chamber's subdued illumination reflecting off his thinning silver hair. "From what we know of the Federation, they would seek peaceful coexistence rather than enter into a dispute over territory. Why, then, would they seek to expand their borders into a region of space that is flanked by two potentially fierce enemies? Surely they know the risks they run by angering the Klingons, and the Tholians are little more than xenophobic reactionaries. The humans and their allies would seem to be asking for war."

Senator Anitra, a woman far younger than most of her companions on the dais but as comfortable with her position as those who had served far longer, rose from her seat and stepped onto the main floor. "According to our intelligence reports, the Federation seems preoccupied with their usual glut of pursuits and would appear all but oblivious to the political maelstrom they've helped to engineer. They have established settlements on dozens of worlds. A handful of those are large, permanent colonies. A network of trade vectors has already been enacted, to say nothing of regular patrol routes for several Starfleet ships assigned to the sector."

When Anitra paused and held up her hand, her dark, calculating eyes locking with his own, Vrax almost surrendered to the urge to smile. What the young senator lacked in age, she more than compensated for with her passion and flair for the dramatic.

Here it comes.

"However," Anitra continued, "as my esteemed colleague has already pointed out, much of this could have been accomplished elsewhere in the quadrant, almost anywhere, in fact, without the risk of angering interstellar neighbors. Indeed, the space station constructed in the region would seem to serve no other purpose except to arouse suspicion and apprehension, if not outright fear of protracted military action."

Stroking his chin, Vrax conceded that the young senator had a valid point. The presence of the starbase, far outside Federation borders, was an unprecedented act. While it could be argued that its deployment was so that it could better oversee military and civilian shipping operations supporting the growing network of colonies in the Taurus Reach, to the Praetor it seemed like too large of a tool for the job.

"Perhaps their mind-set has changed," he said, "and the Federation no longer fears conflict, even if it stands between them and whatever goals they pursue? They might even welcome such confrontation. After all, a few of us have seen the humans acclimate to the needs of a given situation with surprising alacrity."

As he spoke the words, he glanced to his longtime friend D'tran, who nodded in agreement. Even more so than Vrax himself, the aged senator possessed a long and unique familiarity with the humans. Over a century ago, while still a subcommander in the space fleet, D'tran had served aboard one of the vessels that had made the first recorded contact with a ship from Earth. Very little information was gathered during that initial meeting, practically nothing, in fact, and despite several efforts in the years that followed—some of which Vrax oversaw personally—much about the humans had remained a mystery even after Romulus found itself at war with the humans and learned firsthand of the tenacity and adaptability that belied any perceived physiological, mental, or cultural inferiorities they might possess.

In the years that had passed since that bitter, costly conflict—which Vrax had also witnessed firsthand and which had caused far more devastating and lasting damage to the empire than was generally acknowledged—precious little new information had been collected regarding the humans' expansion into the galaxy.

Much of that drought was caused by the shortsightedness of the Praetor in office at that time, who had chosen a path of isolation for the Romulan people, ostensibly for the purpose of rebuilding and reprioritizing their outlook toward internal affairs, rather than pursuing a rigorous program of reaffirming the role of the Romulan Empire as the dominant force in the galaxy. By opting to focus time and energy inward, the Praetor in effect had conceded much of the territory beyond the empire's current borders to the upstart Federation and, to a lesser extent, the Klingons.

Which is why he eventually was "retired" from office, Vrax reminded himself. *Should you fail to chart the best possible course for the empire, you surely will suffer a similar fate.*

Knowing this, in the decades that had passed since Vrax had stepped into the role of Praetor he had overseen an unprecedented series of intelligence-gathering activities. Deep-cover operatives and long-range sensor probes had provided some measure of clarity into the activities of their onetime enemy, which had grown—far beyond the fledgling interstellar coalition it had once spearheaded—into the United Federation of Planets. Much had been learned about the political and communal inroads the humans had forged with civilizations as they moved ever farther into the galaxy, as well as the trials they faced when confronted with new adversaries. Working from the information that had been obtained, it was feared by many political and military experts within the Romulan government that the Federation was on the verge of an unprecedented expansion with the potential to threaten the empire's interests in this quadrant.

The Taurus Reach would at first seem to be but the latest manifestation of that fear, but that theory quickly collapsed when confronted with Sarith's invaluable report of what she and her crew had experienced in the Palgrenax system.

As if reading his thoughts, Senator Anitra clasped her hands before her and bowed her head in his direction. "Based on what we already know of the humans, Praetor, particularly their penchant for adaptability and even their willingness to engage in deception to protect their interests, isn't it logical to assume there is some other motive in play here? Should we not act now, rather than repeat the mistakes of our past leaders?"

Though he was certain she meant no disrespect, it was easy for Vrax to understand the collective murmurings of the other senators in the wake of Anitra's words. Many of the comments being uttered around him were low enough in volume that he was unable to discern their content, but he comprehended their meaning just the same. It was a rare occurrence for a member of the Senate even to present the appearance of calling into question the decision of the Praetor—any Praetor—in a public forum. For someone as relatively new to the chamber as Anitra, who in all likelihood was younger than D'tran's favored senatorial robe, the action bordered on blasphemous.

Not that Vrax concerned himself with such things. He much preferred his senators to be open and honest with him no matter the issue. Should they bring a bit of fire to the floor when they debated their points, so much the better.

Holding up a withered hand, he stifled the muffled yet still animated conversations taking place to his flanks, and regarded Anitra with a mentoring smile. "You have a suggestion, Senator?"

Appreciative and perhaps emboldened by her Praetor's indulgence, Anitra stepped closer to the dais. "The Federation's focus is elsewhere, Praetor. For whatever reason, the Taurus Reach has captured their attention, which brings with it growing tensions between them and the Klingons. It seems logical that, should things continue along that course, both sides will be forced to commit increased resources to cope with that ever-worsening situation."

Turning so that she did not obstruct Vrax's view of the chamber's main floor, she indicated the map of the empire emblazoned upon the interlocked tiles. "Perhaps this is the opportunity for which we have waited. The humans and their allies may be vulnerable where their territory borders ours. We know that many worlds in what is now Federation space are rich with resources vital to the continued survival of the empire, and were lost to us when we stipulated to the treaty that ended the Great War. We could well be in a position to retrieve that which rightfully belongs to us."

When the other senators began muttering this time, Vrax noted the almost unanimous connotation of approval now flavoring the dialogue.

He had to admit that Anitra's proposition was as intriguing as it was bold. If the Federation's interests were concentrated elsewhere, this indeed might be the time to consider aggressive strategies, to probe the Federation's borders and assess their strengths and weaknesses with the aim of reclaiming valuable territory ceded to the humans in the aftermath of the war.

As appealing as that notion was to him, Vrax was well aware that Anitra's proposal was far more complex than had been implied by the discussion to this point.

"While the Federation might be distracted by happenings elsewhere," he said, "that is not to say they are inattentive, or defenseless." He pointed to the floor map. "The observation outposts which guard their border are formidable obstacles. We cannot be sure the cloaking devices our ships carry will offer protection from their sensors." Given the reports received from the ill-fated *Bloodied Talon,* there already was some concern over the technology's perceived vulnerabilities.

"The outposts themselves are literal fortresses," offered Vice-Proconsul Toqel, stepping forward with hands clasped behind her back, "embedded within asteroids and designed to withstand even the most intense assaults."

Standing next to her, Proconsul Sret shook his head. "We have no facts to corroborate what might be nothing more than Federation propaganda," he said. "The truth is that we do not know the outposts' defensive capabilities. They have been allowed to drift unmolested on the Federation's side of the Neutral Zone for more than a century. For all we know, they could be predators which in fact possess no teeth."

"Or they're simply hiding their teeth while awaiting an easy kill," Vrax countered, his tone one of caution. "Regardless, we will not know one way or another until we take some much-needed first steps into the unknown."

"Wise observations, Praetor," Toqel said. "However, what of the Taurus Reach? There can be no doubt that it presents an alarming concern."

Vrax could not disagree with that reasoning. Had the Federation found some new civilization, technology, or other resource that might give them an unprecedented tactical advantage? Maybe they had only found a clue to something unimaginable in its scope or power, unmatched by anything which currently existed, and with the potential to position whoever found it first as the undisputed rulers of the known galaxy.

For that to be anyone but the Romulan Star Empire was unconscionable. Regardless of the cost, no matter if it plunged the entire galaxy into war, Vrax knew he could not allow such change to come to fruition. The Romulan people would never subjugate themselves to anyone so long as life flowed through his aged, feeble body.

Of course, judging from the reports from the *Bloodied Talon,* the Federation might well have incensed a new enemy, one possessing enough power to stake its own claim, rendering all other considerations irrelevant.

Vrax knew that answers lay along only one path.

The path leading back to the Taurus Reach—and whatever secrets it possessed.

The saga of
STAR TREK VANGUARD
will continue

ACKNOWLEDGMENTS

Sincere thanks are in order for editor Marco Palmieri, for inviting us to play in this new section of the *Star Trek* sandbox and trusting us to meet the standard of excellence he has established for all of the other writers with whom he has worked. As longtime diehard fans of the original *Star Trek* series, the chance for us to expand upon that universe and to stretch it in new ways was simply a temptation too enticing to ignore.

Thanks also to David Mack, who took head-on the challenge of writing the first *Vanguard* novel as well as working with Marco to develop the series' larger story arc and what we believe to be one of the most interesting cast of characters to come down the *Star Trek* pike in a long time. He also managed to set the bar quite high for intrigue, excitement, and just plain fun with the series' inaugural volume, *Harbinger*. Here's hoping we did you proud, Mack-Daddy.

And a high-five to the most honorable Dr. Lawrence M. Schoen, he of the Klingon Language Institute, for his invaluable assistance in helping us devise a few new Klingon words. No, we're not going to tell you what they mean. Where's the fun in *that*?

ABOUT THE AUTHORS

DAYTON WARD has been a fan of *Star Trek* since conception (his, not the show's). After serving for eleven years in the U.S. Marine Corps, he discovered the private sector and the piles of cash to be made there as a software engineer. His professional writing career began with stories selected for each of Pocket Books' first three *Star Trek: Strange New Worlds* anthologies. In addition to his various writing projects with Kevin Dilmore, Dayton is the author of the *Star Trek* novel *In the Name of Honor* and the science fiction novels *The Last World War* and *The Genesis Protocol* as well as short stories which have appeared in *Kansas City Voices* magazine and the *Star Trek: New Frontier* anthology *No Limits*. Though he currently lives in Kansas City with his wife, Michi, Dayton is a Florida native and still maintains a torrid long-distance romance with his beloved Tampa Bay Buccaneers. Be sure to visit Dayton's official website at http://www.daytonward.com.

Still reeling from the knowledge that *Star Trek* was a live-action series *before* it was a Saturday-morning cartoon, KEVIN DILMORE is continually grateful for his professional involvement on the fiction and the nonfiction sides of the Star Trek universe for nearly a decade. By day, he works as a writer for Hallmark Cards in Kansas City, Missouri; by night, it's a whole different picture. Since 1997, he has been a contributing writer to *Star Trek Communicator,* penning news stories and personality profiles for the bimonthly publication of the Official *Star Trek* Fan Club. On the storytelling side of things, his story "The Road to Edos" was published as part of the *Star Trek: New Frontier* anthology *No Limits*. With Dayton Ward, his work includes a story for the anthology *Star Trek: Tales of the Dominion War* as well as one for the September 2006 anthology *Constellations* to celebrate the fortieth anniversary of the original *Star Trek*; the *Star Trek: The Next Generation* novels *A Time to Sow* and *A Time to Harvest*; and installments of the original e-book series *Star Trek: S.C.E.* and *Star Trek: Corps of Engineers*. A graduate of the University of Kansas, Kevin lives in Prairie Village, Kansas, with his wife, Michelle, and their three daughters.